John Alexander Logan

Uncle Daniel's story of Tom Anderson and twenty great battles

By an officer in the union army

John Alexander Logan

Uncle Daniel's story of Tom Anderson and twenty great battles
By an officer in the union army

ISBN/EAN: 9783743377103

Manufactured in Europe, USA, Canada, Australia, Japa

Cover: Foto ©Andreas Hilbeck / pixelio.de

Manufactured and distributed by brebook publishing software (www.brebook.com)

John Alexander Logan

Uncle Daniel's story of Tom Anderson and twenty great battles

UNCLE DANIEL'S INTERVIEW WITH PRESIDENT LINCOLN AND SECRETARY STANTON.

Uncle Daniel's Story

OF

"Tom" Anderson

AND

TWENTY GREAT BATTLES.

BY

AN OFFICER OF THE UNION ARMY.

NEW YORK:

A. R. HART & CO., PUBLISHERS.

1886.

UNCLE DANIEL'S STORY.

CHAPTER I.

DARK DAYS OF 1861.—A FATHER WHO GAVE HIS CHILDREN
TO THE COUNTRY.—RALLYING TO THE FLAG.—RAISING
VOLUNTEERS IN SOUTHERN INDIANA.

*" The more solitary, the more friendless, the more unsustained I am, the more I
will respect and rely upon myself."*—CHARLOTTE BRONTE.

ALLENTOWN is a beautiful little city of 10,000 inhabitants, situated on the Wabash River, in Vigo
County, Ind., in the vicinity of which several railroads now center. It is noted for its elevated
position, general healthfulness, and for its beautiful
residences and cultivated society. Daniel Lyon located
here in 1850. He was a man of marked ability and un-
doubted integrity ; was six feet two inches in height, well
proportioned, and of very commanding and martial appearance. In 1861, he was surrounded by a large family,
seven grown sons—James, David, Jackson, Peter, Stephen,
Henry and Harvey—all of whom were well educated, fond
of field sports and inclined to a military life. The mother,
" Aunt Sarah," as she was commonly called by the neighbors, was a charming, motherly, Christian woman, whose
heart and soul seemed to be wrapped up in the welfare of
her family. She was of short, thick build, but rather
handsome, with dark brown hair and large blue eyes,
gentle and kind. Her politeness and generosity were
proverbial. She thought each of her seven sons a model

man; her loving remarks about them were noticeable by all.

Daniel Lyon is at present 85 years old, and lives with one of his granddaughters—Jennie Lyon—now married to a man by the name of James Wilson, in Oakland, Ind., a small town conspicuous only for its rare educational facilities.

On the evening of the 22d of February, 1884, a number of the neighbors, among whom was Col. Daniel Bush, a gallant and fearless officer of the Union side during the late

UNCLE DANIEL TELLING HIS STORY.

war, and Dr. Adams, President of —— College, dropped in to see Uncle Daniel, as he is now familiarly called. During the evening, Col. Bush, turning to the old veteran, said :

" 'Uncle Daniel,' give us a story from some of your experiences during the war."

The old man arose from his easy-chair and stood erect, his hair, as white as snow, falling in profusion over his shoulders. His eyes, though dimmed by age, blazed forth in youthful brightness; his frame shook with excitement, his lips quivered, and tears rolled down the furrows of his

sunken cheeks. All were silent. He waved his hand to
the friends to be seated ; then, drawing his big chair to
the centre of the group, he sat down. After a few moments' pause he spoke, in a voice tremulous with emotion:

"My experience was vast. I was through the whole of
the war. I saw much. My story is a true one, but very
sad. As you see, my home is a desolate waste. My family
consists now of only two grand-children ; wife and sons
are all gone. I am all that is now left of my once happy
family. My God ! My God ! Why should I have been required to bear this great burden? But pardon this weak-
ness in an old man. I will now begin my story.

"In the month of ———, 1861, my nephew, 'Tom' Anderson,—I called the boy Tom, as I learned to do so many
years before, while visiting at his father's ; he was the son
of my eldest sister,—his wife, Mary, and their only child, a
beautiful little girl of two years (called Mary, for her
mother), were visiting at my house. Their home was in
Jackson, Miss. One evening my good wife, Tom, his wife,
my son Peter, and I were sitting on our front porch discussing the situation, when we heard a great noise a
couple of blocks south of us. The young men stepped out
to see what the trouble was and in a very short time
they returned greatly excited. A company of men were
marching down the street bearing the American flag,
when a number of rebel sympathizers had assaulted
them with stones, clubs, etc., and had taken their flag
and torn it to shreds. It seemed that a Mr. 'Dan'
Bowen, a prominent man in that part of the State, had
been haranguing the people on the question of the war,
and had denounced it as 'an infamous Abolition crusade,'
and the President as a 'villainous tyrant,' and those who
were standing by the Union as 'Lincoln's hirelings, and
dogs with collars around their necks.' This language stirred up the blood of the worst element of the people, who
sympathised with secession, and had it not been for the
timely interposition of many good and worthy citizens,
blood would have been shed upon the streets."

Here Col. Bush asked :

"What became of this man Bowen?"

"I understand that he now occupies one of the highest positions the people of Indiana can give to one of her citizens. You see, my friends, that we American people are going so fast that we pass by everything and forget almost in a day the wrongs to our citizens and our country."

"But to return to what I was saying in connection with the young men. Tom Anderson was in a state of great excitement. He said he had almost been mobbed before leaving home for entertaining Union sentiments, and feared that he could not safely return with his family. My son Peter suggested that, perhaps, they (being young) owed a duty to their country and could not perform it in a more satisfactory manner than to enter the service and do battle for the old flag. To this suggestion no reply was made at the time. I said to them:

"'This seems to me a very strange condition of things, to see a Government like this threatened in its permanency by the very people that have controlled and profited most by it.' Tom replied:

"'Uncle, I have given a great deal of thought to this subject. You know I was born in Ohio. My father was an Episcopal minister, and settled in Mississippi while I was but a boy. My father and mother are both buried there, leaving me an only child. I grew up and there married my good wife, Mary Whitthorne. We have lived happily together. I have had a good practice at the law; have tried to reconcile myself to their theories of human rights and 'rope-of-sand' government, but cannot. They are very *different* from our Northern people — have *different* theories of government and morals, with *different* habits of thought and action. The Pilgrim Fathers of the North who landed at Plymouth Rock were men of independence of thought; believed in Christianity, in education and universal liberty. They and their progeny have moved almost on a line due west, to the Pacific Ocean, infusing their energy, their ideas of government, of civil liberty, of an advanced Christian civilization, with a belief in man's equality before the law. These ideas and thoughts have become imbedded in the minds of the Northern people so firmly that they will fight to maintain them ; will make them temporarily a success, and would make them permanent but for their habit of moving so rapidly in the direction of business and the accumulation of wealth, which prepares the mind to surrender everything to the accomplishment of this single object. The Southern inhabitants are almost entirely descended from impetuous, hot-blooded people. Their ancestors that landed at Jamestown, and later along the Southern Atlantic coast within our borders, were of an adventurous and warlike people. Their descendants have driven westward almost on a parallel line with the Northern people to the borders of Mexico, occasionally lapping over the Northern line. Their thoughts, ideas, manners and customs have been impressed upon the people wherever they have gone, by the pretense, always foremost and uppermost, as if a verity, that they were the most hospitable and chivalric of any people in America. Their civilization was different. Their arguments were enforced by the pistol and bowie-knife upon their equals, and slaves subjected to their will by the lash and bloodhound—the death of a man, white or black, being considered no more than merely a reduction of one in the enumeration of population. They have opposed common schools for fear the poorer classes of whites might have an opportunity of contesting at some time the honors of office, that being the great ambition of Southern society. They would not allow the slave to be educated for fear he might learn that he was a man, having rights above the brute with which he has always been held on a par. The aristocracy only were educated. And this was generally done in the North, where the facilities were good; and by sending them from home it kept down the envy and ambition of the poorer classes, where, if they could have seen the opportunity of acquiring knowledge it might have stimulated them to greater exertion for the purpose of storing their minds with something useful in extricating themselves from an obedience to the mere will of the dominating class. Those people, one and all, no matter how ignorant, are taught to consider themselves better than any other people save the English, whose sentiments they inculcate. They are not in sympathy with a purely Republican system of Government. They believe in a controlling class, and they propose to be that class. I have heard them utter these sentiments so often that I am sure that I am correct. They all trace their ancestry back to some nobleman in some mysterious way, and think their blood better than that which courses in the veins of any Northern man, and honestly believe that one of them in war will be the equal of five men of the North. They think because Northern men will not fight duels, they must necessarily be cowards. In the first contest my judgment is that they will be successful. They are trained with the rifle and shotgun ; have taken more pains in military drill than the people of the North, and will be in condition for war earlier than the Union forces. They are also in better condition in the way of arms than the Government forces will be. The fact that they had control of the Government and have had all the best arms turned over to them by a traitorous Secretary of War, places them on a war footing at once, while the Government must rely upon purchasing arms from foreign countries, and possibly of a very inferior character. Until foundries and machinery for manufacturing arms can be constructed, the Government will be in poor condition to equip troops for good and effective service. This war now commenced will go on ; the North will succeed; slavery will go down forever; the Union will be preserved, and for a time the Union sentiment will control the Government; but when reverses come in business matters to the North, the business men there, in order to get the trade of the South, under the delusion that they can gain pecuniarily by the change, will, through some 'siren song,' turn the Government over again to the same blustering and domineering people who have ever controlled it. This, uncle, is the fear that disturbs me most at present.' "

"How prophetic," spoke up Dr. Adams.

"Yes, yes," exclaimed all present.

Col. Bush at this point arose and walked across the floor. All eyes were upon him. Great tears rolled down his bronzed cheeks. In suppressed tones he said:

"For what cause did I lose my right arm?"

He again sat down, and for the rest of the evening seemed to be in deep meditation.

Uncle Daniel, resuming his story, said:

"Just as Tom had finished what he was saying, I heard the garden gate open and shut, and David and Harvey appeared in the moonlight in front of the porch. These were my second and youngest sons. David lived some five miles from Allentown, on a farm, and Harvey had been staying at his house, helping do the farm work. They were both very much excited. Their mother, who had left Mary Anderson in the parlor, came out to enjoy the fresh air with us, and observing the excited condition of her two sons, exclaimed:

"'Why, my dear boys! what is the matter?'

"David spoke to his mother, saying:

"'Do not get excited or alarmed when I tell you that Harvey and I have made a solemn vow this evening that we will start to Washington city in the morning.'

"'For what, my dear sons, are you going?' inquired the mother, much troubled.

"'We are going to tender our services to the President in behalf of the Union. Harvey is going along with me, believing it his duty. As I was educated by the Government for the military service, I deem it my duty to it, when in danger from this infamous and unholy rebellion, to aid in putting it down.'

"Their mother raised her hands and thanked God that she had not taught them lessons of patriotism in vain. She laid her head upon David's manly breast and wept, and then clasped Harvey in her arms and blessed him as her young and tender child, and asked God to preserve him and return him safely to her, as he was her cherished hope. Peter, who had been silent during the entire evening, except the bare suggestion to Tom to enter the service, now arose from where he was sitting, and extending his hand to David, said :

" 'My old boy, I am with you. I shall commence at once to raise a company.'

" David turned to his mother and laughingly said :

" 'Mother, you seem to have taught us all the same lesson.'

" His mother's eyes filled with tears as she turned away to seek Mary. She found her in the parlor teaching her sweet little daughter her prayers. My wife stood looking at the pretty picture of mother and child until little Mary Anderson finished, kissed her mamma, and ran off to bed; then entering the room she said :

" 'Mary, my child, I am too weak to speak. I have held up as long as I can stand it,' and then burst into tears. Mary sprang to her at once, clasping her in her arms.

" 'Dearest auntie, what is the matter ? Are you ill ?

" 'No ! no ! my child ; I am full of fear and grief ; I tremble. My sons are going to volunteer. I am grieved for fear they will never return. Oh ! Mary ! I had such a terrible dream about all the family last night. Oh ! I cannot think of it ; and yet I want them to go. God knows I love my country, and would give all—life and everything—to save it. No, I will not discourage them. I will tell you my dream when I have more strength.'

" Just then my blessed old wife fainted. Mary screamed, and we all rushed into the parlor and found her lying on the floor with Mary bending over, trying to restore her. We were all startled, and quickly lifted her up, when she seemed to revive, and was able to sit in a chair. In a few moments she was better, and said :

" 'I am all right now; don't worry. I was so startled and overcome at the thought that so many of my dear children were going to leave me at once and on such a perilous enterprise.'

" To this Peter answered :

" 'Mother, you ought not to grieve about me. Being an old bachelor, there will be but few to mourn if I should be killed.'

" ' Yes ; but, my son, your mother loves you all the same.'

" Just then a rap was heard at the window. It being open, a letter was thrown in upon the floor. I picked it up. It was addressed to 'Thos. Anderson.' I handed it to him. He opened it, and read it to himself, and instantly turned very pale and walked the floor. His wife took his arm and spoke most tenderly, asking what it was that troubled him.

" ' Mary, dear, I will read it,' he said, and unfolding the letter, he read aloud :

" ' JACKSON, Miss., June — 1861.

" ' DEAR TOM—You have been denounced to-day in resolutions as a traitor to the Southern cause, and your property confiscated. Serves you right. I am off to-morrow morning for the Confederate Army. Good-by. Love to sister.

" ' Your enemy in war,

" ' JOS. WHITTHORNE.'

" ' Mary sank into a chair. For a moment all were silent. At last Tom exclaimed:

" ' What is there now left for me ?"

" His wife, with the stateliness of a queen, as she was, her black hair clustering about her temples and falling around her shoulders and neck, her bosom heaving, her eyes flashing fire, on her tip-toes arose to her utmost height. All gazed upon her with admiration, her husband looking at her with a wildness almost of frenzy. She clenched both hands and held their straight down by her side, and exclaimed in a tone that would have made a lion cower :

" ' Would that I were a man ! I would not stop until the last traitor begged for quarter ! '

" Tom flew to her and embraced her, exclaiming:

" ' I was only waiting for that word.'

" She murmured :

" ' My heavens, can it be that there are any of my blood traitors to this country ?'

" The household were by this time much affected. A long silence ensued, which was broken by David, saying :

" ' Father, Harvey and I having agreed to go to Washing

ton to enter the army, I wish to make some arrangements
for my family. You know I have plenty for Jennie and
the babies, and I want to leave all in your hands to do
with as if it were your own, so that the family will
have such comforts as they desire.'

"David's wife, Jennie, was a delightful little woman,
with two beautiful children—Jennie, named for her
mother, and Sarah, for my wife. I said to David that I
would write to his brother James, who was a widower, having no children, to come and stay with Jennie. I at once
wrote James, who was practicing medicine at Winchester,
Va., that I feared it would be 'unhealthy' for him there,
so to come to me at once. This being done and all necessary arrangements made, David and Harvey bade all an
affectionate farewell and started for their farm, leaving
their mother and Mary in tears. As their footsteps died
away their mother went to the door, exclaiming,

"'Oh, my children! will I ever see you again?'

"That night we all joined in a general conversation on
the subject of the war. It was arranged that Peter should
start next morning for Indianapolis to see the Governor,
and, if possible, obtain authority to raise a regiment under
the call of the President. This having been decided
upon we all retired, bidding each other good night.
I presume there was little sleeping in our house that night
save what little Mary did, the poor child being entirely
unconscious of the excitement and distress in the family.
The next morning Peter took the train for Indianapolis,
Tom went down town to ascertain the latest news, and I
took my horse and rode out to David's farm, leaving the
two women in tears, and little Mary inquiring:

"'What is the matter, mamma and aunty?'

"I rode on in a deep study as to the outcome of all
this trouble. I came to David's house, unconscious for a
moment as to where I was, aroused, however, by hearing
some one crying as if in despair. I looked around and saw
it was Jennie. She stood on the door-step in great grief,
the two children asking where their father had gone.

"'Good morning, my daughter,' I said, and, dismounting, I took her in my arms, and laying her head on my shoulder she sobbed as if her heart would break.

"'O! my dear husband, shall I ever see him again? O! my children, what shall I do?' was all she could say.

"I broke down completely, this was too much; the cries of the little children for their papa and the tears of their mother were more than I could stand. He had never left them before to be gone any great length of time. I took Jennie and the children into the house. There was a loneliness and a sadness about the situation that was unendurable, and I at once ordered one of the farm hands to hitch the horses to the wagon and put the family and their little traps in and get ready to take them to my house, and turned David's house over to his head man, Joseph Dent (he being very trusty) to take charge of until David should return. With these arrangements I left with the family for Allentown. On our arrival the meeting of the three women would have melted the heart of a stone. I walked out to the barn and remained there for quite awhile, thinking matters over to myself. When I returned to the house all had become quiet and seemingly reconciled. For several days all was suspense; nothing had been heard from any of our boys; I tried to keep away from the house as much as possible to avoid answering questions asked by the women and the poor little children, which I knew no more about than they did. But while we were at breakfast on the morning of ——, Jennie was speaking of going out to her house that day to look after matters at home and see that all was going well. Just at this moment a boy entered with a letter, saying:

"'Mr. Burton sent me with this, thinking there might be something that you would like to see.'

"Mr. B. was the Postmaster, and very kind to us. He was a true Union man, but the opposition there was so strong that he was very quiet; he kept the American flag flying over his office, which was burned on that account a few nights later, as was supposed, by Southern sympathizing incendiaries. These were perilous times in Southern Indiana."

"Yes! Yes!" said Col. Bush. "We had a taste of it in Southern Ohio, where I then resided; I know all about it. The men who were for mobbing us at that time are now the most prominent 'reformers,' and seem to be the most influential persons.

Uncle Daniel continued:

"I opened the letter and read it aloud. It ran substantially as follows:

"'We arrived at Columbus, O., on the morning of ——, when there was some delay. While walking about the depot I chanced to meet your old friend the Governor. He was very glad to see me, and said to me, "Lyon, you are the very man I am looking for." I asked, "Why, Governor? I am on my way to Washington to tender my services to the President in behalf of the Union." The Governor answered, "You are hunting service, I see. Well, sir, I have a splendid regiment enlisted, but want to have a man of some experience for their Colonel, and as you have been in the Regular Army and maintained a good reputation, I will give you the position if you will take it. I grasped him by the hand and thanked him with all my heart. This was more than I could have expected. So, you see, I start off well. We are now in camp. I am duly installed as Colonel. Harvey has been mustered in and I have him detailed at my headquarters. He seems to take to soldiering very readily. I have written Jennie all about matters. I hope she and my darling children are well and as happy as can be under the circumstances.

"' Your affectionate son,

"' DAVID LYON.'

"He did not know that I had them at my house, and all were assisting one another to keep up courage. This letter affected the whole family, and caused many tears to fall, in joy as well as grief; joy that he had succeeded so well at the beginning, and grief at his absence. That evening Jennie received her letter from the 'Colonel,' as we now called him, all becoming very military in our language. Her letter was of the same import, but much of it devoted to family affairs. This made Jennie happy. We all retired and rested well that night, after pleasing the children by telling them about their father being a great soldier, and that they must be good children, and in that way cause their mother to write pleasant things about them to their good papa."

CHAPTER II.

"When sorrows come they come not single spies, but in battalions."—SHAKESPEARE.

"THREE days later Peter returned from Indianapolis, with full authority for Tom Anderson to recruit a regiment for the Union service. This was very gratifying to him, and he said to his wife, 'Mary, my time will come.' She appeared happy over the news, but her quivering lip, as she responded, gave evidence of her fears that the trial to her was going to be severe. My good wife then called us into tea, and when we were all seated, Mary said to her :

" 'Aunt Sarah, you have not yet told us your dream. Don't you remember, you promised to tell it to me ? Now let us hear it, please."

" 'Yes, my child. It has troubled me very much; and yet I don't believe there is any cause for alarm at what one may dream.'

" 'Mother, let us hear it,' spoke up Peter; ' it might be something that I could interpret. You know I try to do this sometimes; but I am not as great a success as Daniel of old.'

" 'Well, my son, it was this : I thought your father and I were in the garden. He was pulling some weeds from the flower-bed, when he was painfully stung on both hands by some insect. Soon his fingers began dropping off—all five from his right hand and his thumb and little finger from his left.'

(17)

"Tom laughingly said, 'Uncle, hold up your hands;' which I did, saying, 'You see my fingers are not gone.' Whereupon they all laughed except Peter.

"My wife said to him :

"'My son, what is your interpretation of my dream ! It troubles me.'

"'Well, mother, I will not try it now. Let the war interpret it ; it will do it correctly, doubtless. Let us talk about something else. You know dreams amount to nothing now-a-days.'

"During all this time, Peter wore a serious countenance. We discussed the matter as to how Tom should go about raising his regiment. It was understood that he should start out at once, and that Peter should take the recruits, as fast as organized into companies, and place them in the camp of instruction at Indianapolis. The next morning Tom opened a recruiting office in Allentown, placed Peter temporarily in charge, and started through the country making speeches to the people (he was quite an orator), and soon succeeded in arousing patriotic sentiments in and about Allentown. After raising two companies, he extended his operations, going down on the O. & M. R. R. to Saco, a town then of about 1,000 inhabitants. While addressing the people, a mob gathered and were about to hang him. He stood them off until the Union people came to his rescue and saved his life."

"That is just as it was where I lived," said Col. Bush. I know of just such a case, where a mob tried the same thing ; some of them, however, repented before they went to heaven, I hope."

Uncle Daniel continued:

"He left the town, however, under a guard and returned home. Soon after this he made a second effort, by arming 20 resolute men of his recruits with Colt's revolvers, which he procured from the Governor of the State, and returned to Saco. He at once gave notice that he would speak the next day. When the time arrived, he told his men to take positions in the crowd, scattering as well as they could in his front. This done he commenced his speech. Soon mutterings of the crowd could be heard, and finally the storm came and they rushed towards the stand. He shouted at the top of his voice, "Hold!" at the same time drawing his revolver, declaring he would shoot the first man that advanced another step, and also raising his left hand above his head. This was a signal for his men to "fall in," and they all rushed into line in his front with drawn weapons. The crowd instantly ran in all directions, much to the amusement and gratification of Tom.

"There were some loyal men in that community, and

TOM AND THE MOB.

before leaving Saco, Tom had raised a full company. When the day came for them to leave, they marched with the flag presented to them by the ladies of the town proudly waving, and with drum and fife making all the noise possible. There was no more disturbance there, except in secret. The 'secesh' element murdered several soldiers afterwards, and continued secretly hostile to the success of our army. In a few days after this Tom had recruited another company. There seemed then to be an immediate demand for a regiment, with a brave and daring officer, at the Capital, for some reason not then made known. Tom was ordered to have his four companies mustered in, and, attached to six already in camp; he was commissioned Colonel, and the regiment was numbered the ——— Indiana Infantry Volunteers. Tom Anderson looked the soldier in every respect. He was five feet eleven, straight as an arrow, well-built, large, broad shoulders, black eyes and hair, and martial in his bearing.

"He placed his family in my charge. The next day after Tom had left (Peter Lyon, my son, having gone before him with the recruits), my wife, Mary, Jennie, the three children and myself, were all on the porch, when a tall man, fully six feet, rather fine looking, made his appearance at the gate, and asked if that was where Daniel Lyon lived. As I answered in the affirmative, he opened the gate and walking in, saluted us all with:

"'How do you do? Do you not recognize me? I am James Lyon.'

"I sprang to him and grasped his hand, his mother threw her arms around his neck and wept for joy, the other women greeted him heartily, and the little children rushed to him. Although they had never seen him before, they knew he was some one they were glad to see, as their fathers and uncles, whom they knew, were gone from them. We all sat down and the Doctor, as I must call him (being a physician by profession), gave us some of his experiences of the last few weeks. When he received my letter and commenced getting ready to leave, the people of Winchester suspected him of preparing to go North to aid the Union, and so they threw his drugs into the street, destroyed his books, and made him leave town a beggar. He walked several miles, and finally found an old friend, who loaned him money enough to get to my place."

Mr. Reeves, who was of the party, said :

"I have been through all that and more, too. I had to leave my wife and family, and was almost riddled with bullets besides ; but it is all past now."

"I have been greatly interested, Uncle Daniel," said Dr.

Adams, "and am taking down all you say in shorthand, and intend to write it up."

"The next day," continued Uncle Daniel, "the newspapers had telegrams stating that the troops at Columbus and other places had been ordered to the East for active operations. I said to Dr. James that he must stay with the family while I went to Washington, as I wanted to see the President on matters of importance. The truth was, I wanted to see David and Harvey, as well as the President. I started the next morning, after telling the women and children to be of good cheer.

"When I reached Washington I found the army had moved to the front, and was daily expecting an engagement, but I could not understand where. I at once visited the President, to whom I was well known, and told him my desire. which was to see my sons. He promptly gave me a note to the Provost-Marshal, which procured me a pass through the lines. That night I was in the camp of my son David, who, you remember, was a Colonel. After our greeting we sat down by his camp chest, upon which was spread his supper of cold meat, hard crackers and coffee, the whole lighted by a single candle inserted in the shank of a bayonet which was stuck in the ground. While enjoying the luxury of a soldier's fare I told him all about the family, his own in particular. Harvey enjoyed the things said of him by the children which I repeated. The Colonel, however, seemed thoughtful, and did not incline to very much conversation. Looking up with a grave face he said to me :

"'Father, to-morrow may determine the fate of the Republic. I am satisfied that a battle, and perhaps a terrible one, will be fought very near here.'"

"I asked him about the armies, and he replied that we had a very large army, but poorly drilled and disciplined; that the enemy had the advantage in this respect. As to commanding officers, they were alike on both sides, with but little experience in handling large armies. He suggested that we retire to rest, so that we could be up early, but urged me to stay at the rear, and not go where I would be exposed. To this I assented. Soon we retired to our couches, which were on the ground, with but one blanket apiece and no tent over us. I did not sleep that night. My mind was wandering over the field in anticipation of what was to occur.

Early next morning I heard the orders given to march in the direction of the gaps. Wagons were rolling along the road, whips were cracking, and teamsters in strong language directing their mules; artillery was noisy in its motion; the tramp of infantry was steady and continuous; cavalrymen were rushing to and fro. I started to the rear, as my son had directed, and ate my breakfast as I rode along. About 10 o'clock I heard musket shots, and soon after artillery; then the musketry increased. I listened for awhile. Troops were rushing past me to the front. As I was dressed in citizen's clothes, the boys would occasionally call out to me, 'Old chap, you had better get back;' but I could not. I was moved forward by some strong impulse, I knew not what, and finally found myself nearing the front with my horse on the run. Soon I could see the lines forming, and moving forward into the woods in the direction of the firing, I watched closely for my son's command, and kept near it, but out of sight of the Colonel, as I feared he would be thinking of my being in danger, and might neglect his duty. The battle was now fully opened—the artillery in batteries opening along the line, the infantry heavily engaged, the cavalry moving rapidly to our flanks. Steadily the line moved on, when volley after volley rolled from one end of the line to the other. Now our left was driven back, then the line adjusted and advanced again. The rebel left gave way; then the center. Our cavalry charged, and our artillery was advanced. A shout was heard all along the line, and steadily on our line moved. The rebels stubbornly resisted, but were gradually giving way. The commanding General rode along the line, encouraging all by saying:

"'The victory is surely ours, Press forward steadily and firmly; keep your line closed up;' and to the officers, ' Keep your commands well in hand.'

"He felt that he had won the day. For hours the battle went steadily on in this way. I rode up and down the line watching every movement. I took position finally where I could see the enemy. I never expected to see officers lead their men as the rebels did on that day. They would rally their shattered ranks and lead them back into the very jaws of death. Many fell from their horses, killed or wounded; the field was strewn with the dead and dying; horses were running in different directions riderless. I had never seen a battle, and this was so different from what I had supposed from reading, I took it for granted that, both sides being unacquainted with war, were doing many things not at all military. I learned more about it afterward, however. From an eminence, where I had posted myself, I could see a large column of fresh troops filing into the plain from the hills some miles away. They were moving rapidly and coming in the direction of the right flank of our army. I at once rode as fast as I could to the left, where my son was in line, and for the first time that day showed myself to him. He seemed somewhat excited when he saw me, and asked: 'In Heaven's name what are you doing here?'

"I said: 'Never mind me, I am in no danger.'

"I then told him what I had seen, and he at once sent an orderly, with a note to the General commanding. In a short time, however, we heard the assault made on our right. It was terrific. Our troops gave way and commenced falling back. The alarm seemed to go all along the line, and a general retreat began without orders. Soon the whole army was leaving the field, and without further resistance gave away the day. The rebel army was also exhausted, and seemed to halt, in either joy or amazement, at the action of our forces.

"Just as our army retired I found a poor young officer wounded. I let him take my horse, thinking that I could walk as fast as the army could march. I came to the place formerly occupied by my son's regiment. There I found quite a number of wounded men, and my young son Harvey trying to help one of his comrades from the field.

Neither army was then in sight. I heard the sound of horses' hoofs; looked up, and saw a cavalry troop coming. I supposed it to be our own, and did not move. They dashed up where we were, and Col. Hunter, in command, drew his sabre and cut my dear boy down. I caught him as he fell, his head being cleft open. I burst out loudly in grief, and was seized as a prisoner. I presume my dress and gray hair saved my life. I was torn from my son and made to walk some three miles, to the headquarters of Gen. Jones, who heard my story about

DEATH OF HARVEY LYON.

my adventure and my dead boy. He at once released me and sent an officer with me to that part of the field where my dead child lay. I shall ever respect Gen. Jones. He is still living, and respected highly for his great soldierly qualities. I walked on the line of our retreat until I came up with a man driving an ambulance. I took him back with me and brought my son away from the field to the camp of his brother, whom I found in great distress about Harvey, but he was not aware of what had befallen him. I pointed to the ambulance, he looked and saw him lying there dead. He fell on my neck and accused himself for having brought the young boy away from home to encounter the perils of war. I was going to take his body back to his mother, but the Colonel said :

" 'No; bury him like a soldier on the battlefield.'

"So I gave way, and we buried him that night in the best manner we could. He now lies in the cemetery at Arlington. My sorrow was great then, but I am past it all now, and can grieve no more."

Col Bush here interrupted, saying :

"Uncle Daniel, you made a narrow escape. My heavens! to think of a father carrying his young son dead from the battlefield, slain by an enemy in such a villainous and dastardly way."

"What a blow to a father," said Dr. Adams. "Uncle Daniel, this Colonel was a demon to strike down a youth while assisting a wounded comrade. He deserved to be killed."

"Yes, it would seem so. I felt just as you do, and my son David uttered many imprecations against him. But, you see, we forgave all these men and acquited them of all their unholy deeds. Col. Hunter has become a very prominent man since the war, and now holds a high position in one of the Southern States. You know, in the South, the road to high position since the war has been through the rebel camps."

"Yes, yes! Uncle Daniel, that is true. Not so, however, with us in the North. The road to high position here is not through the Union camps, but through wealth and the influence of what is called elegant society, where no questions are asked as to how or where you got your money, so you have it."

"It does seem so, Doctor, now; but it was not so in our earlier days. I am sorry to confess that this change has taken place.

"After going through the scenes of this battle, now called the battle of the 'Gaps,' and burying my son, I felt for the time as if I could have no heart in anything ; the only thought on my mind was how to break the sad news to his mother. The Colonel said he would keep the name from the list of the dead until I could return home to be with the mother, so as to console her in her grief. I bade my son, the Colonel, farewell. There he stood, quiet and erect, the great tears rolling down his cheeks. I commenced my sad journey alone. In going to Washington I overtook straggling detachments, teams without drivers, and found on the road general waste of army materials, and equipage of all kinds in large quantities. Arriving in Washington, everything was in great confusion. The old General then in command of all the forces was dignified and martial in his every look and movement, but evidently much excited. There was no danger, however, as both armies were willing to stand off without another trial of arms for the present. I saw the President and told him what I had witnessed, as well as my misfortune. I advised that no movement of our forces be again attempted without further drilling and better discipline, as I was sure good training would have prevented the disaster of that day. On my way home I was oppressed with grief, causing many inquiries of me as to my distress, which only made it necessary for me to repeat my sad story over and over again until I reached Allentown. My friends, there was the great test of my strength and manhood. How could I break this to my wife? They had all heard the news of the battle, and were in sorrow over our country's misfortune. On entering the gate all rushed out on the porch to welcome me back, eager for news; but my countenance told the sad story. The Doctor was the first to speak :

"'We know about the battle, father,' said he; 'but your face tells me something has happened to the boys. What is it?'

"Sarah and the women stood as pale as death, but could not speak. Then I broke down, but tried to be as calm as I could, and said :

"'Our dear Harvey is killed.'

"My wife fell upon my neck and sobbed and cried aloud in despair until I thought her heart would break. The children ran out to their mother, crying:

" ' Oh ! mother, what is the matter ? Is papa hurt? Is he shot ?'

" They screamed, and the scene was one that would have melted the strongest heart. James stood and gazed on the scene. When all became somewhat calm, my wife was tenderly placed in bed, and Jennie, after hearing that the Colonel was safe, staid with her. To the others I related my experience on the battlefield, and the death of Harvey, his burial, my capture and release, my arrival at and departure from Washington, and all up to the time I reached home. The saddest time I ever spent in my life was during the long, weary hours of that night; the attempt to reconcile my wife to our sad fate, the fears expressed by the wives of the Colonel and Tom, the questions of the children, and their grief and sobs for their Uncle Harvey— they all loved him dearly ; he had petted them and played with them frequently, entertaining them in a way that children care so much for. Many days my wife was confined to her bed, the Doctor keeping close watch over her. Weeks of sadness and gloom in our household passed before we seemed to take the matter as a part of what many would have to experience in this dreadful and wicked attempt to destroy the peace and happiness of our people. In the meantime, Col. Tom Anderson (as he was now a Colonel), and my son Peter, who had been made a Captain in Col. Anderson's regiment, came home to see us, and tried to make it as pleasant for us as could be done under the circumstances. When Peter heard of Harvey's death, through Col. Anderson, he was very much affected and wept bitterly.

" ' That dream haunts me,' he said, ' by day and by night. I know my fate so well.'

" This amazed the Colonel, and he asked Peter what he meant by this nonsense.

" ' I know,' said Peter, ' but——'

" ' But what ?' asked the Colonel.

" ' Nothing,' replied Peter, and the conversation on that subject dropped for the time being.

" The visit of Col. Tom and Capt. Peter, as we now out

of courtesy called them, made the time pass much more
pleasantly. Col. Tom and the Doctor, both being good
conversationalists, kept the minds of the family as much
away from the battle of the Gaps as possible. The Doctor
having lived in Virginia and Col. Anderson in Mississippi,
their conversation naturally turned on the condition of the
South. The Doctor said 'there are in Virginia many
Union men, but they were driven into secession by the
aggressiveness and ferocity of those desiring a separation
from the Government.

" 'Those people are opposed to a Republican form of
Government, and if they succeed in gaining a separation
and independence, sooner or later they will take on the
form of the English Government. They now regard the
English more favorably than they do the Northern people,
and the most surprising thing to me is to see the sentiment
in the North in favor of the success of this (the Southern)
rebellion. True, it is confined to one political party, but
that is a strong party in the North as well as the South.

" ' One of the dangers that will confront us is the tiring out
of our Union people at some stage of the war, and following on that the success by the sympathizers with the rebellion in the elections North. If this can be brought about it
will be done. This is part of the Southern programme, and
they have their men selected in every Northern State.'"

" ' I have heard this discussed frequently, and their statements as to the assurances that they have from all over the
North—in New York, Ohio, Pennsylvania, Indiana, Illinois,
and so on. In Ohio, their chief adviser from the North,
Mr. Valamburg, resides. Such men as "Dan" Bowen and
Thos. A. Strider, both very influential and prominent men,
are regarded as ready to act in concert with them at any
moment. Should that party succeed, with such men as I
have mentioned as leaders, the independence of the Confederacy would at once be acknowledged, on the ground
that we have failed to suppress the rebellion, and that a
further continuance of the war would only prove an abso-
lute failure; and I fear that our Northern peacemakers
would then cry "peace! peace!" and acquiesce in this

outrage upon our Republic and our Christian civilization.'

"'Yes,' replied Col. Tom; 'but, Doctor, there is a feature preceding that which should be carefully considered. I fear, since I have heard what is going on here, that these Northern secessionists and sympathizers will organize in our rear and bring on war here at home. I was ordered to the Capital to watch this movement. They are organizing all around us. I was about to be mobbed near here for trying to raise troops for the Union army. Thos. A. Strider, of whom you spoke, is doing everything he can to discourage enlistments. He speaks of the Republican President as "a tyrant and this war as an unholy abolition war," and people listen to him. He has been considered a kind of oracle in this State for many years, as you know.'

"Just then Jennie returned from the post-office with two letters from Col. David—one to her and one to the Doctor. This concluded the conversation between Col. Tom and the Doctor. Jennie's letter gave her a more complete description of the battle of the Gaps than any he had heretofore sent. He spoke of my appearance on the ground and the tragic death of Harvey. The household assembled and listened with great attention, except my wife, who went weeping to her room, as she could not hear of her boy without breaking down, wondering why it was her fate to be so saddened thus early in the contest. The Doctor opened his letter and found that the Assistant Surgeon of Col. David's regiment had died from a wound received at the battle of the Gaps, and the Governor of Ohio had commissioned Dr. James Lyon Assistant Surgeon at the request of the Colonel. He was directed to report to his regiment at once. This was very gratifying to the Doctor, as he felt inclined to enter the service.

When his mother heard this she again grew very melancholy, and seemed to think her whole family were, sooner or later, to enter the army and encounter the perils and vicissitudes of war. The next morning the Doctor bade us all good-by, and left for the army of the East. The visit of Col. Anderson and Peter helped to distract our attention from the affliction which was upon us. Peter, however, was very quiet, and seemed in a deep study most of the time. His mother finally asked him if he had thought of her dream, saying it troubled her at times. He smiled, and answered:

"'Mother, I think this war will interpret it. You know there is nothing in dreams,' thus hoping to put her mind at rest by his seeming indifference; but he afterwards told Col. Anderson his interpretation."

Dr. Adams here asked Uncle Daniel if he knew Peter's interpretation.

"Yes; it was certainly correct, and so it will appear to you as we proceed in this narrative, should you wish to hear me through."

"My dear sir, I have never been so interested in all my life, and hope you will continue until you tell us all. I am preserving every sentence."

"The day passed off quietly, and next morning Col. Anderson and Peter left for their command. Mary was brave; she gave encouragement to her husband and all others who left for the Union army. She was very loyal, and seemed to be full of a desire to see the Union forces succeed in every contest. In fact, the letter of her brother to her husband seemed to arouse her almost to desperation; she went about quietly, but showed determination in every movement. She taught her little daughter patriotism and devotion to the cause of our country, and religiously believed that her husband would yet make his mark as a gallant and brave man. She gave encouragement to my good wife Sarah, and to Jennie, Col. David's wife. She told me afterwards, out of the hearing of the others, that she hoped every man on the Union side would enter the army and help crush out secession forever."

CHAPTER III.

" Cease to consult ; the time for action calls,
War, horrid war approaches to your walls."— HOMER.

"FOR a season battles of minor importance were fought with varying success. In the meantime Col. Anderson had been ordered with his command to join the forces of Gen. Silent, at Two Rivers. Here there was quiet for a time.

"At length, however, orders came for them to move to the front. For a day or so all was motion and bustle. Finally the army moved out, and after two days' hard marching our forces struck the enemy's skirmishers. Our lines moved forward and the battle opened. Col. Anderson addressed his men in a few eloquent words, urging them to stand, never acknowledge defeat or think of surrender. The firing increased and the engagement became general. Gen. Silent sat on his horse near by, his staff with him, watching the action. Col. Anderson was pressing the enemy in his front closely, and as they gave way he ordered a charge, which was magnificently executed.

"As the enemy gave back, evidently becoming badly demoralized, he looked and beheld before him Jos. Whitthorne. The recognition was mutual, and each seemed determined to outdo the other. Anderson made one charge after another, until the enemy in his front under command of his wife's brother retreated in great confusion. Col. Anderson, in his eagerness to capture Whitthorne, advanced too far to the front of the main line, and was in great dan-

(31)

ger of being surrounded. He perceived the situation in time, and at once changed front, at the same time ordering his men to fix bayonets. Drawing his sword and rising in his stirrups, he said:

"'Now, my men, let us show them that a Northern man is equal to any other man.'

"He then ordered them forward at a charge bayonets, riding in the centre of his regiment. Steadily on they went, his men falling at every step, but not a shot did they fire, though they were moving almost up to the enemy's lines. The rebel commander shouted to his men:

"'What are these? Are they men or machines?'

"The rebel line wavered a moment, and then gave way. At that instant a shot struck Col. Anderson's horse and killed it, but the Colonel never halted. He disengaged himself, and pushing forward on foot, regained his line, and left the enemy in utter rout and confusion. Whitthorne was not seen again that day by Anderson. The battle was still raging on all the other parts of the line. First one side gained an advantage, then the other, and so continued until night closed in on the combatants. A truce was agreed to, and hostilities ceased for the time being.

"The Colonel worked most of the night, collecting his wounded and burying his dead. His loss was quite severe, in fact, the loss was very heavy throughout both armies. Late in the night, while searching between the lines for one of his officers, he met Whitthorne. They recognized each other. Col. Anderson said to him:

"'Jo, I am glad to see you, but very sorry that we meet under such circumstances.'

"Whitthorne answered:

"'I cannot say that I am glad to see you, and had it not been for making my sister a widow, you would have been among the killed to-day.'

"The Colonel turned and walked away without making any reply, but said to himself:

"'Can that man be my wife's brother? I will not, however, condemn him; his blood is hot now; he may have a better heart than his speech would indicate.'"

"Thus meditating, he returned to his bivouac. In the morning the burying parties were all that was to be seen of the enemy. He had retreated during the night, and very glad were our forces, as the battle was well and hard fought on both sides. The forces were nearly equal as to numbers.

"Col. Anderson did not see the General commanding for several days; when he did the latter said to him :

"Colonel, you handle your men well; were you educated at a military school ?'

"The Colonel answered :

"'No; I am a lawyer.'

"General Silent remarked :

"'I am very sorry for that,' and walked on.

"Tom wrote his wife a full report of this battle. He called it the battle of Bell Mountain. It is, however, called Two Rivers. He said that Gen. Silent was a curious little man, rather careless in his dress; no military bearing whatever, quite unostentatious and as gentle as a woman; that he did not give any orders during the battle, but merely sat and looked on, the presumption being that while everything was going well it was well enough to let it alone. In his report he spoke highly of Col. Anderson as an officer and brave man.

"This letter of the Colonel's filled his wife's heart with all the enthusiasm a woman could possess. She was proud of her husband. She read and re-read the letter to my wife and Jennie, and called her little daughter and told her about her father fighting so bravely. We were all delighted. He spoke so well of Peter also. Said ' he was as cool as an icebox during the whole engagement.' He never mentioned to his wife about meeting her brother Jo on the field until long afterwards.

"The troops of this army were put in camp and shortly recruited to their maximum limit. Volunteering by this time was very active. No longer did our country have to wait to drum up recruits. The patriotic fires were lighted up and burning brightly: drums and the shrill notes of the

2

fife were heard in almost every direction. Sympathizers
with rebellion had hushed in silence for the present—but
for the present only."

"Uncle Daniel," said Major Isaac Clymer, who had been
silent up to this time, "I was in that engagement, in command of a troop of cavalry, and saw Col. Anderson make
his bayonet charge.   He showed the most cool and daring
courage that I have ever witnessed during the whole war,
and I was through it all.   Gen. Pokehorne was in command of the rebels, and showed himself frequently that

THE CHARGE OF COL. ANDERSON'S REGIMENT.

day, urging his men forward.   He was afterwards killed at
Kensington Mountain, in Georgia.   We got the information very soon after he fell, from our Signal Corps.   They
had learned to interpret the rebel signals, and read the
news from their flags."

"Yes, I have heard it said by many that our Signal
Corps could do that, and I suppose the same was true of
the other side."

"O, yes," said Col. Bush, "that was understood to be so,

and towards the end of the war we had to frequently change our signal signs to prevent information being imparted in that way to our enemy."

"There was a Colonel," said Major Clymer, "from Arkansas, in command of a rebel brigade, in that battle, who acted with great brutality. He found some of our Surgeons on the field dressing the wounds of soldiers and drove them away from their work and held them as prisoners while the battle lasted, at the same time saying, with an oath, that the lives of Abolitionists were not worth saving."

"Yes. The Colonel mentioned that in his letter and spoke of it when I saw him. He said it was only one of the acts of a man instinctively barbarous. His name was Gumber—Col. Gumber. He has been a prominent politician since the war, holding important positions. You know, these matters are like Rip Van Winkle's drinks—they don't count, especially against them."

"'But among Christian people they should,' said Dr. Adams.

"'That is true, but it does not. There are two distinct civilizations in this country, and the sooner our people recognize this fact the sooner they will understand what is coming in the future. But, returning to my story, the winter was now coming on, and I had to make provision for the families that were in my charge, so I called the women together and had a council as to what we would do for the best; the first thing was to arrange about sending the little girls to school. After discussing it, we concluded to start them the next day to the common school. Our public schools were said to be very good. So the next morning my wife, Mary and Jennie all started with the children to school. They saw the teacher and talked with her, telling her that their fathers were in the army, and she entered them in school. They came and went, back and forth, and seemed greatly pleased during the first week, but on Wednesday of the second week, they came running home crying and all dirty, saying that some of the school children had pelted them with clods and pebbles, calling them Abolitionists. Little Jennie said to me:

" 'Grandpa, what is an Abolitionist ?'

"I replied : 'One who desires the colored people to be free, and not sold away to strangers like cattle.'

" 'Grandpa, do white people sell colored people like they sell cows ?'

" 'Yes, my child.'

" 'Well, grandpa, is that right ?'

" 'I think not, my child. Would it be right for me to sell you away from your mother and send you where you would never see her again ?'

" 'Oh ! no, grandpa; you would not be so wicked as that. I would cry myself to death; and mamma—what would she do without me, she loves me so ?'

" 'Yes, said little Sarah, 'I love sister, too. I would cry, too, if you sent her away where I could not see her. Why, grandpa, people don't do that, do they ? Your are only fooling sister.'

" 'No, no, child; in the South, where the war is, there are a great many colored people living. They are called slaves. They work for their masters and only get what they eat and wear, and their masters very often sell them and send the men away from their wives and children, and their babies away from their mothers and fathers.'

" 'Grandpa, do they ever sell white people?' asked Jennie.

" 'No, my child.'

" 'Well, why don't they sell white people, too ?'

" 'Oh, my child, the law only allows colored people to be sold.'

" 'Well, grandpa, I don't think any good people ever sell the little children away from their mothers, any way.'

" 'No, my child, nor any grown people either.'

" 'Well, grandpa, you wouldn't sell anybody, would you ?'

" 'No, my child, I would not.'

" 'Well, then, grandpa, you are an Abolitionist.'

" 'Yes, in that sense I am.'

" 'Well, grandpa, I am one, too, and I will just say so at school, and will tell the boys and girls who threw clods at us and called us Abolitionists that they sell people like cows, and that they are not good people.'

"'Yes,' said little Mary Anderson, 'I know what colored people are. They've plenty of them down where we came from. They call them "niggers". They are mighty good to me, grandpa, and my papa doesn't sell 'em. He is a good man. He don't do bad like those rebels, does he, ma?'

"'No, my child, your papa does not sell anybody. He is against it. He never owned anyone. He does not think it right to own people.'

PUPILS ATTACKING THE "LITTLE ABOLITIONIST."

"'No; my papa don't, does he, ma? He is going to fight the people that sell other people, ain't he, ma?'

"'Yes, my darling; but don't say any more. Let us go in and get our tea, and you will feel better.'

"This interference of little Mary and her mother let me out of a scrape, for I say to you, friends, that I was getting into deep water and would have very soon lost my soundings if Jennie and little Sarah had kept after me much longer. You see, the truth is that I had never been an

Abolitionist, but a Freesoil Democrat; but soon I became a full-fledged Abolitionist after our flag was fired upon by the Secessionists.

"However, we all entered the house, and after tea, the children being put to bed, we held another council and decided that inasmuch as there was such great excitement in the country, and Allentown being such a hot-hole of rebel sympathizers, it was not safe even to allow our children to attend the schools. Jennie, however, being a good scholar and having prior to her marriage taught school, we unanimously elected her our family teacher, and setting apart a room, duly installed her on the next Monday morning over our Abolition school, as we found on the evening of our discussion with the children that they had converted the household by their innocent questions.

"The next day I rode out to my son David's farm and saw Joseph Dent, the man whom I had left in charge. I inquired of him if everything was all right about the place, and he told me that he had moved his family into David's house, as he feared some damage might be done to it, having seen several persons prowling about at different times. He did not know who they were, but was sure they meant mischief, as they were very abusive of the Colonel, calling him a 'Lincoln dog,' after the manner of Dan Bowen in his speech.

"Joseph said he was now prepared for them; that he had another man staying with him, and if I would go with him he would show me what they had done. I did as he asked me, he led the way into the house and upstairs, where he showed me a couple of holes cut through the wall in each room, just beneath the eaves, and standing in the corner was a regular arsenal of war materials. I said to him that he seemed to be in for war. The tears started in his eyes, and he said:

"'Uncle Daniel, I am an old soldier; was in Capt. David's company when he was in the Regular Army. I came to him three years ago when my enlistment was out. I will defend everything on these premises with my life. I would be in the army now with the Colonel (I am used to calling him Captain) if he had not asked me to stay here and take care of his farm. These "secesh" will not get away with me and my partner very easily, and should you hear of this fort being stormed, you bring some men with you to pick up the legs and pieces of the fellows who shall undertake it. Do not be afraid ; we will take care of all here.'

"'Yes, Joseph, I see that. I will tell Jennie, and also write the Colonel how splendidly you are doing.'

"'Thanks,' said Joseph, giving me the regular soldier's salute. 'Is there anything wanted at your house, sir ? Tell the Colonel's wife that I will bring down anything that she may be wanting at any time. I will certainly bring a load of wood in to-morrow.'

"We were in the habit of getting many things from the farm—butter, eggs, chickens, potatoes, etc. All our wood came from there. Joseph was very useful in many ways. I returned home satisfied that all was going well at the farm.

"The weather was now getting cold and disagreeable ; too much so, it was thought, for any very serious army movements on our Western lines. The rebels had collected a very heavy force at Dolinsburg, situated on a high ridge, with hills sloping down to Combination River, one of the tributaries of the Ohio. Here they had built an immense fortress, with wings running out from either side for a great distance ; on the outer walls were placed large guns, sweeping and commanding the river to the north. The rebels were well prepared with all kinds of war materials, as well as in the numbers of their effective force, to defend their works against great odds.

"Gen. Silent, who, it seems, always did everything differently from what the enemy expected him to do, conceived the idea that he would try to dislodge them. When the enemy heard that he was preparing to move against them, they but laughed at such an attempt.

"The General, however, made ready, gave his orders, and his army was soon in motion. The direction in which our army was to march was very soon known, as it was impossible to keep any of our movements a secret, on account

of the great desire of newspapers to please everybody and
keep every one posted on both sides, the rebels as well as
friends; which prompted them to publish every movement
made. This was called 'enterprise,' and it has been considered patriotic devotion by many, especially the gold
gamblers and money kings. This was not permitted by our
enemies; the publication of any secret expedition or movement of their forces, by any one inside of their lines, would
cost him his life ; and so in any army save our Union army.
Why was this ? It does seem to me that this ought not to
have been so. I have often thought of it, and concluded it
must have been fear. 'The pen is mightier than the sword'
has been truthfully said.

"Our Congress was afraid of the press, and were not willing to make laws stringent enough for the army on this
subject. The President was nervous in this respect,
and commanding Generals were afraid of criticisms ; so
it was the only class that had the privilege of doing and
saying what it wished to, and, my friends, that is one of
our troubles even now. Our statesmen are afraid to speak
out and give their opinions, without first looking around
to see if any one has a pencil and notebook in his hand. This
is getting to be almost unbearable, to find some person in
nearly every small assemblage of people, on the street, in
the hotel, in the store, even in your own private house, reporting what you have for dinner, what this one said about
some other one, what this one did or said, or expects to do
or say in the future. But I am wandering from my story."

"Well, Uncle Daniel, your discussions on all subjects are
interesting," replied the Doctor.

"I have been thinking of what you said about the press
during the war," said Col. Bush; "and taking what you
said upon the subject of our great ambition here in the
North to get money, and let all else take care of itself, I
can see that the same sordid spirit pervaded the press during our war; fortunes were made by many newspapers in
that way; everybody bought papers then; we sold the news
to our own people for money and furnished it to the rebels
gratis. Get money, get money; that is our worst feature,

and most dangerous one it is, for the country's welfare."

"I agree with you, Colonel," spoke up Maj. Clymer, "but I would rather hear Uncle Daniel talk. On any other occasion I would be delighted to hear you."

"I beg pardon, Uncle Daniel," replied the Colonel. "I will hereafter be a patient and delighted auditor."

"Well, when the army was under way there was great excitement and alarm throughout the North among the Union people. Our armies in the East had not been successful, and the sympathizers with the rebellion all over the country were again beginning to be rather saucy. They would enjoy getting together and reading of our defeats and discuss, to our disadvantage, the failures of our attempts to subdue the rebellion, and in this way made it very uncomfortable for any person who loved his country and desired its success. They would in every way try to discourage our people by saying 'this movement now commencing will only be a repetition of what we have already had so often lately in the East.'

"But our army moved on, and during the march to the vicinity of Combination River they were met by the enemy frequently, who were trying to impede their march, and several severe skirmishes and minor engagements occurred. They were now within some twenty miles of Dolinsburg Fortress, when a sharp and very decisive engagement took place between one battalion of cavalry, two batteries of artillery, and three regiments of infantry on our side, where Col. Anderson was the ranking officer, and therefore in command, and five regiments of infantry, two batteries and one troop of cavalry on the side of the rebels. They were posted behind a small stream, known as Snake Creek, having steep banks. The action commenced, as usual, with the skirmishers. After reconnoitering the position well, the Colonel determined to send his cavalry and one regiment around some distance, so as to cross the stream and strike the enemy's left flank. He could not expect re-enforcements, if they might be needed, very soon, as he marched on the extreme southern road, so as to form the junction with the other troops on their extreme right, touching Combination River to the south of the enemy's works, so as to be the extreme right flank of our army. The enemy, finding his force was superior in numbers, attempted to cross the stream with his infantry. The two batteries were opened and poured shrapnel into the advancing column, dealing havoc and slaughter on all sides. They tried to keep their line, but they soon staggered, halted, and fell back. The Colonel then opened a destructive musketry fire all along the line. Just at this moment he heard the attack of his regiment of infantry and troop of cavalry on their flank. He quickly advanced across the stream, and the enemy was in utter rout.

"He captured all his guns—six 12-pound Napoleons and four howitzers—and a large number of prisoners. He followed closely on the rear of the enemy, gathering in stragglers and squads of men until night closed in and compelled him to desist and go into camp. When safety from surprise was assured, he sent for one of the prisoners to get some information about the road and the fortifications, commands, etc. After ascertaining many things that he considered important, he found, upon further inquiry, that his enemy upon that afternoon was commanded by Col. Jos. Whitthorne, his wife's brother. He turned and said to Peter, who was standing near:

" 'This man seems to be my evil genius. I hope I will not meet him again. It seems hard that I am to continually meet my own kindred in combat. Is it possible that these people are willing to spill the blood of their own friends and kindred, merely because they have failed to retain power longer, and for that reason will destroy the Government?'

" 'Yes,' said Peter; 'they will never be content except when they can control other people as well as the Government. But see here, Colonel, do you see this?' showing him a great rent in the breast of his coat and vest; 'a pretty close call, wasn't it?'

" 'By George! it was that!'

" 'Well, never mind; but was not this about as nice a little fight as you would wish to have for an appetiser?'

" ' Yes, you are quite right; and that reminds me that I have not had a bite to eat since four o'clock this morning. By the way, have you any cold coffee in your canteen ?'

" ' O, yes, I have learned to keep that on hand. Here, help yourself.'

" The Colonel took a good drink, and turned to Peter and said :

" ' What is the matter with that coffee ?'

" ' Nothing ; it is only laced a little.'

" ' Laced ? What is that ?'

" ' Why, I put a little brandy in it, that's all.'

" ' That's all, is it ? Well ! that is something I have learned. Let me taste it again.'

" Which he did, as Peter afterwards said, until there was none left. I tell you these poor fellows were excusable for occasionally warming up after a hard march or a battle. I have learned to look very leniently on the shortcomings in that direction of the poor old unfortunate fellows who are going through this hard world without a penny, after having served their country faithfully. I see them nearly every day, forgotten, neglected, no home, no friends to care for them ; and to see them when they pass by the American flag always salute it. I hope their fate will be a better one in the next world.

" I well remember that during the war every one who cared for his country would say, 'God bless the Union soldier and his family.' We all prayed for them then ; the good women in church, at home, in the hospital, at the side of the sick, wounded or dying soldier, prayed fervently for their safety here and hereafter. We loved him then, and say we do yet ; but we find the same men who reviled him then, complaining about the pension list, and some saying : 'The Confederates fought for what they believed to be right. We are all American citizens. Why not put all on the same footing ? Let us be brothers.' I tell you, my friends, the people of this country are hard to understand. I heard the President of the Southern Confederacy applauded this year. I was saddened by this, and was glad that my time here could not be regarded as of great duration. Can such things be? Am I dreaming? Where am I? Is it possible that I am in Indiana and not in South Carolina? Am I under the Union flag, and not the Confederate?"

Uncle Daniel here bowed his head, and in a whisper to himself, said:

"Is it so? Is it so?

CHAPTER IV.

BATTLE OF DOLINSBURG.—HEROIC CONDUCT OF COL. TOM ANDERSON.—REPORTED DEAD.—HIS WIFE REFUSES TO BELIEVE THE REPORT.

" There was speech in their dumbness, language in their very gesture, they looked as they had heard of a world ransomed, or one destroyed, a notable passion of wonder appeared in them; but the wisest beholder, that knew no more but seeing could not say, if the importance were joy or sorrow; but in the extremity of the one it must needs be."—SHAKESPEARE

"THE next morning the march was resumed. At an early hour the whole army was in motion on different roads with the general understanding that the command would close in line around the west side of the fortress that afternoon. The weather being very disagreeable for marching, there was delay on the roads, but, finally, late in the evening the army commenced closing in and forming its line. The centre was commanded by General Smote; the left, resting north, on the river, commanded by General Waterberry, and the right, resting on an almost impassable slough, connecting with the river, commanded by General McGovern. In moving into position the place was found to be well protected by a heavy abatis and chevaux-de-frise, from point to point, above and below the fortress. This seemed impassable, and the enemy, seeing our army closing in around them, kept up a terrible fire on our advancing columns, causing us very severe loss in getting into position. It was at a late hour in the night (when our lines were only partially formed) that our army rested, as best as they could, in the snow and sleet; but not a murmur was heard. The next morning our lines were advanced to the front and the impediments removed as much as possible; though

(45)

a severe and deadly fire was poured upon our men most of the day. Late in the afternoon an assault was ordered in the centre, and a bloody affair it was; again and again our brave fellows moved on the works, but were as often driven back with severe loss. About 4 o'clock Gen. Silent came riding along with an orderly by his side, his staff having been sent in different directions with orders. He came up to where Col. Anderson was sitting on his horse, watching the engagement in the centre. Gen. Silent, after passing the compliments of the day, said to the Colonel:

"'Your engagement at Snake Creek (that being the name of the creek where the Colonel met the enemy the day before) was a rather brilliant affair as I learn it.'

"'Yes,' said the Colonel; 'it was my first attempt at commanding in a battle, but we had the best of it.'

"'Yes,' said the General; 'and now I want to see if you can do as well here. I wish you to assault the enemy's works in this low ground on the right, in order to draw some of his forces away from the centre; our forces are having a hard time of it there.'

"Col. Anderson gave the order at once to prepare for action—knapsacks and blankets were thrown off, and the assaulting column formed. The General rode away after saying:

"'It is not imperative that you enter their works; but make the assault as effectual as you can without too great a sacrifice of men.'

"The Colonel looked at the ground over which they must pass and viewed the works with his glass, but said not one word save to give the command 'Forward!' On, on they went, and as they moved under a torrent of leaden hail, men fell dead and wounded at every step; but they went right up to the mouths of the cannon. There they stood and poured volley after volley into the enemy, until at last he began to give way, when re-enforcements came from the centre, as was desired. The Colonel's force could stand no longer. Sullenly they fell back to a strip of woods when night closed in, and the battle ceased for the day.

Our lines were much nearer the enemy than in the morning.

"The centre held their ground at last, and all was still. Part of the night was employed in hunting the dead and wounded. Many were wounded and frozen to death, being left on the ground during the night. The suffering in front of Dolinsburg was something almost indescribable—it snowed, sleeted, hailed and froze during the whole of the night. The troops did not sleep, nor did they attempt it; they had to form into squads and walk around trees all night. No fires could be lighted—they were so close to the enemy's entrenchments. Just at daylight the sharp sound of their skirmishers was heard. They had concluded to move out on our right and attack us on our flank, and open the way for the escape of their army. On they came. Our line was soon formed and our musketry opened. During the night one of our batteries had been brought up and given position on a slight elevation to the right of Col. Anderson's centre. The enemy opened furiously on our line, and in a few minutes our battery was knocked to pieces and was charged by infantry. Here there was a bloody conflict; men fell by the score; the snow was reddened by the blood of both patriots and traitors. The smoke seemed to hover around the trees and underbrush, as if to conceal the contending forces from each other. The flame of musketry and the red glare of the cannons lighted up the scene with a lurid tint. Limbs fell from the trees, and the ground was mown as smoothly of weeds and underbrush as if by a scythe. Our right was under orders to hold their position at all hazards. The battle, dreadful and bloody, continued. By degrees the troops on the right of Col. Anderson gave way and abandoned the field. At noon but one regiment besides Col. Anderson's withstood the enemy on the right of our line. They were terribly cut up, and having no food, were nearly exhausted. Their ammunition was growing scarce, none having been brought up to this point for their supply. In this condition they stood like a wall, under the most galling fire of artillery and musketry, their comrades falling like grass before the sickle. At length the enemy's cavalry appeared in the rear; not in line, but as if observing the battle with a view of taking advantage at the proper time of any mishap that might occur in our lines. Col. Anderson seeing this, and feeling that his command was now in great peril, conceived the idea of a bayonet charge on the line to his front, and so ordered it. His line moved forward, in a double-quick, and with a shout drove the enemy, who was stampeded by the impetuous assault. The Colonel, being on foot, led his men right up to the works,

COL. ANDERSON WOUNDED.

the enemy having been driven inside. As he leaped forward to them, with sword in hand, calling to his men, 'Come on, my boys,' he fell, as they then thought, mortally wounded. The enemy seeing this made a fresh assault, and drove our force back. Col. Anderson was left on the field supposed to be dead. The battle raged all along the line. Our right was driven and forced under the brow of a hill. While under this partial shelter a portion of the enemy made their escape through this unoccupied part of the field. At this time our left made a successful assault upon the works of the enemy, capturing their outer line and forcing them into their more contracted lines but more strongly fortified. The centre had made several ineffectual assaults and had lost in killed and wounded very heavily. Re-enforcements came to the right, and a renewal of the assault all along the line was ordered. To the work of blood and death the men again came forward with a heroic will, and for about an hour the battle was like the long roll on a thousand drums. The air was filled with shells; the heavens were lighted up as if meteors were flying in all directions; the rumbling of artillery was heard as batteries changed position, and the loud commands of excited officers. On and on moved the serried masses. As the lines opened by the dropping of the dead and wounded, 'close up, boys,' could be heard. It was now about dusk. One grand charge all along the line, one grand shout, 'up with the flag, boys !'—all was over, the fortress was ours, and the Stars and Stripes floated over Dolinsburg. That night, however, was a night of gloom and sorrow in our army. Gen. McGovern was killed in the last assault. Gen. Smote was badly wounded and died a few days later. Gen. Waterberry, a brave and gallant officer, fell a few weeks later at the battle of Pittskill."

"I remember when Waterberry fell, poor fellow," said Col. Bush.

"Yes, many a poor fellow lost his life in those two battles. We captured a great number of prisoners. Gen. Bertram surrendered. Many of his leading officers were killed and wounded, and some made their escape through the opening in our line on the right, where Col. Anderson fell wounded."

Dr. Adams asked : " Uncle Daniel, did you ever hear of him ? Was his body found ?"

"Yes, Doctor, and the story of that and his recovery is a very singular one. Peter searched diligently for him, but failed to find him ; this distressed him so much that he decided to ask for a leave and return home, so as to stay a short time with the family and do what he could to help us bear the sorrow of the Colonel's supposed death. After our grief-stricken family could have the patience to listen to his recitals, he gave us the story just as I have told it. Mrs. Anderson, although stricken down with grief, insisted that her husband was not killed, or he would have been found among the slain; that a man of such marked features would have been noticed by some one who did the interring. The Captain insisted that there could be no doubt but that he was killed. Time passed on, but little Mary would continually ask, 'If her papa was dead?' 'Was he shot?' 'Who had killed him?' and a thousand other questions which constantly kept her mother thinking of the Colonel's fate, and soon she determined to go in search of him. Peter was leaving for his regiment, now under command of Colonel Rice. Col. Anderson having been reported as killed, Rice had been promoted Colonel, and the regiment had moved with the army in a southwesterly direction some considerable distance from Dolinsburg. Still there had been troops left there, so that it was perfectly safe to visit the battle-field, there being no rebel force in that part of the country at that time. I agreed to go with her, and made all the arrangements necessary for the family; the farm of Col. David having been looked after, and our family-school reorganized under Jennie, which had become demoralized by the news of Col. Anderson's death. In the meantime we had heard from Col. David and James, who were well, and also had letters from Stephen and Henry; both had joined the army: Stephen in an infantry regiment from Ohio, where he lived, and Henry in a cavalry regiment from Michigan, where he had been employed for a time in surveying for a company; so at this time I had one son left not yet in the army, he being my third son, Jackson, who was then engaged in railroading in Minnesota. We had not heard from him for some time, and his mother was sorely troubled, expecting soon to hear of the last of the Lyons being in the army. This, she thought, was a little more than ought to be required of any one family."

"So say I, Uncle Daniel," spoke up several of the listeners.

"True, true; but our country's demands should be satisfied by her citizens, no matter what they may be. Well, when all was arranged, Mary Anderson and I started. We went as far as we could by cars and boat, and then obtained horses and traveled on horseback to Dolinsburg. Coming to the pickets we were halted, and, on telling our errand and where we were from, we were taken to the headquarters of Col. Harden, who was in command of the post. We were well received and most hospitably treated by himself and officers. They all sympathized with Mrs. Anderson; knew of the Colonel's gallant conduct in battle, but all thought there was no use of a search for him; that he was certainly killed in charging the works near the fort. They showed us where he made the assault. After resting for the night we started on our search, Capt. Day accompanying us as guide and protector. We first went to the place where the Colonel fell, but there was nothing but long trenches, where the dead had been buried. We passed over the battle-field, which was mowed down smoothly by bullets. Limbs of trees had fallen in confusion, furrows were plowed in the ground by shell, horses' skeletons, broken muskets, pieces of wagons, parts of caissons, spokes, ammunition boxes, pieces of blankets, coats, pantaloons, parts of tents—everything in pieces, the evidences of a great contest were marked at every step. Late in the afternoon, worn out with walking and the excitement, we returned, very much disheartened. We dined on soldier's fare, which seemed to us delicious. After discussing the battle and the probabilities of the result of the war until a late hour, we retired to the camp cots for a night's rest. Next morning we got ready for a start. Mary Anderson inquired of Col. Harden which way the rebels who got through our lines had retreated. He answered her that they retreated on a road along the river up stream some twenty-five miles, and then crossed on a boat that had come down the river on its way to Dolinsburg, which was stopped by the retreating rebels. Mary said:

"'Uncle Daniel, I am going to that place if I can be al-lowed to do so.'

"I replied: 'This would be a very tiresome and fruit-less trip, my child; but if you will be any better satisfied by doing so, I will make it with you.

"Col. Harden said he would send a small escort for pro-tection, though there was no danger of any force of the enemy, but there probably would be some wicked people there who might do us some harm. He had our horses brought out, and sent Capt. Day and ten mounted men with us. The road was somewhat rough, but very passable for saddle-horses. When we had gone about ten miles we met a colored boy, some fourteen years old, who said he was going to Dolinsburg. Mrs. Anderson rode on with Capt. Day. The escort was in front of them. I asked the boy why he was going to Dolinsburg. He said he lived about ten miles further up the river, and that an old colored woman, called 'Aunt Martha,' had sent him down to see if any soldiers were at Dolinsburg; and if so, to tell them that there was a Union officer at her house, sick.

"'Do you know his name?' I asked.

"'No, sir; but Aunt Martha calls him Massa Tom.'

"I trembled all over. My blood was hot and cold by turns.

"'When and how did he come there?' I asked.

"He said that the rebels had left him. My brain was now dizzy, and I told him to turn back and take me to the place. We rode past the rest of the company while they were resting for a short time. I told them I would ride on to the place where the river was crossed, and wait there for them. Mary was hearing all she could from Capt. Day about the battle, and so she raised no objections. I in-quired of the boy as to the appearance of the sick officer. He described him as very pale, black hair, eyes and beard. I could understand his being pale, and felt sure it was Col. Anderson. I asked the boy if he ever spoke to him. He said he had not, but Aunt Martha talked to him about his wife and little girl and Uncle Daniel. I now was positive it

was Tom. I reeled in my saddle and nearly fell from my
horse. What should I do ? I could not tell Mary, for if it
proved not to be him she would not be able to bear it. So I
rode on. After a long time we came to the house. It was
some hundred paces from the road, a square log cabin or
hut, occupied by an old colored woman ('Aunt Martha')
and her husband ('Ham'), both over sixty years, I should
judge.

The old aunty was in the yard, a smooth, hard, flat piece

UNCLE DANIEL MEETS AUNT MARTHA.

of ground, fenced off by a low fence, about four rails
high, which a man could easily step over. I saluted her
with :

" 'How do you do, aunty, do you live here ?'

" 'Yes, sa, I lives heah—me and Ham, my ole man. What
is you, massa ? Is you Union or is you " Sesh ?"'

" 'Oh ! I am a Union man,' I replied.

" 'Den I is glad to see you. I'll jes' call Ham. He runned
away when he seed you. He's feared; yes, he's dat. He
isn't gwine wid de "Sesh" any mo'.'

"'Well, aunty, have you a Union officer in your cabin, sick?'

"'Well, now, massa, I'se jes' got to know who you is afore I 'fess on dat case.'

"'Well, aunty, I am Daniel Lyon, sometimes called "Uncle Daniel."'

"'Afore God, is dat you, Massa Lyon? Jes' get off yo' hoss an' wait rite heah; I be back in a bit.'

"She hobbled in, evidently to speak to the Colonel. I waited quietly until she returned. Just then the others came in sight, and I sent the boy to halt them. Aunty came out so excited that she could hardly speak.

"'Sho' as you is born'd, dat Massa Tom knows you; but, sah, he's powerful weak, an' you must exclose who yo' is to him in a most delicacious manner, or you'll incite him. He's 'fraid, sah, dat you is a exposter.'

"'O, no, aunty, I am his uncle and benefactor.'

"'Yo' is what?'

"'His uncle,'

"'No, but de oder t'ing what you is?'

"'His benefactor.'

"'Glory to God! Is you? May de Laud shine his light in dis pore house, an' brush away de fears ob dis misfortulate famly.'

"Then she called Ham.

"'Oh, yo' Ham, come heah.'

"I entered the cabin and beheld Col. Anderson, as pale as death, lying on a poor, broken-down bed. I knelt by his side upon the floor and wept aloud. The Colonel could only whisper. Extending his hand, while the great tears were rolling down his face, he asked:

"'Is my wife with you? How is my child?'

"He was greatly excited and very weak. I arose from his bedside and told him who were coming, and begged him to be calm. Aunty brought some cloths and laid on his breast, saying to him:

"'Now, Massa Tom, you mus' be still. Don' be like I tole you. You mussent get 'cited now—nuffin of the kine. Jes' see de folks like yo' allers done. Dey's come a mighty long ways to fine yo'. Wish dey stay away 'til I cure yo'; but spose it's all rite. De good Laud he done knowed de bes'. Maybe de "Sesh" come take him some day afore long, so de Laud he knows what he wants. Bress de good Laud.'

" 'I went out to meet the others. Mary at once asked me what the matter was. I spoke as gently as I could, and said :

" 'Mary, Tom is still alive.'

" She instantly leaped from her horse and made for the cabin, and in an instant was at the bedside of her husband, covering his face with kisses and tears. Tom was too weak to more than whisper 'my dear wife,' and weep in silence. Old Ham had come in, and stood in one corner of the room looking on the scene with his hands locked together over his head. He was heard to say over and over in a low tone :

" ' De Lord bress dese chillen.'

" Aunt Martha took hold of Mary, saying :

" 'Deah Misses, yo' jes' stop dat cryin'. You ought to be 'joiced dat Massa Tom be libbin. You ought ter seed him when de "Sesh" fotched him heah. I tell you dat was de time what fotched me down. I done got rite on my old knees an' axed de good Laud to spar dis good Massa Tom. I knowed him de berry minute I laid my eyes on him. Many's de time I make his bed and cook his dinnah. I tell you all about dat. Why, dem "Sesh," when dey fetch Massa Tom heah in de old wagon, dey des frowed him out like he been a hog, and tole Ham an' me dat we mus' dig a hole and put him in; dat we be killed if we don't. I done went and looked at him, an' tole Ham dat he wasn't dead ; dat he was wa'm an' bredin. So Ham an' me jes' carried him into dis house, an' got blankets and kivers, and wash him wid wa'm water, and took keer on him; setted up all de time, one or bofe on us, and kep' him good an' wa'm, an yo' see he's done gittin' well. De good Laud heah our prayers, an' he whisper to pore ole Marfa dat he gwine to fetch him out for some good he gwine to do for us pore people. Bress de Laud; he is good

to us. I tell yo', de man what said to dig a hole fo' him is
a bad man; his name is Whitthorne. I 'member de name
kase I knowed de Whitthornes in Jackson, Miss., when I
libbed there. Yes, dat so.'

"At this Mary broke down again. She felt sure that this
was some of her people. Aunty continued:

"'Ole Massa Gawge (George), that we b'longed to, move
up heah six year ago, on dis place, from Jackson. He
libbed up dar on the hill in dat white house dat yo' see up
dar, dat am locked up an' no one is in it. Dey got lot ob
t'ings in dar. When de Union whip de Sesh at Dolinsburg, and de Sesh come dis way, gwine home or somewhar, den Massa Gawge an' all de famly dey go, too, an'
take all de niggers 'cepin' me an' Ham. Dey say we's too
ole, an' dey done lef' us to take keer ob de place; dey leabe
de smoke-house so we kin git in an' git sumpin to eat.
Well, dey is plenty in dar, an' we lib all right, and, bress
de Laud, dat save Massa Tom's life. De good Laud fix
it dat way, sho' as yo' born. He take keer ob de good
folks.'

" Old Ham, who had been silent, broke out:

"'Yes, dat's so, massa, dat's so. De Laud do do dis. He
done told me up at de smoke-house to take all dat we
wanted, an' dat when Massa Tom done get well, dat we
mus go wid him 'way from heah an' lib with Massa Tom;
dat de Sesh kill us when dey find out we done cure him
up. Yes, sah, de Laud say dat to me, sho.'

"I said to him: 'Ham, are you sure the Lord said
that; did you not dream it, or was it not Aunt Martha
that said it?'

"'No, massa, no; de Laud told me, sho! I know 'twas
he. De words come right down frough de smokehouse when
I was gittin' meal to make de gruel for Massa Tom. O, no,
massa; Martha was down heah. I told Martha when I
come back.'

" 'Well, Ham, what did Martha say?'

" 'She say dat we must 'bey de Lord; dat he was mo'
our massa den Massa George; don't we b'longs to de Laud
mo' dan to Massa George. Den I say dat's well, Martha;

you know, and if you b'lieve in dat we go. An' we is
gwine wid Massa, sho.'

" 'If you should go, Ham, they would accuse us of steal-
ing you, and have us arrested for it.'

" ' Well, I doesn't know 'bout dat. I knows we can steal
our ownself away, an' go to de place whar Massa Tom lib ;
I knows dat. We's gwine ; dat's done fix; we's gwine.'

"The Colonel had been listening, and smiled to find
that these two good old people loved him so, and he
nodded his head to Ham, which caused him to laugh immoderately.

" 'It's done fix,' said Ham, and he left the cabin.

"I said: ' Aunty, have you any children ?'

" 'Laud bless yo' good soul, we has six chillen somewhar;
don't know whar. Massa George he sole our chillen 'way
from us soon as dey was six year old. I never see any ob
dem since den; neber heard anything 'bout dem. He sole
'em 'way down on de Gulf somewhar; neber would tell us.
Dey done forgot us, or whar we lib, long go; dey so young
when dey taken 'way, O, dey do dat way, so de ole folks
not fine 'em. I tell you, Massa Lyon, 'tis purty hard on ole
folks, to lose de chillen dat way. If dey die an' de Laud
take dem 'way, dat's all rite; de Laud know he own business; but when dey sole 'way, dat hard. You see, dese
people dey got chillen, but dey tink we no keer for our'n.
Dat is whar dey don't know. We does keer jes as much
as de white folks, but we can't help ourself, dats all. I tell
you dat's bad. O, I cry myself nearly to deff 'bout my
chillen; but all do no good; dey done gone ; I neber see
dem any mo'. If I was to, dey would not know me, an' me
not know dem; so no good now to cry any mo'; dey be all
dead, maybe—hope dey am—den dey work for de Laud
and Master all de time, and not be worked all de time fo'
de people for nuffin' an' doin' no good. Yes, I hope dey is
all done dead. Wish I knowed dey was, den I'd be feelin'
good. You see, me an' Ham talked dis all ober. We neber
see our chillen no mo' no matter whar we is ; so we am
gwine where we will be counted wid de people an' not wid
de cattle. Yes, sah ; dat's what we's got in our heads;

dar's no use tryin' to put it out; it in dar, an' dar it stay. We's gwine, sho'.'

" ' Well, well, aunty, all right ; I will see that you go. I will take the consequences. I will not see as good an old couple as you are held like cattle if I can help it.'

" The old woman shouted 'glory,' and hobbled out of the cabin, I presume, to tell Ham what I had said.   •

" By this time the Colonel had recovered somewhat from his excitement, and quietly and in a low voice told us how he came to be there. He said that when he was wounded on the works of Dolinsburg and left for dead, that some one came along and stanched the flow of blood by binding some cloth around the wound saturated with something— his wound was through the right breast, touching slightly the right lung—that in the afternoon, when a portion of the rebel army passed over the ground that he occupied, Col. Whitthorne, his wife's brother, discovered him and had him placed in one of his ambulances, bringing him away; had no knowledge as to what his intention was— whether to take him to some place of safety—some hospital, or let him die and bury him where his remains could afterwards be found by his family; that up to within a few days he had no idea where he was; that these old colored people had kept his whereabouts a profound secret, except among a few of their race whom they could trust; that when he found a force was stationed at Dolinsburg, he got them to send there and give the information, so that he might make some arrangement about getting away, for fear of recapture by the enemy, and they had sent the boy that we met. He was anxious to get away, and thought that he could bear being moved in some easy conveyance to Dolinsburg in two or three days' travel. We consulted together, and Capt. Day sent a messenger back with a letter to Col. Harden, asking him to send an ambulance and a surgeon the next day, we remaining with the Colonel until their coming. There was plenty of fodder at the plantation barns, and the men took care of the horses. Aunty prepared a sufficient quantity of wholesome food for ourselves. We passed the night without much sleep, the Captain and I using our chairs for beds, as there was not sufficient accommodation for us all; Mrs. Anderson slept on the bed by her husband, and the men found comfortable quarters in the stables. We enjoyed ourselves, however, hearing Aunt Martha and Ham tell us how they had taken care of the Colonel ; how they had bathed and dressed his wound once each day with warm water and poultices of white-oak ooze and slippery-elm bark; how they stopped the bleeding with soot from the wooden chimney; how they dosed him occasionally, when his wound seemed painful, with good whiskey that Ham got up at the house on the hill (he had managed to force an entrance somehow); and how every day they asked the Lord to heal his wound and make him well, so he would take them away from their long suffering and unhappy life. The story of the old woman was most interesting as well as very amusing. The next morning we had bread, coffee and chicken, which was relished by all, I assure you. The Colonel was fed on gruel and a piece of chicken. Aunty, who had him entirely under her control, would not allow him to eat anything else. After breakfast was over I asked Aunty how she came to know Col. Anderson, and she in her way told me the story of her having been hired out once by her master to Col. Anderson's family before the Colonel was married, and she said :

"'Laud bress you, chile, I know Massa Tom soon I put my eyes onto him. Yes, sah. I neber let on, doe. He didn't know nuffin when they frowed him out heah like a pig. No, sah. He was mos' dead, sho'. Dat's one time he mos' done gone to glory, sho'. But he all right now; he come out. An' when he do, oh, great Laud, don't I jes' want him to go for dem "Sesh." Yes, I tell you, I do. Dar is no mistake on dat pint.'

" The day passed. The Colonel improved and conversed considerably with his wife. We left them together all we could to enjoy their reunion. He was very desirous of getting away and having the assistance of a surgeon, who, however, could do no more for him than was being done. In the afternoon late, however, there came an ambulance and the Post Surgeon. This seemed to give new life and spirit to all. The Surgeon entered the cabin, and, after pleasantly conversing about the Colonel with us, proceeded to make an examination of his wound. Aunty was determined to be present. She raised the Colonel up, and showed the Surgeon where the wound was, its condition, etc. He said it was healing rapidly, and would be well soon, but that he would be some considerable time gaining sufficient strength to do any service. He said that aunty ought to have a diploma; that she had treated him as skillfully as anyone could have done, and much better than some might have done, Aunty at once replied :

" 'I tell you where you gib de "'plomas." You jes' gib dem to de Laud. He is de one what do dis work. I tell you, He keep Massa Tom for some good. I don't know what, but he is got some good work afore he, sho'. I tells you, de Laud never show dis pore old nigger what to do, des like she be a doctor, less He wanted Massa Tom to do something. He know what He wants. He know all t'ings, de Bible say so, an' dats the book you can't 'spute.'

" We all agreed with aunty, and she was happy. The next morning the ambulance was arranged in the best possible manner and the Colonel tenderly carried out and laid in, his wife and Aunt Martha having a place arranged so they could stay in the ambulance with him. We all started, old Ham tying their belongings up in a couple of blankets and lashing them on a horse loaned him by one of the escort. We were two days in making Dolinsburg, but did it without any very great inconvenience or suffering to the Colonel. When we arrived Col. Harden welcomed us most heartily, and made all necessary arrangements for the comfort of Col. Anderson, as well as the rest of us. I noticed that Col. Harden said nothing about the two colored people, and did not seem to notice them, so I called his attention to them. He looked at me rather quizzically and remarked :

" ' Why, I did not observe any colored people. You did not bring any through the lines, did you ?'

"I took the hint, and said :

"'O, Colonel, what did I say? I was a little absent-minded being up with Col. Anderson; and loss of sleep has bothered me."

"So, you see, I got out of the scrape. Orders then existed against bringing colored people through the ines, as I learned afterwards. He (Col. Harden) always said that he was color-blind, and could not distinguish between the color of people. I remained several days, and Col. Anderson continued to improve. I, however, felt that I ought to go home and look after the family. So old Ham and I got ready, and bade good-by to all, after returning thanks for the kindness shown us. We took the two horses that Mary and I rode to Dolinsburg and made our way through in several days to Allentown. I preferred to go all the way on horseback, to save, perhaps, some trouble about Ham. He claimed to be freeborn and from Ohio, where I formerly lived. This went as sound, and no trouble ensued. Ham lived at our house and did chores for us and made himself generally useful. I related the whole story to the family and made all happy, especially little Mary Col. Anderson's child, who had the impression fixed on her mind that her papa had been killed, like her Uncle Harvey. We received letters from David and James, in the Eastern army; also, from Stephen, who had marched with the regiment to which he belonged to the Army of the Center, then in the western part of Kentucky, and on the way to Pittskill Landing, where the Union forces were now concentrating. Henry wrote that his regiment of cavalry had been ordered to the East to report to Gen. Kilpatterson. Having heard from all our family, except Jackson, we were again happy. We all longed for the day to come when Col. Anderson and his wife would return home, and were anxious also to see the good old colored woman who had been a mother to him during his illness. The children especially asked me every day about Aunt Martha; how she looked? if she was as black as Uncle Ham? and why Mr. George sold her children? and many other questions that could not well be answered."

"Uncle Daniel, I knew Col. Harden, of whom you

spoke," said Maj. Clymer. "He was a good soldier, went all through the war, and died in 1868. He was rather an old man for the service, and was never well after the war closed."

"Yes; I heard of his death; I kept track of him up to that time; he was a good man."

"Uncle Daniel," said Dr. Adams, "the implicit faith of those two old colored people was an example that might well be followed by the masters now."

"Yes; the colored people are the most faithful on the face of the earth, and deserve better treatment than they are getting in the South."

"Why is it that they are deprived of their political rights in the Southern States ?"

"My dear sir, that is easily answered. As I have heretofore repeated in the discussion of other points, the controlling element in the South is now, as it ever has been, an aristocracy of and for power. They do not intend that in any way or by any means, lawful or otherwise, the control of their States shall pass out of their hands; by this means they will control the General Government. It would be the same were these colored people white ; if they were poor and not of the ruling class, they would be deprived of their rights in the same way. They believe that they were born to control, and control they will, unless we shall find men hereafter in charge of this Government with nerve enough to see that the rights of the people are protected and enforced."

"Yes," said Col. Bush, "another war will come some day, and it will commence at the ballot-box. People will suffer just so long and no longer. The idea that I gave my right arm away for a Government that allows its citizens to be bulldozed and murdered merely for desiring to participate in the affairs of the Republic. No, sir ! I fight no more until I know what I am fighting for and also that we will sustain the principles for which we contended."

"This is a curious people. They are nearly ready for any kind of government to-day, when only a few years ago they expended billions of money and rivers of human blood for liberty, and now care nothing for it. They made the gift of franchise to millions at a great sacrifice, and now quietly smile at its surrender. O, yes; but how can you expect anything else. Are we not apologizing every day for what we did? Do we not avoid speaking of the war in the North? Are not some of our great leaders to-day men who aided and sympathized with treason, while we teach kindness to our erring brethren and forgive all? Do we not find our flag despised nearly everywhere in the South? Do they not march under their State flags instead of the Stars and Stripes? Are not all their monuments to rebel leaders and Generals? Are not their school books full of Secession sentiments? Do they not teach the children that we conquered them with hired Hessians? While this is so in the South, and any allusion to the war in the North is regarded as stirring up bad blood, is it not submissive, cowardly and unworthy of any brave people, and will it not result finally in their dominating over us? These are the reflections that annoy me in my old and lonely days."

Here he stopped, was silent for a moment, then said in a low tone:

"Why should I have lived to tremble now for the future of my country."

The tears stood like crystals in his eyes, and he ceased to speak for the present.

CHAPTER V.

" But whether on the scaffold high,
Or in the battle's van,
The fittest place where man can die
Is where he dies for man."—BARRY.

"DURING the suspense great preparations were being made for the various campaigns by the several armies of the Union, which caused much excitement throughout the country. The many prisoners captured at the fall of Dolinsburg had been sent to different camps in the North. The secession sympathizers were vieing with each other as to who should visit them the oftenest and show them the greatest consideration. The whisperings of releasing them and organizing for 'a fire in the rear,' as the saying went, were loud and plentiful. I traveled to Indianapolis and Chicago to see if I could learn anything of a definite character on these points, and at both places heard mutterings and threats that were calculated to produce alarm and also to make any loyal man feel like beginning a war at home. Everything that was being done by the authorities was denounced as arbitrary and despotic—their acts as unconstitutional. In fact, no satisfactory act had been performed by the Administration that was calculated to assist in putting down the rebellion (according to their way of thinking). When I returned home I found a letter from Peter, who had been promoted to a Majority in his regiment. The Lieutenant-Colonel (Rice), as I before stated, had been made Colonel, Major

Pierce Lieutenant-Colonel, and Capt. Lyon (Peter) Major. They had not as yet learned of the discovery of Col. Anderson. I wrote to Peter, giving him in full the details in reference to the Colonel, but told him not to reveal the facts to a soul until it should be reported officially. In his letter, however, he informed me of the massing of the rebel troops at Corin Junction, and the like process going on at the High Banks, on the Little Combination River, now called Pittskill Landing, and that he looked for hot work as soon as the Army of the Center, under Buda, could make a junction with Gen. Silent. When I read Peter's letter all the family were anxious about his fate, should there be another battle fought. Old Ham was present and seemed to be much interested in what I was saying. He had been entertaining the three children with his simple stories about the 'Sesh,' as he and Aunt Martha called the rebels. He spoke up, saying:

" ' Massa Daniel, I tells you da's no danger, sah. I had a dream 'bout dat. Massa Peter am all right, sah; I tells you he is. I neber dreams 'bout anything but what comes out good.'

" My wife asked Ham if he could interpret dreams.

" ' No, missis; I not know 'bout dreams 'cept my own. I knows dat Massa Peter all right.'

" There was no way getting the cunning old darkey to tell his dream. My wife said to him:

" ' I am troubled about a dream that I had at the commencement of the war. It distresses me still.'

" She then related her dream, and he broke out into a laugh, saying :

" ' Yes, but you see, massa got all he hands, all he fingers; dey all dar—none done gone. Dat dream all good, kase, you see, he fingers all right. O, dat's nuffin. De bug he be Sesh; skare you, dat's all; bite de chillen little spec, dat's all.'

" We all laughed at the curious speech of old Ham, and yet he sat down and commenced counting his fingers, and said :

" ' How many chillen yo' got, misses ?'

3

" ' Seven.'

" ' Ham became silent, and nothing more could be got from him on the subject of the dream. He never spoke of the matter again to any of us, except to Peter. I found after all was over that he and Peter had the same interpretation—strange, yet so true."

" Uncle Daniel, what was the interpretation, may I inquire the second time ?" said Dr. Adams.

" It was very strange; but the interpretation is disclosed by the casualties of war, and as we proceed you will recognize it. But to my story: The rebel and Union forces were now confronting each other, and each was constantly on the lookout for the movements of the other. About midway between the camps of the two armies they were almost constantly having skirmishes, sometimes with cavalry, and sometimes with infantry. The successes were about equal. Peter related the story of an old colored man, I presume something after the style of old Ham, meeting him while he was making a reconnaissance with his regiment. The old darkey was tall and very black, and was walking in great haste when Peter called to him:

" ' Uncle, where are you going ?'

" ' Ise gwine to de ribber, sah. Ise ti'd ob de wa'. Ise been cookin', sah, for de ' Sesh.' He say he gwine to whip dem Yankees on de ribber,—dat dey am gwine to come right on and drive dem in de ribber and drown dem like cats ; dat's what he say, sho'. I heah him wid dese old ears, I did.'

" ' When did he say he was coming ?'

" ' Well, massa, he say he comin' right off, sah ; he say he kill 'em an' drown 'em all afore de res' ob de Yankees come for help dem; dat's what he say.'

" ' Who was it said this ?'

" ' Why, sah, it wah de big Gen'l—de one what boss all de res'; he name wah Massa Sydenton Jackson. He say he kill all ob you stone dead—he not leab one ob em.'

" ' If he is going to kill all of us, you don't want to go to our camp and get killed, do you ?'

" ' No, sah ; I doesn't spec' to git killed; I 'bout 'cluded dat I wait till de shootin' git goin' pretty libely, den I jes' skip de ribber and neber stop 'til I be done gone whar dey done got no wa'.'

"'How many soldiers have they in Gen. Jackson's army?'

"'Well, I dunno, but I 'spec' dar am somewhar near a million ob dem, sah. Dey's got de woods full ob hoss sogers, an' all de fiel's full ob 'em what walks. Den dey got big guns wid hosses. Oh, Laudy, massa, I dunno, but dey's heaps ob dem.'

"'What were they doing when you came away?'

"'Dey was campin' 'bout ten miles, I 'spose. I walk mighty fas', and I is monstrous tired. When dey start dis mornin' I get outside and go in de woods and keep whar I see dem all de way. When dey stop I keep on. Dey be here in de mornin', sho'. I knows dey will, massa.'

"This being about all Peter could ascertain, he thought perhaps it would be as safe back towards the main army, so he returned, bringing old 'Dick' with him, that being his name. When Peter reported with Dick at headquarters the General cross-questioned the old man in a manner that would have done credit to a prosecuting attorney, and said to Peter:

"'Major, I guess the enemy intend to try our strength very soon.'

"He then said to Dick:

"'You can go around behind my quarters. You will find some colored people there, with whom you will remain until after we have this fight. You can then go where you please.'

"'Bress de Laud, Massa Gen'l, you gwine to make me stay heah and get shotted?'"

"'Well, I don't know whether you will get shot or not but you will stay as I direct.'

"'Afore God, Massa Gen'l, you see dese heah 'backer sticks, (meaning his legs), 'dey go, dey go if dey shoot; I can't hole 'em. I tried dem one time, an' I tell you dey won't stay. You can't hole 'em, no, sah; dey git ebery time—when you 'spec dem be stayin' dey's gwine.'

"The General laughed at his peculiar expressions and sent him away. The position of the Union forces was an exceedingly good one for defensive operations. The country all around was covered with heavy timber and very thick underbrush, save a small opening or field on the right center and to the rear of our right flank. The ground was very uneven, full of streams, gulches, hills and hollows. The line of the Union troops stretched from Hawk Run to Bull Gulch and Buck Lick Junction, the right resting on Hawk Run and the left at or near the Junction, the center in heavy timber quite a distance farther south than either flank. The right of the line was commanded by Gen. Sherwood, the left by Gen. Prince; two divisions were in reserve, commanded by Gen. Waterberry. The Army of the Center, under Gen. Buda, was within communicating distance, but advancing very slowly, causing some fear that they would not get to the field prior to the attack being made by the enemy, who was in great force ready to be hurled against our comparatively small army at any moment.

The suspense must have been terrible for the time, but at last it was over, for on the morning of the third day after Dick made his revelation about the enemy's movements, our forces having become a little careless on their front, the enemy were upon them without much warning. Just as Gen. Sherwood was about to take his breakfast skirmishing commenced not more than a mile from his camp, and nearer and nearer it seemed to approach our lines. The 'long roll' was sounded and 'to arms' was the cry all along the lines. The roads passing through the camp were leading in almost every direction, affording the enemy ample opportunity for unfolding their line all along our front by a very rapid movement, of which they took advantage, and in rapid succession threw their divisions in line of battle and moved with quick motion to the assault which was made simultaneously along our front. From Peter's description it must have come like a thunderbolt. They struck Sherwood's command on the center and right flank and drove him from his first posi-

tion back on the reserves and a part of his command entirely from the field. So thoroughly were they demoralized that they could not find time to return to their places
during that day. Sherwood tried to rally them, but could
not; so he joined his remnant to the first command he
found, and continued resistance to the impetuous assaults
of the Confederates.

"The battle was now raging all along the line ; our
troops were in good condition, and the ones that had won
the victory at Dolinsburg were in no wise discouraged.
They came into action like veterans and stood the first
shock of the battle without the least movement to the rear
or panic. Our lines were again adjusted on the right, and
one continuous rattle of musketry from one end of the line
to the other could be heard. There was no chance for the
operating of cavalry on either side. Artillery was run up
to the front by both armies. How the different arms rattled and thundered. Batteries to the front, right and left
rolled amid confusion and death. Closer still the armies
came until their eyes were seen and aim taken as if in target practice. To the rear and front, as the armies gained
or lost a little of their ground, lay the dead and the
wounded. The shrieks and groans of the wounded and
dying were unheeded; the crushing of bones might also be
heard as the artillery rushed from one part of the lines to
another. In this way the contest continued for the greater part of the forenoon. At last our center was penetrated
and our right was forced back again with the center for
the distance of perhaps a half mile. Our left, having a
better position, under Gen. Prince, held their ground, and,
turning their fire partially on the advancing column
that was forcing our right, checked them somewhat in
their rapid advance. At this critical moment our reserves
came up in good style and entered the conflict. The enemy were now steadily driven back to their original position.

Over the field the Union and rebel soldiers lay side
by side, dead and wounded alike. They were seen helping
one another, their anger and fury soon subsiding when

they found themselves helpless by the side of each other, and, perhaps, often asking 'Why are we thus butchering one another ?'

This bloody battle raged with a deadly fury unparalleled on the continent up to that time. Louder and louder roared the artillery and more steadily and sharply rattled the musketry. The smoke was rising in great clouds from the field of carnage. Gen. Silent was very impatient on account of the non-arrival of Gen. Buda, as well as Gen. Wilkins, whose division was some six miles away to the rear, and was expected to come rapidly forward and strike west of Hawk Run, on the left flank of the enemy; but no Buda and no Wilkins came. The battle was then raging with great slaughter on both sides. The entire Union force was now engaged, and the rebel commander was bringing his reserves forward and re-enforcing his lines. He could be seen re-organizing his forces and putting his reserves in line. Gen. Jackson and his staff were seen riding along giving directions. He had on his staff one Gen. Harrington, who seemed to be very active in moving about. Soon another assault was made on our lines. The fresh troops seemed to inspire them with new zeal, and on they came, steadily and firmly, with a constant and heavy fire pouring into our lines. The assault was resisted for some time. It seems that during this assault, their Commander-in-Chief, Gen. Sydenton Jackson, was shot through the breast, falling from his horse dead. At the fall of Jackson, Gen. Harrington seemed to become crazed and rushed madly on, directing that every Yankee be killed. 'Bayonet them!' 'Kill them like cats!' 'Let none escape!' he cried. So on they came like a line of mad animals, sending forth such unearthly yells as to induce the belief that all the fiends of the infernal regions had been turned loose at once and led on by old Beelzebub himself. On, on they came. Our line reeled and staggered under the assault. A fresh column came up under Gen. Bolenbroke, and advanced rapidly against our right flank, and bore down so heavily that our line on the right and centre again gave way. In falling back, Gen. Waterberry, a gallant officer who had brought up our reserves on our first repulse, was killed while trying to rally his men.

His death seemed to create a panic, and Gen. Sherwood was unable to hold the men to their line. He would form and reform them, leading them himself; but when he would look for the command he was trying to bring to the front, he would find them going to the rear, making very good time.

Peter's command was in this part of the line. He could hear this man Harrington, as the rebels came rushing on, crying out : 'No quarter !' 'Kill every Yankee !' 'Let none escape !' 'Rid the country of the last one !' 'Take no prisoners !' The panic continued on our right, and at least one-half of this part of Sherwood's command broke, and was utterly disorganized, hiding behind trees, in hollows and ravines, to cover themselves from the enemy. In great numbers they sought roads leading to the rear, and followed them without knowing to what point they might lead. In this demoralized condition of one portion of our army, despair seemed to set in. Gen. Silent sat on his horse looking sadly at this condition of things. He spoke not a word. Riding up to Sherwood, who was greatly excited, he said:

" 'General, can you not send word to Prince to fall back slowly ? I see the enemy will soon be on his flank.'

"As the General rode away he said : 'I cannot understand the delay of Buda and Wilkins.'

"He sent orderlies immediately to hurry them up, giving imperative orders to them 'to move to the field of battle as rapidly as possible.' In the meantime Gen. Hudson had gone to the support of Prince ; our forces on the right having steadily fallen back. It was too late, however, to save him. The enemy had surrounded him before Hudson could form on his right, and he was compelled to surrender with a portion of his command, the rest having fallen back and thereby saved themselves. Hudson joined on the remainder of Prince's command and made resistance to the further advance of the enemy. Our line, being again intact, fell back behind a ravine that crossed the battlefield from northwest to southeast—from Mocassin Run to the river. The enemy by this time were in possession of the camps of the Union forces, and partially giving themselves up to plunder, the battle gradually slackened until darkness closed in on the contending armies The enemy occupied our camps during the night, intending the next morning to capture what was left of our army. During the first part of the night they kept up a fearful noise, evincing their joy over what they thought a great victory. Gen. Silent, however, was engaged in arranging his forces for an attack at daylight, being satisfied that he could surprise the enemy and defeat him, as he would not expect our forces to fight, and, therefore, take the noise of preparation for a retreat. The column under Gen. Wilkins came up early that night and was posted on the right of our army, with its right on Hawks Run.

Gen. Buda also arrived during the night and was given position on the left, his left resting on the river. The center, held by Sherwood, was re-enforced by Hudson and that portion of Prince's command not captured. The artillery was put in battery in the center and on the right center, and orders given for the men to replenish their boxes with ammunition, to sleep on their arms, and at 4 o'clock in the morning to make a simultaneous attack all along the line with infantry and artillery, moving the artillery rapidly to the front. This being understood, all were quiet. The enemy were so confident of having our army at their mercy that they lighted fires and made night hideous with their howls. During the night the leaves and grass were set on fire by some unknown means and burned over the battlefield, causing great consternation, as many of the wounded were yet lying where they fell. Their shrieks and appeals for help would have made the tears come to the eyes of the most heartless. An allwise Providence, however, heard their prayers and appeals for help, and the windows of heaven were thrown open and the flood poured forth and subdued the flames, saving many a poor fellow from dreadful torture and death. The storm continued nearly all night, swelling the little streams that ran through the battlefield, causing the roads to become almost impassable. The stragglers were collected and returned to their commands.

At 4 o'clock the crack of musketry was heard, and soon after the artillery from our lines opened and we were upon the rebels. They were taken by surprise and thrown into confusion. The hurrying of officers from one part of the field to another was distinctly heard by our men and greatly encouraged our forces. On they moved, driving the enemy pell-mell from our former camp. It was impossible, under our galling fire, for the enemy to form in any compact line. They fell back as our troops advanced. We struck them in front, on the flank, and, as they sometimes turned in their retreat, in the rear. The slaughter for a time was terrible and sickening. They were at last driven into the woods where they had formed the day before. Here a lull came in the contest, and they took advantage of it to form their line again, believing that our advantage could only be temporary, having no knowledge of the number of our re-enforcements. When they were in a condition to do so they advanced and took the aggressive. On they came. Our line stood as immovable as a rock, received the shock of their first assault, and then poured the missiles of death into their ranks as if they were being rained down from the heavens. For a time the lines both advanced slowly and dealt death into each other. The commands from each army could be distinctly heard by the other. Harrington on the rebel side was heard to say:

"'Charge the Lincoln hell-hounds! Give the cowardly dogs the bayonet!'

"This gave our troops that heard it a contempt for the man, and a determination to receive the charge in a soldierly manner. They stood silent until the enemy was within close musket range, and at the order—the batteries having come up—everything opened and poured volley after volley into the advancing columns, which swayed and halted; no power could press them forward. Our forces seeing this, advanced steadily, firing as they moved. At last the rebel line gave way and fled to the woods on their left, taking shelter among the trees. The ground between the lines was now literally covered with the killed and wounded. On our extreme left the battle was still raging, and seemed to be going to our rear. Gen. Silent rode away to this part of the field. Finding that our forces had fallen back nearly to the junction of Bull Gulch and Buck Lick Run, he ordered Hudson to move rapidly and strike the enemy in flank where the line had been broken by the falling back of their left and center. This order was executed with much alacrity and was a great success. Hudson struck the detached portion of the enemy's army in flank and rear, and doubled them up (over the very ground from which our forces had fallen back the day before), capturing many prisoners and several pieces of artillery. Here he met a young officer whom he had noticed moving rapidly to the front and assaulting the enemy with his command at any and every point where he could hit him.

" Hudson rode up to him and inquired his name.

" 'My name, sir, is Stephen Lyon. I belong to an Ohio regiment. I joined the Army of the Center only a short time since, and this is my first battle. I have lost many men; my Colonel and Lieutenant-Colonel were both killed, and I am the Major and now in command of the regiment.'

"This was my fifth son in line of birth, and sixth in the service. I am digressing, however. Their conversation was here cut short, as Gen. Buda had ordered an advance along his line, which was the left wing of the army. The advance was duly made. The rebels, however, in the meantime had been re-enforced on this part of their line. The contest, therefore, became a very stubborn one on both sides. The advance of Buda was soon checked, and the fighting became desperate. Both armies to our right seemed to have partially ceased their advance, seemingly to understand how the event was being decided on this part of the line. The enemy was driven slowly to the rear for some distance. A halt then came and a rally on the part of the rebels. They organized into column of regiments and made a desperate attempt to break the center of our left. Buda massed his artillery against them, keeping it well supported, and mowed them down with shell and canister until they lay in piles on the ground. They advanced to the assault three times with a heroism and desperation seldom witnessed in any ancient or modern battle, but each time back were their shattered columns sent in utter confusion. Thus the battle continued until late in the afternoon, when both parties reorganized for a last and desperate struggle. The lines of the enemy showed all along the skirts of timber, leaving the open space to our right and center, and extending to Buck Lick Run.

Both seemed eager to make the attack, but our forces were first in motion, and with a quick-step movement they advanced against the enemy. The firing opened all along the line. First one and then the other line staggered and swayed to and fro. The forces on both sides seemed determined to win or die on their ground. At last Wilkins crossed Hawks Run and struck the enemy in his flank, causing consternation to seize him, and he gradually gave way, his left flank doubling back on the main line nearer the center. At this moment Gen. Silent ordered an advance with infantry and artillery simultaneously. This was executed in good order, the firing again became general. The roar of artillery now was almost deafening. The yell of the enemy was heard in every direction as though assaulting, but they could no longer stand against our determined forces. Steadily on the advance continued; the enemy stood, delivering his fire with deadly results, until our army approached to the point where one or the other must give way. The rebels, seeing that our force was coming with a steady step and determination unmoved by their fire, broke in different parts of their line, and finally the moment arrived when they could no longer stand our deadly aim, and their whole line gave way. They retreated through the woods and on different roads in great disorder; our forces followed up their lines of retreat and kept a constant fire upon them until night intervened, which protected them from any further disaster. This closed one of the bloody battles of the war. That night our army again slept upon their arms. Some supplies were brought to them during the night, which stayed their hunger. The next morning the enemy was nowhere to be seen or heard; he had made his retreat in the night, leaving many wagons, ambulances and guns. The roads being made almost impassable by the rain of the night before, their dead and wounded were left in our hands, save those whom they had removed to the rear the night of the first day's contest, when they held the ground. The battlefield presented a ghastly and sickening sight, — the dead, the dying, the wounded; the hospital in the rear, near the river; the parties burying the dead, finding Union men and rebels piled up in heaps together; the long trenches being prepared; the soldiers being wrapped in their blankets and buried without any knowledge of who they were, or to what command they belonged; the words of the dying to be taken back to their friends; the messages to fond wives and blessed children; the moans and shrieks of the wounded as they were carried on stretchers from where they had lain and suffered, some of them, for two days and nights.

These things, when first recited to me by my son Peter, filled me with deep sorrow and pain. O, my friends, the suffering of our poor men for their country was great— it was heartrending to hear of it. When the sick, wounded and dead had been cared for, of course the army could not move again very soon,—it must have rest and reorganization. So the camp for the present was established a little in advance of the battle-ground. Many were furloughed for a short time and returned home. My son Peter came home on a leave, having been wounded late in the evening of the second day. His wound being in his foot, he was unfitted for duty for some time. His Lieutenant-Colonel having been killed that day, he was promoted to the vacancy.

"While Peter was kept in the house (where he was confined by his wound), he constantly entertained us by his recitals of all of these incidents and movements that I have given to you in my poor way. It is a matter of great interest to me to follow the history of men on both sides, and see what their good or bad fortune may have been

since. Now, on our side in this great battle, Gen. Waterberry, one of our leading generals, was killed on the first
day. Gen. Hudson went through the war creditably and
died away from home in some of the South American
states. Gen. Buda soon left the army under a cloud, and
I do not know what became of him. I think, however,
that he is dead. Wilkins went through the war with some
credit to himself, but was killed in Mexico afterwards in
some of their periodical revolutions."

"Uncle Daniel, do you know the history of the rebel
generals since the war, who commanded in this battle of
which you have been speaking?" asked Dr. Adams.

"Oh, yes! You know Sydenton Jackson was killed on
the first day. Bolenbroke was in the rebel army up to its
surrender, but died soon after from dissipation, as I have
been informed."

"I am curious to know what became of Dick, the darky,"
he said.

Uncle Daniel smiled and said: "Dick, poor fellow, has
not been seen since his 'backer sticks' ran off with him,
just as he said they would."

"What became of Harrington, who wanted every d——
Yankee killed like cats—bayoneted—without any quarter
being shown, etc. ?"

"He went to Mexico after the war closed ; could not live
under 'Yankee' rule. He there tried to assist in establish-
ing an empire. Was regarded by some of the Imperial-
ists as suited to become a Duke. When the Empire fell,
and no further hope of a dukedom arose before his flattered
vanity, he came back, and is now one of the leading
governmental reformers and placed in official position by
his party (how strange to say 'reformers'. They were
once known by a different name). But things are changing with the seasons now.

"You see, this great battle of Pittskill Landing, following
so soon after the battle of Dolinsburg, had marked influence
on the country. The people began to see that the question of courage did not depend so much upon where a man
was born as it did on the amount of it he had when he

was born, and the principle for which he was contending, as well as drill and discipline in his duty. The people in the North were beginning to learn that every hill in the South was not mined and ready to be exploded, blowing up everything that approached. After becoming cool they would ask themselves as to where the powder could have been procured, etc."

"Yes," said Dr. Adams, "I remember well when it was reported, and believed by many, that all the hills in Virginia, near Washington, were mined, and that masked batteries were behind every bush."

"Yes, I know many would speak of those things to prove that the rebellion could not be conquered, or any headway made against it. Just as though a masked battery was any more dangerous than a battery uncovered ; and without reflecting as to the quantity of guns that would have been required, and the number of men supporting the batteries at every place where they were by the vivid imagination of many whose stories were invented for the purpose of frightening the ignorant."

"The truth is that it was and is to me one of the great wonders how we ever succeeded in putting down the rebellion, with nearly the entire South in arms, while there were but few that were not in arms who did not sympathize fully with those who were; and in the North a strong political party, as an organization, prayed and worked for the success of secession and rebellion. The only ones of the party who did not sympathize with the rebellion were a few old men who knew the benefits of a government, those who entered the Union army, those who had friends in the service, and those who were taught to revere the Union in early youth. The remainder of that party who desired our success were but few and far between. They are now the ones, however, who saved the Government, preserved the Constitution, the flag, and our honor, and are going to reform all abuses and make everybody prosperous and happy. The Colonel here, who lost an arm for his country, is laid aside as 'worthless crockery'; and as for myself, who gave seven sons to the service of my country, I am of no use whatever. Of course, I am very old, but I supposed that it would be considered an honor to me to have made so great a sacrifice. So I went out to one of the Reformers' meetings last Fall, and instead of being invited on the stand and referred to as an old man who had given up his whole family for his country's cause, I was permitted to sit on the ground and hear an old Secessionist and rebel sympathizer extolled to the skies, with great applause following, and one of our best and most gallant soldiers ridiculed and abused as if he had been a pirate during the war. So it is and so it goes. I am poor. So are all who spent their time in aiding our country. The mistake we made was not to have staid at home and made fortunes, and let these men, who "feathered their nests" during the war, have gone and served in the army and showed their love of country. We would now have been the patriots and the ones to be intrusted with public affairs.

"But why should I care? I think I should not. But it is impossible for me to lay aside my feelings on the subject of my country's welfare. I will go down to my grave with the feeling that those who so loved their country that they risked their lives for it are the safer ones to trust with its control. I cannot see how those who did not wish the success of our country and those who exerted every nerve to destroy it can be the best persons in whose hands to place our vast interests.

"I may be wrong about this, however, and, therefore, will return to my story, believing that the Lord doeth all things well.

"Peter and our family at home were sitting in the parlor. Jennie was wrapping Peter's foot in cloths and bandages, when the conversation turned on Col. David and Col. Anderson. Jennie had a letter from David but a day or so before, which gave us the news of the good health of himself and James, the doctor. It also informed her that Henry had been assigned to duty in the same command with himself, which made it very pleasant for them. My wife, Aunt Sarah, had received a letter from Mary Anderson a day or so before which brought the gratifying intel-

ligence that the Colonel was improving rapidly and would
be able soon to return to Allentown and once more enjoy
for a time the quiet of our home. He was informed that he
must not return to take the field again for some months.
While I was at home, trying to arrange the difficulty about
the colonelcy of his regiment, inasmuch as his discovery and
return to Dolinsburg had not been officially announced, I
wrote to the President the situation, telling him the whole
story and calling his attention to the reports of the battles
in which the Colonel had participated, and asking that he
give him recognition by promotion to a Brigadier-General-
ship. With this request the President had kindly complied, and I had his commission in my possession, which
fact I kept a profound secret. Just then Peter said to me:

"'What can be done to arrange matters in Col. Tom's
regiment? There is Col. Rice, who, when Tom takes command or when the facts are ascertained, will be reduced in
his command as Lieutenant-Colonel, and I will go back as
Major. This I do not care for, but Col. Rice is a proud
man, and will dislike this, I fear.

"'Then he will show himself an unworthy officer. He
should be glad that his Colonel is alive and yield up the
command gracefully.'

"'There is no other way for him to do,' said Peter; 'that
is true.'

"Old Ham was sitting off to one side with little Mary
Anderson on his lap. The child had been listening to what
was said about her father. She spoke to Uncle Ham, as
she, with the rest of the family, had learned to call him,
and asked:

"'When is papa coming home? Is he well? Is mamma
well? How will they get home?' and many other questions.

"Ham said, 'I doesn't know. Hopes he git heah all
right.'

"The old fellow seemed rather serious, and finally he
asked Aunt Sarah 'If dat letta didn't say nuffin 'bout my
ole woman Marfa.'

"'Oh, yes,' said my wife. 'Uncle Ham, you must pardon me; I was so engaged talking to Peter and Uncle Daniel about our sons that I really neglected to tell you. I will get the letter and read you what Mary says about your wife.'

"She took the letter from her pocket and read to Uncle Ham that Martha was well and so kind to Col. Tom, calling him her boy and saying 'the good Laud' had saved him for some good purpose, and sent her love to her 'dear ole Ham.'

"Ham broke into a laugh and said: 'Dat's it; dat's good. I knowed she say jes' like dat. 1 tell you, Aunt Marfa, she be all right. She know somethin', I tell you she do.'

"He then entered into a disquisition on Aunt Martha to little Mary, until she seemed to feel as much interested in Aunt Martha as did Uncle Ham.

"While we were enjoying the rest of the evening in conversation we heard a noise coming from the children's bedroom. Jennie at once left us and proceeded to the room and found little Sarah Lyon—David's youngest child, then four years old—very sick with a violent attack of croup. We at once sent for a physician. He came, examined her and pronounced her very ill. He very soon gave her relief, that proved to be only temporary. We watched her during the night. In the morning she had a violent fever, and seemed to be very flighty. Everything was done for the blessed child, but all in vain. That afternoon she passed away. This was another stroke to our whole family. Jennie, her mother, was nearly frantic. This was the first misfortune of any sort that had happened in David's family. We were all cast down in grief, as we loved little Sarah. She had been named for my wife, who had made the child a special pet. Little Mary and Jennie were almost heartbroken by her death. They cried continually, and could not be pacified for several days. I telegraphed her father, but it seems my dispatch, for some unknown reason, was not delivered for three days. When it was he was almost crazed by the unwelcome news. It was too late, however, for him to come home. This seemed to sad-

den him.   He was never himself any more during his life.
Little Sarah lies in the cemetery at Allentown."

Here the old man broke down and wept bitterly for a
time.   When he recovered he said :

"My friends, it seems to me strange that I should weep
now.   My sorrows are passed.   I am only waiting here below for the reward that true devotion must bring in the
other world.   There is no recompense for it here.   At
least, I have only found that which comes from the affections of a loving family.   Oh! why should my family all—
all have been taken from me as they were ?   Who has had
such a hard fate as mine ?   Yes ! yes ! when I come to reflect, many have.   Yes ! when all are gone—one or many—
that is all ; we can lose no more.   My country, O ! my
country, it was for thee they died."

CHAPTER VI.

" The bay trees in our country are all withered,
And meteors fright the fixed stars of heaven—
The pale faced moon looks bloody on the earth,
And lean-looked prophets whisper fearful change,
Rich men look sad, and ruffians dance and leap."—SHAKESPEARE.

"THE loss of little Sarah had spread such a gloom over our household that I felt a desire to be out at David's farm, away from the house, as much as possible. Peter also seemed much depressed and showed a great desire to return to his regiment. On one occasion, when Ham and I returned in the evening, the conversation drifted in the direction of the absent ones in the army, and to Harvey, who fell at the battle of the Gaps. My wife at once alluded to her dream, which seemed to be preying upon her mind almost constantly. Peter was silent, but I noticed that he dropped a tear. After a moment he said:

"'Mother, you should not be constantly thinking of your strange dream. You will become morbid on the subject, unless you drive it from your mind. There is nothing in it that worrying will or can change. There can be nothing sure in dreams, and if there is, you can only discover it in the future. The war will reveal it all to you should there be anything in it."

"Ham must speak; it was thought by him to be his time.

"'Yes, missus, de wah 'splain it all. Massa Peter and me talk 'bout dat. No danger come out ob dreams, you know.'

"'Why, Ham,' said Aunt Sarah, 'I thought you dreamed

(63)

about Peter, and said he was all right. You assured us of it; and you said that you always knew by your dreams when matters were all right.'

"'Yeas, yeas, missus; but, you see, I be fool on dat. You see, Massa Peter come back wid a so' foot, shot up putty bad. I got fool on dat dream. You see, Marfa allers tells me 'bout de dreams. So you see, I jes' thought I could tell, too. I miss it. Yeas, I miss him dat time. Marfa, she know, she do. She tell you all 'bout dem when she comed.'

"Then he laughed a regular darky laugh, as I found he was sure to do, if he concluded he had drawn you off on a 'false scent,' or heard anything that pleased him.

"Aunt Sarah was relieved. The fact that Ham admitted that he was humbugged by his own dream seemed to quiet her nerves; so she did not allude to her dream again for a great while. But I could see plainly that Peter was very much depressed whenever allusion was made to it. O, it was prophetic, 'twas a revelation of dire calamities to follow, one after another.

"I could see it all when time unfolded the mystery, as it did, in regular order. It was a warning so strangely imparted. But why, why this warning, and why the calamities? That is the question which has been demanding an answer so long; and yet no answer comes that seems to satisfy my mind. Well, well, let that pass for the present.

"The next morning I sent Ham to the farm on horseback to bring some vegetables. Early in the forenoon we heard a noise as if the running of a horse down the street, and looking out saw Ham coming under heavy pressure, with sails spread. I ran out on the porch, and Ham pulled in opposite the little yard gate. I called to him, and asked what was the trouble. The old darky was so scared that he stammered and made motions, but I could get nothing of an intelligent character from him. I made him dismount, tie up his horse, and come in. By this time the family were all out inquiring into the trouble. Ham sat down on the edge of the porch near the entrance and fanned himself with his hat. Great drops of perspiration were rolling down his face. He seemed to be in much distress. Finally Jennie said to him :

"'Ham, where is the lettuce, the asparagus, and the butter we sent you after ?'

"Ham, finding by this time that he was not dead, essayed to speak. He raised himself to his full height.

"'W'y! W'y! Yeas! Yeas! De—de—de—dey done gone !'

"'Gone where ?' asked Jennie.

"'Dey done gone on de road, missus. I jes' tell you-uns dey's Sesh in heah. 'Spec dey got dem, dey eat dem for dey dinner. Dey got dem, sho.'

"'Well, what about the "Sesh," as you call them ?'

"'O, I tole you all 'bout dem. 'Fore de Laud, I mus' rest fust. I is powerful tired, missis—I is.'

"'Well, Ham, put up your horse and get over your fright, and then perhaps you can explain more satisfactorily what has happened to you.'

"'Yeas, missus, I 'spect dat am de bes' way.'

"So, when Ham had cooled off, we had him give us his experience. He said :

"'Well, Massa Daniel, I jes' go to de farm and dar seed Massa Joseph Dent. He fix up de littis, de 'sparagrass, and de eggs; and when dey all fix up I get ready to come home. He says, "Ham, you see dem fellows down de road dar ?" I looked and seed 'em, and say "Yes, sah." Den he say, "Dey bad man's dey is; kase dey's done bin heah all de mornin' lookin' round like dey wants sumfin, and I watch 'em close; if dey bodders me dey ketch it, sho;" dat's what he say ! I done told Massa Dent dat I not feared. But dat was a story, kase me was some skea'd. I gits on de hoss and comed right on jes' like I wa'n't skea'd at all. I rides slow doe, kase as how I wa'n't sho' 'bout dem mans. So I gits 'bout half way down the road home, and dem mans—dar war free of dem; dar war free, sho', dey jes' steps right in de road afore me and de hoss. I say "Good mornin," and takes off my hat like a gemman. Dey say "Whar you goin', nigga ?" Den I know'd who dey is. When dey say "nigga," dat's nuff for dis child. I know'd

dey be "Sesh." Dat's what "Sesh" all call us—"niggas."
I tells you, den I's ska'd. One ob dem say, "What you got
dar, nigga?" I say "wegetables for de house." Den dey
say "Who house?" I told dem Massa Daniel. Den dey
say, "Dat ole Lyon? Dat ole Ablishner? Dat ole scoun'el
what want to whip de Souf? To free de niggas 'mongst
us?" I say, "Don' know 'bout dat. Massa Lyon not say
nuffin to me 'bout dat." Den dey say, "Whar you come
from, anyhow?" I tole 'em I comed from up in de State

HAM ENCOUNTERS THE REBELS.

whar Massa Daniel comed from. Den dey swar dat I a
liar; dat dey know'd Massa Daniel; dat he fetched no
niggas hyar from 'Hio. Den when dey say "'Hio," golly, I
be glad; kase I could't smell out de name afore; forgot him
clar, sho'. Den I say I comed from 'Hio awhile ago, an'
stay wid you, kase I know'd you back dar in 'Hio. Den
dey ax me w'at town I comed from. Den dey get me. I
skea'd den. One of dem say, "O, he a d—d fool; he not
know nuffin." I say, "Yes, sah, sho'; dat's fac'. I doesn't
know nuffin 'bout dem matters what you say." Den dey

laff. Yes, sah, dey laff. I start on. Den dey say, "Nigga, stop dat hoss." De hoss stop. Yes, sah, den I be orful skea'd. O, dey was de mos' wostest lookin' disciplinous "Sesh" you eber did see wid yo' eyes. Dey had ole brown jeans coat an' britches. Dey look like de "Sesh" what I seed when dey lef' Col. Tom at my cabin.'

" 'Well, said Peter, 'they were escaped prisoners, I have no doubt, from some place, and are hunting their way South.'

" 'Yes, sah,' said Ham; 'dat's it; dey 'scape and is gwine back to de reb's army, sho': dat's who dey is. I know'd dey was "Sesh." '

" 'Well, go on, Ham; tell us the rest,' said Aunt Sarah. I was so much amused at Ham's story that I kept rather quiet.

" 'Well,' said Ham, 'den dey took de hoss by de bridle and made me git off. I s'posed dey was gwine to take de hoss, but dey looked de hoss ober, and say he no good, and gib de hoss back. I got on and dey all pull out pistols and tell me to "git;" dat's wa't dey say, and sho' you bo'n, I git—an' de lettice go one way, de 'sparagrass go anoder way, and eggs go de Lord knows whar—to smash, I reckon. Dey all gone, sho,' an' I's hyar. Dey shoot when I go. I 'spect I be kill; but I'm hyar, sho'; dis is ole Ham; he 'scape.'

"We all laughed—in fact, could not help it. I told Ham that I would go out with him the next day and we would see about this matter. Ham withdrew, scratching his head and looking very serious.

"The next day I had the horses hitched to the wagon, and Peter feeling that he had so far recovered that he could stand the ride, we went out together. When we came to the place where Ham had met his three suspicious looking friends we examined the spot, found Ham's lettuce, etc., scattered somewhat over the ground, but could not see much evidence of anything else.

"Ham said but little. Finally, I asked him which direction his friends had gone from here. He at once pointed the way, saying, 'Doesn't you see de track? Dar he go. Turn 'roun' and go back de same way he come.'

"We could see some indications that Ham's story might be true, but not enough to be very satisfactory. However, we went along. When we arrived at the farm and found Joseph Dent we had Ham relate his experience. Joseph Dent said to come in the house. When we had all been seated, Joseph said:

"'Well, I have no doubt as to the truth of what Ham says. The same three men (at least, I suppose them to be, from the description), came here last night and forced me to let them stay in the house. I was not very fearful of their doing me any harm, as I was watchful. My partner and myself could have handled them if they had made any demonstration. We gave them their suppers and a mug of ale and got them going, and found that they were escaped rebels, who had been in prison camp at Indianapolis. They told us that there was a plot to let all the prisoners loose and to raise an army out of their friends North to commence war here, and in that way to have the rebellion succeed.'

"Peter inquired how they came to tell so much about their plans.

"Joseph answered that he and his partner pretended to them that they were in full sympathy with the rebellion, and were staying here only to have the influence of Col. David to keep them out of the Union army, and that if compelled at any time to join either army they would join the rebels.

"'Where have they gone?' inquired Peter.

"'They have gone into the country some twenty miles, to Collins Grove. There is to be a political meeting there to-morrow, and they expect, as they told us, that Thomas A. Strider, of Indianapolis, and Dan Bowen, also of Indiana, were to be there, and through one of them they thought they could obtain aid; that while in prison they had been initiated into a society called the "Knights of the Golden Circle," which was a secession organization, intended as an auxiliary force to the rebel army; that Dan Bowen was one of their main men, and so called "Agitator"; that Thomas A. Strider was Chief Counselor to the organization in Indiana; was to be in Washington most of the time to "watch things" and to defend them at all times when any of their order should be arrested or in any danger.'

"Peter and I went out to the barn and talked the matter over, and thought that in such a case as this we would be justified in resorting to any means or strategy to discover this secret organization and ascertain the designs of its members. We concluded to get Joseph Dent, who was an old soldier, and very bright, with an excellent memory, to join it and find out all that he could about the organization. Agreeing to this, Peter hobbled back on his crutches. He being a soldier made the proposition to Dent, which he readily acceded to, saying:

"'I had thought of that myself, but feared that you might take me to be too intimate with these people. I call them Secessionists and rebels. I think, that if you agree, I will go down to this meeting to-morrow, and when I come back will come to Allentown, as they might keep a watch on me here.'

"With this understanding we returned, instructing Joseph Dent to stay as long as might become necessary, in order to learn all that he could as to the design of these people. After getting our supplies in the wagon we returned home. On arriving we found all feeling very joyful over the fact that Col. Anderson would be home in the course of a week. He had so written to me. Aunt Sarah had opened and read the letter. Little Mary was so delighted that she ran out and tried to tell us all that her father had written. She would talk and stammer and draw a long breath, and then commence again, and repeat until I had to tell her to rest and begin slowly. When we got in we heard all. The two children were delighted at the prospect of seeing Aunt Martha almost as much as seeing the Colonel and his brave wife. Peter and I had to keep quiet about our program with Joseph Dent, and therefore discussed other matters. During the evening Peter concluded that he would not attempt returning to his regiment until Col. Tom should arrive, so that he could arrange about the command and take some word back to Col. Rice. (I said not one word about Tom's commission as Brigadier, but continued the suggestion that Col. Rice could not think of doing otherwise than turning over the command to Col. Anderson.) Just then the post-boy came again with a letter. I opened it and found it to be from my son Jackson, at St. Paul, Minn., (where he resided and was engaged in railroad building,) stating that he considered it his duty to enter the service of his country. Being young and healthy, he said, no patriot in this crisis, blessed with good health, could afford to remain out of the army; that the day would come when the question would be asked of all such persons, 'Why did you not go to the war and fight for your country?' Poor boy, if he were living now he would ask himself the queston: 'Why did I go; for what did I peril my life?' Yes! yes!

"Well, I kept this from my wife, Aunt Sarah, for the time. She was so worried about our family that I thought best to wait for a day or so, inasmuch as she did not see me get the letter. A couple of days passed and Joseph Dent came to our house. After seeing and speaking to Jennie about the farm and her interest generally, and telling Aunt Sarah about Ham's scare and joking him somewhat, he spoke to Peter and myself, and said that he wanted to see us alone.

" We all went out to the barn, and there he told us all that he had heard and seen—that he had gone to Collins' Grove; that there was a large political meeting there; that Dan Bowen spoke in the most excited manner of the wrongs and outrages, as he termed them, of the vile abolition adminstration; that the Union soldiers were mere hirelings; that he hoped none of his party would join the Abolition army to assist in robbing and murdering our brethren down South. (Dent had noted these sayings in his memorandum; he was a man of fair education and a close observer.) Bowen was vociferously applauded during his remarks. Thos. A. Strider spoke also; but he was not so vehement and abusive as Bowen, but was equally strong against the war for the Union. Strider spoke of it as

an unholy war on our part, and all the acts of Congress
and the President being 'unauthorized and unconstitutional,' and that the war would be a failure and ought to
be; that he would not see money appropriated, if in his
power to prevent, to carry it on; that if the Government
undertook to draft his friends in Indiana as soldiers, he
would defend any of them (free of charge) that resisted
such an unconstitutional proceeding. He continued in
this vein for an hour. These utterances were loudly applauded by the majority of the audience. But, continuing,
he stated that on that day he came across the three escaped prisoners heretofore mentioned, and staid with them
during the speeches and agreed to all that was said, so as
to satisfy them of his strict adherence to their principles.

They said to him that if he would remain that night they
would initiate him into their mysterious organization. He
acceded to their proposition without hesitation, and remained—not leaving them for an instant. In the evening,
shortly after dark, they were all conducted to a large
empty barn near by, and on entering it Dent found Thos.
A. Strider presiding, and Bowen lecturing on the designs
and purposes of the Knights of the Golden Circle.

After he had explained the objects of the organization,
an obligation was administered to all who had not before
been admitted and obligated. Dent, being one who had
not before joined, with others took the obligation, and was
then instructed in the signs, grips and passwords. He said
that he played it pretty well, so that he was thoroughly
instructed, and kept repeating them to himself, so that he
might not forget any part. The obligation pledged them
to use all possible means in their power to aid the rebels
to gain their independence; to aid and assist prisoners to
escape; to vote for no one for office who was not opposed
to the further prosecution of the war, to encourage desertions from the Union army; to protect the rebels in all
things necessary to carry out their designs, even to the
burning and destroying of towns and cities, if necessary, in
order to produce the desired result. They were also directed
to give information at all times of any knowledge they

might have of the movements of our armies, and of the
coming of soldiers to their homes; to use their influence to
prevent their return to the army. They were not even to
disclose the murder of any returned soldier or Union man,
if done by any one belonging to this organization. They
were told in the instructions that men were sent into our
prisons to obligate and instruct all prisoners, so that they
could make themselves known in traveling, should they
escape; also, that the organization extended into Canada,

KNIGHTS OF THE GOLDEN CIRCLE MEETING IN A BARN.

as well as every State in the North; that men in our army
belonged to it, who would retreat in battle, or surrender
whenever they could do so; they could always make themselves known to the rebel commanders; that the members
were in every way possible to foment jealousies and ill-feeling between the Eastern and Western troops, and especially between the commanding Generals of the two sec-
tions; they were to encourage the Western volunteers not
to allow themselves to be commanded by Eastern officers,
and especially were they to tickle the fancy and pride of

the Eastern officers and men, by encouraging them not to allow themselves to be subjected to the control of the uneducated men of the West—in short, every kind and character of argument was to be resorted to. In the event of failure, any other means, no matter what, was to be employed to cause failure on our part and success on theirs.

Peter wrote down every word told us by Dent, being very careful about the signs and passwords. This being done, we cautioned Dent to be extremely careful in his conversations with others, and never to speak of this organization to any one, for fear that he might get into trouble or suffer in some way from its members. Dent bade us good day and left for home. We returned to the house and there read over Peter's memorandum carefully, and studied the signs and passwords so as to fully comprehend them. This, to us, was a serious question. Peter felt as though there was much in this to cause our country great trouble in addition to what was already upon us. I said to Peter that I would at once write to the President and send him all the statements as they were made to us by Dent, as well as suggest to him the necessity of having this conspiracy (as it was nothing less) ferreted out at once, which I did that day, and also suggested the arrest and trial of all that could be found who were engaged in getting up these organizations. I soon received a letter, not from the President, but from another, which satisfied me that my letter had been received by the one for whom it was intended.

"Very soon the whisperings and newspaper gossip showed plainly that there were jealousies in the Army of the East as well as in the Army of the Center. Officers were complaining of each other, and some were charging ill-treatment on the part of the Administration, showing clearly that there were influences silently at work. About this time I received a note from Washington requesting me to come to that city. I prepared for the trip. Bidding good-by to our family, and requesting Peter not to leave until I should return, I was off, no one but Peter and my wife holding the secret of my leaving home at this time. When I arrived at Washington I proceeded to the

Executive Mansion, sent in my name, and was at once admitted. The President met me most cordially, and asked me to be seated. He wrote a note and sent it out by a messenger, then turned to me and entered into conversation about the health of our people, the crops of the country, and the sentiments I found generally held among the people of the West in reference to the war. I said to him that among the Union people there was but one sentiment, and that was that the last man and last dollar must be exhausted, if necessary, to put down the rebellion. He grasped me by the hand warmly and said :

"'Lyon, my good friend, I am exceedingly glad to know that. I have been hearing curious stories about your part of Indiana. The Governor of your State seems to fear trouble from some cause.'

"'My dear Mr. President,' I said, 'do not misunderstand me. I do not mean to say our people are united; it is only the Union people I had reference to. There is a strong party in the State who are utterly opposed to the prosecution of the war, and they are led on by very strong and influential men.'

"'Yes,' said the President, 'this man Strider is at the head of that party. He is a smooth-talking fellow—rather an "Oily Gammon," very shrewd, and hard to catch at any open or overt act. He has a way of setting others on and keeping out himself. At least, I should so conclude from what I have seen and know of him.'

"'Yes, Mr. President, you have estimated the man correctly,' was my reply.

"'Just at this point in the conversation, the Secretary of War came in. The President was going to introduce me.

"'No introduction is necessary, Mr. President,' said the Secretary; 'this is one of my old neighbors and friends.'

"'Our meeting was full of warmth and friendly greetings, having been friends for many years in Ohio prior to my leaving the State. We were all seated, and after some general conversation between the Secretary and myself, the President remarked that he had sent for me, and on my presenting myself he had sent for the Secretary of War for the purpose of having a full conference in reference to the situation in the rear of the army out West, and that from my letter to him he did not know of any one who could give him that information better than myself.

"'By the way,' said he, 'what about your nephew, Anderson? He must be a glorious fellow and a good soldier. Of course, you have received the commission that the Secretary and I sent you for him?'

"'Yes! thanks to you, Mr. President. He is improving very fast. His wound will soon be well, and he will then be ready for the field again.'

"'Tell him,' said the President, 'that I will watch his career with great interest. Coming from where he does, he must have good metal in him to face his friends and relatives in taking the stand he has.'

"'Yes, sir,' said I; ' he is a true man, and his wife, though a Southern woman, is one of the noblest of her sex, and as true a patriot as ever lived.'

"'Your family are nearly all soldiers, I believe, Mr. Lyon,' said the Secretary.

"'Yes, Mr. Secretary; I had seven sons—five are in the army, one was killed at the battle of the Gaps, and the seventh is on his way from St. Paul to join it. God knows I have some interest in our success, and I will go myself at any time should it be necessary.'

"'The President here interrupted:

"'No, Mr. Lyon, you must not. You have done enough. If this Government cannot be saved without the eighth one of your family putting his life in peril at your age, it cannot be saved. We will accept no more recruits from the Lyon family.'

"'The President then asked me to give to the Secretary and himself the situation in the West as nearly as I could, and especially in Indiana.

" I proceeded to state the situation—the bitterness of the opposition to the Administration, as well as to the war, then being manifested by the anti-war party, or, in other words, by the Democratic party as an organization ; the organized lodges of the Golden Circle, their objects and designs, the influence they were to bring to bear, how they were to operate and in what directions, the jealousies they were to engender between the officers of the East and the West; the fact that they were to release prisoners and to destroy towns and cities in the North, should it become necessary.

"The President and Secretary both listened with grave attention, and seemed to fully comprehend the situation.

"The President finally said :

"'Mr. Secretary, this is a very serious matter, and is becoming more so every day.'

"'Yes,' replied the Secretary; 'you know, Mr. President, that we have talked this over heretofore, but this revelation seems startling. I can begin to see where the influence partly comes from which gives us so much trouble with some of the officers of the Eastern army. At first I was induced to believe that they were jealous of each other, but I am beginning to think it comes from political influences in opposition to the Administration, having a desire to change the policy of the Government in reference to the war. Several of the senior officers in different commands act as though they thought more of promotion and being assigned to large commands than the success of our cause. They will not serve under any but their own selection of commanders—at least, make opposition to doing so. There seems to be a little coterie who think no one is suitable to command except themselves. They have not been very successful so far, and act as though they were determined that no one else should be. We have relieved their chief and brought a new man to the field, and I do believe that some of these men will not give him a cordial support. We must wait, quietly, however, for developments. One thing is strange to me, and that is that I find these complaining gentlemen all have been and now are in sympathy with the party which is found in a great degree opposing the war. I do not mean by this to impeach their patriotism, but to suggest that the influences which operate upon them and flatter their vanity by suggestions of

presidency, cabinets, head of the army, future power, great-
ness, etc., are not coming from the people or party in full
accord with the Administration and in favor of such a
prosecution of the war as will insure ultimate success.'

"'Well,' said the President, 'we are in their power at the
present, and their demands upon the Administration are
of a character to induce the belief that they are preparing
the road to an ultimate recognition of the so-called Confederacy; but, gentlemen, they will not succeed.' (This he
said with much warmth.) 'I will not let them succeed.
The Lord, in his own good time, will raise up and develop
some man of great genius as a commander, and I am now
patiently waiting for that time. I cannot put these men
aside now. The country would sympathize with them and
feel that I do not know as much about war as they do;
but they will tell the tale on themselves very soon, and
then we will be completely justified in getting rid of them.
This war must go on for some time yet if the Union is to be
restored, and I have faith that it will be; but I am just
now bothered more about the condition in the rear than
in the front; that will come out all right in time. But if
these Golden Circle organizations spread, as they seem to
be doing, in the West, where a great portion of our troops
must come from, and the people should once get the idea
fixed in their minds that the war must be a failure, and a
fire in the rear is started of great proportions, then what?
Then will come the serious question. And should the people pronounce at the next election against a further prosecution of the war, there will be a secret understanding
with those who come into power that the so-called Confederacy is to be recognized, and that will be the end.'

"'But, Mr. President, do you look for such a result?' I
asked.

"'No, sir,' responded the President; 'I was only putting
the worst side of the case—just as I would look at the
worst side of a client's case in court. The people of this
country love this republic too well to see it go down marred
and destroyed merely for the purpose of upholding the
crime and infamy of slavery. No, gentlemen, this Union

4

will be restored. All the rebels of the South, and all the sympathizers and Golden Circles of the North cannot destroy it so long as there is one patriot left qualified to lead an army. They will have to burn every city and assassinate every leading man who is able to be a leader before our flag will go down in gloom and disgrace. This they may try. God only knows what desperate men will do to uphold an unholy cause.'"

"How prophetic this thought was," said Dr. Adams.

"Yes, it was really so. The very things mentioned were attempted, and an organization completed for the purpose. They accomplished a part of their hellish design, but they did not succeed to the extent contemplated.

"But to return to the conversation with the President and Secretary:

"The President then asked me if I would, in my own way, further ferret out what was being done by this organization in the West and post him by reports in writing as often as I could conveniently do so.

"I responded that I could not go into the lodges myself, but I would, in every way that I could consistently, through others, obtain information and send him.

"'This,' he said, 'was all that he could ask me to do, situated as I was.'

"This being all that was desired, the Secretary of War made out a pass authorizing me to enter any and all of our lines or camps of prisoners, to visit any and all hospitals—in fact, to go to and pass through all places under military control in the United States. With this pass in my pocket I bade good-by to the President and Secretary and left for home.

"When I returned I found that Col. Tom Anderson, his wife, and old Aunt Martha had arrived. The family had a joyful meeting and had become settled down. All were glad to see me. Col. Tom, his wife, and Aunt Martha had many pleasant things to relate—how Tom recovered so rapidly; how kind Col. Harden had been; what a good man Surg. Long was; how a band of rebels came down the river to old George's farm, where Tom had been so long;

how they were surprised and captured by one of Col.
Harden's reconnoitering parties, and that they said they
were sent to take Mr. George's property away and to bring
with them old Ham and Aunt Martha.

Old Ham, being present, broke out in one of his charac-
teristic laughs.

"'Ah! He-ogh. Fo' de good Laud, dat's de time dey
miss der cotch. Dis darky was done gone when dey comed.
I know'd dey'd be dar sometime for dis cat, and Marfa, too.
I tells you, dey want her, dey do. She know how to cook
and do things, she do. Be a cole day when dey gits dis
cat agin, sho's you born'd.'

"Aunt Martha came in and said to Ham :

"'What you doin' heah, Ham?'

"'I's sympensizen wid dem "Sesh" what comed down
to ole Massa George's place back yonder for to fotch me
and you back to de Missip. De cat done gone. He-ah!
he-ah!'

"'Yes; but you ole fool, dey'd got you if it had not bin
for me. I beg you afore you goes to go wid Massa Daniel,
you knows I did.'

"'Yes, Marfa, dat's so. I tole dem all de time dat you
knows de bes'. Don't I, Massa Daniel?'

"'Oh, yes, Ham,' I said. 'You always speak well of
Martha, and what she knows.'

"'Deed I do, Marfa; dat's so; I does, all de time.'

"'Dat's all right den, Ham. I forgib you all what you
do, so you jes' git out in de kitchen; dar's whar you
b'long. Dese folks spile you ef dey don't mind deyselves.

"The family, or a considerable portion of them, again
being together, we naturally drifted in our conversation as
to the war, it being uppermost in everybody's mind at
that time; so I found an opportunity to tell Col. Anderson
and Peter all about my trip, what had occurred, and what
I had promised to do. Peter said that I would have to
be very cautious, and that the first thing was to understand whether or not the Postmaster here could be trusted.
Should he allow it to be known that I was frequently
communicating with the President, the enemies at Allen-

town would manage in some way to discover my communications, and thereby my life would be in danger.

"I knew the Postmaster, however, and that he could be trusted; so that part of the matter was settled.

"Colonel Anderson suggested that there should be no haste in settling the arrangements; that it was of such importance that a little reflection would do no harm; so we laid the matter over for the present."

"Uncle Daniel," said Col. Bush, "we who were in the army felt the influence of the Knights of the Golden Circle. There was one time during the war when we would have hundreds of desertions in a night; nor could we stop it for a considerable length of time. We finally discovered that the people opposed to the war were engaged in every possible way in influencing the relatives of the soldiers. They would sometimes get their wives to write about their sufferings, sickness in their families, and in every way that it could be done they were rendered dissatisfied."

"Yes," said Maj. Clymer, "that is true in every respect. Part of my command deserted, and I have found since the war that they were induced to do so by these very influences."

"The situation at that time was very critical," said Dr. Adams. "I remember well when mobs were organized and when soldiers were shot down on the road in this vicinity while returning to their commands after being home on a leave of absence.

"O, yes, those were perilous times for all who were in favor of their country's success. Returning, however, to family matters:

"On the morning of the next day, after Peter, Col. Anderson and myself had talked over the matter of my Washington trip, and sat down to breakfast, Col. Anderson found a paper under his plate. All eyes were upon him, and he turned his upon the paper. He read it, and looked at me as though he understood it all, yet it was evidently a very happy surprise; he said not one word, but handed it to his wife, supposing that the rest knew of it. She jumped up from the table and threw her arms around my neck and wept for joy. This procedure seemed to puzzle the rest of the family, as they were totally ignorant of the contents of the paper.

"'Mother,' exclaimed Peter, ' what is all this ?'

"Col. Anderson said : ' Aunt, do you not know what it is ? '

"' No, indeed,' she replied.

" I then revealed the secret of my keeping the fact quiet about Tom having been commissioned as a Brigadier-General.

"Peter at once said : ' Well, that settles the question in our regiment; and I am truly glad, for two reasons : first, that Col. Anderson has been promoted, and, second, that it leaves our regiment intact.'   .

" All congratulated the Colonel and were happy over it. Old Aunt Martha who was waiting on the table that morning shouted out ' Glory !   Dat's jes' what I sed; dat de good Laud was gwine to keep Massa Tom for some big thing, so he do good.   I know'd it.'

" We all felt that it was due him and all were glad. Upon looking up I discerned tears in Jennie's eyes, I knew in a moment her thoughts, but said not a word. Her darling child, Sarah, had died, and of course she was sensitive and easily touched. After breakfast I took the first opportunity to say to her: ' My dear child, don't feel badly; your husband's promotion will come very soon.'

"This seemed to cheer her up, and all went on well and pleasantly. No one seemed to understand Jennie's tears but myself, and I was very quiet on the subject. Sure enough, the very next day she got a letter from David, telling her that he had been promoted and assigned to the command of a brigade. This made us all doubly happy, and caused us to forget our grief for a time. The two children did not quite understand all this. But Aunt Martha, to whom the children had become quite devoted, was in her very peculiar way explaining it all to the children, and yet she knew but little more about it than they did, and between her explanations and their understanding of it, made it very amusing indeed.

"Two days afterwards Peter left for his command, which was still encamped on the battle-field of Pittskill Landing. He felt as though he could do camp duty if no more. He wore the same sad countenance that had become fastened upon him since he had been pondering over his mother's dream.

"Col. Anderson was still very weak, but was nervous about the future and extremely anxious to recover sufficiently to take the field. His bloodless face and trembling motion showed that he couldn't perform field duty for some time to come. He made a request, however, for the detail of Capt. Day, of Col. Harden's regiment, as one of his aides-de-camp. The order for the detail, in accordance with his wishes, he soon received, but delayed sending it forward, leaving Capt. Day with Col. Harden until such time as he should be able to be assigned to duty. In talking over with Gen. Anderson the situation and the mission I had to perform, we concluded, inasmuch as he was only slightly known through the West, that he could travel through Ohio, Indiana and Illinois on a prospecting tour and be less liable to suspicion than myself, known as I was in many parts of the country, and that the journey was just what he needed to give him strength.

"Preparatory to his undertaking the expedition we thought proper to visit Joseph Dent on the farm, and have the General more fully posted in the mysteries of the Golden Circle. We at once repaired to the farm. While there Dent instructed him thoroughly, he having it at his tongue's end, as he had been meeting with the Circle frequently in the neighborhood, under the advice of Peter and myself. Gen. Anderson carefully wrote down everything in his pocket memorandum book, and after frequently going over the signs, manipulations, passwords, etc., with Dent, we left for home. All the preliminaries were then arranged, so that the General was to start as soon as he considered himself sufficiently strong to undergo the fatigues of the journey.

"Late in the evening the form of a tall, well-proportioned man appeared at the door and rapped. I said

'Come.' He entered, saying, 'Father, how are you?' I saw it was my son Jackson, from St. Paul, Minn. After hearty greetings, I introduced him to Gen. Anderson and wife. Aunt Sarah soon entered the room, and the meeting between mother and son was most touching. In the conversation that ensued Jackson soon disclosed the fact that he was on his way to join the army somewhere, not entirely defined in his own mind ; but came by to pay a visit to us first.

"Gen. Anderson seemed at once to take a fancy to Jackson, and proposed that he make application for a Captaincy in the Regular Army and be assigned to him as one of his staff officers. This was readily acceded to by my son. The papers were made out, and Jackson started for Washington the next morning to make the request of the President, the understanding being that he was to return to my house and await the future movements of Gen. Anderson. His mother, hearing of this arrangement, was better satisfied with it than she would have been if he had started out in some regiment; but she wept bitter tears at the thought of all her sons endangering their lives.

"She said to me:

"'Daniel, if our whole family, or a greater part of them should be lost, who will remember it to our honor, and where will sympathy for us come from ? You know the youth who fired the Ephesian Dome is remembered, while the builder is forgotten.'

"These words of my good wife are constantly ringing in my ears. How true! how true!"

CHAPTER VII

TRAITOR KNIGHTS—ORGANIZATION OF REBEL SYMPA-
THIZERS IN INDIANA AND ILLINOIS—SIGNS AND
SECRETS—GEN. ANDERSON'S TOUR OF INVESTIGATION
—THE GOLDEN CIRCLE.

" O, Conspiracy, shame'st thou to show thy dangerous brow by night,
When evils are most free ?   O then, by day,
Where will thou find a cavern dark enough
To mask thy monstrous visage ?   Seek none, conspiracy."
— SHAKESPEARE.

"SEVERAL days elapsed before Gen. Anderson felt that he could undertake the journey contemplated. Finally he concluded that he would make the effort. He thought it best for him to pass into Illinois first, as he would not be known in that State. After arranging his matters and leaving word for Jackson to remain at my house, (on his return from Washington, should he succeed in obtaining the desired appointment,) until he returned from his tour of investigation, he started.

"The first stopping place of the General was at Colestown, in Charles County. There he remained several days, and found the most bitter feeling existing between the political parties. He passed very easily among the anti-war people for a Southerner and rebel. He made the acquaintance of one Maj. Cornell, who was home on leave of absence. The General, finding him a very intelligent and apparently an honorable, high-minded gentleman, explained to him that he was not a rebel, but on a mission for the Government. This made him all right with the loyal element, that could be privately communicated with and trusted.

"He had noticed a gentleman, rather fine-looking, with the movements and general appearance of a Southerner. He

managed to get a good look in his face, and recognized him
as Mr. Jas. Walters, of Arkansas. He spoke to him. The
recognition was mutual ; the General invited him to his
room, and there the knowledge of the Golden Circle was at
once manifested. Neither disclosed at first anything
about himself, but finally the General told Walters that
he was up here North for his health, and to spy out the
situation and report the same. They soon became very
confidential, and Walters unbosomed himself to the General. He told him that he was traveling under the guise
of a real-estate agent, selecting land for some large and
wealthy firm, but in reality he was organizing the Knights
of the Golden Circle; that he had organized, some ten
miles southeast of the town, a lodge of sixty members.
He gave all the names. In Colestown he had another
lodge, seventy strong, with Col. O. B. Dickens as Chief of
the Order for that Congressional district.

"During that evening he showed the General his lists
and gave him the names of men to go to in Vernon
County, Jeffersonville, Fayetteville, Franklin, Perryville,
Fultonville and many other places in the state.

"Chicago being the main headquarters, he directed
him (if he should go there) to Morrison Buckner, John
Walls, N. Judy Cornington, C. H. Eagle, and many other
prominent men who belonged to the organization and were
in direct communication with Windsor, Canada, where a
portion of the main directors and managers were stationed,
and from whence they were sending out organizers for the
West. Walters told him that Indianapolis, Ind., was one
of the 'Head Centers,' and that Dodgers, Bowlens, Millington, Dorsing and Byron were the Chiefs, with several
so-called Agitators, and that Mr. Strider was Supreme
Counsel; that the organization was spreading rapidly; that
in Ohio, at Dayburg, was the Head Center; that along the
great river there were very many lodges and quite a number of members, but that it had not been so long at work
in Ohio as in Illinois and Indiana. Also, that the Supreme
Commander lived in Dayburg, O.; his name was given as
Valamburg; that in Kentucky and Missouri nearly all the

people were joining the order and sending men as fast as they could to the rebel army, and at the proper time, when things were ripe for the people to rise, one of the most popular officers in the rebel army, who lived in Missouri, would be sent there with enough troops to protect himself until the Knights could join him.

"He went on to say that Col. Burnett, of St. Louis, was Supreme Commander for Missouri, and Marmalade was Chief Agitator; John Morganson was Supreme Commander in Kentucky; that he was gathering men from there all the time; that he was not only Supreme Commander of Kentucky, but appointed to make excursions and raids into Ohio and Indiana, whenever the organization should be considered strong enough to protect him. This, he said, was considered one of the measures to be resorted to in order to frighten the property-holders of the North, and thereby drive them into a peace-policy; that if the North could be once thoroughly alarmed about the safety of their property, the anti-war party would then carry an election, and that would secure the recognition of the Southern Confederacy; that a perfect understanding of this kind existed with the leaders of the Confederacy and the leaders of the anti-war party North. He told the General that this organization was first started in New York city by a man by the name of McMasterson and some gentlemen from Richmond, who had passed through the lines and gone there for this purpose; that there were at that time 100,000 Knights in the State of New York; 30,000 in Ohio; 75,000 in Indiana, and 50,000 in Illinois.

"He said it was thought that it would require about one year yet to get the organization perfected and in good working order; that they had to work very cautiously, and would have considerable trouble getting the right kind of arms into their hands. There was no trouble, he said, in having them all armed with pistols; 'for,' said Walters, 'these Yankees are so fond of money that you can buy arms anywhere, if on hand. You can get them made at some of the private arsenals, if you could assure them against discovery. The intention, however, is to get all things ready by the time of the next Presidential election, and if we do not whip them before that time we will resort to such methods as will insure the election of one of our friends, or one who believes that we can never be subjugated.'

"The General responded to what he had said, and remarked that it did seem that if those plans could be carried out that success must certainly follow.

"'Yes,' said Walters; 'we must not and cannot fail. I

DRINKING TO THE SUCCESS OF TREASON.

tell you, when these money-loving Yanks see their towns and cities threatened, prisoners turned loose, maddened by confinement, and commence applying the torch, you will hear peace! peace! for God's sake, give us peace! This will be the cry, sir! Mind what I say!'

"Col. Walters by this time had disclosed the fact that he was a colonel in the rebel army; he had pulled at his flask frequently, and was growing quite eloquent. Gen. Anderson could not drink, and his looks gave him a good excuse for not doing so. Finally Walters said:

"'Anderson, how did you get here, anyhow? The last time I saw you was at Vicksburg, four years ago, attending court.'

"'Well,' said the General, 'I might have asked you the same question.'

"'Now, don't play Yankee on me in answering my question by asking me another.'

"'Well, said the General, 'I was in Kentucky, and when I crossed the river no one asked me any questions. I looked so ill and emaciated that they thought I told them the truth when I said I wanted a change of climate —and then, I am also playing the Union role, you know.'

"'Is it not very curious,' said Walters; 'I have traveled all over this country, and no one has asked me a question as to where I came from or what I am doing. In our country we would both have been in prison or hung before this as spies. Don't you think so?'

"'We would have been in great danger,' said the General.

"'Danger! Thunder!' said Walters; 'we would have pulled hemp before this.'

"It was then getting quite late, and the General began to excuse himself on account of his health, and they finally spoke of meeting again sometime, and bade each other good night. The General retired after arranging to leave on the train in the morning for Chicago. Leaving Colestown at an early hour, he arrived in Chicago that evening and put up at the Richmond House. In the course of the next day, by proper management, he got acquainted with Walls, Morrison Buckner and Mr. Eagle. This hotel seemed to be the common meeting-place for this class of men. The subject of the war was discussed very freely by all of them. They seemed to be very much exasperated about the course of the Administration, denouncing its acts as revolutionary, arbitrary and unconstitutional. Eagle seemed to be rather a good-natured fellow—dealt measurably in jokes, as I took it. He said that he did not owe allegiance to any country, as he understood it; that his father was French, his mother was German, and he was born on English waters under the Italian flag ; and that he should claim protection from all until his nativity could be settled.

"The General said he rather took a liking to him. He finally explained to the General, however, that he was from the South, but left there because his health was not good enough to go into the Confederate army, and he knew if he staid he would have been compelled to do so. In Chicago there was no danger of having to go into either army; that a man could stay and help the rebels more than if he we were South, and if they wanted him in the army he could hire some fool to go and get shot in his place for a hundred dollars. He said that there was another advantage—that the people went so fast that they forgot which side you were on in a month, and that you did not have to live there always to become a citizen. You could go to Congress after you had been there a week, if you only knew how to handle the 'boys.'

" The General said that he was really amused at the fellow, but very soon the Grand Head Center of the State came in and he was introduced to Mr. N. Judy Cornington.

"The General gave him the sign, which was at once recognized, and the wink went round that the General was a brother. They conversed freely about the condition of the country; the ultimate result of the war; what must be done to bring about peace; how the Administration must be changed and peaceful commercial relations established with the South, and the Southern Confederacy recognized. To all this the General responded :

"'Yes; but suppose these things that you mention do not bring about the result. What then ?'

"' What then ?' you ask. 'We will then resort to any and every means, no matter what, for success. We are now in the same condition as the rebels South. Should they fail we will have to go South, or forever be under the ban of treason. You do not suppose that these people who support the Union will ever trust any of us or any of our party again, should our friends South fail, do you ?'

"' Well, what of it ?' asked Mr. Buckner. 'I do not now,

nor do I expect hereafter to ask these people for anything. I am actuated by principle purely, without reference to the future. Let the future take care of itself.'

"'Yes, that is well enough, Mr. Buckner,' said Cornington, 'as a sentiment just now; but some day we will feel differently, and our people, who are now taking desperate chances, will want to have something to say. You do not suppose that all these brave men who are now in the rebel army, and their friends North, are going to allow these Abolitionists to run this Government, even if we should not succeed.'

"'Do you think that these people North will care (after this thing is over) anything about who shall be in power,' said Mr. Eagle. "I tell you, Mr. Cornington, that they will soon forget all about it. You show them where the least taxes are and the most money to be made, and they will throw patriotism to the dogs. Why, if the rebellion fails, I expect to see Jeff. Davis' Cabinet, or part of them, running this Government, with him behind them directing things. Yes, sir; no matter what occurs, we only have to let these people go on making money, and we will look after the politics. They will not take time to do it.'

"'Why, gentlemen, I expect to run the politics of this State yet. I intend to make money now, and when the thing blows over I will then have leisure. I do not care for the amount of money these Northern men want. When we Southern men get enough to have a small income to live on, we turn our attention to politics; and there is no trouble to run things if you only attend to it. These rich fellows think all you have to do is to have plenty of money, and if you want anything done in politics, buy it. There is where they make their great mistake. You must work the boys—give them a show along with you. The people all have their ambitions—some great, some not so great, but all want a show. There are some men here in this city who think they can buy the whole State. But they are mistaken; when they try it they will discover their error. They will find the fellows that play politics play the game well,' and so rattled on this man Eagle. The

General said that when he got started he was like a wound-up clock—you either had to let it run down or smash it.

"'Well,' said Cornington, 'Eagle, you seem to take rather a rosy view of things. I do not look at matters quite in the same light that you do. I want to see success assured; then matters may assume the shape you say. But I fear if we fail the result will be otherwise.'

"Said Eagle: 'I tell you, sir, that no matter what happens, the brains and courage and aggressiveness of the Southern people will control this country, Union or no Union, and you will see it yet, if we live. But that belief must not prevent us from doing our duty manfully. We must hang together and terrify the Northern people.'

"'Yes,' said Cornington, 'as was said by one of our fathers in the Revolution, "we must hang together, or we will hang separately."' This caused Eagle to laugh.

"'Oh!' said he, 'those old fellows were frightened into success, and you must know that to alarm the North about their money and property being in danger is the only road to success. You can't scare them about their lives. Our people are mistaken on that point. They care much less for their lives than for their "oil."'

"The General, after getting all the information he could as to the extent of the organization, their designs and intended future operations, which corresponded with what he had learned from Walters, promised to see them again, and left that night for Dayburg, Ohio. On arriving there he tried every way to obtain an interview with the Supreme Commander of the Golden Circle of the United States, but in vain. His attempts were all thwarted in one way or another. The Commander (Valamburg) must have had some fears in reference to strangers.

'For three days the General tried to get a chance to see him, but could not. He met, however, three men,—Pat Burke, Tim Collins and John Stetson,—with whom he formed a slight acquaintance, and, on giving them the signs and passwords of the Circle, was taken into their confidence. They took him riding into the country and showed him

several large barns where they were in the habit of holding their meetings, and gave him full information as to
their prospects in reference to future operations.   The
three men were Agitators or, in other words, Organizers.
    "John Stetson had been in Dayburg about three months;
was a Colonel in the rebel army ; had been a prisoner at
Camp Chase, but in some mysterious way was permitted to
escape by putting on different clothes from his own, which
in some manner were smuggled in to him.   He had shaven
off his whiskers and made a close crop of his hair, and was
so changed in his appearance that no one would have suspected that he was the same man.   He was known in
prison, and so entered on the records, as Col. Jacob Reed,
13th Ky. (Confederate) infantry.   This man Stetson, alias
'Reed,' was very communicative ; told the General that if
they did not succeed in working up sufficient feeling in the
Northern States to change the course of the Administration that they would have to resort to other and more severe methods—such as raiding in the North, destroying
property, burning cities, etc.; that the Confederacy must
be successful; that they were now in for it, and there must be
no faltering; that there must be no sickly sentiment about
the means to be adopted hereafter; that fire and flood and
desolation were perfectly legitimate if necessity should
ever demand the use of different means from the present.
He said that they could raid from Kentucky and Missouri;
that New York, Cleveland, Cincinnati and Chicago had
been agreed upon as the cities for destruction, if the time
should ever come for such action ; that their friends in
those cities could make themselves whole from the wreck
—at least, all that they particularly cared for; so far as
the property-holders who pretended to be their friends
were concerned, they did not care for them,—that they
would not help them any, and only wanted to fill their
pockets out of the general misfortunes of the Southern
people.
    "After the General had traveled around considerably
with these men as their friend and guest, he wished them
success and health, bade them a hearty good-bye, and left

for Indianapolis to see the Governor, not wishing to try experiments there, where he had been in camp so long. When he arrived and had time to visit the Executive, he found him greatly perplexed at what he had ascertained about the secret treasonable organization in the State of Indiana. He asked the General a great many questions about his recovery, his promotion, etc., and finally said:

"'I want you to help keep up the reputation of our State in the army.'

"Gen. Anderson replied:

"'I hope, Governor, you will never have any cause for complaint in that direction.'

"'No,' said the Governor; 'I hope I shall not! But,' said he, 'it begins to look as though we might have trouble at home. These Golden Circles are bound to give us trouble, and I fear very soon,'

"'Yes,' said the General, 'they are getting pretty numerous, and very bold and exasperating at the same time. How many do you suppose there are in this State, Governor?

"'I suppose there must be twenty or thirty thousand— enough for a pretty good army. If they had any bold man to lead them, they could release our prisoners here and destroy our city.'

"Seeing that the Governor exhibited some alarm, the General was afraid to tell him then how many there actually were in the State. But very soon his Adjutant-General came in, and in conversation raised the figures to some forty or fifty thousand. The Governor looked surprised, and the General thought that he might then disclose the facts as to numbers, and told the Governor that he had found out means of ascertaining, and that their claim for Indiana was 75,000. This seemed to startle him. He at once asked his Adjutant-General how many regiments there were now in camp near the city, and was informed that there were four, with a great many recruits in the camp of instruction. He made many inquiries of the General as to how he obtained his information. Gen. Anderson told him that he had obtained it in various

ways; that some of his friends had joined the organization
and, not believing in it, had posted him, under the seal of
confidence.

" 'Do you believe them ?' inquired the Governor.

" 'I most certainly do,' responded the General.

"The General then gave him the names of Strider,
Bowen, Bowlens, Millington, Dorsing and Byron as the
leaders—Organizers, Agitators, Commanders, etc.—for the
State of Indiana. The Governor was surprised at hearing
some of the names, and said he had no doubt of Strider
being at the bottom of it, but that he would not be
caught; that when the trying time should come, if ever,
he would turn up as counsel, and in that way would get
out of it, and thereby seal the mouths of the criminals.

" He advised the Governor to keep a watch on some of
these men, and he would soon discover them; that they
had not been long enough at this thing to understand the necessary precaution. None had yet been
caught and punished, and they were not looking to
the serious consequences to themselves should they be exposed.

"He also asked the Governor to apprise the President
of the United States of the condition of these matters in
the State, but at the same time not to mention his name
as the source of information. He bade the Governor
good-by and left for Camp Chase, Ohio, having, while
in Indianapolis, determined to return to Ohio and inves-
tigate the prisoners at Camp Chase. When he arrived
there, having no authority, he could not converse with
the prisoners alone; but, becoming acquainted with the
Colonel commanding the Camp, and explaining in confidence who he was and his mission, he was allowed free ac-
cess to the camp and to the prisoners. He soon picked
out a young man from Virginia—his appearance would
indicate his age to be about eighteen years. He told the
General that he lived in the extreme south-western part of
what is now old Virginia. His name was Ridenbergen.
He said to the General that he had no cause to fight
against the United States, but that he was in now and pro-

posed to fight it out. The General having played the Southern dodge and sympathy with the rebellion in such a way as to satisfy him, and also having given the sign of the Circle, which this young Virginian seemed to well understand, there was no longer any necessity for withholding anything in reference to their condition, expectations of succor, release, etc. He told the General that John Stetson, alias Col. Jacob Reed, of Dayburg, had been there frequently; that only a few of them recognized him; of course no one 'peached,' as they knew he was working for their benefit.

"He said our commander of the prison was not very observing ; that quite a number had escaped, and nothing was known or said about it ; that others answered for them, reported them sick, or gave some other excuse which was always taken ; that Stetson had brought in the rituals of the Golden Circle, and that all of them who were intelligent enough to understand it, were posted, and that some of the guards belonged and were constantly making the signs to the Confederate officers inside. He had no doubt that sooner or later they would be released. He had the same idea about how they would ultimately succeed. This idea pervaded the minds of all with whom he had spoken on the subject. Many leading men in Ohio were in accord with all that they contemplated with reference to their release and the future success of the Confederacy.

"He also said that the party in Ohio who were in sympathy with the rebellion were quite outspoken, and were under the lead of a very able and bold man. The General inquired of whom he had reference, and he said Valamburg, of Dayburg.

"'Yes,' the General responded, 'I have heard of him frequently; but is he a military man ?'

"'No,' replied Ridenbergen; 'but we have them in the State in many places, from the Confederate army, just waiting the sound of the bugle. But the fears I have are as to the time. It takes so long to get everything ready— our people have to move so cautiously.'

" 'Have you heard that we are organizing for raids from Canada at some future time ?'

" 'Oh, yes ; that is understood. Many of our best and brightest men are over there, at different points, preparing for it; but that is to be done only when we must strike in Northern cities for the purpose of terrifying the Northern property-holders ; we must strike then where the greatest amount of wealth is concentrated.'

"The General then said to him:

" 'Mr. Ridenbergen, you are a young man. I hope to hear good things of you in the future,' and bade him good-bye.

" The General arrived at Allentown the next day. After the family greetings, kisses from his wife and little daughter, and a 'How ar' you, Marsa Tom ?' from Ham and a 'Bress de good Laud, heah you is agin!' from Aunt Martha were over, the General related his trip to me in minute detail, and told me that matters were much worse than he had any suspicion of prior to his investigations. In speak·ing of those he had seen, and his many talks with members of the Knights of the Golden Circle, his utter contempt for them, and especially for many leading men who claimed to be loyal to the Union, but did not like the unconstitutional manner of prosecuting the war, he remarked :

" 'There was but one of all of them that I have seen for whom I have any sympathy or respect, and he is the young Virginian, Mr. Ridenbergen. I rather liked the frankness of this young man. I am satisfied that at heart he is not a rebel, but is young, and, after engaging in the rebellion, will go as far as any one to make it a successful cause.'

. "Just then Jackson came from the train and entered the house.

" 'My ! how well you are looking, Gen. Anderson, compared with your appearance when I left. You must have been to some water-cure or have used some kind of elixir of life,' was his first greeting.

" ' No, sir,' replied the General ; ' I have been marching, and it has brought me out wonderfully.'

"'Yes, it has. Well, Jennie, I saw David, Dr. James and Henry. They are all well and "spilin'" for a fight. David thinks that his brigade can thrash the whole rebel army.'

"Little Jennie rushed to her Uncle Jackson, saying:

"'Did you see my good papa ?'

"'Yes, dear, I saw him, and he sent you a thousand kisses and asked all about you.'

"Turning away, he said, 'Poor David, his heart is broken over the loss of his little Sarah.'

"Gen. Anderson said, 'Sit down, and tell us all about your visit. Were you successful ?'

"'Oh, yes ; I am a full-fledged Captain in the 13th U. S. Inf., and assigned, by order of the Secretary of War, as Aide-de-camp to Brig.-Gen. Thomas Anderson, the hero.'

"'Stop, stop,' said the General ; 'you must not com-mence that too soon. The taffy part must be left off if you are to be on my staff.'

"'My dear,' said his wife, 'he can say that about you to me ; for it's the truth. Capt. Jackson, I will not get mad at you for speaking in a complimentary manner about my husband.'

"'Hereafter I will repeat all the good things which I may have to say about him to you; but you will tell him, and then he will get mad at me.'

"'No, he will not be mad ; don't you know what peculiar animals men are ?'

"'Well, yes; they are rather peculiar," said Jackson. 'They like compliments when not deserving ; but when deserving they then dislike them. Is that not about the way with most men ? I notice women are somewhat dif-ferently constituted ? Are they not ?'

"'Yes, indeed ; they always like compliments. Do they not, my dear ?' addressing her husband.

"'I have usually found it so,' replied the General. His wife ran into the house, and laughingly said :

"'Well, I guess Tom has been trying his compliments on some one else. Has he not, aunty ?' addressing Aunt Martha.

"'God lub you' sole, chile, dese men, you can't tell nuffin

'bout dem, sho'; but Massa Tom be all rite, I 'spect ; I
knows him; no fear 'bout him; de good Laud spar' him for
good work, sho'.'

" 'I asked the General to write out a full statement of
all he had reported to me. He did so that night, and the
following day I mailed it to the President with a private
note accompanying.

"During the day Jackson entertained us with his visit
to Washington, to the army, and the pleasant time he
passed in camp with his brothers. He said that there was
something wrong in that army; that the machinery did
not seem to work very smoothly, but that never having
been a soldier, perhaps he could not form a correct opinion.
The sequel told the tale, however."

" Well, Uncle Daniel, this Golden Circle discovery was
most extraordinary," said Dr. Adams.

"Yes. It grew into greater proportions later on, however."

"I feel an interest in knowing what became of that
young Virginian whom Gen. Anderson met at Camp Chase;
his name I forgot, but have it written down."

" Yes; you mean Mr. Ridenbergen ?"

" Yes."

" I have learned that he went through the war on the
rebel side unharmed, after the war married in Pennsylvania, and is now one of the most prominent men in
Virginia. He espoused the advanced policy of the men
who saved the Union, and is now one of the leading opponents of the unreconstructed in that State."

Uncle Daniel becoming very weak and exhausted, by
an agreement with us, the continuance of his story was
postponed until another time.

CHAPTER VIII.

BATTLE OF PAGELAND—A VICTORY TURNED INTO A DE-
FEAT BY TREACHERY—DEATH OF GEN. LYON—ON THE
TRAIL OF THE KNIGHTS OF THE GOLDEN CIRCLE.

> " *Sorrow breaks seasons, and reposing hours,*
> *Makes the night morning, and the noontide night.*"
> —SHAKESPEARE.

URING the two weeks intervening, Dr. Adams was engaged in carefully writing from his very full shorthand notes the relation of facts as given by Uncle
Daniel. At the appointed time all were again present, eager for a continuance of this interesting and remark-
able history of events only a short time past, and yet
almost forgotten. When all were seated Uncle Daniel
began :

" The time between the sending of my report to the
President of Gen. Anderson's trip and his answer, with
further instructions, was considerable. Finally, I received
a letter from the Secretary of War, who seemed very much
gratified about the information that had been gathered, as
also at the manner in which it had been obtained. He requested that I send or go myself to Canada and ascertain
such further facts as I could in reference to the conspiracy
and the movements of the conspirators. Gen. Anderson,
my son Jackson, and myself held a consultation as to my
going. They thought the undertaking too hazardous for
me to attempt, and finally Jackson proposed that he
would go himself, saying that it would be at least two
months before Gen. Anderson could again take the field
for active operations ; in the meantime he (Jackson) could
be profitably employed in this business for the Government. This was agreed upon as the better course to pur-

sue. Jackson was at once given all the secrets of the Circle as far as the General knew them. He studied the passwords, signs, and their instructions until the General pronounced him sufficiently well informed for a first class conspirator. And as soon as he could get himself in readiness he started for Montreal, C. E., by way of New York. During all this time the Circle had been busily at work, and the excitement was increasing all over the country.

"The alarm for fear of the enemy in our rear was producing such a condition of things as to endanger the safety of the people everywhere in the West, and at this time much encouragement was given to our enemies at home by the many failures of our armies in the East. The army, as before stated, had been put under a new commander, Gen. Pike, and the displeasure created among the ranking officers was easily to be seen by their language and manner towards him. This feeling was constantly fed by disparaging articles in the opposition press. The enemy in arms could easily see that this was a golden opportunity, and they availed themselves of it. They commenced a movement which indicated an advance against our forces. Gen. Wall, of the rebel army, had by rapid marches put himself between Gen. Pike and his base. This forced a movement on the part of our troops to the rear, and necessitated an immediate attack upon Gen. Wall in order to drive him back from the threatening position he occupied. The troops were moved rapidly back in the direction of Cow Creek, where it was intended by Gen. Pike to assault him.

"The army was at last all collected in easy supporting distance, and Pike moved out with Gen. Horn's corps and assaulted Gen. Dawn's division of Wall's army. The contest was a spirited one, and lasted until well in the night. Dawn finally retreated. During the night all arrangements were made for an advance. The next morning the General-in-chief of the rebel armies was moving by forced marches in order to join Wall prior to any serious engagement, and Pike was determined to attack Wall before the main army of the enemy could arrive; but, to his utter astonishment, his forces under Farlin, ordered to join him from the base of supplies, were not in motion as yet, as he ascertained; and so with Fitzgibbon, who had been repeatedly urged to come with all dispatch. This left Pike in such a condition that he must delay his attack, which delay might bring great disaster to his army. Pike sent his staff officers to notify those Generals of his desires and intentions, which was done; but all manner of excuses were given for the delay. Finally, the next day, when part of his forces had arrived, Fitzgibbon coming up leisurely with his corps of magnificent soldiers, he was forced to commence the battle in the absence of Farlin and his corps. He moved out, putting his cavalry on the right flank, near Siddon Springs, threatening the left of Wall's army, who were formed in line of battle at or near a small town called Pageland. Rackett holding Pike's right, Shunk in the center, and Brig-Gen. David Lyon on the left of Shunk, his left resting on the edge of a grove of thick timber. The extreme left of the command was held by Gen. Fitzgibbon's corps. It was understood that Fitzgibbon would attack the enemy during the engagement on his right flank, and in that way measurably destroy him.

"The troops being thus disposed they were ordered to advance. The battle soon commenced by slight cavalry skirmishing on our right. Our cavalry having met the cavalry of the enemy, he, discovering our movements and positions, moved out to meet us. The firing and cracking of carbines increased, until finally musketry was distinguishable on the line fronting our cavalry. They soon asked for support, which was sent, and the enemy driven back. At this time skirmishing opened in several places on our infantry line, and continued until our whole line was formed and advanced. The enemy having advantage in position, did not advance to meet our forces, but held themselves in readiness to receive any attack that our troops should make upon them, Wall intending to save his men as much as possible, and to hold out until the main rebel army should arrive. Finally an assault was ordered all along the line, and Wall was driven back to a deep depression in the ground, behind which, on the rising slope beyond, he reformed his line. Our forces pressed forward and assailed his left with great energy. Wall gradually gave way and was being easily driven back, when all at once a dash was made from the position to which they had been forced. This onslaught was so vigorous and irresistible that our forces had to give way and fall back to the main line. Gen. Rackett, seeing this dash of the enemy, at once said :

"'These are fresh troops. They are re-enforcing from some other part of the line.'

"This being communicated to the commanding General, he said they must have weakened the center. In order to test this he ordered an assault to be made at once upon their center. In this opinion he was correct. The assault upon the enemy's center dislodged him and drove him in much confusion back to another position. Our left then moved forward rapidly with the same result, and the battle was going well and very satisfactorily. Our right being then re-enforced, the enemy was driven from his line at every point. Gen. Pike believing that he had the enemy in a position where he could easily beat him, if his other forces would come up promptly, sent to the rear to find Farlin, but he could not be found. He said to one of his staff officers :

"'Does not this look as if I was betrayed ?'

"The staff officer, now dead, replied :

"'General, this is what I have feared for some time. The movements of the enemy look as though they were only fighting for time. You see how easily they are forced back—in numbers engaged more than equal to ours.'

"'What of Fitzgibbon on the left ? I have not heard a gun in that direction.'

"'Nor will you,' replied the officer.

"'But he has orders to attack at once. He must attack very soon, I am sure. How can he see and hear a battle like this without engaging ?'

"The officer made no reply. The General thought he would ascertain, and ordered his staff officer to proceed to the line of Gen. Lyon, and ask him to feel out from his left for Fitzgibbon, and to open communication with him. This order being executed, Gen. Lyon reported that he could not find any force to his left, but at the same time reported that there was much noise and dust in his front on the main road, and he feared re-enforcements for the enemy.

"Just then Gen. McIntosh reported with his command, which had been marching from Fitzgibbon's rear for some time in order to reach the battlefield. As soon as he had reported Gen. Pike directed that, as soon as his command could rest, so as to be in condition to move forward, he desired him to move up in support of Gen. Lyon; as he feared re-enforcements were moving to his (Lyon's) front.

"Just about this time Fitzgibbon had discovered much dust rising in the direction of the south. He called the attention of some of his officers to it, and proposed a retreat. But his command did not think a retreat without losing a man or testing the enemy would look quite soldierly, and the retreat was abandoned for the present; but in a few moments an immense flock of wild pigeons (having been by some means disturbed,) came down like a great cloud, and the roaring sound they produced in their flight so startled Gen. Fitzgibbon that he thought a large corps of cavalry were charging upon him. Thereupon he immediately ordered his men under cover and to prepare for retiring, at the same time announcing that our forces were evidently beaten. Gen. McIntosh moved forward and at once engaged the enemy, and the battle became general.

"The enemy, then evidently being re-enforced, made several desperate but unsuccessful assaults upon our center; but soon fresh troops were thrown in its support, and our lost ground regained. Our right at this time pressed forward, and at once were hotly engaged. Our artillery now opened from the different positions occupied by our batteries. The enemy's batteries promptly replied. Our cavalry were ordered to try and penetrate to the rear of the enemy. Here was a contest between cavalry. Carbines cracked and rattled almost like the heavy musketry of infantry. Many a horse was seen going at full speed over

the field riderless. Many a cavalryman fell. At last a
charge with sabers drawn was ordered. The sight, as described to me, was one of grandeur to behold. On to the
charge they went, each saber flashing in the sunlight.
Crash went saber against saber. Sparks flew as if from
heated steel. 'Forward?' was heard on both sides. Flashes
of sparks and ringing sounds from the steel as saber came
against saber. Arms were gashed, hands and faces were
cut, heads were cleft, and sabers pierced the bodies of the
troopers on either side.

HENRY LYON IS CAPTURED.

"Back went the rebel cavalry and on against them our
men were thrown, until infantry came to the enemy's support, accompanied by a battery of artillery. A deadly fire
from both was poured into the ranks of our horsemen.
Our lines staggered, then recovered again, but could not
withstand both the infantry and artillery. They were
compelled to fall back. Many were unhorsed and quite a
number captured. Among them was my son Henry,
of the Michigan Cavalry. His horse was killed, and his

own back injured in the fall, so that he could not make good his escape. (He was sent to the rear. I heard nothing from him for months—only knew that he was taken prisoner.) But the command again rallied and held their line on the flank of our infantry. The artillery on the left of our line were having a regular duel with several batteries of the enemy. Our center was being sorely pressed again. Column after column assaulted and checked our advance. Gen. Pike was very anxious about his support, and repeatedly sent to find Farlin, but the same report was made each time, ' Not in sight; cannot be found.' At last a report came that Farlin was some twenty miles away, and moving very leisurely.

" ' My God !' exclaimed Gen. Pike, ' my army is sacrificed. These men will not support me. The battle is to be lost, and perhaps all depends upon the issue here to-day. To win this battle makes our success sure ; to lose it may be the loss of all.'

" He called an officer and said, ' Take this written order to Fitzgibbon. He must attack at once.'

" Fitzgibbon was found beneath the shade of a broad oak. He had not fired a gun; his men were panting for a chance to enter the contest. As the officer passed along they cried out, 'Why not put us into the fight ?' 'How is the battle going ?' ' Are we driving them ?' ' The rebs are being re-enforced ; we can see troops coming down by Pageland.' (The town was in full view from where they were impatiently waiting for the command 'Forward!')

" Gen. Fitzgibbon paid no attention to the order, except to say, ' Pike doesn't know what he is doing.'

" The officer said, on returning, Fitzgibbon's men were lying by their arms, (which were stacked,) and could be put into line instantly. The General could not believe that the attack would not be made by Fitzgibbon. The battle now was at white heat—infantry, artillery and cavalry were all engaged. The lines swayed, sometimes the rebels were gaining slight advantage, and then the forces on our side. Gen. David Lyon's command was now all engaged.

He drove the enemy through the woods where his left first rested. He was handling his troops well. The commanding General came along where he was engaged and complimented him very highly for the manner in which he was succeeding on his part of the line. He then asked David (Gen. Lyon) if he could hear any firing on his left. Gen. Lyon answered him in the negative.

"'Is it possible? Are you not mistaken? It seems to me that I can hear it.'

"'No, Gen. Pike,' said Gen. Lyon; 'you imagine so; for I assure you I have watched and listened for some movement on my left. There has been none whatever.'

"Gen. Shunk came up just at that moment and said:

"'Gen. Pike, Gen. Rackett is killed.'

"'Is that so? He was one of my most faithful Generals.'

"He sent an officer back to see that the next officer in rank should take command at once.

"Gen. Shunk said to Gen. Pike:

"'I fear that re-enforcements for the enemy are coming up. I have just captured some prisoners, who say they have marched fifteen miles to-day, and were put into the battle as soon as they arrived. They also say that the commander of the rebel armies is not more than ten miles away with at least 20,000 men.'

"'Yes, that may be so; but if Fitzgibbon will attack on the left, as I have ordered him positively to do, and Gen. Farlin comes up—who is not farther away than the rebel troops—we will be their equal in numbers.'

"'Do you think Farlin is trying to get here, General?'

"'Why, he knows we are engaged. He is an old soldier and ought to do his duty.'

"'True enough; but if he did not know his duty, and was not an old soldier, he might come sooner than he will, knowing it. I do not like to say so, General, but I have my suspicions that Farlin and Fitzgibbon do not wish you to win this battle.'

"The conversation was here broken off. The enemy having made a desperate assault on Shunk's command, he rode quickly away. By this time the battle was terrific, and the slaughter terrible on both sides. The field was beginning to look more like a slaughter-pen than anything else to which it could be compared. Men were being brought to the rear on stretchers, and also carried by their comrades without stretchers; in fact, you know it was a very common thing for several men to take hold of one to help him to the rear when sometimes the soldier had but a scratch.

" Gen. Horn, who had been in reserve up to this time, came up with his command and supported Gen. McIntosh, who was now hard pressed. When Gen. Horn entered the field he could be heard far away, having a stentorian voice. He advanced rapidly and drove the right of Wall back far from his main line; but here, in close supporting distance, lay Longpath, with his fresh troops. He waited until Horn's line was clear in advance of the main line, and at once set upon him with great ferocity, driving him back on McIntosh, that portion of our line giving way for the moment. Gen. Lyon's command was then furiously attacked by fresh troops. They stood the shock, but had finally to give way. Pike witnessed this terrible fighting, and said again, 'Can it be possible that Farlin will not get here in time to save this battle?' He again rode up to Gen. Lyon and asked if he still heard nothing on his left. The General answered ' No.' He then directed him to send a courier through and communicate with Fitzgibbon. By this time the heaviest fighting was on the right and center, the firing having slackened on the left. The courier was gone but a short time, when he returned and reported the enemy marching down a road to our left and forming at right angles with our line. This was easily understood, and as soon as possible our left was changed to face the troops so forming on and across our flank. New troops were thrown in at this point, to enable proper resistance to be made, their attack on our angle being made as a diversion.

" This attack now having been repulsed, the enemy were driven back, and quite a number of prisoners captured; the soldiers became much elated and commenced cheering, which was taken up all along the line. On our left our

officers took it that Farlin had arrived, or that Fitzgibbon
had sent word that he was going to attack at once and relieve the situation, the position of the troops facing our
left being such that he could attack them in the rear. But
all were doomed to be disappointed. The rebels forming
on our left were troops just arriving and under the immediate command of the General-in-chief of the rebel
army. They were soon in position, and. their skirmishers
moving through the woods in the direction of our refused
left. The situation was critical indeed. The commanding
General ordered all the artillery that could be brought into
battery to be placed in position on this flank. The line
then held by Wall on his left could not be abandoned, nor
could he draw from his center, as he was being pressed all
along that part of the line. But on they came through the
woods. None but infantry could get through without
great delay. They opened fire. Our line gave way, and
fell back to the support of the batteries. Finally the batteries all opened, and like the roar of mighty thunders was
the noise. The earth shook as though an earthquake
was disturbing it. Fire was vomited forth as though it
were from the mouth of some burning volcano. Destruction and death were dealt out unsparingly to the enemy.
They started to charge the batteries, and with that hideous yell that they seemed only to employ or understand, on
they came. But finally, when they could stand against
the torrent of shot and shell no longer, they broke to the
rear in great confusion.

"Gen. Pike saw the success, and exclaimed :

"'If my other troops would only come up, or Gen. Fitzgibbon attack, the day would soon be ours.'

"But he was doomed to further disappointment. They
did not come up, neither did they attack. The rebel General soon took in the whole situation. He put his artillery
in battery on a hill to the right of our refused line, so as
to concentrate his fire on the flank of our batteries and
force them to change position. This being done he
opened some eighteen guns. This forced a change in the
position of our batteries, and there and then commenced

one of the most destructive artillery duels that was ever witnessed. Battery horses were killed on both sides. gunners blown to pieces by shell, officers and men mangled, Gen. Mosely, on the rebel side, had his head shot off, and a Colonel and two Captains were blown to pieces on our side. While this duel was going on the rebel General was reforming his men for another infantry attack on our left. At this moment Gen. Pike said to Gen. Lyon:

" ' General, I hear guns over to our left.'

Gen. Lyon listened, and answered :

" ' Well, General, I believe you are correct. I think I heard a gun.'

" Pike then elieved that Fitzgibbon had made an attack, and would compel the enemy to withdraw their forces directly on our left. But he was mistaken. No attack was made except the one by the rebels. Very soon afterwards they had completed their line, and, knowing the value of a flank attack, again assaulted in the same manner as before. They came this time with more caution than before, but with a stronger force. They opened fire on both sides about the same time. The battle was now renewed all along the line—cavalry, infantry and artillery. The lines wavered occasionally on both sides. The left of our line gave way at first, but rallied again. Gen. Lyon rode up and down his line, cheering his men. He led them again and again against the seeming adamantine wall of rebels, and finally forced them back slowly, holding all the ground gained. By this time our center was penetrated and broken. Our troops could not be rallied for some time. The rebels seeing our confusion took advantage of it, and with the intrepidity of so many demons made another attack on all parts of the line and forced our whole line some distance to the rear. It looked for an hour as though all was lost. At one time our lines seemed to be melting away and becoming disorganized. They were rallied again, however, and formed a new line about a mile in the rear of our first. Both armies were exhausted. Fresh troops then to our aid would have settled the fortunes of the day in our favor But they did not come. Gen. Pike

5

thought that whoever made the first attack would be successful, and ordered our line forward. They moved cautiously, but steadily, attacking and driving the enemy back. He kept falling back until he occupied his first line and we ours. Our left, however, was soon struck by a division of fresh troops, and was driven back some distance through the woods with great loss. My dear son, Gen. Lyon, here, while rallying his men, was shot through the heart and instantly killed."

The old man wept bitterly, and many tears rolled down the cheeks of his listeners. When he could resume he said :

"If Fitzgibbon had attacked as was expected, our flank could not have been turned, and the great slaughter that occurred on this part of the line would have been avoided. Night here closed the day's slaughter with our left completely turned and our troops demoralized. They passed the night on their arms. The next morning at daylight the attack was resumed by the rebels and our army was beaten. Gens. Stepleton and Kearnan fell on that day, with many other brave officers and men. No battle lost during the war fell with more crushing effect upon the loyal people than did the defeat of the Army of the East at the battle of Pageland. The battle was lost by the failure of Farlin and Fitzgibbon to support Gen. Pike. They did just what the President and Secretary of War feared they would do—that was, fail in supporting Pike, the new commander. Their idea was to dictate the commander or not fight. One would think that men who had fed upon the charity of the Government from youth to middle age would be inspired by a more lofty feeling and sentiment. But this is a mistake. You cannot infuse patriotism by drilling at a college or in the field. This comes from the nursery of the mother. Nor can you put brains, commonsense or courage where God has refused it. The question with these men was, 'Do you belong to a certain chosen few?' If so, that was put above every other consideration. A volunteer, no matter how much he might develop a genius for military affairs, could have no recognition at their hands.

"The fact that Julius Cæsar and Napoleon Bonaparte were great generals without military training except in the field proved nothing.   If men like those who first commanded our army in the East, and who formed the coterie, had lived during the Revolutionary War, Washington and the best of his generals would not have been permitted to have commanded a brigade, if these men could have controlled as they did at the outbreak of the rebellion.   The same feeling has grown among our people since the war,

DEATH OF GEN. LYON.

until the brains of a man cuts but little figure in matters connected with governmental affairs.   He must belong to one of two classes : either a snob or one who has made a fortune.   No matter whether he made it selling rotten blankets to the Government, worthless arms for the soldiers, bad meat, diseased horses, small mules, rotten and poorly-put-together harness, or procured his money in some other way—if he has it, the conclusion is at once that he is a great man and full of wisdom.   These things are unfortunate in a government like ours.   But this is the tendency,

and has been for many years.   Dash and swell is the motto
now; it is growing more in that direction every day.   But
I have wandered away from my subject.   The battlefield
of Pageland and its surroundings was a sight to behold the
day after our defeat.   The private soldiers felt outraged
and officers were discouraged, and many good people de-
spaired of our final success.   Even the President was more
despondent than he had ever been, but still had faith in
God and our cause.   The losses on both sides were very
great.   The country all around was by both sides turned
into a great hospital.   The army was almost disorganized;
it certainly was most thoroughly demoralized.   Gen. Pike
was relieved, and McGregor put in command again.   Fitzgibbon was sent to the rear without a command.   Farlin
was everywhere by every friend of his country severely
censured.   Fitzgibbon was denounced as a traitor to his
superior officer.

" The mournful part to myself and family had only in
part come upon us.   Dr. James Lyon, having cut one of
his hands in making an amputation, feared bad results
from the wound; for that reason he procured a leave of absence, and accompanied the remains of his brother David
home.   I will not attempt to describe to you the depth of
grief in our family, from the oldest to the youngest. It was
greater than I now wish to recall, even though so many
years have passed since that melancholy scene.   Suffice it
to say that Gen. David Lyon fills the grave of as gallant
and noble a soldier as ever drew a sword.   He rests beside
his wife and little daughter Sarah in the cemetery at
Allentown."

The old man, overcome by this recital, could not speak
for some time, but finally continued :

" Gen. Anderson was very sad.   Dr. James was very restless with his hand, which had commenced swelling and was
becoming extremely painful.   My wife Sarah and Jennie
(David's widow) were stricken down with fever, requiring
the constant attendance of Mary Anderson and Aunt
Martha for many days before their recovery was assured.
In the meantime Peter arrived, the wound in his foot hav-

ing broken out again.   When he came to his mother's bedside she said :

"'O ! Peter, my son, that horrible dream haunts me
still.'

"This dream from the first had a very depressing effect
upon Peter, though he pretended to think nothing of it.
We now commenced casting about to see if there was any
way to have Henry exchanged. He being merely a private
soldier, this was not so easy of accomplishment, as if he had
been an officer.   During the evening, while we were engaged in conversation in the parlor, Aunt Martha came in
and said :

"'Uncle Daniel, dar's a young lady on de porch who
wants to see you very bad, she say, on mos' obticlar
bizness.'

"'Tell her to come in,' was my answer.

"In a moment a very modest and rather pretty young
lady walked in.   She was evidently greatly embarrassed.
I arose, and extending my hand asked her to be seated.
She sat down for a moment, and then hesitatingly said :

"'Your wife is unwell, I understand, Mr. Lyon ?'

"'Yes,' I replied; 'very unwell.   She has had a great sorrow recently.'

"'Yes, sir; so I understand.   I very much desired to see
her, but will not annoy her at this time.   I had a matter about which I wished to speak with her.   You know,
women give their confidence to one another; but I hope
you will allow me to give mine to you, as your wife is sick ?'

"'Yes, my good girl; you can say what you wish to me.'

"'Well, Mr. Lyon '—— she then hesitated.

"I encouraged her to proceed.

"'Well, I am on my way South, and I wish your good
offices in getting through the lines.'

"'How can I assist you, my child ?'

"'I hear, sir, that you are a great friend of the President, and I thought perhaps you might intercede for me.'

"'May I inquire for what purpose you wish to go South?
Do your people live there ?'

"'No, sir; I live in Michigan.   I was never farther South

than this place, and this is my first visit here. My name is Seraine Whitcomb. I am going South to see what I can do to have a young man exchanged who is now a prisoner in the hands of the rebels.

"'Is he your brother?' I inquired.

"She blushed, and replied :

"'No, sir, he is not a relative; but one in whom I am much interested.'

"I saw through the whole matter at once, but did not press the young lady further. If I had only known whom she meant I would have embraced her as the greatest little heroine living. She said she only wished a letter from me to the President; that she would do the rest herself. This letter I gave her without further questions. She was so modest and yet so brave. She took the letter, bade me good-by, and left. As she went out she remarked :

"'Do not be surprised if you should receive a letter from me at some future time.'

"After she had gone Peter remarked that perhaps she was sent down South by the Golden Circle, and I might be bestowing favors on the wrong person. I said, 'True, but I will take my chances on that girl's being honest, and, not only honest, but a regular little heroine.'

"Here the conversation on this subject came to an end, and we took up the condition of the army. Peter said the jealousies between officers in the Army of the East were strange; that there was nothing of this kind among the Western troops; that all seemed to have the same common purpose, and that was success; but, said he, it may be partly accounted for in this, that we are all alike unskilled in the arts of war, and do not know enough to get up these conspiracies and jealousies. We are all volunteers, save two or three, and all obey orders, and go into a battle to win, each one believing he is doing the best fighting. It seems that at the battle of Pageland the only object of some of the leading commanders was to find some way to lose the battle and at the same time save their own scalps.

"Gen. Anderson said:

"'Well, I do not know how I may succeed as a commander; but I will have the courage to relieve any man, and send him to the rear, of whom I may have the least suspicion, whether it be for cowardice, want of good intentions toward the Government, good faith toward his superior officer, or for any other cause that might give uneasiness about his properly performing his duty.'

"'That would seem to me to be the proper course for any commander of forces,' I replied."

"Uncle Daniel," said Dr. Adams, "I am curious to know what became of those two generals—Farlin and Fitzgibbon."

"Well, sir, the same power that is now rewarding those who struck us the heaviest blows, both North and South, is paying homage to these men. They are both held in high esteem by many people, and you would think they were the only loyal men that were near the battlefield on that day."

"Yes," said Col. Bush; "to have lost an arm or leg on the Union side is like the brand of Cain nowadays; but to have been a rebel or to have belonged to the Golden Circle, or failed in some way by which the rebels profited or gained advantage, entitles one to a medal or some high position of honor and emolument."

CHAPTER IX.

" Yesterday was heard,
The roar of war; and sad the sight of maid,
Of mother, widow, sister, daughter, wife,
Stooping and weeping over senseless, cold,
Defaced, and mangled lumps of breathless earth,
Which had been husbands, fathers, brothers, sons,
And lovers, when that morning's sun arose.

—POLLOCK.

"GEN. Anderson, Peter and myself concluded that we would again visit the farm. There we found poor old Joseph Dent in utter despair on account of his 'poor Captain' (as he called David) having been killed. He talked of him in the most enthusiastic manner, and would then weep, saying 'the only friend I had is gone, and I will not be satisfied until I can get even with these rebels.'

"Gen. Anderson said : 'Well, Joseph, what will you do ?'

"Joseph was silent ; as an old soldier he knew how to keep his thoughts to himself.

"'Will you go to the war ?' continued the General.

"'No, sir; I will stay here and take care of this farm for Mrs. Lyon and little Jennie. They shall not suffer while I am able to look after them.'

"Old Ham thought he had a point, and said : 'Dat's good; dat's jes' what I 'tend to do when Massa Tom git killed. Jes' so.'

"'Shut up, Ham. Your Massa Tom, as you call him, is not going to get killed. There have been enough of the Lyon family killed already,' said Peter.

(136)

" 'Dat's so, Massa Peter. I not got dat in my kalkerlate, you see ; but I tell you I is monstrous feered 'bout dese matters; deys is heaps of people gittin' killed, and most of dem is good peoples, so dey is. Can't tell who nex', massa; can't tell, sah !'

" ' Well, Joseph, there will be no trouble about your staying. We want you here on the farm,' I said. ' We are all very much distressed, but, at the same time, we must look out for our country somewhat; and our family all being in the army, of course we must expect some misfortunes. Have you heard any more of the Golden Circle in this neighborhood ?'

" ' Yes, Uncle Daniel; they are at work, and since the defeat of our forces at the battle of Pageland, they are outspoken about what they intend to do ; not only in aid of the rebellion, but they threaten the Union people here at home—threaten to destroy their property, and make war in Indiana if it becomes necessary, just as you have heretofore understood. I am keeping close watch, and they will not be able to do any very great harm here without my knowing it.'

" We cautioned Joseph, and told him to come in to our house frequently and let us know what was going on.

" On returning home we found Aunt Sarah and Jennie much improved, but Dr. James was suffering very great pain. The swelling was extending up his arm from his hand. I said to him perhaps we had better have a physician. ' You are suffering so much that I fear you are not in a condition to attend to your own case.' He consented, and one was called in. On examination he pronounced the trouble blood poisoning. James was greatly alarmed at this. The physician commenced at once with the most radical treatment. The next morning James seemed much easier, and looked as if he was coming out of it all right.

" The next day, while we were sitting on the porch, the postman brought me a letter, written in a delicate female hand. I read it and then called Gen. Anderson and Peter to listen:

"WASHINGTON, D. C.

"My Dear Mr. Lyon, Allentown, Ind.:

"Thanks for your very great kindness. I have the President's pass through our lines; when you hear from me again, I will let you know about your son Henry.   Very respectfully,

"Seraine Whitcomb."

" 'Well, well,' said Peter; 'that tells a tale. Now, father, I agree with you. She is a brave girl; there is not more than one in a thousand like her.'

" 'Yes; but what does she mean by saying I will hear from my son?'

" 'It will reveal itself,' said Peter. 'She is in love with Henry, and has gone to look after him.'

" 'Do you think so?' I inquired. 'Well, I do sincerely hope so.'

"Just then we saw Jackson coming. He came in, and after salutations and greetings between us, he entered the house to see his mother, the Doctor, and Jennie. He was much broken down over the death of his brother. The news of the battle and the list of the dead in the papers having contained David's name, he hastened home. He had, however, been very successful in laying the foundation for probing many things which might be of vast importance in the future.

"When he left home he first went to New York and had an interview with McMasters and B. Wudd, who were the leading spirits in New York, and one of them the principal man North in starting the organization. From these men he learned much about what was going on in Canada; the fact that there was no doubt that quite a number of Southern men were there with a large amount of money with which to carry out any scheme that might be agreed upon. These men in New York were in constant communication with those in Canada; also, with leading men in Richmond. He managed to obtain a letter of introduction from McMasters to the leading Knights of the Golden Circle in Canada; this letter introduced him as William Jackson, of Memphis, Tenn., and was directed to the Hon. Jacob Thomlinson. With this letter and the information he had now obtained, he made his way home, feeling that he could not undertake the further prosecution of his mission without returning and consoling his mother and the family as much as he possibly could in their distress. Knowing his mother's feeble condition, he feared the consequences of the heavy affliction that had fallen upon her during the battle of Pageland—with one son a prisoner and another killed outright.

"I wrote the President, and promised that later on I would have the Canada mystery solved. Our people were in desperate straits. Our army had been outnumbered and forced back to the position in front of Pageland; defeated there, and forced to shelter itself in the rear of Cow Creek. It was now broken and shattered, lying in defenses near the Capital, discouraged and worn down by fatigue, wounds and disease. The outlook was anything but bright. Commanders had been changed. Some of our best fighting generals had lost their lives at Pageland. The country had but little confidence in the staying or fighting qualities of the commander, Gen. McGregor, as he had made no success heretofore. The rebel commander, well understanding the situation, was moving rapidly up and along the south line of the Grand River, evidently intending an invasion of the loyal States by penetrating our lines and crossing at or near Brown's Ferry. Our lines were held at this point by Gen. Milo, having in his command 10,000 men, who were all surrendered at the demand of Gen. Wall without very much resistance. Wall had slipped through the mountains like a cat, and was upon Milo before he knew of his approach. This was very strange though, and hard to understand, and only increased the fears and suspicions already existing that something was out of joint, so that the machinery was working badly in that army.

"The enemy now had no impediment in the way of a rapid movement except high waters, which seemed to interpose as the only power that could stop their advance into the interior of our country and to the rear of our capital, cutting off all communications to the North with the loyal States.

"The administration was now in a position of great danger, in many respects, not before contemplated.

"The rebel sympathizers and Golden Circles were loud in their denunciation of the war and the party sustaining it. Thos. A. Strider and Dan Bowen were traversing the state of Indiana, making inflammatory speeches, and all over the North the same policy was being pursued by the anti-war party. They alarmed the people by declaring that unless the war was stopped our homes North would be invaded; that our armies could not cope with the rebels. The only thing that seemed to put a check to their hopes, operations and denunciations was the fact that our armies in the West were having a continuation of victories.

"This being the situation of the armies and the condition of the minds of the people, the loss of another great battle at this time would have greatly prolonged the war, if it would not have been fatal to the ultimate success of the Union cause. The authorities at Washington were doing everything in their power to allay the excitement among the people, and at the same time were trying to have the Army of the East put in motion so as to pass down to Pottstown and interpose in front of the enemy; he evidently intending to move by way of Brown's Ferry, throwing part of his force on the Brown's Ferry road and a portion over into the Sheepstown road, making a junction at or near Shapleyville. The Union forces were expected to move across by Fardenburg, down the sloping mountains of Cochineal and along and across Mad Valley to Pottstown, and take position behind Antler's Run. But it seemed to be almost impossible to get Gen. McGregor to put his army in motion. Many were the excuses made ; want of this thing to-day, and something else to-morrow—shoes, clothing, blankets, and many other things—protracted the delay. Finally, the President and Secretary of War being out of patience with his hesitancy and excuses, the President directed the Secretary of War to order Gen. McGregor to move without further delay. This seemed to be understood by McGregor, and the next day everything about the camps was in a bustle, and the Army of the East was again in motion; but the movements were slow, and made in such a manner as not to inspire very great confidence in our immediate success. The men and subordinate officers seemed resolute and determined, but there was something surrounding all the movements that was mysterious.

"The papers were full of all the movements, and were discussing the probabilities, etc. Seeing this Gen. Anderson was fired with a desire to at once return to the front. On account of his very weak and feeble condition we tried to detain him, but in vain.

"He said : 'No, I am going to the front, and I wish to go to the East. Will you ask by telegraph for such an assignment for me ?'

"I answered that I would, and did so immediately.

"The next day he received a telegram from the Secretary of War, directing him to report to Gen. McGregor for assignment to duty.

"Gen. Anderson said to Capt. Jackson : 'Your invasion of Canada will be postponed until later. You will be ready to start in the morning with me to the Army of the East.'

"He called old Ham, and repeated the order to him to be in readiness.

"Ham said : 'Afore de Lord, Massa Tom, you isn't gwine to be fitin' agin, is you ?'

"'Yes ! You get ready. Have your bedding and all your traps ready, if you think you can stand to be shot at by the rebels.'

"'Shot at ! Is you gwine to put me out to be shot at ? Me done thought thar war 'nuff white folks to get shotten at, widout de poor darkies like me.'

"'Yes; but you want to be free, do you not, Ham ?'

"'Yeas; Massa Tom, I wants dat—I wants it bad; but how is gwine to come ?'

"'Fight for it. You are no better than I am, are you ? Had you not as well be shot as for me to be ?'

"'Yeas, sir; dat am so. 'Specks de darkies got to fight. I'll fight, Massa Tom, if you say so. Yes, I do. I stay wid you, I will sho'.'

" Old Martha happened to hear this, and broke forth :

" ' Well, well, Massa Tom, I's sorry you is gwine to de wah agin. But it all right. I tells you dat de good Laud save you up for some good. I jes' know he do it all right. I take care of Missus Mary and de little gal; don't you hab no fears 'bout dem. But you isn't gwine to hab Ham go, is you ? If you doz, dat ole fool he git kill. I 'spect he got no mo' sense dan jes' git rite in whar dey is fitin'.'

" ' No, no, Marfa; you is wrong dar. I tell you dat you is. I stay by Massa Tom.'

" Peter and Jackson laughed, and said to the General:

" ' Ham thinks you will be in a safe place during the fighting.'

" ' Yes, he seems to be of that impression. I think I may, perhaps, relieve his mind somewhat,' said the General, with a smile.

" The General telegraphed Capt. Day at Dolensburg to report at once to him at Gen. McGregor's Headquarters, Army of the East. The preliminaries being arranged, all were to be ready early the next morning. The General and Capt. Jackson having arranged and got ready their proper uniforms, horses, mess-chest and everything that would be required in the field, they spent the evening quietly. The Doctor was very sleepless, and suffered more than usual, but was thought not to be in any immediate danger. My wife and Jennie were now also quite recovered.

" The next morning, the General having procured a car for their horses, camp equipage, etc., they took leave of the family, who were in tears, the two little girls, Mary and Jennie, crying aloud. As the General, Capt. Jackson and Ham walked away, Aunt Martha called after Ham :

" ' Now, Ham, ef you eber spects to see me agin, don't you forgit your prares ob a night, and de good Laud will fotch you back ef you do dat ; but He let you git kill like a cat when you done forget it. Do you mine me, Ham ?'

" Turning to me, she continued: ' I 'spect de rebs git dat darky,' then going to the kitchen she gave vent to her

grief.   The poor old woman felt as badly to part with her
Ham as did Mary in parting from her General, but gave
expression to it in her own simple way.

"The General, Jackson and Ham arrived safely at
the headquarters of Gen. McGregor, which were in the
valley to the north and east of Cochineal Mountains. His
commands of infantry and artillery were variously located
on the mountains and in the valley, with his cavalry at
Pottstown. It so happened that one of the division com-

GEN. ANDERSON TAKING COMMAND.

manders had been taken seriously ill, and was sent to the
rear. This gave an opportunity for Gen. Anderson to be
placed in command of a good division at once. To Anderson's great delight Gen. McGregor ordered him to take
command of this division. Having reported, he sent immediately for all the commanding officers of the division and
made their acquaintance. He was greatly pleased with
them and they with him. He learned all he could in so
short a time about the troops, and at once took measures
to put them in good condition. In a few days Capt. James

Day reported, and the General's military family was organized, he having taken an Adjutant-General from the command.

"The army was now being rapidly put in good shape ; a complete re-organization was being effected, and all were feeling less discouraged. They seemed to well understand that there was to be a great battle fought, and the imperative necessity for a victory by our forces East at this particular time.

"The enemy found means by which to pass the obstructions in his way, and moved through the country in different directions. Finding that the movements of our army were slow, he seemed to feel that there was no immediate danger of a serious engagement. But the surrender of our forces under Gen. Milo (who died immediately afterwards) so elated the rebel army that they were determined to attack our forces whenever and wherever opportunity offered. Both parties were, however, maneuvering for some advantage; the General of the rebel forces holding McGregor off until his force under Wall could come up from Brown's Ferry. The cavalry of both armies were now scouting continuously for many miles on the flanks of the armies. The pickets were out quite a distance in advance of the opposing forces. No conflict had yet occurred between any of the outposts. Finally the commander of the rebel forces selected his position and gave challenge to our forces, with his rear to the Grand River, covering two main roads leading to the rear, his front facing the winding course of Antler's Run, his right resting on a bridge at the main crossing, his center occupying a ridge commanding the open fields in his front, the right of his left and right center resting on the junction of the two main roads, his extreme left refused so as to form an angle at his left center, extending along and through a skirt of heavy woods; his reserves to the rear on the roads, so as to be thrown easily to the center or either flank in case of necessity; the country to his front, right and left being very uneven, full of gulches and ravines, difficult of passage, especially under fire. So posted he flaunted the rebel flag in the face of our

army, although at this time his main support had not arrived from Brown's Ferry. But no doubt existed in his
mind, I presume, as to their coming up in good time. Mc-
Gregor did not then seem inclined to accept the challenge,
His command was moving slowly. Farlin, still in command
of a corps (for shame be it ever to our indulgent chiefs), was
some distance away and did not arrive on that day. So the
armies rested. In the meantime Gen. Anderson was eager
for the fray. He visited Gen. McGregor's headquarters and
indicated his desire to bring on the engagement, saying
very soon the enemy would be so securely posted that it
would be exceedingly difficult to dislodge him. To this
McGregor replied that he could not risk a battle without
Farlin's forces being up and in readiness to support our line.

"During the night Farlin came up. A battle must then
and there be fought. The whole country stood with bated
breath awaiting the result, as all understood that the rebels must be driven back on what they claimed as their own
ground, or our country was in imminent danger of becoming demoralized should they see the battlefields changed
to the North.

"When the morning came, the commands being in readiness, the movement of our forces commenced. It was soon
discovered that the main crossing of Antler's Run was held
by a strong force of the enemy, which compelled our troops
to seek for some other and less dangerous passage. This
was found to our right, facing the left of the enemy. His
left being refused gave a safer passage over the stream.
The plan of battle was to throw Gen. Horn's Corps at the
upper crossing, assail the rebel left and, if successful, to
cross the left of our forces, under Gen. Broomfield, by assaulting the enemy at the lower crossing, and if he could
be driven from there, to cross and assault his right, his
center being too strongly posted to risk an attack on it
then. (Gen. Anderson had been assigned with his division
to Gen. Horn's Corps.) The crossing over on our right was
effected without much difficulty, and the enemy pressed
back in the heavy woods. The enemy were evidently holding and waiting, as no general engagement ensued. An-

other corps crossed in the rear of Gen. Horn's and formed
ready to assault. Our left had not as yet been able to cross
in front of the enemy's right, and in this position we found
ourselves,—part of our army on the one side and part on
the other of Antler's Run, in front of the enemy ; thus the
two armies rested that night. Our intention being thus
revealed to the enemy, he had only to wait the attack,
which they must have concluded would be commenced
at an early hour in the morning. The night was most
beautiful ; the vault of heaven being studded with stars,
so that either army was in plain view of the other, at no
very great distance separated. During the night another
of our corps crossed the Run at the same crossing that
Gen. Horn had passed over in the morning, and moved
down to the left and in front of the rebel center. Occasionally the movement of this corps would be responded to with
a few musket shots and a few shells from a battery posted
on the ridge in the rebel center. At an early hour in the
morning the Union forces took the initiative and hurled
Horn's Corps against the rebels' extreme left. The struggle was a severe one—re-enforcements could not well
be sent to the rebel left for fear of the movement being now
made against their right. The battle on the left was at
full height, and the lines swayed to and fro. Gen. Anderson made a movement around a skirt of woods near a
chapel, and charged the enemy's lines, with sword drawn,
leading his men in person. The assault was of such an impetuous character as to send dismay into the ranks of the
enemy, and they gave way in confusion. Gen. Horn, however, advanced his left and center farther to the front than
should have been done without other troops being in position to sustain the movement, and the rebel center, with
their left reformed behind the woods, fell upon Horn's left
and center with great energy and determination. The two
columns now engaged with dauntless courage on both
sides. The combatants, equal in mettle, faced each other in
open field at very close range; each holding his ground until
it appeared as though none would be left alive on either
side. Neither line wavered, and it seemed as though the

contest would only be determined by a complete demolition
of the two forces. Gen. Horn fell, mortally wounded, and
the command fell upon Gen. Simmons, who was killed
soon after taking command. At this time the killed and
wounded of the superior officers were such that it left Gen.
Anderson the ranking General of the corps. He at once
assumed command, and could everywhere be seen giving
his orders and encouraging his men to stand. This they
did until the slaughter on both sides became a shocking
sight to behold.

"Gen. Hughes and Gen. Baily had fallen on the rebel
side. The batteries from our side were playing from a hill
on the east side of Antler's Run, pouring a galling enfilad-
ing fire into the rebel line. Thus these lines stood amid
death and desolation in their ranks until the men themselves on both sides, in order to stop the cruel slaughter of
comrades, with one accord ceased firing, and the officers
sat on their horses looking at each other as their forces
slowly retired each to his rear. At this time, if Gen. Farlin had moved forward the day would have been won without further slaughter. Gen. Anderson repeatedly sent
word to him that if he would attack the enemy he could
be routed, as their left was almost destroyed; but he did
not assault at the opportune moment.

It was then seen that nothing more than skirmishing
had been going on between the forces on the Union left
and the rebel right. Gen. Broomfield had not succeeded
in crossing the run, and was held at bay by a small force,
thus enabling the rebel commander, after discovering this
hesitancy on our left, to concentrate on his left and center
for the purpose of renewing the conflict. His re-enforcements had now arrived from Brown's Ferry, and he was
eager to make an assault, being now satisfied that he should
take the aggressive. Our batteries had crossed the run,
and were supported on elevated ground by sufficient infantry, as we thought, for their safety. The rebel forces
moved from their cover behind the woods, and were advancing to the crest of the ridge that ran across the open
field from north to south, the best position to occupy for

vantage ground. Gen. Anderson seeing this, determined
to meet the attack and contest for this ground. Both
forces were now in motion, each determined the other
should not occupy this ridge. Orders were given to Gen.
Broomfield to cross the run at once and attack the enemy's
right. Gen. Mausker was ordered to move on the left of
Gen. Horn's Corps, now under Gen. Anderson, and attack
at once ; Farlin being in reserve, perhaps, because he could
not be got anywhere else.

"The artillery was all across the run and ready for action. The cavalry had crossed some miles above and to
the north, and were ordered to charge the enemy in the
flank as soon as the engagement should be renewed. So
on came the troops of both armies, and when in close
range, the firing commenced again on our right and the
rebel left, it continued all down the line until all were engaged. The firing was terrible and most destructive. Our
batteries opened, and on in full charge came our cavalry.
The rebel infantry on the left prepared to receive the cavalry, kneeling on one knee with fixed bayonets. What a
charge that was, and what a slaughter ! On came the
cavalry; on, on to the bayonet came horse and man. Clash
against bayonet came saber. Many the horse and man
went on and over the bayonet in that charge. Part of the
cavalry halted and hesitated, some retiring to the rear.
Many an infantryman that did the same. Infantry and
cavalrymen were piled together in the long slumber of
death. At last our cavalry had to retire. While this
tragedy was being enacted, the infantry on the right, left
and centre were also playing the role of death. Column
after column were hurled against each other, only to be repulsed. Our two corps first drove the enemy back and occupied the ridge, and for awhile held this advantage, until
the whole rebel army, save a skirmish-line, was withdrawn
from the right and center, and concentrated on and against
our right. It looked as though the contest was now to be
continued only on this part of the line. Farlin was now in
line on the left of Mausker. Many of the enemy's troops
were thrown in at this point who, not having been en-

gaged, were comparatively fresh. Their column was
formed in two lines. On and against our lines in quick
succession they were thrown. Another great slaughter then
commenced and continued, line facing line in open field.
Gaps were made by falling men. The command on both
sides could be heard, ' Close up !' Never did men stand
more courageously amid slaughter and death. Gen. Anderson rode to the line and along its full length, sword in
hand, with a large white plume in his hat, that his
men might recognize him. Artillery roared and musketry rattled as if they were the hail and thunder
from a hundred clouds. Groans and shrieks were heard.
The ground was strewn with the dead and dying. As the
lines finally gave way, the spot could be designated by
rows of the dead. Our line was now distended and no reserves. The rebels were again re-enforced, Their dash
and desperation broke our center, and Farlin fell back.
Gen. Mausker now fell, shot through the head. His corps
became demoralized and fell back in fragments. Gen. Anderson tried to rally the lines, but could not, and was
compelled to fall back to the rear, where the artillery was
posted. The situation at this time was most critical.
The General in command was desperate. To lose this
battle was his disgrace, having more troops than the
enemy, as it would also probably in a measure seal the
fate of his whole army. He at once gave Broomfield an
imperative order to cross the run at the point of the bayonet, and to advance upon and assault the enemy's position, being his extreme right. This was done in good
style, the enemy driven at the point of the bayonet from
the crossing and from his position on his right. The contest was now changed from the enemy's left to his right.
Troops were thrown in on his right quickly, and the battle became desperate on this end of the line.

"Gen. Anderson, discovering this, without orders rallied
his men and all others that he could, and made a furious
attack again on the enemy's left, driving him from the
open field into the woods. He then ordered the artillery
to advance to the ridge occupied by our line, and from

there poured shot and shell into their ranks. The enemy became demoralized and broke in many parts of his line, ours still advancing and Gen. Anderson moving his artillery to the front as he could get position for it. The enemy on their left commenced a retreat down the Sheepstown road in great disorder. The batteries poured their deadly missiles after them, doing great damage. Gen. Anderson pressed forward, believing that their army could now in a great measure be destroyed before they could get back to a strong defensive position for protection. Many prisoners were now being captured. Gen. Broomfield was following upon the Brown's Ferry road, when darkness set in. An order was now received from Gen. McGregor to desist from any further pursuit for the present. Gen. Anderson put his troops in position for the night, and ordered up stores and supplies for their comfort and made all necessary arrangements for an early movement in pursuit of the enemy the next morning. After attending to these matters he left Capt. Jackson Lyon and Capt. Day, both of whom had been by the side of the General during this terrible battle. The General with an Orderly retired to the headquarters of the commanding General, which he found in a small farmhouse some two miles to the east side of Antler's Run. When he arrived he was welcomed very heartily and highly complimented by Gen. McGregor.

" The General said :

" ' Anderson, we will not attempt to follow these rebels. Our army is worn out and so terribly damaged and demoralized that it would not do to risk another assault, should the enemy make a stand, inasmuch as they would have an advantageous position, which they certainly will, as they can select where they will fight if we pursue.'

" ' Yes,' said Gen. Anderson; ' but, General, could we not press them so close and worry them so as to keep them on the run, and virtually destroy them before they can get back to their own ground ? You know that while our army is terribly mangled, the enemy is certainly in no better condition.'

" ' That is true,' said Gen. McGregor ; ' but I never have,

nor will I ever fight my army when in bad condition. But
we will not discuss the matter any further now.   You will
stay and get a bite to eat and take some rest, but before
doing that take a glass of wine.'

"'Thanks, General; I think I would enjoy a glass about
this time.'

"After taking a glass together they sat down and had
quite a conversation on the events of the day.   The
house being very comfortably furnished with beds and

ANDERSON OVERHEARS THE CONSPIRACY.

cots, Gen. McGregor said to Gen. Anderson, 'Lie down
and rest while the servants are preparing the supper.'

"The General did so, and dropped off to sleep.   Soon
some general officers came in and were seated at a table,
imbibing rather freely. The noise they were making
aroused the General from his slumbers.   He recognized
Farlin ; to the others he was afterwards introduced, being
Gen. Bowlly Smite and Gen. William Cross. The General
did not rise, nor did he, by any means, exhibit any knowledge of their presence.

"In the conversation between these three Generals they were discussing the probable success of the war and the course of the Administration.

"Farlin said : 'I am very decidedly of the opinion that this war will last for ten years, and finally the South will gain their independence. The North will tire out, and the property-holders will get tired of paying taxes. This war is very expensive, and the debt will eventually alarm the country, so that they will be ready to accede to anything.'

"Said Smite : 'Well; but what will become of everything ? This Government is not strong enough to stand this strain. It has not power, except it be usurped, to prosecute the war against these Southern States. I do not believe in a Republic anyway. We ought to have a government of central force and power—a military government, or a monarchy, such as England. Suppose we had such a government as that. We would not be afflicted every now and then with new commanders that we who make soldiering our profession know nothing and care nothing about, and cannot allow to be placed over us when we can avoid it.'

"'Well; but,' said Cross. 'what can we do ? That is what we should think about. For instance, here, to-day, we have won a great battle. It is not likely that either of us will be put in command of anything higher than a corps. The command of the different armies will be given to some of those pets who want to free the niggers; and I was told the other day in Washington by Mr. Thos. A. Strider, who is one of the ablest men in this country, that this Abolition President was going to try to set the slaves free and thereby impoverish the South, so as to force them to lay down their arms. He said that if this was done he would not be surprised if Indiana would rise up in revolt.

"'If that be true, I will leave the army myself, said Smite.'

"'No, you are wrong,' said Cross. 'If this is the intention of the Administration, we ought to organize the army on a better basis than it now is, have McGregor relieve every one who is not his friend; and let us urge him to march upon the Capital and there we can install him Dictator, recognize the South's independence, with the understanding that they in turn will send their army to the front near to us, so as to sustain him.   We could seize all armories, arsenals and war materials.   The people would then be powerless. England would at once recognize the South, and if we can maintain ourselves six months, which we can easily do, the whole of Europe would recognize our government.'

" ' Just at this moment Gen. McGregor entered the room and said :

" ' Gentlemen, I hope you have been enjoying yourselves. I have been out to my Adjutant-General's office, dictating my orders for to-morrow. I hope you have helped yourselves to my sherry and champagne. I had quite a good lot of it brought on, not knowing how long this campaign might last.'

" Farlin said : ' General, I would think that the campaign for the present is almost over ; our troops are in no condition for further offensive operations.'

" ' Do you think so ?' said Gen. McGregor.

" ' Yes ; most assuredly.'

" ' Yes,' added Smite ; ' we are in no hurry; this war cannot be rushed through ; and if this Administration is going to do what I understand it is, there are some of us who will not submit.'

" ' What is that ?' inquired McGregor.

" ' Free the negroes. We will not stand that. We want you to be up and dressed. We will put you in place of the Administration, and have the country governed properly, make peace with the South and stop the war.'

" Gen. McGregor here put his finger to his lips, indicating silence on their part; and looking in the direction of the bed on which Gen. Anderson was resting, all became silent on this subject, and commenced speaking of the quality of the wine. Very soon supper was announced, and the messenger was told to call Gen. Anderson. The General, turning over and groaning as if awakening from a deep sleep, arose, and addressing Gen. McGregor, said :

" ' General, I would have slept till morning, without intermission, had I not been called.'

" ' He was then introduced to Generals Cross and Smite, and all repaired to their elegant meal, and there discussed the occurrences of the day, the merits of the several officers who had fallen, etc.

" When supper was over, which continued quite late, Gen. Anderson repaired to his own headquarters, which had been moved up to and in a depression or cut near Antler's Run, on the east side. There he found his Adjutant-General, a few darkies, and old Ham.

" ' How are you, Ham ?' inquired the General. ' Are you still alive ? You did not stay very close to me, to-day, so that you "might be safer," did you Ham ?'

" ' No, Massa Tom. When you fust start out, I was gwine long wid you, but you lef' me, and den you said nuffin 'bout me comin' wid you, and I spose you not kear 'bout habin me bodderin' you. Dat's all how it war, Massa Tom.'

" ' Yes, Ham, I see. Well, it is all right. You stay with the headquarters and take care of my traps, and I will not ask you to take command of my troops in time of battle.'

" Ham laughed one of his peculiar guffaws.

" ' Yah ! yah ! Massa Tom. I speck dat is de bes' way. Doz you want sumfin to eat ? Got plenty of chicken. Dey git skeered at de fitin', and jes' cum rite to de camp, sah. Yes, sah, dey am 'fraid of de Sesh, dey is; dey know der friends, dese chickens do.'

" The General laughed, saying, ' Ham, are you quite sure they came into camp alone ?'

" ' Well, sah, dey got in heah some way. I not fotched dem in. De fuss I seed dem, dey in de corner ob de tent all scrouched up, so I spose dey hidin' from de Sesh, and I jes' took 'em in to sabe dem. Yes, sah; dat's de way it war.'

" Ham retired behind a tent, and laughed immoderately, saying ' I spect he not keer bery much; I feels my way pretty good, I does.'

"The troops rested during the night, and next morning there were no rebels in sight, and they were ordered into camp, and no further pursuit of the enemy contemplated by the commanding General. They, however, were soon required in another direction, for the purpose of protecting the Capital of the Nation. Gen. Anderson's old wound re-opened, which caused him to turn over his splendid command. At the suggestion of his surgeon, he with his two Aides-de-camp and old Ham, returned to Allentown until such time as he could again recover sufficiently to perform his duty. The President hearing of his skill in maneuvering troops, and his gallant conduct on the battlefield, at once promoted him to be a Major-General.

"Their return home, of course, made our family very happy again—only marred by the continued severe illness of Dr. James. He had lingered for months, sometimes improving, and then again suffering severely. He seemed to revive and gain strength on the return of his friends. Capt. Day took up his abode at Young's Hotel, and Capt. Jackson remained at home with us. Peter returned in a few days, his foot being in a very bad condition, he fearing that an amputation might become necessary without great care and immediate rest. Thus our family were once more partly together, and although some were suffering greatly, we enjoyed the recital of the battle of Antler's Run, by both Capt. Jackson and the General. The story of his lying on the bed and hearing the suggestions of a conspiracy by the superior officers of the Army of the East, caused me serious reflection. The details of this conversation he gave me in confidence, having never revealed it even to his staff officers. I at once repaired to the Capital, and saw the President and Secretary of War, and stated to them the whole of the conversation and the proposed scheme. They were almost dumbfounded. The President thanked me saying :

"'I have now declared the slaves free. We will see what we will see.'

"He then remarked :

"'I have my eye on the man the Lord I think is raising

up in order to complete the work we have begun. These men must be held in our hands until the right time arrives;' which he thought would not be very long.

The Secretary of War was not so mild. Under a promise that I would still prosecute my inquiries further into Canada and elsewhere I left for home. On my arrival I found the Doctor much worse, and the family greatly distressed. He lingered but a few days and passed away. You can see our household was again in deep gloom. I will not speak of our grief. We were a sorely stricken family."

CHAPTER X.

BATTLE OF MURPHY'S HILL.—THE MOST SANGUINARY
FIGHTING OF THE WAR.—MURDER OF STEPHEN LYON.
—UNCLE HAM GETS A STRONG DISLIKE TO WAR.

Generals 'gainst Generals grapple gracious God,
How honors Heaven heroic hardihood!
Infuriate, indiscriminate in ill,
Kindred kill kinsmen, kinsmen kindred kill,
Labor laid levels, longest, loftiest lines ;
Men march 'mid mounds, 'mid moles, 'mid murderous mines.
—FINLEY.

"AFTER the lapse of considerable time Gen. Anderson
was considering whether or not he had recovered
sufficiently to again take the field. His staff officers and his wife were protesting that his strength
was not sufficient.

"I said : 'Well, we will consider this matter at another
time.'

"Aunt Martha called us ; we all walked in and sat down
to tea, Capt. Day with us, having been with Gen. Ander
son almost daily since his return. While at the table my
wife spoke of the absence of Stephen and Peter, wishing
them with us, and again alluded to her dream, saying that
she had dreamed it all over again last night. and that she
thought there must be some kind of a warning to her in it.

"Just at this moment I discovered old Ham standing in
the corner very much absorbed in counting his fingers. He
seemed to be considerably bothered, however, in making
up the proper count. Aunt Sarah discovered him, and
said :

"'Ham, what are you doing ?

"'Ham saw that his manner caused my wife (Aunt Sarah)
to be disturbed, and the old fox (for he was very sly) said:

(157)

"'Yes, missus, I's—I's jes' seein' how many is here, and how many dey is wid de oder boys what goed away, so dat I know how many you is when you'uns is all togedder. I tell you, dis am a big family—dat's all.'

"Old Martha, who was attending the table, spoke to Ham in her usual way, saying:

"'Ham, you jes' git out, you ole fool; go to de kitchen, whar you b'longs.'

"When Ham left we finished our tea, but Aunt Sarah showed plainly that she was very much troubled. She soon retired for the night, and the rest of us conversed about the situation and Gen. Anderson's condition; he claiming that he was strong, the rest of us to the contrary. We concluded to settle it for the present by visiting the farm the next morning, which we did, taking Ham with us as driver of our wagon. When we arrived Joseph Dent invited us all into his house, and while making inquiries of him as to his health, the condition of his stock, etc., a man came to the gate and called for him. When he returned he said that this man was notifying him that he must come to a meeting that night of the Golden Circle; that the Circle had some very important business on hand. We encouraged him to go, and to report to us at Allentown the next morning. Dent consented, saying that the Circle had been exceedingly active; that an agent had been there from Canada and had required them to make a selection of agents of their Circle to be ready to do some particular work, which would be explained at the proper time. He also gave us the names of two men, one of whom resided in Allentown. This caused us to think seriously about the danger that we might be in, as men coming from Canada might discover us in some way and afterwards recognize any of us who should be in that country prying into their designs. We left for home, and on the way noticed that Ham was unusually quiet, but watchful. Finally, he concluded that it was his time to speak, and turning to Gen. Anderson, said:

"'Massa Gen'l, did you see dat man out at de barn, sir?'

"'No,' said the General.

"'Well, sah! dat was the wussest lookin' Sesh I eber did see. He war lyin' in de hay, and when he look at me I lef''; yes, sah, I lef'. Somefin wrong dar, sah. You better ax Massa Joseph, when he be down to de house, 'bout dat.'

"We satisfied Ham by agreeing to find out on the next day; so we came home, and were sitting on my portico talking about what was best to do, when the General received a dispatch from Washington, stating that Gen. Rosenfelt, commanding the Army of the Center, had asked for Gen. Anderson to be assigned to him, which would be done whenever he was well enough to take the field. The General was somewhat disappointed, as he wished to return to the Army of the East, for reasons that you can understand from what occurred in his hearing while at Gen. McGregor's headquarters. He was a true soldier, however, and said not a word, but promptly telegraphed, thanking them for the assignment, and saying he would report very soon. He felt that he would be able to attend to duty without very great danger to himself; so he directed Capt. Jackson, as we now called him, to get ready, also Capt. Day, who had come in a few moments after the receipt of the telegram. The young men seemed particularly well pleased. Capt. Jackson felt that he would be with Peter and Stephen. Stephen had been promoted and was now a Brigadier-General. So all seemed pleased, though I knew how Gen. Anderson felt.

"The General sent a telegram to Gen. Rosenfelt, who was then encamped between Nashua and Stone Run, Tenn., informing him that he would start for his headquarters in about two days. He did not get away, however, as soon as he stated.

"The next day Joseph Dent came, and was greatly delighted at something. So we gave him a seat and cleared the decks, as you must know that these secret matters about how information was obtained of which we were coming in possession, other than in the ordinary course of things, was not told to the whole household. Before proceeding, however, we asked him to tell us who was in

the barn at the farm the day before, that had so alarmed
Ham. He laughed and said it was his partner; so we
dropped further inquiry, but did not tell Ham.

"Joseph Dent said he attended the Circle the night before, as he had promised, and that they were in great
trouble. They had been advised that the agents would
not be needed for the present; that some scheme that was
on foot had been postponed, and that a consultation was
to be held in order to come to an understanding as to what
course was to be pursued. He said a man who was a
stranger to him stated that two of their principal men who
were to carry out the scheme (whatever it might be) had
been sent to Europe, and that this left them in a condition
so that they could not proceed until they could work up
their plan; that their plan or scheme was being matured
by the men, who were to obtain their material in England; that it could not be done here without suspicion being aroused. This, he said, was all that was said or done.
So you see, this meeting evidently had reference to some
desperate undertaking, of which their leaders in Indiana
seemed to be posted as to the fact that something was to
be done, without knowing the details. This proved
to us that they had communication one lodge with another all over the country, and also with the heads of
the conspiracy, and therefore we would have to take every
precaution in all of our movements; but as we acted only
through persons that we could trust with our lives, we
considered the matter comparatively safe, and were very
sure that we would be able to post the President at all
times as to what might be danger in the way of our
success.

"The next day, when the family were informed that the
General, Capt. Jackson and Capt. Day must leave us, our
house again became a scene of distress. My wife cried all
day long. Mary Anderson was nearer breaking down than
I had ever seen her since we heard that the General (then
a Colonel) was killed at Dolensburg. Jennie also nearly
gave way. The two children begged them most piteously
not to go away to fight (as they termed it) any more.

"Ham seemed rather serious, and did not relish the renewal of his acquaintance with the Sesh. The next morning, all matters being arranged, the General and his two aides, with old Ham, after taking leave of all the family, left. The scene that followed in my household I will not attempt to describe. Ham lingered a little behind, but finally he embraced Aunt Martha, and said:

"'Good-by, Marfa; I guess I'se a gone darky dis time. I tell you I do not like de dream what I had.'

"'Go long, you ole fool; dreams 'mount to nuffin. You eats too much cabbage las' night. Dats all what ails you. Dar's no danger you git kill. You jes' go long wid Massa Tom. Dat's what you do.'

"'All right, Marfa, I do it. Good-by.'

"They arrived at Gen. Rosenfelt's headquarters (which were with his army) and reported. Gen. Rosenfelt was very glad to see the General, and told him that he would assign him to the command of a first-class division under Gen. Papson, his army then being divided into three full corps, commanded respectively by Papson, Gen. Critsinger and Gen. McCabe. His army numbered, embracing all arms of the service, some 56,000 effective men, and was well supplied with all necessary material for any kind of movement.

"On the next morning Gen. Anderson was assigned to the command of such a division as mentioned. He was well pleased with his corps commander, who was a fine-looking man of middle age, very quiet and unostentatious. The whole army seemed to be in splendid condition for a campaign. On looking through his division that day he found Stephen Lyon in command of his Third brigade, and Peter in command of one of Stephen's regiments. This delighted the General, and he quickly said to Capt. Jackson:

"'Gen. Rosenfelt and Gen. Papson both being old friends of Uncle Daniel, I suspect one of his letters might be found amongst the papers of both Rosenfelt and Papson.'

"Capt. Jackson laughed and said:

6

"'Well, father has nothing else to do except to keep the President posted and look after his children, which he faithfully does.'

"'Yes,' said Gen. Anderson; 'he does his duty in all respects.'

"That afternoon Gen. Stephen Lyon and Col. Peter Lyon (being their respective rank at that time) visited Gen. Anderson's headquarters, and of course enjoyed themselves, each thanking the good fortune that had brought them together. They discussed the situation, and Stephen was decidedly of the opinion that unless we advanced at once and gave battle that the enemy would do so, and the position we occupied not being a favorable one for defense, he thought we could force a battle where our position would be better.

"The enemy at this time were also in good condition, and were commanded by Gen. Biggs, with three full corps, commanded respectively by Gen. Polkhorn, Gen. Chatham and Gen. Harding. Biggs's command was disposed as follows : Polkhorn's corps and three brigades of Harding's were at Murphy's Hill; the remainder of Harding's corps to the southwest some twenty miles, forming the left flank; the remainder of Biggs's army lay some twenty miles to the south and east; on and in advance of his extreme left was one division on the Nashua and Franktown road. In this position lay the rebel army, in easy supporting distance to the center and main line, it having been selected by Biggs as a good position on which to make his stand against our forces, his outposts being ordered to fall back should our forces advance. The position was a good one, as it forced our army to cross Stone Run in his front in any direction that our troops might approach him.

"During the evening a lady came to our picket line and asked to be taken to Gen. Rosenfelt's headquarters. This was done. When she appeared, Gen. Rosenfelt recognized her as Mrs. Lotty Houghton, who had been employed, it seems, by Jardine, Marshall & Co., northern manufacturers of cotton goods, to purchase cotton and get it through our lines. They had a permit to do so from the Treasury

Department of the United States, and it seems she was quite successful as one of the agents. The enemy were eager to sell their cotton and our people anxious to get it. She went to and fro with passes from both sides, neither believing she could give any information that would be of importance to either side. She, however, was an exceedingly bright woman, who noted in her mind everything she saw or heard. She was as true and as loyal to the Union as any commander we had. She asked the General for a private interview, and gave him the position of the enemy, as I have before stated. This was the only certain information he had up to this time as to their exact position. She also told him that the reason she came to him now was that all the enemy's main force of cavalry were gone. That of Morganson and Forester were far away on raids, and would not be able to return in time to aid in a battle, should Gen. Rosenfelt feel like assuming the offensive. She proposed to him that she would go to Nashua and from thence down the Franktown road, pass through the lines of the enemy, and come in their rear to Murphy's Hill, where she was well known; remain there quietly with a lady friend, and when she discovered anything that she considered absolutely important, she would get through the lines some way and come to him with the information. He was delighted at this proposition and said to her :

"'You shall be well rewarded for this.'

"She said, in reply :

"'No, sir; you mistake me. I am no spy! I give this information because it comes to my knowledge without my seeking it, and not in any confidence. I do this for the good of my country, and not for reward.'

"The General bowed and applauded her devotion to her government. She then bade him good-by and left for Nashua, refusing an escort.

"Gen. Rosenfelt sent for his corps commanders that evening, and explained the situation as he understood it. After examining the map and showing his officers the manner he desired an assault to be made, should he determine to attack, all agreed that there was no cause for delay.

The troops were in fine condition and 'eager for the fray.' The General commanding told them to be ready to move at 4 o'clock in the morning. He would send them written instructions in the meantime. So he prepared his orders and sent them out. First, his headquarters would be with those of Gen. Papson's corps; that the army would march by three different roads, leading from Nashua in a southerly direction. Gen. McCabe, with his command, would march on the Franktown road; Gen. Papson, with his command, being the center, on the Nolton and Shelltown Road; Critsinger on the Murphy's Hill road. McCabe was to assail Harding's forces on his road; but if Harding should fall back on the main rebel line, in that event McCabe and Papson were both to bear to the left, so as to present an unbroken front or line at or near Stone Run, opposite Murphy's Hill. The movement commenced the next morning, but not so early as directed. During the march McCabe ran against Harding's pickets, when a skirmish began. The rebel forces fell back on their main line. Gen. McCabe was delayed for some reason and did not reach Harding's main position that day, but on the next. And when he did arrive, Harding had left and was far away on his road to join Bigg's main force. The rain was now falling in torrents, and Papson and Critsinger were troubled to get their trains through the mud over very poor roads. When Gen. Rosenfelt's forces were finally concentrated he was compelled to rest one day, *he* thought, in order not to engage the enemy with his army in a tired and worn-out condition.

The enemy had to march about the same distance, however, in order to make their concentration of forces. The ground over which the battle must be fought lies between Stone Run and Overman's Creek; it is slightly rolling ground, with sticky, clayish soil, in which the roads are tortuous and easily worked up by teams so as to become almost impassable. There were clearings on this ground, but they alternated with a chaparral that was almost impenetrable. There are three roads through this valley, between the two streams, which converge on Murphy's Hill.

"Rosenfelt, after resting, formed his line with McCabe on the right, Papson in the center, and Critsinger on the left, leaving Stone Run between the enemy and himself. One or the other must cross this stream sometime and somewhere during the engagement, in order to attack his opponent. There is much in the first assault if made with decision. In the evening, just before dark, one of McCabe's brigades struck one of Wittington's (rebel) brigades. The contest was a severe one, in which our forces were damaged very much. This ought to have proven that the enemy were intending to cross the run and strike our right flank. But it did not seem to disturb our commander in the least. That night Rosenfelt laid before his corps commanders his plan of attack, which was to throw his left across the run and attack and drive the rebel forces from Murphy's Hill, and get between the hill and the enemy, and use the high ground for artillery on the line and flank of the enemy; at the same time strike him in the center with Papson, leaving McCabe to merely hold his line to resist and not to attack.

"This being understood, all were to be ready the next morning to carry out the plan of the battle laid down by the General commanding. During the day Mrs. Lotty Houghton heard directly from one of the rebel officers that they were to move that night all their available forces to our right and attack us on our flank in the morning. So she concluded to leave that day, in order to be out of the way of the battle, and started south. After traveling several miles outside of the enemy's lines, she cut across to the west and took the road leading from Nashua to Pulaston. Traveling on that for some distance she struck across to the road from Nashua to Murphy's Hill, following that until she came to our pickets, and there asked to be shown to Army headquarters. She got in very late, and the Sergeant made a mistake and took her to Gen. Papson. He did not know her and was rather suspicious. She told him of the movement of the enemy. He took her into his headquarters and sent out to find Gen. Rosenfelt.   But he could not be found.   He was out somewhere looking after his lines. This caused delay. He was not found until morning, and then not until after the movement had commenced on his left.   Critsinger was crossing the run in front of Murphy's Hill.   When Gen. Rosenfelt was informed that Mrs. Houghton was in our lines, and of her statement made about the enemy, he said :

" 'It cannot be so.   Biggs cannot suspect our movement. But even so, I will crush his right, which he has left exposed, and carry out my plan before he can do anything.' Gen. Rosenfelt superintended the crossing of the run in person.   He saw the moment approaching when he could throw himself with a vastly superior force upon the isolated division that Gen. Biggs had left at the hill—the rest of Biggs's command having crossed the run to his left. At this juncture skirmish firing was heard, and in a very short time sharp musketry burst forth on our extreme right.

"At once Rosenfelt questioned in his mind, could Biggs have guessed the movement by which he was menaced ? Was he endeavoring to forestall it, or was this one of those encounters between pickets ?   Or had Mrs. Houghton brought to him the correct information ?   He at once sent to have her brought to him.   But she had left for Nashua on the turnpike road, so as to be out of the way, as well as out of danger.   Very soon the facts were revealed to him, when too late, however, to retrace his steps.   There was nothing left but to attack the isolated force at once, as McCabe had stated that he could hold his position against any force that might attack him.   The battle had commenced on his right, and the rebels were pressing forward and gaining very great advantage.   Our forces were taken completely by surprise on our right—the soldiers were in their tents, the officers scattered ; the Chief of Artillery was at the headquarters of Gen. McCabe ; the artillery horses had been taken to water, and in the great haste to get under arms each regiment formed in front of their tents.   On came the rebel division, pouring a terrific fire

into our ranks, advancing at every discharge, and loading
as they came. Our artillery was mixed up and the portion
of it that could be got into position was operated in vain.
The two forces came together and fought hand to hand
amid a musketry fire that struck friend and foe alike.
Gen. John's brigade held their ground manfully, but could
not long withstand the impetuosity of the attack and the
superiority of numbers. Their line broke in several places,
and the batteries, deprived of horses, fell into the hands
of the enemy. Gen. Willis's brigade was totally routed
and he made a prisoner. Kirkham's brigade was broken
to pieces and routed. The first assault did not last long,
but was extremely damaging to our forces. Thus attacked,
our lines were falling back in the direction of Overman's
Creek, when Lawting's rebel cavalry fell upon their flank,
capturing many prisoners, guns, and much camp equipage.
Polkhorn now assaulted Gen. Davies' division with two
fresh divisions. Davies repulsed the first assault, but was
struck in flank by Clayber, which forced him back. Pot-
ter's brigade was by Clayber entirely dispersed. By this
time our right flank had been broken and driven back on
Hospital Hill, and finally from there.

"The rebel cavalry then came charging down, capturing
many prisoners. Our wagon trains, ammunition and rations were only saved by the action of one regiment of
our cavalry charging the rebel flank and forcing them
back. News reached Rosenfelt that his right was completely routed. He at once countermanded his order to
attack with his left, and moved to the right in order to
save a great disaster and perhaps his army.

" In the meantime Biggs was preparing to attack the center, and on came one of his divisions in double column and
struck the troops of a general who was in waiting to receive
them (Gen. Sherlin). The attack was quick and terrible,
but they were rolled back, attacked in turn, and the rebel
loss in one brigade was one-third of its force. Gen. Sull,
one of our brave officers, here lost his life while leading a
charge. Rosenfelt and Gen. Papson now commenced forming a new line, which had to be done under a heavy fire, as

the battle had extended down to and on the center.
Sherlin had fallen back to form on the new line. Rosen
felt had become excited, and was riding over the field with
his hat off, ordering everything he came to—batteries, regiments and companies. Papson, who was always cool and
calm in battle as on dress parade, had his corps well in
hand, and ordered Gen. Anderson, who was on his right
and adjoining Sherlin, to receive the enemy and give him
the bayonet. There had been a cessation of fighting for an
hour, and the broken troops had commenced to re-organize
and get into line. Biggs, seeing that postponement would
not do, ordered up the division from Murphy's Hill, and
again the battle commenced with renewed vigor. Sherlin
was assailed first by Polkhorn. Gen. Anderson now seeing
his chance, moved quickly to Sherlin's support, and with
a dash struck one of Polkhorn's divisions in flank, and almost annihilated it. One of his brigades, Stephen Lyon
commanding, was ordered to charge against another
division. This was handsomely done, and the rebels fell
back rapidly. At this time Biggs came into the fray, and
led back his broken brigades in person, but they fared the
same as before. In this assault Sherlin lost his other two
brigade commanders, and had his troops somewhat demoralized for a time; but they soon recovered and the attacking commenced on our side. Our lines were moved
forward and the battle was furious; first an advantage
was gained on the one side and then on the other. At last
our men became encouraged and were fighting with a firm
conviction that we were gaining ground and driving the
enemy back. During an hour of hard stand-up hand-to-hand
fighting, officers and men fell like the leaves of Autumn
after a bitter frost. Night then closed in, leaving the two
armies facing each other.

"A profound silence prevailed during the night, interrupted only by the groans and the shrieks of the wounded
and dying, after a constant strife, which had lasted for ten
hours. No more sanguinary struggle for the length of
time was ever witnessed. During this day there was not a
single regiment of our troops that had not been more or

less engaged. The enemy's cavalry had crossed the run below our army and captured and destroyed a great quantity of our provisions, ammunition, etc. That night no rations were distributed. The poor boys gathered around the campfires and anxiously inquired about missing comrades, and what of the day to-morrow. Many of the soldiers thought our army surrounded. Three of our Generals had fallen during the day, and many thousand poor soldiers were killed, wounded and captured.

"That night Gens. Anderson and Sherlin met for the first time, and in talking over the morrow both agreed that they would die on that ground or win the battle, and they infused this same determination into all they met.

"Biggs thought that Rosenfelt would retreat during the night. He could not believe that he would undertake to maintain himself in the position in which he had been forced. He thought that he had only to wait until morning to gather the fruits of a great victory. He was mistaken. The next morning he found the Union forces in a compact line skirting the timber, with hastily thrown-up earthworks. If Rosenfelt had made his movement, on the information given by Mrs. Houghton, earlier in the day, instead of the afternoon, he would, perhaps, have met with no disaster. But the next day, when he found that Biggs did not attack, he determined to do so. He made the same movement that he began the day before, and was driven back in his first attempt to take the hill. He then began a general assault, and retook all the positions lost the day before. The loss of the enemy was very heavy, and the victory of the second day was complete. Gen. Anderson moved out with his division by the side of Sherlin, and the two seemed to vie with each other as to which could face the greatest danger. The rebels lost two Generals, killed that day. In the two days' fighting the losses on both sides were most serious. In the evening, after the battle was concluded, as General Anderson was riding over the field near Hospital Hill, he discovered a rebel officer leaning against the root of a tree. There were two rebel soldiers with him. He was very pale, and not able to speak in louder tones than a whisper. The General dismounted, giving his reins to his orderly. Approaching the group, the two soldiers arose and said :

"'General, we surrender.'

"The General replied :

"'That is not my purpose. I do not come to make prisoners, but to know if I can be of any service to this wounded officer.'

"As the General spoke, the wounded officer said, in a whisper :

"'Tom, is that you ?'"

"'Yes,' said the General, reaching out his hand to Capt. Whitthorne, in whom he recognized his wife's cousin.

"Capt. Whitthorne took his hand and said :

"'I am dying. I want you to tell cousin Mary that I have never forgotten her ; I love her, and wish I could see her now. We will not speak of our differences now ; the approach of death softens our hearts. You are a brave man, Tom. I am proud of you, even as an enemy. When I die, as I will in a few minutes—I can only last a little while—will you bury me just where I fell? There is the spot,' looking over his left shoulder and asking one of the men to mark it.

"This exertion caused the blood to flow profusely, as he had been shot through the lungs.

"In a few minutes he breathed his last. Gen. Anderson had him properly interred at the place where he requested, and marked it with a headstone with his name upon it. He wrote to his wife the facts as I have given them to you. Gen. Anderson never alluded to him afterwards except in the most respectful terms. When Mary, the General's wife, received a letter giving an account of her cousin's death, she wept, but said nothing.

"But to return to the results of the battle : Biggs retreated and left the field to Rosenfelt, who concluded to go into winter quarters instead of making pursuit. He said it was necessary that his army should recuperate. Wishing, however, to cover Nashua, he sent a command

out to the west from Murphy's Hill, on the road to Franktown.   It fell upon Stephen Lyon's brigade to go.   He was
quite unwell, but would by this station have an independent command—his brigade and two regiments of cavalry
and two batteries of artillery—consequently he was gratified by the order.   In marching the command moved slowly,
there not being an urgent necessity for their presence at
Franktown.   On the second day's march they halted and
had a luncheon at a spring by the roadside.

THE MURDER OF STEPHEN LYON.

"Gen. Stephen Lyon was lying on a mattress in an ambulance.   When the command had rested he sent them forward, remaining at the spring himself, saying to his officers
that he would come on after resting, as he could soon over-
take them.   He kept with him only one officer (Lieut. Curtis),
two orderlies and the driver, not dreaming of an enemy
being in that part of the country, as Biggs's army was
many miles south of Stone Run, or rather to the southeast at Tullahoming.

"Col. Joseph Whitthorne (then Brigadier-General), with

a detachment of cavalry, came dashing up.   He captured
Lieut. Curtis and the two orderlies and driver, and then
asked who the officer was that was lying in the ambulance.
On being told that it was Gen. Stephen Lyon, he replied :

"'I have sworn to kill him if I ever met him, for sending
a spy into my camp.'

"Stephen was unarmed, and protested that he knew nothing about the charges alleged against him.   But it did
no good.   Whitthorne ordered his men to shoot him, and
it was done and my poor boy was in this cold-blooded way
murdered by this gang of bushwhackers.   My other sons
had his body taken back to Murphy's Hill and buried.   I
never knew who murdered him until the war was over."

The old man again broke down and for a time was unable to proceed, but at last said :

"You can see how the fates were against my family.
When the news was received at home my poor wife could
not rally under these successive blows, and she lay sick for
months.   I thought she would soon follow the poor boys.
When she did recover it was only partially.   She was never
well afterwards.

"After the battle, Gen. Anderson thought he would
look up his military family, as his headquarters had
been sent to the rear during the conflict.   Capt. Day
and Capt. Jackson were near him all the time, and were
no better posted than the General as to where the headquarters were.   Finally they were found some three miles to
the rear.   The orderlies, driver, cook, etc., were found
established at the headquarters; but old Ham, poor old
man, was nowhere to be found.   A general search was at
once instituted, and finally he jumped up like a rabbit
from some thick underbrush.   When he came out he looked
all around, and at last realizing who the parties were that
had discovered him he threw up his hands and exclaimed :

"' Bress the good Laud, and you'uns are not all killed.
Afo' de Laud I never 'spected to see any you good people
agin.   And heah is Massa Gen'l Tom, and Massa Jackson
and Massa Capt. Day.   Well ! well ! if dis isn't a sprize to
ole Ham.'

" The General said :

"'Ham, how did you get here? What made you run away? I thought you were going to stay with us.'

" 'Yes, sah, I thought so, too; but, sah, de shell, de guns and de bums dey all come rite down over whar I was, and I not know how to fight. One ob de mans git me a gun and fix it up, and I git behind a tree and poke it out and pull de trigger, and bress de Laud it shoot de wrong way and I fine myself knocked ober away off from de tree. Den I said dis is no place for dis darkey, and I gits; dats what I does, and I comed along pretty fas' and I got wid de wagons, and pretty soon de hossmen ob de Sesh—I b'leves dey calls 'em cabalry—dey come on de run and burned up de wagons and slashed 'bout and cussed about de Yanks and swared about de niggers and skeered me out ob my breff. Den I gits in de woods and creeps under de brush and dar I stay, and sho' you born I thought ebery one was killed, I wouldn't never come out if you hadn't found me, sho'. I done thought I neber see Marfa no more. O, bress de Laud, I's hungry doe.'

" 'Well, come along, Ham; I guess I will have to send you home; you seem not to take to war.'

" 'Well, sah! Massa Gen'l, 'spect it be de bes'; for afore de Laud I feels curous when you is fitin'. Somehow I doesn't jes' feel rite all de time dey is shootin'. It seems dey would kill a darky jes' as quick as dey do a white man.'

" 'Yes,' said the General; 'why not?'

" 'Well, sah, I doesn't know why; it 'pears like dey wouldn't kill the darkies when we work for dem so long. But de Sesh dey is quar folks dey is; dey fight doe, don' dey, Massa Tom?'

" 'Yes; they fight like other people.'

"By this time they were at headquarters, and Ham got hold of his namesake and devoured it as a wild beast would have done. Ham was very serious and finally said :

" 'Massa Tom, I guess dey not fight any mo' berry soon, does dey?'

" The General replied that he did not know.

" ' Well,' said Ham, ' I guess I stay wid you a while longer. You won't write home 'bout me gittin' in de bush, will you'uns ?'

" ' No; if you wish us not to do so.'

" ' O, for de Laud's sake ! Marfa she d neber lib wid dis darky no mo' if she know what I do. You won't tell her, Massa Tom, will you ?'

" ' No, Ham; I will keep it a secret from her.'

" ' Well, den, I will try him once mo'. I 'spects I stay here nex' time. I knows I do. O, I knows de nex' time, sho.'

" All right, Ham; you get around now and get our things together, and look after my " traps." '

" ' Yes, massa, yes.'

" ' Ham's conduct and explanations afforded great amusement for the boys around headquarters for some time.

Capt. Zeke Inglesby said :

" Uncle Daniel, I did not know before that Gen. Stephen Lyon, who was murdered at Bethesda Springs, was your son. I know all about his murder. I belonged to his brigade. That dastardly murder was considered by all soldiers as one of the most outrageous acts and cold-blooded murders ever known in civilized warfare."

" Oh, yes. I grieved over his death very greatly, he being the second one of our dear boys murdered outright —the fourth dead since the war began. It chilled the blood of our whole family. The strangest thing to me was how Gen. Anderson, Capt. Jackson and Col. Peter could restrain themselves so as not to mention the name of his murderer, in all their conversations about his death; but, as I said, I never knew who did it until after the war. I could easily understand the reason for their not telling the name. Mary Anderson, being his sister, was never told the facts ; nor my wife nor any of us at the time, the boys fearing that it might cause an unpleasant feeling even to know the fact that a near relative of one of our family could be such a barbarian.

"I was kept quite close at home for some months with our family, being their only protection within call. During this time no man ever suffered more in spirit. I can see it all before me now: my poor wife's agony, the sorrowing of David's widow, Mary Anderson's trouble, the two poor little children—their questions about their Uncle Stephen, who killed him, and why? These questions I could not answer."

At this point Dr. Adams inquired if Gen. Rosenfelt ever expressed any regret at not listening to the information imparted to him on the morning of the battle.

"No, sir; I did not so understand."

"Uncle Daniel, did you know anything of Mrs. Houghton after this?"

"Yes; she continued to do good service for our cause, as you will learn hereafter."

Uncle Daniel here called in Mrs. Wilson. She was a bright and beautiful woman. He took her in his arms and said to us:

"This dear child and one boy, the son of another of my boys, are all of whom I can now boast."

His speech at this point was so pathetic and saddening, that the whole party were unconsciously moved to tears. His voice trembled, and he slowly walked out of the room, overwhelmed by the sad memories he had awakened.

CHAPTER XI.

"But mercy is above this sceptered sway,
It is enthroned in the heart of kings,
It is an attribute to God himself;
And earthly power doth then show likest God's,
When mercy seasons Justice."—SHAKESPEARE.

"GEN. BIGGS having taken up his position in the
angle of the headwaters of Goose River and Cane's
Fork, near Tullahoming, in the midst of a rich
valley, Rosenfelt at once commenced repairing the
railroads and throwing up earthworks near Murphy's Hill,
which almost encircled the entire place. There he remained
during the winter and following spring. The two armies
were principally engaged in watching each other, neither
being willing to risk an advance against the other. For
several months this situation continued. The only operations that marked this long period of inaction on the part
of the two armies were a series of small exploits which were
calculated to cause the two armies to degenerate into small
bands, that could only be employed in harassing their
enemies. The rebels got ready, however, and made the
first attempt. Gen. Weller, with a brigade of cavalry,
pushed his way up within a few miles of Nashua, burned
a railroad bridge, then descended on the right bank of the
Le-Harp River to the banks of Combination River, and
there seized several of our transports, which were loaded
with supplies. He burned these with all their cargoes.
One of our gunboats reached the scene of action just in
time to also become a prey to the flames.

176

"This act on the part of the rebel cavalrymen in its audacity seems to have completely paralyzed our mounted troops, and Weller was permitted to return entirely unmolested. In a very short time, elated by his success, he concentrated a force of some 3,000 men under Gens. Forrester and Lawting, with two batteries, within twenty miles of Nashua. Gen. Rosenfelt, seeing that the rebels were riding all around and about him with impunity, sent Gen. Davies with one division of infantry, and two brigades of cavalry commanded by Gen. Minting, in order to hem Weller in and 'bag him' and take him into camp, as the soldiers would say. Davies marched from Murphy's Hill to Eagle Cove; Sleeman marched from Nashua with a division of infantry, upon Tyrone; Minting moved away to the south by way of Franktown, where the forces were all to close in like pulling the drawstring of a bag and closing it over your game. But when opened there was no Weller inside. The next heard of him he had pushed on far to the northwest, and while our forces were closing in at Franktown, Weller had again reached the borders of Combination River at Mariam's Crossing, and appeared before Dolinsburg on the next day. You remember the great battle fought at Dolinsburg, where Gen. Tom. Anderson was thought to have been killed, but was found by me in the darky's cabin?"

They answered: "Yes; that could not be forgotten."

"Well, gentlemen, this place was still commanded by good old Col. Harden. He had but 700 men all told. The place was encircled by parapets commanding the ravines north and south. In the center the Colonel had constructed large earthworks, and mounted thereon one 32-pounder. He also had a section of field-guns. The rebels lost no time in making their dispositions, and were ready for the assault. Col. Harden hastily made preparations to receive the enemy. He placed his women and sick on a transport that lay at the wharf. That being done, the old Colonel said to his men: 'Boys, here I will die before I will lower that flag,' and his command all cheered him, and said 'we agree to that sentiment.'

"Weller was now ready; he ordered Forrester and Law-ting to advance and attack. But before doing so he thought it would be the more correct warfare to summon the garri-son to surrender. He did so by sending a flag of truce and demanding a surrender of the fort. Col. Harden inquired by what authority the surrender was demanded. The reply was that Gen. Weller demanded it 'in the name of Jefferson Davis, President of the Southern Confederacy.'

" ' Tell Gen. Weller that if Mr. Davis is here in person I will see him ; but if Gen. Weller wants this fort he must take it at the point of the bayonet. Col. Harden never surrenders to the enemy.'

" This was reported to Gen. Weller, and he remarked, ' We will see.'

" Forrester deployed his command and moved forward up the hill, but as he galloped up under a heavy fire his loss was severe. The soldiers who were defending that part of the outer works retreated inside of the heavy fortifi-cations. A murderous and destructive fire was now opened upon the enemy from all sides of the works.

" Forrester fell back and formed a new line, and Weller put his whole force in action. Lawting joined Forrester on the right, and the assault was made.

" Old Col. Harden said: ' Boys, here they come; let them charge close up before you fire. Fill that old 32-pounder with bullets on top of the shell;' and they did.

" So Forrester charged with his men right up to the works. Col. Harden gave the command ' Fire !' and with one volley from muskets and the old 32-pounder the cav-alry retreated in every direction; many horses and men fell under this terrible fire. Our men leaped out of the works, and with bayonets fixed charged down against For-rester's men and captured many of them. Forrester's best Colonel was killed and his command routed and demoral-ized. Lawting had captured the Cemetery Ridge, where some of Col. Harden's men had made a stand, but finding they could not hold it, fell back into the fort. Darkness here closed in and the old flag still floated over Dolins-burg. During the night a gunboat came to the rescue.

" The next morning there were no rebels in sight, save killed and wounded. Dolinsburg was never again assaulted by the enemy during the war. Col. Harden was a brave man, and dearly beloved by my whole family; not alone for his bravery, but for his kindness to Gen. Anderson during his stay at the Colonel's Headquarters.

" Weller was being followed up by Davies, who had finally gotten on his track. But he took another tack; he moved a short distance, as if intending to meet Davies, and then suddenly wheeled to the right and reached Centertown by way of Pinche's Factory, along the line of Goose River. After fording the river he called a halt at Colesburg. His men were now worn out with fatigue, and his horses totally unfitted for further service until thoroughly recuperated. This ended Gen. Weller's exploits for a considerable length of time. Just then another raider appeared upon the scene—one Gen. Van Doring, in command of some 5,000 fresh cavalry. This new force gave the enemy courage, and they at once renewed their former audacity. They were determined to wipe out if possible the terrible and painful result of their attack upon Col. Harden at Dolinsburg, and immediately advanced within a short distance of Rosenfelt's main encampment, drove in his outposts, and threatened his short line of communication with Nashua. By this time large re-enforcements had arrrived by way of transports up the Combination River to Nashua. Sleeman's division had moved forward to the main force at Murphy's Hill. The General felt that he must rid the country of these raiders, or his situation would become intolerable. His detachments, except in large bodies, could not venture out of camp without danger of being attacked by rebel cavalry. Later on, one day, a report came that our outposts were attacked and part of them captured within a few miles of his main army. Rosenfelt was greatly excited to think that with his force of cavalry—one brigade at Nashua, one at Franktown supported by a division of infantry at each place, and two brigades at his main position—the rebels were audacious enough to come in sight of his camp and menace him. Just at this moment Gen. Sherlin, a small man, but a great soldier, came into his headquarters and said:

"'General, how would you like to have an infantry commander take one of your detachments of cavalry and try his hand on Van Doring, who, I understand, is running round your camp playing marbles on your boys' coat-tails?'

"'Well, sir,' said Rosenfelt, 'I wish we had some one like old Col. Harden at Dolinsburg after this fellow Van Doring. Do you think you can run him back on his own ground?'

"'I will try.'

"'Well, sir, you may try your hand to-day.'

"'All right,' said Sherlin; 'I am now ready, and I want only 1,000 men.'

"The General ordered two regiments to report; they did so promptly, and were off. They started with Sherlin at their head, and were not long in reaching Brady's Wood, where the enemy was strongly posted. Without hesitating for one moment Sherlin attacked them and charged, saber in hand. The contest was of short duration. The rebels had not seen that kind of cavalry fighting before. They were soon routed and driven in great disorder back to and across Goose River. Sherlin returned the next day with 200 prisoners and a command of encouraged men. This aroused great jealousy with the cavalry officers, and made him the subject of many remarks. But he went quietly back to his command of infantry without any exultation or mention of his victory.

"Gen. Sherlin and Gen. Anderson that evening were speaking of our cavalry, when Sherlin remarked that they only wanted some one to teach them how to fight.

"'That is true,' said Gen. Anderson; 'we must obtain consent to go out and attack the enemy whenever and wherever we may find him. We now have re-enforcements, our army is fresh and well supplied in all respects.'

"The General commanding finding this feeling existing, and seeing that his re-enforcements had all come forward and were in camp, amounting to some 14,000, while Biggs had only received the 5,000 cavalry under Van Doring, he felt that he could afford to make a forward movement and attack his antagonist wherever he might be found. So he commenced by directing that our forces were to make Goose River our line for the present, by first driving the enemy to the south side of the same, and if possible force him out of this part of the country.

"Sherlin's division and two brigades of cavalry were to march to Eagle Cove and thence to Columbiana; Sleeman's division, with other troops, were to form the center; the left was to move on Shelltown;—the whole to concentrate on and along the north bank of Goose River. Gen. Corbin, being in advance on the road leading to Columbiana, met Van Doring at Spring Hill, and after five hours' hard fighting surrendered his whole command. When this news reached Rosenfelt, who was still at Murphy's Hill, it disturbed him much. The troops having now marched for a week over very bad roads through rain and mud, he directed them to return to their former positions, 'having accomplished all that the commanding General desired,' as he said.

"Kentucky was at this time infested with raiders and guerrillas. Gen. Broomfield, who had about that time been sent to the West to command the Department of Kentucky, soon cleared that State of these pests. Their mode of warfare on either side was merely harassing without accomplishing any great results. Very soon Rosenfelt's troops were again within his old camp lines, and Forrester commenced annoying him in many ways. Gen. Papson being at Rosenfelt's Headquarters, in conversation remarked:

"'If you will allow Gen. Anderson, of my corps, to take command of a division of your cavalry, and give him instructions that Forrester must be driven beyond Goose River and kept there, I will guarantee good results.'

"Rosenfelt readily assented, and the arrangements were made and the order given. The command started, and by rapid marches came up to Forrester at a point near Auburnville, and drove him as far as Winter Hill, a point where the general headquarters of the rebel cavalry had been for some days. Gen. Anderson charged down upon them with his whole force in regular old English cavalry style, with drawn sabers. The rebel cavalry made stubborn resistance, but our force drove them from their position with much slaughter. They retreated in great confusion, and were closely pursued and sorely pressed until they were forced to cross Goose River at different points. The country was now cleared of them for the present. Gen. Anderson returned with 500 prisoners. This ended the raids, and our army was not subjected to these harassing exploits again while it remained at Murphy's Hill. During these many annoyances by the rebel cavalry our troops were sent after them so frequently and marched so rapidly, and at times such great distances, that they often became weary and footsore.

"The day after Gen. Anderson returned from driving Forrester out of this portion of the country a division of infantry under Sleeman returned from a very long and circuitous march. On the detail for guard duty that night was a boy from one of the Michigan regiments, (the 1st Michigan I think,) who during the night was found asleep on his watch. He was arrested and taken to the guard-house. The young man was greatly troubled. He had been a good soldier; had never shirked any duty imposed upon him. The next day he was reported by Serg't Smith as being found asleep while on duty. This was a serious matter,— the penalty being death if found guilty. The report was taken to Gen. Sleeman, and by him transmitted to Gen. Rosenfelt with a request that he order the Court-Martial, if one should be decided upon. The General at once ordered the Court. I never have believed that severe punishments in the army were productive of good discipline. The best soldiers are the kindest men, and the most successful are those who inflict the fewest severe punishments upon their men. The detail for the Court was made and the charges filed.

"The Court held its sessions at Gen. Rosenfelt's Headquarters. The poor boy was brought out of the guardhouse in the presence of the Court. He was 20 years old, very slight, light complexion, light auburn hair, large blue eyes, delicate frame, and, in fact, looked almost as much like a girl as a boy. His appearance made a deep impression upon the members of the Court; great sympathy was felt for him. The Judge-Advocate asked him if he had any objections to the Court, which was composed of officers from Gen. Sleeman's Division, with Gen. Sleeman as President of the Court. The boy answered that he had no objections; 'for,' said he, "I do not know any of the officers. I know but few persons in the army. I know only my messmates. I am not acquainted with any of the officers of my own company. I know their names, but have no personal acqaintance with either of them.'

"'Do you never talk with any of your company officers?' inquired the Judge-Advocate.

"'No, sir,' replied the youth; 'I have never asked a favor since I have been in the army. I have obeyed orders, and strictly performed my duty and asked no questions.'

"'Have you any relatives?'

"'Yes, sir; I have an aged father and mother, and one sister.'

"'What was your business before entering the service?'

"'I was a sales-boy in the wholesale dry-goods store of Baldwin & Chandler, in Detroit, Mich., where my parents live.'

"'Have you written to your parents or sister since your arrest?'

"'No, sir; I asked permission to do so, but it was refused me.'

"Gen. Sleeman, an old man, full of sympathy and kind feelings, on the impulse of the moment said, 'That was an outrage.'

"The Judge-Advocate reminded the General that such remarks were not proper in the presence of the Court.

"'Yes,' said the General, 'I spoke before I thought; but the impropriety of the remark does not change my opinion.'

"The charges were read to the boy, charging him that in this, 'he, James Whitcomb, a private soldier, was regularly detailed and placed on guard duty, and that he slept while on post in the face of the enemy, thereby endangering the Army of the United States.'

"The Judge-Advocate advised the boy to plead 'not guilty,' which he did.

"Just at this moment Capt. Jackson Lyon came along where the Court was in session, and for the first time heard of this trial. He listened for a moment and heard the name of the boy mentioned, and it struck him at once that it might be Seraine's brother. He waited until the Court adjourned and asked permission to speak to the boy. It being granted, he ascertained that James Whitcomb was the brother of Seraine, who had gone South in search of Henry. He told the boy to be of good cheer—to admit nothing; that when they proved the charge, as perhaps they would, to ask permission to make a statement, and then to tell all about his march; the reason for his inability to keep awake, and all about his condition on that night, and that he, Capt. Jackson Lyon, would look after him; but not to mention him as his friend, but as one only feeling a sympathy for him.

"Jackson wrote to me that day all about the case, and thought it was best that his father and mother should not be made aware of his arrest and trial, but that I should write to the President all about the case, and do no more until he (Jackson) should arrive. My son Jackson was a very cool-headed man, and always did everything in the manner that would create the least excitement or suspicion. You see, he had a plan in a moment for the safety of this poor boy.

"Well, to get back. The next day the Court reassembled at 12 o'clock and proceeded with the trial. The witnesses were sworn. Serg't Smith exhibited the detail for the guard, as well as the detail from the boy's company, and the report of the detail to him with James Whitcomb's name on the same. He then showed the time for the boy's guard-duty to commence on that relief, and finally, by the Officer of the Guard who went around with the relief guard, that the boy was found asleep and did not arouse from his slumber when he was challenged, but that the Sergeant of the Guard had to shake him quite hard to arouse him. This, you can see, was very strong and hard to get over."

"Yes," said Col. Bush, "that was a strong case. I was hoping to hear that there was a mistake about it."

Maj. Clymer said: "Well, I hope he was acquitted. I have slept many a time on my horse during a hard march, when if I had been placed on guard-duty I would have gone to sleep in five minutes."

"So have I," said Capt. Zeke Inglesby.

"Yes, yes. I have no doubt of that; but it is not the men who commit acts against law that are always punished, but those who are caught. These men seemed to think this a terrible crime in this boy, and yet, perhaps, there was not one of them who could have done differently under the same circumstances.

"After the witnesses had been heard against the poor boy, he showed great mental suffering and agony; the disgrace to his parents and sister was what troubled him so much. His company officers were sworn, and stated that prior to this no complaint had ever been made against the boy. That although they only knew him as a soldier, they had always observed his neatness and soldierly appearance and bearing; they all thought that the march the two days before and until 9 o'clock the night on which he was found asleep on post, was calculated to tire out a boy of his frail organization.

"The Chief Surgeon stated that a boy of his constitution would be very likely to drop to sleep anywhere after such a strain upon his physical strength.

"This closed the evidence with the exception of one witness. The boy asked if he could make a statement to the Court. Some discussion arose on this point. The Court was cleared, and Jackson said that he afterwards learned that old Gen. Sleeman grew very angry at the idea of refusing an innocent boy a chance to say a word in his own defense. Finally, it was agreed that the boy might make his statement. He arose, and, with a tremulous voice and much agitation, said:

"'Gentlemen of the Court: I am a poor boy. My life is of no value to me, and but little to my country. I have risked it several times without fear or nervousness. For

my parents' sake I would like to go through this war with
an honorable record. To take my life would do me but
little harm. I can meet death as a true soldier. But what
can this great Government gain by taking my life? You
can inflict ruin, distress and misery upon an old man and
woman, and upon my queenly sister, who is now going
through more perils, if I am correctly informed, than any
of us. I came to the army not for gain. I was getting
much more pay without risking my life, but I felt it
my duty to aid in sustaining our Government. I did not
dream, however, that in the event that I should escape
death from the hands of the enemies of our country that,
for an unhappy result entirely unavoidable, my comrades-
in-arms would hasten to make a sacrifice of me. Were I
guilty of anything that I could have avoided, then I would
not ask for leniency; but this I could not avoid. That I
slept on my post I will not deny; but I pray you hear my
excuse. It is this: Two days before this offense was committed, we had marched through rain and mud some
twenty miles in pursuit (as it was said) of Forrester's cavalry. I did not see many horse tracks in the road, however, and took it that our forces had captured all their
horses, and that the rebels were taking it on foot, as we were.'

"Here Gen. Sleeman laughed, and said *sotto voce:*

"'That boy ought to be put in command of our cavalry,
instead of being shot.'

"'The night of this march my messmate, John Martin, a
boy of my own age and my neighbor before coming to the
army, was taken quite ill. It was his turn to be on guard.
I took his guard duty that night, and was entirely without
sleep. When not on post I was attending to him, as he
would have done for me. The next day John was not able
to carry his knapsack and gun on the march, and as we
had no transportation, I carried his as well as my own.
The burden was very great for me, and when we arrived in
camp I was completely exhausted. John was not able to
stand my guard, and when I told the Sergeant my condition, he would not excuse me, and gave as a reason that I
had no business to carry John's gun and knapsack, inas-

much as I had no orders from him to do so. I think the Sergeant would do much better as a General than as a Sergeant. I may do him injustice, and I would not do that for the world, but I do believe that he entertains the same high opinion of himself that I do of him.'

"At which remark old Gen. Sleeman laughed again, and said, so as to be heard, 'That boy will be a man some day, and, by the eternal, it would be a crime—yes, a murder—to shoot him.'

"Continuing, James Whitcomb said: 'This, gentlemen of the Court, is my excuse, no more, no less. I hope that John Martin may be called to verify my statement.'

"When the boy sat down the whole Court were in tears.

"John Martin was called, and he did verify everything that had been stated by James Whitcomb. This closed the evidence in the case. The Court adjourned until the next day at 12 o'clock. When they met they began the consideration of the verdict. The Judge-Advocate charged the Court that the evidence was clear and conclusive; that the law fixed the penalty; that there was no way out of it; they must find the fact that he did sleep on his post, and that fact being found, the verdict must be death.

"The Court was two days coming to a conclusion. When they did, my God, it was enough to make a man's blood run cold in his veins. They found him guilty on all the charges and specifications, and sentenced him to be shot to death, with only ten days' respite. The sentence was approved, and orders given to manacle the boy and double his guard. Gen. Sleeman raved like a madman, and came near resigning; said if the boy was shot he would at once resign. As soon as the judgment of the Court was known, Jackson took a leave of absence for ten days and left on the train that evening for home. He came, and on his arrival was looking like a ghost. All ran to him to welcome him.

"He soon assumed his wonted calmness, and talked with his mother, Mary Anderson and Jennie, as well as the little girls, telling them all about the army. His mother was still sick in bed over the murder of our son Stephen; but we all enjoyed seeing Jackson, and were glad to know that Peter and Gen. Anderson were well. Our family, you will observe, was not very large at this time. Jackson made Aunt Martha happy by telling her that Ham was well, and was behaving splendidly.

"'Thank de good Laud for dat. I always 'spects to hear he killed. But I knows Ham; he am awful coward. He allers runs off when dere is any danger. I have to look out for dat.'

"Jackson had a full report of the proceedings of the Court-Martial so far as the testimony and the boy's statement was concerned. He read the whole statement over to Jennie (David's widow), Mary Anderson and myself. As he read the boy's statement the two ladies burst into tears. Mary Anderson arose and walked the floor, looking like a Queen, and seemingly much excited. Finally she said—I shall ever remember her words:

"'My God, what does all this mean? Has the great Father forsaken this family? Four have already lost their lives, and one now suffering in some loathsome prison if alive; my husband and Peter nearly at death's door on more than one occasion; Seraine Whitcomb, a lovely girl, with her only brother in the army (he a mere boy), she leaves her old father and mother to take the chances of her life through the lines searching for one of our family, and now her only brother under sentence of death for what he could not help doing. Capt. Jackson, what do you propose?'

"Jackson replied that some one must proceed to Washington at once, and that he thought it was not best to let the boy's parents in Detroit know the facts, they being old people and alone (according to the statement of the boy), and as the young lady is doubtless searching for Henry, as we all surmise from her letter to our father, it is certainly our duty to look after this boy's case ourselves. I have only ten days' leave from my duty, and therefore brought these papers, thinking that father might perhaps go to see the President.

"Mary Anderson spoke up at once and said:

"'No, sir; no, sir. Your father will not go. He must

not leave Aunt Sarah in her present condition. I will go; yes, I will go at once. Get me a ticket, I want no trunk; my satchel will do. I will be off on the first train.'

" Jennie said, ' Why, Mary, you will not go, will you?'

" ' Yes, I am going. I am determined to do so. It is settled; so do not attempt to stop me.'

" ' Well,' said Jennie, ' Uncle Daniel, what shall we do? '

" I replied, ' She is determined on it, and we will just help her to get off at once.'

" So the ticket was procured and Mary was off with a good-bye, taking with her a full statement of the case made out by Jackson, also his letter, and a letter from me to the President. Under the circumstances this was a painful trip to her—the anxiety as to her success; the fact that she knew nothing about the family in whose behalf she was enlisted. She a stranger to the President, how should she approach him? What could she say to him? Suppose he would refuse to interpose in behalf of the boy? And a thousand inquiries would come to her mind to annoy her. She slept none on her way, but finally arrived safely in Washington, and went directly to the Executive Mansion without stopping to take a mouthful of food'or a moment's repose.

" When she reached the threshold of the mansion she came near fainting; her courage and strength both seemed to leave her all at once. Presently her strength returned, and she asked to be admitted. The usher said, 'I will see,' and took her name to the President; also my letter. The President was alone. She could not speak. The President came forward and took her by the hand and greeted her most kindly, saying that he almost knew her; that he knew much of her through me, as I had spoken of her in connection with her husband. The President said :

" ' Your brave husband is so well known to me through my friend Mr. Lyon, and through his daring on the field, that you would need no introduction more than that I should know who you are; and I take it that you are on an errand of mercy, as I am sure you could not be here to ask anything for your husband, as I would do anything

for him, as he knows, merely for the asking by himself
or my friend Lyon.'

"'No, Mr. President; you will never be troubled by me
in that way. I am truly on an errand of mercy and justice'; and here she broke down and wept.

"When she recovered she said:

"'Mr. President, my errand is to save the destruction of
a good family.'

"She then recited the facts as to the two old people, and
that Seraine, the only daughter, was now on an errand of
mercy South somewhere.

"The President replied that he remembered giving her a
letter at the request of his friend Daniel Lyon, and said :

"'My dear Mrs. Anderson, there is hardly anything that
I would not do for any of Mr. Lyon's family, as well as Gen.
Anderson and yourself ; and, certainly, if to prevent a calamity to such a family as you describe Mr. Whitcomb's to
be, I would do anything that would be proper and reasonable for me to do.'

"She was very much encouraged by these remarks, and
began to feel more at ease.

"The President, seeing this, asked her many questions
about her husband's health, and also about my family.
When she spoke of Stephen's foul murder, the President
walked the floor and remarked :

"'Most diabolical—fiendish.'

("Little did he or she then suppose that it was her own
brother that had committed this wicked and cruel murder.)

"By this time she was so much encouraged that she
handed him the letter and statement of Jackson.

"The President read the letter, and then read and re-
read Jackson's statement. Great tears rolled down his
bronzed cheeks as he read the statement. He tapped a
bell, and sent for the Secretary of War. The Secretary soon
came, and greeted Mrs. Anderson very cordially on being
introduced. The President asked him to take a seat, and
handed him the statement. He read it, and said :

"'I will at once see if any papers in this case have been
forwarded.'

"During all this time imagine the suspense and fears of Mary Anderson.

"The Secretary sent to the Judge-Advocate-General, and found that the papers had just arrived.

"The President said :

"'Let them be brought to me immediately.'

"When they were placed before him he read them over carefully, remarking, when he had finished, that they were exactly as stated by Capt. Lyon. He handed them to the Secretary and asked him to read them, which he did, and laid them down without a word of comment.

"After some conversation between the two men, the President turned to her and said :

"'Mrs. Anderson, cheer up, weep no more ; your friend shall not be hurt ! Instead of showing himself unworthy of clemency he has proven himself a noble boy. The kindness which he showed to his messmate and neighbor boy was enough to have commended him to mercy. He should have been complimented for his kindness and excused from duty, instead of having it imposed upon him. You can go home and bear the glad tidings to his father and mother that their boy shall be saved for a better fate.'

"Mary Anderson, trembling with emotion, said :

"'Mr. President, you are so very kind, sir. But, if you will pardon me, his father and mother know nothing of their boy's trouble. We kept it from them, believing it would have caused them great distress. We desire to keep it from them.'

"'Do you say that his father and mother do not know of this, nor that you are here ?'

"'Mr. President, they are not aware of the case.'

"'Mrs. Anderson, that was very considerate in your friends and yourself, to keep this from them for the present at least.'

"The President then wrote, with his own hand, a telegram, ordering the suspension of sentence against James Whitcomb—that he had been fully pardoned—signed it and sent it to the office with directions that the dispatch be sent at once. Mary Anderson on her knees thanked the

President from the fullness of her heart. He bade her rise; said he had done nothing that she should thank him for; that if he had permitted such a sentence to be carried out he never could have forgiven himself. He bade her go home and carry the good tidings to her friends. He told her to give me and my family his kindest regards. She then left with a light heart.

"She went directly to the train, forgetting that she had eaten nothing during the day. She returned to us one of the happiest persons that ever lived, and you may depend upon it that we all shared in her joy. Capt. Jackson had returned to his command prior to Mary's return from Washington. When we all got through with the family talk and Mary had eaten her dinner, she gave us a full account of her trip, her agonies and sensations on meeting the President. She was exceedingly happy in her details about her trip and her success; but, strange to say, she never alluded to it again voluntarily, and would, as much as possible, avoid conversation on the subject when spoken to in reference to it.

"Gen. Anderson had asked that James Whitcomb be detailed from his regiment and assigned to him as an Orderly at his Headquarters, which was done. And again all was moving on quietly in the field."

"Yes," said Capt. Inglesby, "as I before stated, there would have been warm times in that camp had they shot that boy. The whole camp had heard the facts about his helping his comrade, and the soldiers with one voice said he should not be executed. His pardon was a Godsend to the officers who were intending to carry out the sentence. During all my experience (and I was through the whole war) I never knew such a mutinous feeling in the army as that sentence created."

Dr. Adams remarked that in all his reading and experience in life there had not been a female character brought to his notice who had shown the will, determination and good judgment that Mrs. Anderson had from the beginning of the war; her fixed Union principles; her determination to make any and all sacrifices for the cause of her country;

her persistence in hunting for her husband when all others were sure of his death at Dolinsburg—few women like her have lived in our time. "God bless her, whether she is living or dead!"

The tears rolled down the old man's cheeks, but he uttered not one word in response.

7

CHAPTER XII.

> "*If that rebellion*
> *Came like itself, in base and abject routs,*
> *Led on by bloody youth, guarded with rage,*
>   *   *   *   *   *
> *You revered father, and these noble lords*
> *Had not been here to dress the ugly form*
> *Of base and bloody insurrection.*"—SHAKESPEARE.

"AFTER the long-continued idleness of the Army of
the Center around Murphy's Hill, the people began
to clamor for a movement of some decisive character. During Gen. Rosenfelt's inactivity, Gen.
Silent had moved with the Army of the West against Gen.
Pendleton, who had continued to obstruct Conception River
by holding Victor's Hill, as well as the grand bluffs below.
Gen. Silent had made some of the most wonderful marches
and successes ever known. He had opened ways for the water
to flow from the river into the lands; had cut canals through
at different points; had run the batteries of an hundred guns
with his transports laden with supplies for his army;
marched on the opposite side of the river below Pendleton,
crossing his army below the Grand Bluffs in one day and
night; moved out against the enemy, who was in superior
force, cutting loose from his own base of supplies, and
fought him in six hardly-contested battles with victorious
results each time, and he finally succeeded in hemming Pendleton inside his fortifications at Victor's Hill and forcing
him, with his entire army, to surrender unconditionally.

"The President had also in the meantime placed Gen.
Meader in command of the Army of the East on account of

the constant failure of other commanders during the Spring campaigns. Soon after assuming command Meador had gained a great victory over the enemy at Gotlenburg, and had driven him back across Grand River to his own ground. The enemy had become so encouraged by his victories over our armies heretofore, that he concluded to try a second invasion of the loyal States.

"The people who desired the success of the Union forces were greatly rejoiced over the victory at Gotlenburg and in

MORGANSON'S RAID.

the West by Gen. Silent, and by them Rosenfelt was constantly urged to do something by way of giving some activity to his army. But he hesitated and thought the heat of Summer was too great in that climate for his men to march and endure the fatigues of a campaign. This was so discouraging to his troops that many of them sought relief by obtaining a leave of absence and returning home for a few days. Among those who returned were Gen. Anderson and my son Peter. When they arrived at home all greeted them with many hearty welcomes. My wife by this time had so far recovered as to be up a portion of the day, and the return of the General and Peter seemed to revive her drooping spirits. The children were overjoyed and Aunt Martha was as much delighted as any of the family, and repeated her confidence in the "good Laud's" having saved the General for some good purpose. Finally she could not restrain herself any longer, and said:

"'Massa Gen'l, what you do wid Ham? Whar is he? I 'spect he be kill and you done 'cluded you not tell ole Marfa'.

"'No, Martha,' said the General; 'Ham is well. I left him with Capt. Jackson and Capt. Day to take care of our traps.'

"'Well, dat's all right. I feered he kill.'

"'No, Aunty; he is all right.'

"The next day Joseph Dent came in from the farm and told us he had learned the night before that a meeting of a few of the leading men had been held at Windsor, Canada, and that meetings were to be held at different places in the Northern States by prominent Knights of the Circle to consider what was best to be done, and also to appoint delegates to meet somewhere in Canada at a time and place to be hereafter designated, and that several propositions were being considered about work which would be undertaken very soon; such as destroying property, raiding in the North, releasing prisoners, etc.

"This information was of such a character that we deemed it important to have a full report of what was at the time being done in Canada, as that seemed to be the base of the enemy's operations for our part of the country, and inasmuch as Peter had promised James Whitcomb, now Orderly to Gen. Anderson, that he would go to Detroit and visit his aged parents and satisfy them of his innocence should they have learned of his misfortune in having been court-martialed and condemned, we concluded that this would be an excellent opportunity for him to pass over to Windsor or elsewhere in Canada and gather what information he could. This being understood, he left at once, desirous that no time should be lost during his leave of absence.

The family being gathered in the parlor that evening, Gen. Anderson said:

"'Mary, now give us your experience as a visitor at the White House; how the President appeared to you, etc.'

"Mary related what had transpired in a modest way, saying in conclusion that nothing but the feeling aroused in her breast by the outrage that was about to be perpetrated upon that poor, innocent boy could have induced her to have undertaken such an expedition. She said she could do anything except to ask favors. Said she:

"'Tom, my dear, you need have no fears about my ever becoming a lobbyist in Washington, or a courtier at the White House. I have tried appealing to the President once, and although successful that time, and treated courteously and kindly by that big-hearted and noble old patriot, yet I have hardly recovered from my scare up to this time; and now I do hope that you will never mention this again, for it does really give me a palpitation of the heart whenever the subject is alluded to. I am a coward, I know I am, and am frightened still.'

"'Well, Mary, you did a noble act, and I am the prouder of you for it.' He kissed her and she sank down in her chair overcome with emotion. We then changed the subject, and the General entertained us by recitals of the trials and vicissitudes of the army. We were all enjoying the visit of the General very much and hoped to have a pleasant time, but a few days after his arrival the country about Allentown became greatly alarmed and excited.

"Gen. Morganson, of whom I have heretofore spoken, had crossed from Kentucky at or near Louis City into Indiana, and was raiding the country, taking horses, wagons, and all kinds of property that could serve any purpose whatever in aiding the rebellion or in facilitating its movements. Stores were pillaged, houses plundered, banks robbed, and farms laid waste. The people were taken entirely by surprise, and the only thing that could be resorted to to meet the emergency that was upon them, was for the loyal citizens along the raider's path before and behind to assemble and make resistance and obstruction to his march. Gen. Anderson, comprehending the situation, at once gathered together a few men and started in pursuit of Morganson. He collected men and material as he went. He also aroused the people to action everywhere. Morganson's force was being recruited from the Golden Circle as he passed through the country.

"That community was never so thoroughly excited before. Many murders were committed on his line of march, and this one had lost his horses, that one had his house plundered ; this town had been sacked, and in some instances burned, and so on.

"Gen. Anderson made his march as rapidly as he could with raw men and horses. He finally struck Morganson's rear and forced him to make a stand. Gen. Anderson dismounted his men and told every man to cover himself behind a tree where it could be done. The contest lasted for about an hour, when a small body of men who had been gathered together in advance of the raiders, struck him in the rear, as he was then facing, and caused a great stampede, and his force broke in various directions through the woods. Morganson turned upon this small force and drove it back, making his escape. Gen. Anderson followed him up closely, however, forcing him to change his course in the direction of the river. Gen. Broomfield had withdrawn a small force from Kentucky, which finally joined Gen. Anderson. Morganson was preparing to cross the river at a point near an island, the water being shallow there. Gen. Anderson with his raw recruits and about 100 of Broomfield's men at once assaulted him, broke his line, and killed and wounded many of his men as they were attempting to cross the river. After hard fighting for a few moments Morganson and those of his command that were still with him surrendered.

This ended the raiders and their foolish exploits. The men who had volunteered to follow Gen. Anderson were of all ages and sizes—from the schoolboy to the grandfather. None of them had been in the army or at any time seen service, so that they were without any sort of discipline, with the exception of a few who were at home on furlough from their regiments, and some of Gen. Broomfield's command. But Gen. Anderson said that they fought like veterans, each one in his own way. Morganson and his command were taken to Camp Chase for safe keeping, and Gen. Anderson returned to Allentown to enjoy the leave of absence interrupted by the raiders.

"Joseph Dent came in the next morning after Gen. Anderson's return, and told us that when Morganson entered Indiana on his raid the Golden Circles were notified, and were getting ready to join him and make war all over the State, but that he appeared too soon for them; that on account of his (Dent's) illness he had not been able to advise us earlier."

Dr. Adams inquired who this Gen. Morganson was.

Uncle Daniel said: "He was part of Forrester's command, that had raided around Rosenfelt so much during the previous Winter and Spring. He had crossed the Combination River to the east of Rosenfelt at Carthage, moving nearly due south by way of Greenberry, avoiding all points at which there were Union troops. He doubtless believed either that the members of the Golden Circle were ready to join him, armed and equipped, or that his raid would strike consternation into the hearts of the people, inasmuch as our armies were all far away from where he proposed to lay the scene of his audacious exploits. But he made a mistake when he began to take horses and other property from all alike, whether Union men or rebel sympathizers. This changed the sentiments of many people very rapidly."

Said Maj. Clymer: "What has become of Gen. Morganson? I have not heard of him since the war."

"He was killed somewhere in Tennessee soon after his escape from Camp Chase, so I have been informed.

"During Gen. Anderson's absence in pursuit of Morganson, Peter was traveling rapidly through Canada. He returned the day following Gen. Anderson's from his capture of the raiders.

"The people everywhere seemed to be greatly rejoiced at the General's success. He received a great ovation from the citizens of Allentown, and they cheered whenever he made his appearance. This caused him to keep very close to the house, as he was not fond of demonstration. The people, however, flocked to see him, and many of them could see great virtues in our family who, prior to that time, did not know us because we were not good enough for their society. So you see their own safety was the patriotic spark that burned brightly in their bosoms. But this is human nature. Selfishness seems to pervade nearly all, as is evidenced every day. Many of those who wanted the rebellion to succeed did so not because they were really rebels, but because they had said that we could not conquer them, and were willing to see our Government destroyed, merely to get a chance in the future to say to every one, 'I told you so.' These people now want the Government placed in the hands of its enemies for the same reason, so as to say, 'You cannot keep the control out of the hands of such able and brave men as these.' Thus, you see, it is in many merely a selfish pride of former expressed opinions."

"That is a new idea, Uncle Daniel," said Dr. Adams; "but I am not sure but there is much in what you say."

"Yes, Doctor; experience and close observation have taught me many things that I would have been slow to believe years ago. I am wandering, however, from what I was stating.

"The next evening after Peter's return we were all at tea and while at the table Aunt Sarah, my good wife, asked Peter the condition of his foot. Peter replied that it was nearly well; he did not suffer from it except occasionally when he caught cold in it.

"'You must be very careful, Peter,' said she; 'I am fearful about it. You know how your brother James lingered and finally died with a mere cut on his hand. I was disturbed about your wound last night in my sleep. I was dreaming about it.'

"'Well, mother,' said Peter, 'you seem to be dreaming something constantly, and will continue to do so, so long as you allow yonself to be worried.'

"But Peter ceased speaking on the subject, and his face took the sad expression that seemed to have fixed itself upon him. I then spoke up to relieve the matter and said, 'Wife, you must not worry so much. You are just able to be out, and I fear you will make yourself sick again. Peter will take care of himself,—at least I hope so.'

"Aunt Martha seemed to be listening to our conversation, and (having been greatly indulged by all our family on account of marked kindness to Gen. Anderson as well as to all the rest of the family) here chimed in and said:

"'Marsa Lyon, I tells you dat you is wrong on dat pint. De mans don't know how to take kear of demsefs. Now, dars Ham. He's like to get kill any day, he am. He don't know nuffin, he don't.'

"Gen. Anderson and Peter laughed when she spoke of Ham getting killed. Peter seemed to lose for the time-being his sad countenance, when he remembered about Ham getting under the brush at Stone Run.

"Aunt Martha knew nothing about Ham's precipitate retreat during the last battle, so she continued by saying:

"'Jes' see, Massa Tom, de Gen'l dar. Whar he bin if he lef' wid de mans when he got shotted at dat fight at Dolinsburg? He done bin dead sho. Dars whar he bin. I tell you de good Land know who he trus' him wid; yes sah, he do. So he put him wid me and den he make my ole head cifer out de cures what fotched him out. Jes' kase he want Marsa for good work, dat's why. What would Ham do curin' him up? No, sah, he not know how, and de Laud no trus' him.'

"Peter said: 'Aunt Martha, you rather like the Lord, I take it.'

"'Yes, sah, I do. He be good. He fotched de poor darkies out ob workin' all de time for nuffin for dem Sesh, and he know what he doin'. He goin' to let dem Sesh 'spect dat dey whip dem Yanks affer while, but he not let dem do it. He jes' coaxin' dem on till he git good men hold of de army, den dey all git smash up. Jes' like Gen'l Tom, de Laud save him for dat. Don't you see dat? My!

when Marsa Tom git after dem Sesh, dey done gits ebry
time, dey do; don't dey, Marsa Lyon.'

"I agreed with her and the rest laughed. She finally cut
her speech short and retired to the kitchen.

"After tea Gen. Anderson gave us quite an amusing account of his little improvised army that followed Morganson. He said no braver set of men ever marched, but that
it was very hard to tell his men from the raiders when
they got together; that some were riding in saddles and
some without, substituting a doubled up blanket or quilt;
some were on old and some were on young horses; some
were on ponies and some on mules, some wore 'stove-pipe'
hats, some caps, some straw hats, and some were without
either. Some had on frock, some dress, and some round-
coats, and many entirely without coats of any kind; some
with boots, some with shoes, and some entirely barefoot.
Take them all in all, they were in dress à la Falstaff's troop,
but they were a success, and did what the Army of the
Center, under Rosenfelt, had failed to do, and that was to
capture the rebel cavalry. This raid of Morganson was an
audacious adventure, doubtless encouraged by the Knights
of the Golden Circle, and had he waited long enough I have
no doubt that we would have had an uprising in Indiana
that would have been very troublesome to put down. It
was quite fortunate that it occurred when it did."

"Yes," said Dr. Adams; "I have no doubt that plans
were being perfected about that time and later on for a
general raiding and plunder of many cities, as well as portions of the North outside of cities, where we could be seriously damaged."

Uncle Daniel resumed, saying: "During that evening we
discussed matters generally, but Peter felt very much disappointed at his being absent in Canada while Gen. Anderson was bagging Morganson. He said that it was just his
luck to miss everything of this kind, but that he always
had the luck to get into some hard place in front of the
enemy, and usually get hurt in some way or other, but that
when it came to getting rebels into a place where they could
be easily whipped or captured or chased out of the country,

the luck seemed always to fall to Gen. Anderson. He turned to the General, and with a twinkle of the eye asked him if he had Ham with him to assist in hiving these Sesh. The General laughed and said no; that Ham was back watching out for the Army of the Center and keeping Gen. Forrester from coming in some morning and taking away our trunks and camp equipage. At this they both laughed.

"Peter said: 'Ham will not have quite the trouble that we have all had heretofore since Forrester's command has been depleted by Morganson's capture.'

"'No,' replied the General; 'he will only need to watch one of them now.' The conversation then turned on Peter's trip into Canada.

"I inquired if he saw Mr. and Mrs. Whitcomb. He said that he spent one night at their house; said they were nice old people, very religious, and lovely in every respect; that they were very proud of their children and spoke of James as a brave and good boy. They knew nothing whatever about his having been in trouble. When he told them that he knew him and that he was on duty with Gen. Anderson, they were delighted, and asked many questions about the army, our prospects, etc. They spoke of Seraine as their lovely daughter; knew about her mission, her fondness for Henry, and, in fact, gave him much information about Henry prior to the war that we did not know. Altogether his stay with them was very pleasant. After hearing about these good people, in whom we all felt an interest, I insisted on his now giving us a full report of what he had found out about the situation in Canada in reference to the conspiracy and conspirators.

He stated that on leaving Detroit, Mich., he went directly to Windsor, and while there became acquainted with several gentlemen, one from Chicago in particular by the name of John Wall. Peter, having learned all about the Golden Circle, their signs, passwords, etc., had no trouble in making himself known, and, as he represented that he was from Nashville, Tenn., he got along without being suspected by any one. Wall and he became friends at once, and as they had rooms adjacent at the hotel they were together the first night in Peter's room until very late. Wall knew all about Morganson's raid, but not about his failure and capture. Peter learned that on his way home from the Detroit papers. Wall told Peter that he feared Morganson would not succeed in obtaining many recruits, as the authorities in Canada at the head of the organization had not furnished the arms that were promised to their friends in Indiana and Ohio; that he was at that time there for the purpose of procuring arms for Illinois, and that he had been sent there to see Mr. Jacob Thomlinson and a Mr. C. C. Carey on that business. He said he was to have the arms smuggled through to Chicago, where they would be subject to the orders of one Mr. N. Judy Cornington, and that the intention was to release the prisoners at Chicago and Rock Island at a time to be agreed upon for Camp Chase, Chicago, and other places. At this point Gen. Anderson inquired if Wall was a man about five feet eight inches in height, heavy build, gray eyes and light hair mixed with gray, about half and half. Peter replied in the affirmative. The General said

" ' He is the same man Wall that I met in company with Cornington, Buckner and Eagle when I was in Chicago on my voyage of discovery.'

" 'No doubt of it,' said Peter. Peter continued by saying that Wall gave him full particulars as to what was intended. He said that so soon as arms could be procured and the prisoners released it would be made so hot for the Abolitionists, as he called the Union men, that they would be glad to call their army back from the South in order to protect themselves against fire and plunder in the North; that men were now organizing to burn many of the cities North, and if that did not bring the Abolitionists to terms other methods would be resorted to, but that the destruction of property would be effective, as the North cared more for their property than they did for the Government. The next day they met a man by the name of Tucker, who was on his way to Montreal, where he was to meet Jacob Thomlinson and Mr. Carey, in order to consult with them about what was to be done in the direction mentioned by Wall.

He said that arms must be procured at once; that the friends North were ready but that no means had yet been provided so that they could act. He thought that if Jacob Thomlinson did not have the arms in Canada he should at once proceed or send to England for them; that he was ready himself to perform the journey. To this Wall replied 'That is all that is wanted in Illinois.' Tucker said that already men were in England procuring and preparing material only recently discovered that would burn up all the cities of the North without endangering the parties applying it, and should this fail something else must be resorted to; that the Confederacy could not and must not fail. He was in favor of assassinating every leading man North if absolutely necessary to procure their independence.

"Peter met several other Southern men while in Canada, as well as quite a number of Northern men, who were in the conspiracy, and said that they all seemed to be imbued with the same feeling and spirit—a determination to have the rebellion succeed at no matter what cost. In their desperation he thought they would resort to any means, no matter how destructive, barbarous, or murderous. He left Wall and Tucker, and visited one or two other places, and then returned, as he thought he was meeting too many Southern men who might afterwards recognize him. His statement only strengthened what we already had reason to believe. Peter also said that this man Tucker and Wall placed great reliance in Valamburg, of Ohio, and Thomas A. Strider and Bowen, of Indiana, and felt sure that they would arouse the people of the North against the Administration to such an extent that the war men would be put out by the people, and anti-war men put in their places, so that a recognition of the Southern Confederacy would be assured. The only thing that seemed to alarm them was the success of Silent at Victor's Hill and Meador at Gotlenburg. They said they had fears that these two men were their greatest enemies, and would relieve from the Union army all the officers who were not Abolitionists. They seemed to mean all who were opposed to the Administration. They appeared to understand but two classes of men in the North —their sympathizing friends, and Abolitionists.

"I made Peter write out his statement and leave it with me. I sent it to the President, and soon received his thanks through his Secretary.

"Two days later Gen. Anderson and Peter left for their commands, and on their arrival at the Army of the Center they were most enthusiastically received by officers and men. An officer said:

"'General, you had to go home to get a chance at the rebs.'

"'Yes,' the General replied, 'Morganson and his men were merely visiting up North during the vacation.'

"The General found his staff officers, orderlies, and old Ham at his Headquarters. When he had seen them all and inquired as to their welfare, he told James Whitcomb about Peter having seen his parents. This delighted the boy very much to think that any of us should care enough about him to seek out his father and mother. Ham, being present, concluded that it was about his time to say a word, so he inquired of the General about Martha. The General told him that she was well, and sent love to him, and said she prayed for his safety.

"Ham laughed and said: 'I's not killed yet, but I 'spec' I will be some day; for de nex' time I's gwine right into de fight, so I is. I jes' tell you, Marsa Gen'l, I done sleep on dis, and jes' make up my mind dat I fight dem Sesh de berry nex' time we git at em.'

"'Well, Ham,' said the General, 'I am not sure that we will need you to do any fighting; but we would like it if you would stay around where we could find you, the next battle in which we are engaged. Will you do that?'

"'Yes, sah! I will, no mistake, dis time.' He got up pretty close to the General, and said, 'Marsa Gen'l, you didn't tole Marfa 'bout I hidin' in de bush, did you?'

"'No, Ham; we said nothing about it to any one.'

"'Thank you, Marsa Gen'l; thank you, sah. I go now an' look after de hoses; I guess dey hungry.'

"'All right, Ham,' said the General; 'go on.'

"Gen. Rosenfelt at this time was reorganizing and putting his army in shape for a forward movement.

"Gen. Papson had been home, and had just returned and was changing some of his divisions. In this change he had assigned some three more regiments to Gen. Anderson, thereby making his division very strong. After the reorganization had been completed, Rosenfelt called several of his Generals together at his Headquarters and talked over the proposition to advance upon the enemy, and found perfect unanimity among them in favor of an early advance. He then said to them that he should move within ten days. His Quartermasters and Commissaries were put to work and were busily engaged in procuring supplies and having them loaded into the several corps and division train-wagons. Everything was active in camp. The horses and mules were being re-shod, and the sound of many anvils could be heard both by day and by night. Officers were supplying their mess-chests and obtaining extra supplies, as they supposed there would not be another opportunity very soon. At this time the Army of the Center numbered some 60,000 effective men, and was in splendid condition as to health, but had grown somewhat lazy after so long a rest in camp with nothing to do. Gen. Biggs, who was in his front, had scattered his forces very much, and while he had fewer infantry than Rosenfelt, he had more cavalry. His cavalry, however, had been diminished by the silly exploit of Morganson, who, as we know, had been captured with many of his men, and those who were not captured had concluded that raiding was unprofitable and did not return to Bigg's army again. His force was divided about as follows: Polkhorn was at Shelltown with about 20,000 men; Harding was at Waterhouse, to the right some distance, with some 10,000 men; and at Tullahoming, with about 15,000 men, lay Chatham in a well-intrenched position, his cavalry to the front and left of his army about 8,000 strong. Gen. Bertram, who surrendered Dolinsburg to Gen. Silent, was now holding Knoxburg and Chatteraugus with some 18,000 men, about equally divided between the two places.

"Rosenfelt was now compelled to attack his intrenched position or move to the left, thereby endangering his communication to the rear. This was somewhat perplexing to him. In marching forward he would be obliged to leave forces behind him to guard his communications, thereby constantly diminishing his strength, while the enemy in falling back would lose none of his strength. Looking at the situation after he was ready, he again concluded not to move. This caused a terrible clamor both in and out of the army. Finally he was ordered peremptorily to move forward against the enemy. He obeyed the order, the army was put in motion, and a forward movement began. The question was how to out maneuver Biggs. A feint was made on Shelltown, which lay in the direct route of his march. This caused Biggs to concentrate his forces at this point. While this movement was being made our main forces were moved by rapid marches to Munster on the enemy's right, which jeopardized his communications with Chatteraugus and the valley south.

"Biggs now finding his forces flanked, and seeing the danger of being cut off from a junction with Bertram, fled precipitately over the mountains to Fayette. Rosenfelt finding that Biggs had retreated in such hot haste, was deceived into the belief that Biggs had gone into Georgia at or near Romulus, and on finding that Bertram had left Chatteraugus with his command, concluded that the enemy were re-enforcing the rebel army in the East, and therefore thought to push on with force enough to attack and defeat him, at the same time holding the strong points in the rear. So he sent Gen. Critsinger with his corps to Chatteraugus, and with the rest of his force marched over the mountain into the valley, intending to have the larger portion of Critsinger's Corps join him in the valley, and then to move south. Instead, however, of Gen. Biggs having sent any portion of his army to re-enforce the rebel army in the East, he was concentrating all his forces at Fayette and quietly awaiting re-enforcements from the East. Gen. Longpath, with a corps of 20,000 men, was moving on railroad cars as rapidly as possible to the sup-

port of Biggs. Gen. Rosenfelt was now on the road between Bridgeton and Fayette without any knowledge as to
the whereabouts of Biggs, and yet he was now within fifteen miles of him, and Biggs with somewhere about 80,000
men was lying in wait for Rosenfelt's advance. During
this afternoon a lady came into camp and asked to be shown
to Gen. Rosenfelt's Headquarters. When she appeared to
the General he at once recognized Mrs. Houghton, who had
made such a trip just before the battle of Murphy's Hill, in
order to give the General the movements of the enemy on
his right the night before the assault. The General was
exceedingly glad to see her. She was invited to partake of
soldiers' fare, and was very pleasantly entertained. As soon
as she could get an opportunity she said to the General:

"'Are you going to meet Gen. Biggs with your army?'

"The General responded: 'Yes, if I can ever find him.'

"'Well, General, if you continue marching in the direction that you are now going, you will find him to-morrow.'

"The General laughed and said, 'I hope so; but, my
dear lady, he is near Romulus.'

"'No, General, he is not; he is at Fayette.'

"'At Fayette?' said the General with astonishment.
'You say he is at Fayette?'

"'Yes, sir, I do; I saw his camp this day; was not in the
camp, but in sight of it. I have been at Smallwood, some
fifteen miles south of Fayette, and know that Gen. Longpath, with his corps from Gen. Law's command in Virginia has joined Biggs. The last of these troops passed on
yesterday for Fayette, and I was told by a well-informed
person that the corps would increase Bigg's army to between eighty and ninety thousand men.'

"'Impossible!' said Rosenfelt; 'he would not have more
than sixty thousand with these.'

"'Yes; but, General, you must know that 20,000 of the
Victor's Hill paroled prisoners captured by Gen. Silent
have been collected together and organized into a corps
under Gen. Stephenson, and are now in camp with Biggs.'

"'Is that so?' inquired Rosenfelt.

"'Yes, General; what I have stated is true, and I hope you will believe me this time. I once before took the chances of my life to give you correct information, and had you believed my statement as then made to Gen. Papson many a poor soldier might be living to-day who sleeps beneath the sod. I come now as I did then, merely because I love my country, and for no other reason. These rebels treat me kindly and never ask me a question which would indicate their suspicion of me. I do not dislike them personally, but I am an inborn Union woman, would make any sacrifice for the preservation of our Government. General, you are in the greatest danger of having your army destroyed. If I were a man and a General in command of this army I would fall back at once to Chatteraugus and make resistance, as they are sure to attack you in a very short time. The understanding with them is that they must crush your army before re-enforcements arrive to your support from the Army of the West, that army having cleared that portion of the country of the enemy.'

"Rosenfelt said: 'If you had seen the army and made an estimate of its strength, I would then have no doubt, but I am persuaded that you are mistaken as to the whole rebel army being at Fayette. They say so to you, but there is merely a force there to impede my march. It is a mere outpost. Their main army is at Romulus, Ga.'

"'Well, General, I should not like very much to see you move on this outpost at Fayette, and I beseech you to send your scouts and find out the exact situation before you make any further movement, as I assure you that you will not proceed very far on this road without a great battle, and one that you will have cause to remember the rest of your life.'

"And so he has."

"The General said: 'Well, it is best to proceed with great caution at all times, and inasmuch as I know you feel sure of what you say, and having given very correct information heretofore, I will halt for the day and send my cavalry to Fayette and let them clear the town of the rebels.'

"Mrs. Houghton laughed and said: 'General, you had better give orders to have what will be left of them (if you should send them there with such orders) return and let you know which road will be left to you to march on, which ever direction you may wish to go.'

"'Yes,' said the General, 'you seem to think we will not be strong enough for the enemy.'

"'General, he has a great army.'

"Gen. Rosenfelt concluded that perhaps he had better be prepared, so he placed Gen. McCabe's Corps on the right, Gen. Critsinger in the center; Gen. Papson being some ten miles to his left near Cherokee Run, was allowed to remain. His cavalry, under Gen. Straiter, was ordered to take the main road to Fayette, and to enter the town if possible; but at all events to feel the enemy and ascertain his position and force. The cavalry were late in getting in motion, and when they had gone some ten miles the darkness of the night impeded any rapid movement. But their orders were such that they must move on. Soon they struck the rebel pickets, who retired before them. Finally they approached the rebel camp which was lighted and stretching out for miles to the east and south. The rebels had discovered the approach of the cavalry and sent two regiments of infantry on a side road to their rear, who opened on them from an unsuspected quarter. This forced Gen. Straiter to strike off to his left, following a road leading from Fayette to the old Mission House. By doing this he made his escape with small loss, but was completely cut off from his retreat back to Rosenfelt's Headquarters. He traveled all night and struck the left of Gen. Papson's Corps at daylight, giving this information to Papson, which was at once sent to Rosenfelt. Messengers were sent with all dispatch to inform him of the situation, and not only so, but to say that it looked as though the enemy were about moving, and Gen. Papson thought they would be most likely to strike our left. This Rosenfelt did not credit, as he could not see, if they intended an attack, why they would not attack our right. In this he was mistaken. The enemy were intending to turn our left, take possession

of the Mission House road, and interpose between Chatteraugus and our army, secure Chatteraugus and Bridgeton,
thereby taking possession of the lines of railroad between
there and Nashua, forcing Rosenfelt away from his base of
supplies, and, eventually, to destroy and capture his army.

Gen. Papson, taking in the situation, ordered one of his
divisions, with Straiter's tired cavalry, at once on and across
the road in rear of Cherokee Run, holding two of the main
crossings, at the same time notifying Rosenfelt of his position and the reasons for it. In the meantime Rosenfelt
had concluded that the information given him by Mrs.
Houghton was in part correct. Having said this much to
her, she asked to be permitted to go into Chatteraugus,
which she could do by crossing over in the rear of the army
to the Mission House road. Her request was granted,
and she started on her way. She had not traveled far before she heard cannonading. She was then sure that the
battle had begun. Rosenfelt was greatly perplexed. Finally he agreed to Papson's suggestions, and ordered Critsinger's Corps to the left, and to join on to Papson's right.
By this time he could hear the sound of artillery in the distance, but held McCabe, believing that the attack would
most likely be made on that road and on his right. Gen.
Papson, seeing that one brigade of the enemy had advanced
to the crossing on Cherokee Run, did not hesitate, but
ordered Gen. Anderson to attack it, which he did at once.
The contest was a sharp one, but the enemy were driven
back very much broken up, with heavy loss in killed and
wounded. Papson then threw Palmerston's division in on
the extreme left, on high ground, covering the road and
crossing well with artillery. In the afternoon a strong force
under Polkhorn advanced, and furiously attacked the two
divisions under Anderson and Palmerston. The contest
raged for over an hour.

Palmerston was driven from his position, and our cavalry,
which had been posted on his left, was broken into fragments. Gen. Anderson changed front with his left brigade
and struck Polkhorn in flank and forced him back on his
main line. Palmerston was now supported by Sherlin's

division and his former position retaken. By this time Longpath had come up on Polkhorn's left and had assailed violently Critsinger's left, and after a severe struggle, in which the loss was great on both sides, our lines gave way and the rebels came through and down the slope of the hill in perfect swarms. Papson, quietly and coolly, as if in church, threw a portion of his corps into the breach and checked the advance. He then adjusted Critsinger's line and moved at once against Longpath's right and broke it, driving it back in great confusion. He then advanced his whole line and drove the enemy back for some distance through the woods on to his reserves, and in this position night closed in on the two armies. During the night Rosenfelt came up with McCabe's Corps, which was now posted on a ridge to the right of Critsinger. This being done, he had his corps commanders assemble at his Headquarters, now near Papson. When all were together the manner of the enemy's assault was stated and various views given as to his number. Some contended that his whole army was engaged; some, his right wing only.

"General Papson was of a different opinion. He thought that the day's battle had been fought on the part of the enemy by his advance merely; that he was marching rapidly, believing that he could pass around our left flank on the Mission House Road, by way of Roseville, into Chatteraugus without much of a struggle, thinking our army all to be on the Bridgeton and Fayette road; that in the morning they would attack with their whole force; and for that we should prepare during the night. Rosenfelt agreed that all arrangements for a great battle must be made during the night. He directed that the lines be adjusted and made as compact as possible, and all be ready to receive their assault by daylight in the morning. He then sent out to find his cavalry commander, Straiter. When found it was ascertained that part of his command had retreated to Roseville.

"The General ordered him to get his command together that night and move by daylight in the morning around our left, and on the right of the enemy, and attack his right flank; to dismount his men and fight them as he would infantry, and to fall back on Palmerston's left and there take his position, and to maintain it if possible. He directed McCabe to refuse the right of his line and to close up on the left with Critsinger. Papson he directed to take command of the left and center and to advance, if he should drive the enemy in the direction of the Mission House road, so as to get the enemy across it if possible. The two armies could be heard during the entire night moving into different positions. The movements of the artillery sounded at times as if it was coming into the other's line. Hospital parties could be heard on both sides in search of the wounded. The light of the fires could be seen for miles on either side, where the men were getting their scanty meals and perhaps their last one. Rosenfelt was busy all night in giving directions for the morrow. He rode all along his lines during the night.

"Biggs intended to make the assault at the opening of day the next morning. Polkhorn was to move around and make an assault on our left and center with one wing of the rebel army, composed of two corps. This attack was delayed, however, by a heavy fog that hung over the field, lasting for some two or three hours, giving Gen. Papson time to strengthen his lines. At length the breathless suspense came to an end. Bolenbroke with a full division had moved around on Papson's left flank (our cavalry failing to get round as ordered) and made a most desperate assault. This was taken up by successive Confederate divisions toward the center with a view of getting possession of the road to Chatteraugus. Gen. Papson was equal to the occasion, and Bolenbroke was soon hurled back in utter rout, two of his Generals killed—Helmer and Deshling— and many of their men and officers killed, wounded and taken prisoners.

"In the same manner were all attempts to break Papson's line abortive. While these things were going well and Papson's command proving itself the superior of the enemy, rolling him back in dismay, a terrible disaster befell us on the right, which endangered the safety of our whole army.

In the morning, very early, Rosenfelt, in passing along the lines of his army, discovered that McCabe was stretched out like a string, with no solidity whatever in his line; that Davies with his division was entirely detached from the main line and isolated; and Critsinger was also stretched over entirely too much ground. He at once ordered the proper dispositions to be made, which was not attended to until late, and in changing these divisions the movement was attended with the most fearful results to our troops, a gap being opened in our front by the withdrawal of one of our divisions to the rear, the place not being closed up, as it should have been. On its discovery by the enemy, Long-path threw Hoadley's division in at this point, at the same time assaulting our right flank with Bertram's force. By this movement and assault on our flank our whole right wing was utterly disorganized and demoralized. They rushed in every direction. The commanders seemed to be stampeded and worse demoralized (if such a thing could be) than even the men. The woods swarmed with disorganized bands of men without officers. The whole right became a confused mass, mingling together without any reference to organization. In this mixed and confused condition they came like a rushing torrent through the woods in all directions; but finally, getting the direction to the northward, they bore everything along in the same direction. Rosenfelt, by some means, was carried along by this moving mass in the direction of Roseville, and, being now separated from the rest of the army, he continued his way to Chatteraugus, the presumption at least being that he went to Chatteraugus in order to collect together and reform his shattered divisions, that Papson might be properly protected in his looked-for retreat with the remainder of the army.

"When Papson was looked for he was not to be seen coming on the road. He had met the shock which came upon him after the General commanding and the whole right wing had abandoned the field, leaving him and his command to take care of themselves. Papson stood like the pillars of Hercules, and met every assault of the com-

bined army of Biggs with his single corps. Gen. Gregor
came back from the retreating column with his command,
as also did several other brigades. They were reconstructed hurriedly and formed in line in support of Papson.

"He soon distributed these troops and strengthened his
flank. He fell back to a ridge across the road over which
the enemy were moving, and here reformed his lines and
encouraged his men. Gens. Anderson and Sherlin were
gathering and putting in line anywhere that they could do
so the men who had been lost from their commands on the
right. The rebels were now advancing on Papson with
the assurance of an easy and triumphant march upon
Chatteraugus, where they expected to make prisoners of
Rosenfelt and his entire army. Papson was still receiving
companies and regiments returning to the field after finding that a portion of our army stood its ground. Batteries
that had been abandoned on the field by McCabe and Critsinger in their stampede were gathered and put in position
with other artillerymen to work them. Gen. Gregor was
moved to the right with his returned forces (who redeemed
themselves at once), he hurled one of Longpath's divisions
from a hill on Papson's right, where a flank attack was intended by the enemy. By this success we gained the position that entirely protected our right. Papson now with
his small force was in a strong position. The fighting
continued on different parts of our line. Palmerston had
been again driven from the left and Gen. Anderson again
sent to his support. He fell upon the enemy with his command and drove him back with great slaughter. Palmerston was again re-established, and, with his position
strengthened, could now hold it. The battle raged with
great fury the full length of the line, and never did a Spar-
tan band stand more firmly than did our gallant men. At
four o'clock like a mighty tempest in all its most terrible
fury did the musketry and artillery of the enemy burst
forth upon Papson's devoted columns, the entire rebel
forces moving down upon him in solid phalanx. Our
forces replied with all their artillery. The roar of the artillery, with its blazing fire, the rattle of the musketry on

both sides, equaled any ever heard or witnessed. Solid masses boldly marched up in front of Papson's lines, where they were literally mowed down by our musketry and discharges of shrapnel and canister from our batteries. They would recoil and then move forward again into the very jaws of death. You could see them fall almost in heaps, as it were.

"This character of contest continued until darkness set in, our columns not moving or swerving in the least. At dark the enemy retreated. The victory of Gen. Papson was complete. Had the whole army remained and supported Papson during the day a great battle would have been won by our army, and Biggs driven out of the country, although his army was so greatly in excess of Rosenfelt's in numbers. As the battle closed Papson received orders from Rosenfelt at Chatteraugus to fall back to Roseville, which was done. They encamped there for the night. Gen. Anderson and staff were worn out and hungry. They hunted their Headquarters, but Headquarters were not there. Old Ham was nowhere to be found, and no provision had been made for anything to eat. Gen. Anderson was greatly annoyed, but thought perhaps there was some excuse for it, as most of the men seemed to get lost during the day.

"Capt. Day and my son Jackson said to the General: 'Perhaps he is with Rosenfelt, assisting him in reorganizing the army in Chatteraugus.' Matters were really too serious for jokes to be very amusing or interesting at that time, so the conversations on the subject of Ham and his whereabouts ceased. The next day they marched to Chatteraugus without disturbance from the enemy. Many of our men remained on the battlefield that night (compelled to do so from exhaustion) and came on to camp next morning without the enemy coming in sight. Gen. Rosenfelt stated his loss at 16,000, and Biggs admitted his to be 18,000. The army of Rosenfelt was all collected and concentrated at Chatteraugus.

"When Gen. Anderson came into camp he had a search made for Headquarters wagons and tents, as well as for

Ham. Finally one of the orderlies found Ham down under the bank near the river and brought him to Gen. Anderson. When Ham saw the General he was delighted and called out:

"'My Laud, Marsa Gen'l, I 'spected you done dead!'

"'Yes,' said the General; 'but it seems you did not wait to see.'

"'No, sir; dat am so. I staid doe, Marsa Gen'l, jes' as long as anybody else do whar I been. I tell you, our mans all git, dey do; and when I seed dat big Gen'l what's ober all ob you'uns (what am his name)—when I seed him a gittin' from dar, I 'cluded it war about time for dis ole nigga to march on dis way, too. Dat Gen'l, he not ride slow, I tell you; he go fas'. And, afore de Laud, I 'spected you ebery one killed or cotched by dem Sesh; den whar's de use ob me stayin' any mo' at dat place, Marsa Gen'l?'

"'Well, Ham, did you ever study law?'

"'No, sir; I 'spect not; I dunno what it am.'

"'I think you would have made a good lawyer, Ham.'

"'Well, Marsa Gen'l, de truf is, ole Ham no good for nuffin'. I cannot stand dis fitin'; dat am de truf, Marsa Gen'l. So, you see, I is no good. I stay all right jes' as long as it am all quiet; but whar am de use ob me stayin' by myself?'

"The General laughed and said that was too good to keep. He let Ham off, sending him out with Capt. Day and Jackson to get some tents and camp equipage from the A. Q. M. The next day he amused himself telling Papson and Sherlin what Ham said about 'no use for him to stay by hisself when de big Gen'l gone.' They all enjoyed the joke except those that came in early. Ham came back after a while to the General and begged him to promise not to tell 'Marfa,' and then went off satisfied.

"Biggs soon followed up and took possession of the ridge to the east running from the old Mission House to the Little Combination River, called Middleton's Ridge, and also a spur branching off from the regular chain of mountains down to the river west of Chatteraugus, known as Looking-Glass Mountain. The line thus formed was in the

shape of a horseshoe, and, with the river washing the north
side of the town, Rosenfelt was completely encircled; the
object of Biggs being to force a surrender by starving him
out, Biggs now fully commanding all Rosenfelt's communications both by rail and river.   This was the position of
the two armies at this time.

"Gen. Silent was ordered to leave Victor's Hill and proceed to Chatteraugus, sending as many troops as could be
spared from the Army of the West.   Gen. Meador was directed to send 20,000 men from the Army of the East, in
order to protect the communications of the Army of the
Center.   In the meantime Broomfield had been ordered to
move with his force, then in Kentucky, on Knoxburg.
Gen. Hord had come on transports up the Combination
River to Nashua with his corps from the Army of the East,
and had sent them in advance to protect the railroad between Nashua and Bridgeton.

"Gen. Silent learning the situation, sent the troops forward from Victor's Hill and hastened to the scene himself.
The first order he issued in connection with the Army of
the Center was that of relieving Rosenfelt of his command
and placing Gen. Papson in his place.   The condition of
the Army of the Center by this time was really frightful
and perilous, and to relieve this situation was the thing to
be done, if possible.   To this end all the energy of the Chief
was directed.   To do this before an unprovisioned army
would be forced by starvation to surrender was the prob-
lem.   Gen. Silent telegraphed to Papson to hold out, and
the answer came, 'We will hold out until we starve.'"

"What a noble old Roman," said Dr. Adams.

"Yes," said Col. Bush; "the old man had no superior in
the army, either as a patriot or fighter; he was like a rock
when he once took his position and got his lines formed."

"I knew him well," said Inglesby; "he was a noble
man.   He would have starved to death in Chatteraugus
before he would have surrendered."

"Uncle Daniel, what has become of Gen. Rosenfelt?" inquired Maj. Clymer.   "He was a kind man, and I liked
him very much, barring some faults."

"Yes. Well, he became soreheaded and got mad at the Administration, and was exceedingly bitter on Gen. Silent for relieving him, and soon took shelter under the wing of the anti-war party ; but I have not heard of him for many years. I think he went to some foreign country, then came back and went to mining. I have no knowledge of his whereabouts now, however."

CHAPTER XIII.

GEN. SILENT GUIDED BY A SPECTER.—ARMY OF THE CENTER.—BELEAGUERED AND HALF STARVED IN CHATTERAUGUS.—MIDDLETON'S RIDGE.—GEN. SILENT'S FORCES SWEEP THE REBELS FROM THE CREST.

———

"O thou whose captain I account myself,
Look on my forces with a gracious eye.
Put in their hands thy bruising irons of wrath
That they may crush down with a heavy fall,
The usurping helmets of our adversaries.
Make us thy ministers of chastisement,
That we may praise thee in thy victory.
To thee I do commend my watchful soul.
Ere I let fall the windows of mine eyes,
Sleeping and waking, O, defend me still."
—SHAKSPEARE.

———

"THE Army of the Center was now in a most deplorable condition. Gen. Biggs's lines extended to the river above and below, so that the Union army inside of Chatteraugus was practically invested, the rebel army being so situated that every movement of our troops could be watched as carefully as if they were all of the same army. The enemy persistently threw shells into our camp and made it very uncomfortable both by day and night. The rains had so swollen the river and damaged the roads that there was no direction from which supplies could be drawn in wagons of sufficient quantity to be of any very great assistance, had the rebels only held the line of communication by rail. Our whole command had to be placed at once on half rations. Over 3,000 wounded soldiers were in camp and hospital, suffering and dying for want of proper food and nourishment. Forage for the animals could not be procured, and more than 10,000 died in and about Chatteraugus. One-third of the artillery horses died, and the remainder were unfitted for service.

"Biggs had cut off a train of supplies of medical stores for the wounded, and the ammunition of our army was reduced to the minimum. In the battle of Cherokee Run the men had thrown away and lost their blankets, so they were exposed to the hot sun and the chilly nights, without blankets, tents, food, or any of the comforts that even soldiers usually enjoy in the field. When Rosenfelt started on the campaign his order was to take but one blanket to each man, and no overcoats. In this condition they could not retreat. They seemed doomed to surrender at no distant day.

"The enemy well knew the condition of our troops, being in possession of the route to our depot of supplies, and the one by which re-enforcements would reach our army. They apparently held our forces at their mercy. For these reasons the enemy deemed it unnecessary to assault and lose lives in an attempt to take what seemed secure. All that Biggs had to do, as he thought, was to wait, and Chatteraugus would fall into his hands without a struggle. Starvation would soon force terms, as retreat or re-enforcements were considered alike impossible. No other portion of our armies was reduced to such a terrible extremity during the war.

"This was the situation of the Army of the Center when Gen. Silent took command of it. Biggs had sent his cavalry to the interior to watch all movements on our part, and especially to prevent supplies from being brought to or concentrated anywhere for our almost famished soldiers. Weller and Lawting, in command of the rebel cavalry, captured and destroyed in the Sewatch Valley 1,000 wagons loaded with supplies. They also captured 700 wagons at Macklinville, with about 1,000 prisoners, and at the same time destroyed millions of dollars of other property.

"Gen. Silent had just arrived at Nashua, and, finding that the raiders were burning wagon trains and railroad trains loaded with supplies, collected all the cavalry he could, obtained horses and mounted two regiments of infantry. Under a skillful officer he started them in pursuit of Weller and Lawting, chasing them into Northern Ala-

bama and capturing near one-half of their commands.
Gen. Silent had no means of getting into Chatteraugus
until Biggs's force at Bridgeton and on the river between
there and Chatteraugus could be dislodged and driven out
of Looking-Glass Valley, which ran down along the mountain side to the river. He had difficulty in getting all the
positions correctly.

" Finally he met Mrs. Houghton, who had come out from
Chatteraugus prior to its investment. She gave him the
most satisfactory detailed statement that he had received
from any one as yet. In the interview she told him what
she was doing in that country and where she had been;
what she had said to General Rosenfelt the night before
the battle of Murphy's Hill, and what she told him the day
before the battle at Cherokee Run. The General questioned her as to the number of the enemy, the names of the
commanders, etc. When she gave the names of Longpath
and Stephenson, the General said :

" ' They are sending troops here from the rebel army
East ? '

" ' Yes, General,' she replied ; ' 20,000, I am sure, and I so
told Gen. Rosenfelt.'

" The General said : ' They are using the Victor's Hill
prisoners ? '

" ' Yes,' said she ; ' Gen. Stephenson is said to be in command of 20,000 of them.'

" ' But they have not been exchanged as yet ? '

" As to that she did not know, but they were now in Gen.
Bigg's army. Gen. Silent thanked her and invited her to
come to Chatteraugus when he should take it; ' which,' he
said, ' I mean to do in ten days from the day I open the
lines of communication, so as to get food to those starving
soldiers.' He then left her with many thanks for the information.

" The next day Mrs. Houghton sought Gen. Silent again
and said to him:

" ' General, there is one matter, which may be important, I
did not think to mention yesterday in our conversation.'

" ' Pray, what is that ? ' said he.

"'Gen. Longpath is to start in a day or so to Knoxburg with his command, in order to drive Broomfield from there, who they understand is now in possession of that place.'

"'Well,' said the General, 'that is of more importance to know than anything you have told me.'

"'I am exceedingly glad then, General, that I thought of it.'

"The General then said to her: 'I am extremely curious to know how you learned this.'

"'Well, sir, I visit hospitals on both sides, and many things are there said that would not be told to anyone in camp. I had seen a sick rebel who had just come into the city in citizen's clothes to be taken care of by his friends, and you must not ask me who or where he is.'

"'No,' said the General, 'I will not. Good-by!'

"Gen. Silent at once ordered Gen. Hord to concentrate his whole force at Bridgeton as quickly as possible, and in three days the 20,000 men from the Army of the East had secured Bridgeton and crossed over Little Combination River on the road to Looking-Glass Valley. They moved forward, driving Biggs before them, until they reached the western base of Coon's Mountain, in order to pass into Looking-Glass Valley. At the point where he was to enter the Valley the rebels made an assault upon his head of column. Hord deployed his troops, advanced to the attack, and very soon routed the enemy. The enemy now could very plainly detect and understand the movement. Our troops went into camp at about six o'clock.

"The rebels could see that if this movement was successful re-enforcements as well as supplies to the Union army would immediately be the result, and they were bewildered and chagrined. At about one o'clock the same night, Hord was attacked in force by the enemy. Gear's command first received the assault. Hord at once moved to the support of Gear, but before reaching him found a large rebel force posted on a range of hills which completely commanded his line of march. These hills were steep and rugged. There was, however, but one course left, and that was to assault. This was done in a most gallant style. The hills were scaled and the enemy driven from them with a loss of many prisoners, as well as killed and wounded. Gen. Gear meanwhile had been contending against a superior force for two hours, and though almost enveloped at one time by the enemy, he finally succeeded in repelling the assault. The moonlight was so bright that the firing seemed to light up the whole heavens, as if meteors were in every possible space. The yells of the rebels, the running away of teams, the heavy sound of artillery, were enough to 'frighten the souls of fearful adversaries.' Mules broke away from their wagons and hitching places, some with halters, some with harness and singletrees dangling at their heels. Horses neighing and mules braying, all dashed in the direction of the enemy, who mistook the fleeing animals for a cavalry charge, and fled in disorder and confusion. At daylight the enemy had been repulsed at every point and our route to Chatteraugus secured.

"Gen. Silent had managed to communicate with Gen. Papson, and directed that one of his divisions should cross over the river in front of his camp in plain view of the enemy, and while the enemy were watching these movements pontoon bridges were being laid across the river by the Engineer Corps, they passing down the river beyond the left flank of the enemy in the night time. Over this bridge crossed Palmerston's Division and joined Hord, and by the next morning all the heights commanding the bridge and Looking-Glass Valley were secured and communication opened by way of the north side of the river by crossing the pontoon bridge, and on that very day rations for the men were taken into Chatteraugus. Such a shout as went up from the throats of nearly 50,000 men was perhaps never heard before nor since. Gen. Silent entered Chatteraugus with the supplies for the hungry, and was most gratefully received by officers and men. When this line was opened the boys christened it 'Silent's cracker line.'

"The scene that followed the opening of this line of communication is not to be described by any one. Poor fellows, they had suffered long and much. They were patriots; but how many people remember it now?"

8

At this point the old man grew eloquent, and finally bowed his head for a moment. Resuming, he said:

"In a very short time every one had gained confidence and courage, and was again not only ready but eager for the fray. Biggs at once saw his peril. Longpath was at Knoxburg trying to dislodge Broomfield, while Gen. Papson was being rapidly re-enforced. And now the tables were turned. The rebels no longer jeered at and tantalized our boys with inquiries as to when they proposed to start for 'Pine Forest Prison.' Jeff Davis, the Confederate President, had only a few days before visited Biggs's army and looked down upon our starving soldiers. Our boys knew this, and would ask if Jeff Devis would like to dine with Gen. Silent on hard-tack?

"Just at this time our forces were anxiously looking for the arrival of the troops from the Army of the West, which they knew were marching with all the energy they could to the aid of their comrades. So the next morning the rebels were saluted with a shout that rang from the valley up to the top of Looking-Glass Mountain and along Middleton's Ridge. It was the arrival of Sherwood from Victor's Hill with two full corps of as good soldiers as ever marched under the American flag. Cheer upon cheer from both our armies rang out and gladdened the hearts of all.

"The next day Gen. Silent was handed a note by a cavalryman. He examined it, and found that it bore information to the effect that Longpath had failed to capture Knoxburg, but had been repulsed by Broomfield and was then marching rapidly to re-enforce Biggs. On inquiry the General found that the note was written by a lady, who was then some ten miles away at a farmhouse. The cavalryman stated that she was very anxious that Gen. Silent should get the note that day, and that she had also told him to say to the General that she was the same lady who had given him certain information at Nashua some days before, and that she informed the bearer of the contents of the note and requested him to destroy it if in danger of being captured. Gen. Silent consulted Gen. Papson and found that he had implicit faith in her statements, as he said

she had given Rosenfelt truthful and important information twice as to the numbers and movements of the enemy.
Gen. Silent said:

"'This being so, we must drive Biggs from his position
before Longpath can join him.'

"It was then raining and blowing a perfect gale, and
Gen. Papson said that it might be well to delay until the
storm was over. This Gen. Silent assented to, but directed

THE SPECTER APPEARS TO THE GENERAL.

that all preparations be made for the attack, so as to be in
perfect readiness at a moment's notice.

"Sherwood, however, had not yet succeeded in getting
to the position assigned him. He was struggling against
rain, wind, and high water. In crossing Little Combination
River to the north side the pontoon bridge gave way, and
Gen. Osterman and his division of Sherwood's command
were completely cut off and left on the south side of the

stream. Silent ordered him to proceed up the river to a
point opposite Middleton's Ridge with the remainder of his
command. By this time the freshet was so great that it
was impossible to repair the bridge. So Osterman was
ordered, if he could not get across by eight o'clock the next
morning, to report to Gen. Hord. Sherwood finally succeeded in moving the rest of his command to the point indicated. Pontoons were now necessary for bridging the
river at this point in order to cross the troops again over
to the south side to assault Middleton's Ridge, the point
of it sloping down near to the river, on which rested the
rebel right flank. There were but few pontoons to be
obtained, and here the genius of man came well into play.
Rafts and boats of a rough character were at once improvised, and by the morning of the 24th of November Sherwood's command was once more on the south side of the
river, with men, horses and artillery, ready for the assault.
He was moving in a drizzling rain, and as the clouds hung
low his movement was pretty well covered. He pushed
forward with great rapidity and seized the smaller hills
near the river, driving the enemy therefrom, and at once
fortified them securely.

"The rebels now seeing this advantage made an ineffectual assault to dislodge him. He had possession of two hills,
with a depression in his front between him and the main
ridge, it being his objective point. The mist and heaviness
of the day prevented the enemy on Looking-Glass Mountain
from seeing or understanding the movement of Sherwood
on the right. Night closed in, and as the clouds cleared
away, the light of the camp fires revealed the position of
both armies. Indeed, the night was beautiful. The lights
on the north side were made by those guarding the camp
of Sherwood, left in his movement, across the river. These
lights of the camp fires of both armies now formed a complete circuit, making a grand picture. The stillness of the
night was a warning to all that in the morning work was
to be done.

"About the hour of ten Gen. Silent was out looking at
the lights, and in order to form some opinion of the con-

dition of the weather during the next day, he strolled along the river bank alone. Stopping at no great distance from one of the sentinels, he sat down upon a stone under a large tree, the shadows of which obscured him from view. While sitting absorbed in thought as to what the future would be to the army then preparing for a desperate battle, a strange form seemed to appear before him. He was at first startled, and then felt as though he had dreamed, and was thereby deceiving himself. The object was apparently a woman dressed in a long flowing robe of pure white. The features were regularly formed; she had large blue eyes, long, auburn hair, and a light shone about her which made every feature plain and visible to him. This strange apparition did not speak, but pointed to Looking-Glass Mountain, and passed her hand, extending her forefinger, as though tracing the mountain along to where it dips down to the Roseville road. At this point she held her finger pointing for some seconds. She then turned and pointed to the end of Middleton's Ridge, near the river, and there hesitated; then turned and pointed to the center of the ridge, near where Gen. Biggs's Headquarters were afterwards located. Here she seemed to trace two lines on the side of the ridge by passing her finger twice back and forth. She hesitated at this point for some moments, finally pointing to the sky as though calling attention to the stars.

"At this moment Gen. Silent arose quite excited, and the strange specter vanished. He stood for some moments motionless. He could not move, and was trembling with nervousness. Finally he aroused himself and stepped to the spot where the strange figure had appeared. There was nothing that could have been by dreamy imagination distorted into such a form. He said to himself, 'I dreamed; I must have dreamed; how could this be otherwise?' Just at this moment he saw a sentinel walking his beat some paces away and approached him cautiously. The sentinel challenged, and Silent went forward and gave the countersign. He then told the sentinel who he was, and inquired if anything unusual was going on. The sentinel replied in the negative. Silent then inquired if he had seen nothing unusual.

" ' No,' replied the sentinel, 'except that you have been sitting on the stone under this tree for some time. I have
been watching you, as I was not aware of your business. '

" ' You saw nothing else ?' said the general.

" ' No, sir,' was the reply.

" The General then bade him good night and returned to
his headquarters, feeling pretty sure that he had fallen
asleep and dreamed while sitting under the tree. Yet he
had a half lingering superstition on the subject, and it annoyed him very much. He could not divine the meaning
of it ; whether a dream or not he could not decide. He
walked back and forth in a very unusual manner. One of
his staff inquired if anything had gone wrong in the movements of the army. He said not, but inquired if all the
Orderlies were at their posts, saying :

" ' I will want them very soon to take orders to the field.
They must be cautioned, also, as they will be in some
danger in passing to where they must go.'

" He then sat down and commenced dictating his orders.

" At midnight they were sent out to the different commanders. Hord was to attack with all his force, assisted by
Osterman's division, in the morning at the earliest moment
possible, and scale Looking-Glass Mountain. Gen. Papson
was to make a demonstration against the rebel center.

" The mountain is very steep and covered with trees and
underbrush. Crags jut out at every turn all over its sides,
and at the summit a high crest rises almost perpendicular
50 or 60 feet. Around the point of the mountain nearest
the river the enemy had heavy earthworks, held by one
brigade. The ridge or crest of the mountain was held
by some 7,000 men, with many pieces of artillery. Hord's
command was all on the west side of the mountain, entirely
obscured from the sight of any of our troops who were in
the town of Chatteraugus, so that nothing could be seen
except the rebels who occupied the crest of the mountain.
The movements of the enemy proved clearly that some
advance was being made.

" Gens. Silent and Papson stood on an earthwork on the
north side of the town near the river, where they could

plainly see all the rebel lines. Very soon the smoke and sounds of battle were seen and heard. Osterman had attacked the rebels in their works at the foot of the mountain nearest the river and driven them pell-mell out of their intrenchments, killing, wounding and capturing a great number. At the same time Gen. Gear was pushing up the mountain, his right passing directly under the muzzles of the enemy's guns which were on the summit, climbing over logs, boulders and crags, up hill and down, dislodging and driving the enemy wherever he opposed. Up and on went our brave boys to the mouths of cannon and into the very jaws of death. Gen. Silent, addressing Papson, said :

"'General, our men must be climbing up the mountain's side. The enemy would not fire so rapidly nor such volleys unless our men were near them.'

"'No, I should think they would not,' said Papson.

"The fire flashed from their guns and muskets in the sunlight as though the heavens were in a blaze. Soon batteries could be seen pulling out and moving on the table of the mountain in the direction of the south.

"'Do you see that, Papson?' said Silent. 'They are getting ready to retreat. See, they are sending their batteries out of danger!'

"Papson looked, but said not a word. Soon a portion of their infantry moved in the same direction. The noise of artillery firing could be heard no longer, but the rattle of musketry was becoming more distinct. The men and officers who were not in the demonstration against Middleton's Ridge, which was not a very heavy one, were standing and looking in breathless silence at the upper table-land of Looking-Glass mountain. Finally our line was seen moving up the crest, the men firing as they came, and such a yell as arose from our men in the town of Chatteraugus was of the kind to bring joy to a patriot's soul. On they went, the fire flashing from the muzzles of their muskets. The rebels began to retreat, our men pressing them until they were driven entirely from the mountain and across the valley near the old Mission House, and nearly to the foot of Middleton's Ridge. Papson's movement against the ridge,

which was the enemy's right, ceased, and Looking-Glass
Mountain was ours. Joy was unconfined among our troops.

"The poor fellows, who were nearly starved, acted as
though they were perfectly well and hearty, although they
had had but little to eat for weeks.

"This was only the beginning of the end at Chatteraugus. Gen. Silent thought the rebels would now retreat into
Georgia; but in this he was mistaken. They strengthened
their line on Middleton's Ridge and extended it across the
valley to where Looking-Glass Mountain slopes down to the
road from Roseville to Chatteraugus, and there they seemed
bent on staying. Two days later, finding the enemy again
preparing for battle, Gen. Silent issued his orders for a general
assault. Sherwood at early dawn was to attack the enemy
on his right and drive him back if possible on the southern
portion of the ridge; Papson was to be ready to assault in
front at the moment when the commanding General should
think the proper time had arrived; Gen. Hord was to cross
from Looking-Glass Mountain over to the Roseville road
and attack his left flank.

"The morning was clear and cold. Biggs's Headquarters
could be seen on the crest of Middleton's Ridge, near the
center of his line. Gen. Silent occupied a knob or high
point near our lines that had been wrested from the enemy
in a skirmish the day before. All were anxiously waiting
the assault and final result. Now and again a shot would
be heard, and then a volley. There were skirmishings occasionally in different directions. On Hord's line, as he advanced, slight skirmishing was kept up, and at the base of
the ridge a shot would be fired in the direction of where
Papson was forming his line. Finally shots were heard on
our extreme left, then more, then a piece of artillery, then
a volley, then a battery opened, then commands were heard
and the battle began. Sherwood was moving against the
enemy's right flank.

"He attacked as ordered, but found the enemy in strong
force and very stubborn. The battle continued on this
part of the line without any very material advantage to
either side. At about three o'clock Gen. Papson was or-

dered not to delay his attack any longer, so at this time the
movement of the whole army against the enemy commenced. Papson attacked in double column, Gens. Anderson and Sherlin leading the assault with their divisions.
In the center, at the first assault made on the rifle-pits at
the base of the ridge, our forces were not successful, and
falling back for a short distance they readjusted their lines,
changed some of the regiments, and moved forward again
to the attack. This time the movement was as if it were
machinery in motion.

"When close to the enemy a bayonet charge was ordered,
and against the foe they drove the instruments of death.
The men who were in this deadly charge will never forget
it. As they came with bayonets fixed and directed, the
enemy, seeing their determination, poured a deadly fire
into their ranks. Many a brave man fell, but on the lines
swept over the trenches. Here the rebels were killed and
wounded in such numbers that they lay one across another
in great numbers. The enemy fell back, giving up the
trenches to our victorious troops, and retreated to their
main works on the top of the ridge.

"Our troops moved right on up the slope of the ridge,
facing a shower of shot and shell and musketry most destructive and deadly. Anderson and Sherlin led the way.
Commanders of corps, divisions and brigades vied with one
another as to who should reach the crest first. For a time
it seemed doubtful if any of them would succeed in accomplishing it. Our artillery was in battery playing on the
enemy from an eminence on the plateau east of the town
and between the two lines. Finally the guns of the enemy
were disabled, some dismounted, and others driven from
their position. Our whole line then made one desperate
effort to scale the ridge and charge the rebel works. With
a mighty shout and 'Come on boys!' from Sherlin and
Anderson, the heights were scaled, and amid sickening
scenes of blood and death our brave boys stormed and captured their breast-works. Their center was pierced and
broken. They wavered and finally retreated down the opposite slope of the ridge. Gen. Anderson seized one of our

flags, mounted the rebel works, and held it up so that our
whole army might see it, and they did.   The sight of the
old flag on the rebel works on Middleton's Ridge, filled our
men with joy and enthusiasm.   They rushed forward,
shouting as they went.   The men who had been shut up
and nearly starved, wept with joy unspeakable.

"Sherwood now doubled the enemy's flank back until
they were retreating and falling back on the two divisions
of Anderson and Sherlin, who turned and poured volleys
into their rear.   The retreat of Biggs's army now became
general.   We captured many prisoners.   Just at this moment a rebel cavalry officer on a white horse was seen dashing down the ridge from the direction of the rebel left.   He
came within a short distance of our line and took off his
hat to our troops, as if he intended to surrender.   Turning
on his horse he drew a revolver and fired.   The ball struck
Gen. Anderson in the right shoulder, inflicting a severe and
painful wound.   Gen. Anderson turned and saw him as he
escaped down the side of the ridge.   Anderson recognized
him, but did not say a word.   Many shots were fired at him
by the soldiers, but he made good his escape.   (It was Gen.
Joseph Whitthorne, the fiend.)   Gen. Anderson was taken
by Jackson and James Whitcomb (who had been by his
side during the whole of the engagement) back to the town
to be cared for by the Surgeon.   Gen. Anderson inquired
after Capt. Day, and upon inquiry it was found that he
had been severely wounded during the last charge up the
ridge, and had been carried in an ambulance to the hospital.

"The battle was won.   No rebel flag was in sight, and
the Stars and Stripes w   ed over Looking-Glass Mountain
and Middleton's Ridge once more.   Longpath just reached
Ringgold's Gap in time to meet his flying friends, who were
in a great state of demoralization.   They had been utterly
routed and broken to pieces.   Our army was in great glee
and full of joy that night and for many days thereafter.
The Army of the Center had been in such bad condition
for so long a time—being hemmed in and starved—that it
became necessary to go into quarters for recuperation, and

also to refit and refurnish it with horses, mules, harness, etc. The troops were, therefore, distributed at the most convenient points on the lines of our communications.

"Gen. Silent, now having put Gen. Biggs and his army in a condition of harmlessness for the season, took up his headquarters at Nashua.

"The next morning after the battle, my son Jackson left Gen. Anderson (who was comparatively easy, for his wound, though painful, was not considered dangerous,) to search for Capt. Day. He found him in the officers' hospital, wounded severely, shot through the bowels. He died that night. This was sad news to the General, for he loved him as if he had been a brother. He was buried at Chatteraugus. His friends were notified, and removed his remains to the cemetery near Bloomington, Ill. He was a gallant soldier, and had been so kind to Gen. Anderson that we all loved him. His death caused nearly as much sadness in my family as the loss of one of our own sons.

"My son Jackson, James Whitcomb and old Ham staid close by Gen. Anderson, doing all they could to alleviate his sufferings. There was no suspicion as to who had shot him. One day, however, he was suffering with a severe fever, and in a delirium remarked :

"'Jo Whitthorne is my evil genius. He intends to murder me.'

"This he repeated so often that when he was sufficiently recovered Jackson asked him if he remembered saying this? He replied that he did not. Jackson told him that it had aroused his suspicions on the subject. He then revealed the secret to Jackson under the seal of confidence, as he said it would kill his wife if she knew it. Jackson afterwards revealed the same to me, but no mention was ever made of it by either of us.

"Old Ham was so attentive and kind that no one asked him as to his whereabouts during the battle. Jackson, however, found him under the bed when they brought the General back from the field. The old man said that he had been sick all day, and got under the bed to be out of the way. When they came back he said to the General; 'I

know you be kill' dat day or hurted bery bad, kase I dream
it. De good Laud tole me so when I sleep. No 'sputin' it,
sho, for de Laud allers tells me 'bout dese matters; and
you can ax Marfa if it is not so when you go home.'

"When the General recovered so as to think of these
matters he dictated his report to Jackson, who wrote it for
him, in which he recommended Peter for promotion, among
many others, for gallant conduct, and also recommended
Orderly James Whitcomb for a Lieutenancy in the Regular
Army.   These recommendations were complied with at
once, and Peter was assigned to the command of a brigade.
James Whitcomb was assigned to the 13th U. S. Inf., and
detailed at Gen. Anderson's request as an Aide-de-Camp in
place of Capt. Day. The President sent Peter's commission
to me and I took it to him at Chatteraugus, in accordance
with the wish of Gen. Anderson, who desired to see me,
and at the same time to keep from his wife and our family
the fact of his being wounded until he should be able to
come home. I found my sons both well and Gen. Anderson
improving when I arrived. I remained several days. I
met Gen. Silent and had several conversations with him. I
found him well posted as to all matters North as well as
South. He said there was no danger of Biggs during that
Winter. He could not more than recuperate his army, and
in the Spring, in all probability, the rebel army in the center would have a new commander, as Biggs was a great failure; that if he had moved against our forces when he had
them caged up before re-enforcements came, our army
would have been compelled to surrender. He also spoke
of our danger in the North from the anti-war party. He
regarded it more dangerous than the rebel army. If they
could succeed in carrying the election the Confederacy
would by them be recognized and the Union dissolved.

"In a few days Gen. Anderson was adjudged by the Surgeon to be strong enough to travel. He was granted an in-
definite leave of absence by Gen. Silent, who regarded him
very highly as an able officer. Gen. Anderson, myself,
Jackson, James Whitcomb (now lieutenant), and Ham
started for Allentown. On arriving at home the family

were overjoyed, surprised, and grieved all at the same time
—overjoyed at our return, surprised that they had not heard
of the General being wounded, and grieved at his suffering.

"Lieut. James Whitcomb was introduced to the family,
who were delighted to see him. He left the same evening
for his home in Detroit, and we were together once more,
save two sons, Peter and Henry. The meeting between
Ham and Aunt Martha was very affecting. Their manner
and queer remarks were laughable. Soon Aunt Martha
came in to see her Marsa Gen'l Tom. She hugged him and
got down on her knees and prayed for him, and then said
to me:

"'Uncle Daniel, I bress de good Laud, for you bring
Marsa Tom back. I cure him, sho. I knows what to do;
de Laud tell me, he do. He not goin' to let Marsa Gen'l
Tom die; no he not! He want him to whip de Sesh, he do.
I knows; de Laud tell me bout dat in de dream. He not
fool dis old 'oman; he neber do. Ham, he dream 'bout dat
when he down to de fight. He say he sick when dey fight.
How is dat, Uncle Daniel? Did Marsa Tom tell you? Was
he sick? He awful coward, Ham is, but if he sick, den all
right; but when he not been sick he must stay wid Marsa
Gen'l to keep he things all right. Ham say he do dat. I
'spect he do; he say so.'

"We told Aunt Martha that Ham was all right, and that
pleased her, poor old woman. She was pure gold; God
never made a better heart under any white skin than she
had under her black one.

"Gen. Anderson had the best of attention, and improved
daily until he could walk about without pain, but he was
not fit for duty for a considerable time. The two children
were delighted, and were full of questions of all kinds.
One day when they were trying to entertain the General,
his little daughter asked him who shot him. I saw the
tears come into his eyes, and he arose and walked out on
the porch without making any answer."

Just at this moment Mrs. Wilson came into the room, and
Uncle Daniel took her on his knee and kissed her, saying:

"Jennie, you are my all and only hope, save my poor

grandson, that I now have left. My time will soon come, however, when I can quietly quit this world of trouble and care and find a home where works will have due consideration; where those who serve in the army of the Lord will at least be considered the equal of those who have been in rebellion against him.

"My good friends," said Uncle Daniel, "you may think strange of my melancholy mood; but why should I desire to live longer and see what I do and feel as I do constantly on account of the manner in which things are now being conducted."

"I am not in any way surprised at your feeling as you do. I have felt and do feel the same, though my misfortunes and troubles have not been severe in comparison with yours," said Col. Bush. "But, Uncle Daniel, to call your attention away from your sorrows for a moment, I am very desirous of knowing what became of Mrs. Houghton."

"She remained in that part of the country during that Winter and until our combined Armies of the Center and West commenced their next campaign, during all of which time she kept our commanding Generals posted as to the movements of the enemy, his strength, when troops were sent east or west, where and how many; and when the troops were moved south in the Spring she returned to New York, and, I have been informed, married again. I hope she may be yet living and enjoying great happiness. She was a true woman. I have not heard of her for many years, however."

"She was a heroine sure," said Col. Bush; "her movements were of a most important character, Uncle Daniel."

"Yes, Colonel, she was a true patriot, and loved her country for her country's sake, and I hope the Lord has thrown fortune and pleasure in her pathway. There were a great many patriotic and daring acts performed by women during our war. God bless the good women. To our poor sick and wounded soldiers they were like ministering angels, both in the camp and hospitals."

CHAPTER XIV.

SERAINE WHITCOMB'S EXAMINATION OF THE REBEL
PRISONS AND HENRY LYON'S RELEASE.—MAN'S IN-
HUMANITY.—SERAINE WHITCOMB VISITS THE SOUTH-
ERN PRISON PENS.—A SAD TALE OF WOE.—GRAPHIC
PICTURE OF SUFFERING, WRETCHEDNESS AND DEATH.

"Oh war, thou son of hell,
Whom angry heavens do make their ministers,
Throw in the frozen bosoms of our past,
Hot coals of vengeance."—SHAKESPEARE.

UNCLE Daniel Lyon resumed his story by giving us a
history of the adventures of Miss Seraine Whitcomb,
who, as had been discovered, was the sister of James
Whitcomb, now Aide-de-Camp to Gen. Anderson.
He continued by saying:

"Miss Seraine's journey to Richmond was accomplished
by overcoming the greatest of difficulties. The President's
authority was good at every point in and through the
Union lines. But when she reached the rebel pickets at or
near the Rapidan she was placed under arrest as a spy,
and taken to the headquarters of the commander of the
rebel army. She then stated her case in a modest way,
presenting the note given to her by our President. Her
story was so simple and reasonable that she was permitted
to enter Richmond in order to lay her case before President
Davis. At the same time the authorities at the rebel army
headquarters had a lurking suspicion of her on account
of (as they thought) her pretended perilous undertaking.
Yet she was conducted to Richmond, and there took lodg-
ings at the Virginia Hotel, where she was subjected to a
constant watch over her every movement. She was in
much doubt for several days what course to pursue.
There was great activity going on in making preparations

for some movement of the rebel army. She was not permitted to leave her hotel.

"She finally wrote a note to President Davis, stating that she wished to be permitted to have an interview with him on a matter of grave import to her; that she was alone and under a vigilant watch; that she thought she could satisfy him of her harmless intentions.

"To this she received a very polite answer permitting her to see him at 11 o'clock the following day, and informing her that he would send an escort.

"The next day, promptly at the time, an officer appeared and inquired if Miss Seraine Whitcomb was in. She readily responded, and directed that he be admitted. Presenting himself, he said he was Capt. T. P. Redingson. The arrangements were soon agreed upon, and the two started for the Executive office. The detention in the ante-room was but slight, before they were ushered into the presence of Mr. Davis. Seraine said he was seated in an arm-chair, rather oldish and common. Mr. Davis rose and greeted her pleasantly. He looked care-worn and haggard, and seemed thoughtful; but at no time during the interview did he forget his genial, polite manner toward her. She hardly knew what to say. After a short time he broke the ice by asking her if he could serve her in any way. She gained courage enough to tell him her whole story. She told him she would not give information of any kind to any one in reference to what she might see or hear while under his protection; that she wished to examine the prison records for the name of her friend, Henry Lyon, who she hoped, through his kindness, to find, and have exchanged.

She seemed to touch a tender spot in his nature. He gave her a letter of safe conduct through all the rebel lines, and authority to examine the prisons and hospitals, exacting at the same time a pledge from her that she would, when satisfied, return by way of Richmond and make a report to him of all she should see and hear that was of interest in connection with the prisons, the army, or other kindred subjects. With this understanding and pledge on her part she gave him her thanks, with many good wishes for his health. She then bade him good good-by and returned to her hotel.

"Capt. Redingson, her escort, was very polite to her, and promised that he would call the next day and make arrangements for her to visit the prisons and examine the records or rolls of prisoners in Richmond. The next day at ten o'clock the Captain called and escorted her to Libby. There she saw such suffering as made her almost frantic, but she indulged in no remarks. As she passed along the pallets of rotten straw, the tears would roll down the sunken cheeks of their occupants as she uttered some kind word to them. The rolls did not disclose the name of the one for whom she was in search, and she returned with the Captain to her hotel. That night she could not sleep. She had seen that day such sights as she had never expected to witness, and could not have believed had she not looked upon them with her own eyes. Men eating rotten food; many, very many, sick, sore and distressed; quite a number without sufficient clothes to cover their persons; no blankets; no way to send word to friends; no privileges granted, their treatment harsh and brutal. For the least delinquency inhuman punishment was inflicted. No prospect of help or relief of any kind. All kinds of stories were told them of disasters to the ' Yanks,' as the rebels called the Union soldiers. It was really a sickening sight to behold.

"The next day they visited Belle Isle, and there found the same condition of things. After an examination of records they returned to the Virginia Hotel. Miss Seraine then concluded to leave for Salisbury. She asked the Captain if he would be kind enough to see to getting her tickets and placing her properly in charge of the conductor, with such instructions as might enable her to avoid annoyance on her route. The next morning she was feeling dull and heavy on account of having passed a restless night. The shadows of that which she had seen during the day were continually before her eyes. She got ready, however, and was soon put on the train by Capt. Redingson, who knew the conductor and explained to him her situation and desire to avoid annoyances. Then bidding the Captain good-by, with many thanks for his kindness, she sat down in the car to pursue her weary journey, with many ill forebodings. She looked out of the window over valley, hill and stream, and as she passed on through that picturesque country her eyes fairly feasted on the majestic scenery beautified by the pines that tower heavenward along the line of the railroad.

"In her loneliness she could not resist the floodtide of hopes and fears that swept through her mind—now hoping and then fearing that she would not find Henry. If she should, would he be in the condition of the poor, starved skeletons she had seen at Libby and Belle Isle? Could it be possible that her lovable and gentle Henry could be so starved and harshly treated by these people, who had been so polite and kind to her? 'No! no!' she thought to herself; 'it cannot be.' The train sped along, and at night she was in Salisbury. There she was taken to a hotel of limited accommodations and worse attendance, as it was of the character so common to that country in the days of slavery. Quite a number of sick rebel officers, who had been sent there to recuperate, were in the hotel.

"The next morning it was discovered that a female 'Yank' was in the house, and, the gossips whispered 'a spy!' Miss Seraine was unsuspecting, and acted as if she had been a mere traveler in her own State. But very soon an officer came and sat down by her and began a series of questions, all of which she answered frankly. She told him her mission, and made inquiry about the prisoners there, wishing to look for her friend, Henry Lyon. This officer left her and went to the authorities and had her put under arrest. At this she was frightened almost out of her wits. She wept and begged, but nothing would do but she must have her baggage (merely a satchel) examined. This done, they sent a lady with her to her room and searched her person. Being so much alarmed, she did not think of her letter from Mr. Davis. This was found in her pocket and declared a forgery, as they thought if genuine she would have produced it sooner. Finally the conductor who had brought the train through from Richmond returned, and finding how matters were, relieved her situation by explaining it to the authorities. The officers and Mayor then hastened to make apologies for their action and afterwards treated her very kindly, and offered her every facility for the examination desired. Her search at the place was as fruitless as heretofore. She found the condition of things here as elsewhere with our poor prisoners—nothing but extreme suffering and ill treatment. It was hard for her to understand how any civilized people could find it in their hearts to treat human beings so barbarously.

"She left Salisbury the first moment it was possible for her to do so, and made her way in great sadness to Pine Forest Prison, meeting with many perplexing things on the way. As she neared Pine Forest she became nervous and almost sick with fear that her mission would be a failure. Her strength and resolution all at once seemed to fail her. But on she went, between hope and despair. En route to this horrible place, all kinds of phantoms rose before her mind. She would first see a starved human being, and then a wild beast pursuing him; then the butchery and murder of the victim; so that when she arrived at the village she was almost frantic and nearly insane. A gentleman, seeing her lonely and peculiar situation, assisted her to a house, where she procured quarters.

"It was not until the next morning that she made known her desire to visit the prison. The lady of the house seemed to take in the situation, and, instead of regarding her as a spy, felt a sympathy for her and willingly rendered her all the assistance she could. Miss Seraine told her whole story to her, and sought her aid in making the proper investigation. This lady, Mrs. Lawton, made all necessary arrangements for the two to visit the Superintendent at three o'clock that afternoon. Promptly at that hour they started, and when they entered the Superintendent's office outside the prison-pen they were received most courteously by Mr. Hibbard. At the same time his face wore an expression that made Miss Seraine shudder. His movements were sluggish, his manner uneasy. She hastened to make known to him the cause of her visit, and at the same time presented Mr. Davis's letter. He scanned the paper very closely without making any remark. The arrangement being made to come at twelve o'clock the next day, they returned to Mrs. Lawton's house.

" Mrs. Lawton was kind, and readily engaged in conversation, giving the most horrible description and picture of the prison and the inhuman treatment the prisoners were receiving. Seraine was silent, and refrained from expressing opinions or making any remarks save to say that she had been treated with great kindness and consideration by the officers she had met. Mrs. Lawton gave her to understand that she had great sympathy for the prisoners, and that she was not entirely in harmony with the rebellion, although she had been a sufferer by the war, having lost her husband in the Confederate service. She said she was living there merely to make what she could by selling things to the soldiers when she was permitted to do so. She had a great contempt for Mr. Hibbard, then keeper of the prison. It seems Hibbard was only there temporarily.

" Miss Seraine slept but little that night,—she was so eager to ascertain if Henry was, or if he had been, there. Next morning she arose early and was ready for breakfast, though she ate but little. When the hour of twelve o'clock arrived she and Mrs. Lawton repaired to the office of Mr. Hibbard as per appointment. They were received in a very polite manner, and informed that a guard would be sent through the grounds with them. They asked if he could not accompany them, as they were very timid about passing through without his presence. He finally consented to attend them as guide and protector.

"On first entering at the south gate they met a stench that almost stifled them. As they passed along they saw the prisoners in groups, standing and gazing at them with a stare like that of maniacs. Some were moderately well clad, others almost in a state of nudity. The pen, for that was what it really was, was in the most filthy condition that human mind could imagine. As they passed along they could see the blush of shame mantle the cheek of their escort. They walked through the center of the grounds, being the dryest and most cleanly. To describe accurately the suffering of the men, the filthy condition of this pen, and the ghastly looks of those poor creatures, was more than any tongue or pen could do. They came to where a portion of the sick were lying under a very poor shelter, and there saw sick men with but little clothing and in all the conditions of human suffering possible. Many were covered with ulcers from scurvy, some were sick with fever, some with their teeth dropping out, some dying with dysentery, some with old wounds not healed, some with fresh ones made by their brutal keepers, and nearly all were literally swarming with vermin.

"Miss Seraine became so sick at these sights that she was almost fainting, and asked to return to the house and be permitted to come earlier the next day, so as not to be in the pen during the midday heat. Her request was granted, and they left the prison. She was greatly alarmed for fear she would find Henry among this suffering class of sick men. The next day they entered the prison at nine o'clock, and passing around on the north side of the grounds found many cooking and eating their meals. There were no satisfactory conveniences for cooking. A little fire and a few pans and cups were all. The meat, what little they had, was broiled on coals. Many took their meal and stirred it in a cup with the most disagreeable water ever used, and drank it down without cooking. Hundreds had died within a few days—some from sheer starvation, as they could no longer take the food into their stomachs; some from scurvy, some from fever, and some were murdered by the guards for passing beyond where ordered. How any one could live in that polluted and poisonous atmosphere was the wonder. In the inclosure there was a dirty, swampy piece of ground, with water stinking with filth of a character sickening to behold. When the rain fell all were subjected to the drenching cold bath. On the ground and in the mud and the damp they lay. Many were there who during the prior Winter had been so exposed as to have their feet frozen, until in many instances they were rotting off.

"These sights were so shocking in all respects that Miss

Seraine was afraid to speak, (except to say a kind word, when permitted to do so,) to any of the unfortunate men. It seemed to her that Hibbard knew where Henry was, but was avoiding bringing her into his presence. So she said not a word, but looked well at all in view as she passed along.

"The punishments for any and every little breach of discipline were of the most outrageous character. She saw many persons with their hands tied behind them, and others standing, with their thumbs run through loops of cords tied up to posts. The guards were insolent and were constantly damning the prisoners. Take it altogether—their dirty, filthy food, their mode of cooking, their scanty rations, their clothes, the stinking water they were forced to use, the treatment of the sick, the punishments they were compelled to bear, the dirty, vile pen they were in, and the poisonous atmosphere they were forced to breathe, there is no account anywhere in the barbarous ages that ever did or could equal Pine Forest Prison.

"Miss Seraine became sick and tired of the horrible sights, and at last said to Mr. Hibbard that she did not wish to go around any more to look upon the suffering prisoners, but desired to be taken where Mr. Lyon was, if in the prison. He replied that he thought he was in the main hospital. They directed their steps thither. On entering it she beheld so many ghastly men at one view that she recoiled, and for a moment hesitated. Recovering herself she proceeded. While passing along she beheld a young man with sunken eyes, pale and ashy cheeks, lying on a board cot, so emaciated that she had no thought of who it could be. But in a moment she heard her name whispered, and saw a lean, bony hand reaching out towards her. She looked at him, took his cold, withered hand, and spoke to him, asking if she could do anything for him. He said :

"'I am Henry Lyon, Seraine. Do you not recognize me ?'

"She fell into Mrs. Lawton's arms, exclaiming : 'My God !' When she revived she fell upon Henry's neck and wept bitterly, exclaiming :

"'My Henry! my Henry! Can it be possible, can it be possible?'

"After some little conversation between them, she telling him that all were well at home, etc., Hibbard informed her that the rules of the prison would not allow any further interview at present."

"What a brute," interrupted Dr. Adams.

"Miss Seraine asked to see Surgeon Jones. She ascer-

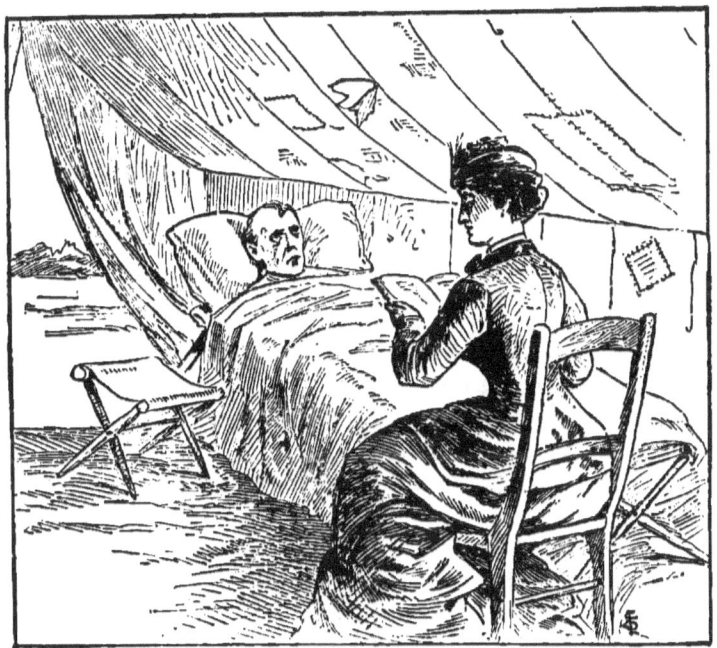

SERAINE WITH HENRY AT PINE FOREST PRISON.

tained that Henry was just recovering from an attack of typhoid fever and was now out of danger. She obtained permission from the Surgeon to visit him daily while she remained, and to bring him certain delicacies to eat. She then returned to Henry and bade him an affectionate good-by, with a promise to see him again. With a sad heart she retraced her steps to Mrs. Lawton's. Retiring to her room

she gave way to her grief and spent the remainder of the
day in tears.

"The following day Mrs. Lawton again accompanied
Seraine to the prison-pen. They took some wine and cake
to Henry. After being refreshed he and Seraine had a
long and pleasant interview, in which Seraine told Henry
all about her trip, etc. She told him she had decided to
leave soon for Richmond, and thence for home, but would
try and arrange with the Surgeon, (who seemed to have
some humanity left,) for Mrs. Lawton to visit and bring him
some nourishment. The prison and the sights beheld by
her had quite affected her nerves. On returning to Mrs.
Lawton's she was suffering with a violent headache, and,
going to her room, she remained in bed for three days.

"Mrs. Lawton was very kind. She sat by her bedside
and gave her a detailed account of her own trials. She was
a daughter of a Union man, and had never lost her venera-
tion for her country and the old flag. Although her husband had lost his life in the Confederate army, she had not
changed her smothered feelings for the Union. She related
to Seraine the many villainous outrages perpetrated upon
the Union prisoners by the inhuman keepers and guards of
this vile den. She told graphically of seven fine-looking
young men who were brought out of the prison for attempting to escape, and shot in the presence of a crowd of jeering
devils. Said she:

"'If a man wishes to learn of "man's inhumanity to
man," this is the place.'

"She expressed her great desire to leave the place, as it
was like dwelling on the verge of the prison for the souls of
the damned. Seraine talked to her of her mission and what
she desired to accomplish; also asked her to keep a watchful
eye on Henry, and when the time should come for an exchange of prisoners to remind Hibbard of Henry as one to
be sent away, provided she could arrange the matter.
Henry had been a prisoner now for more than a year, and
was naturally near the time for his exchange if any one
would look after the matter. After quite a delay on account of her being taken sick again, the time came for her

to leave for Richmond, and after thanking Hibbard for his courtesy, and tendering manifold thanks to Mrs. Lawton for her kindness and great care of her, as well as leaving some money with Mrs. Lawton for Henry's benefit, and promising to write from Richmond if permitted to do so, she embraced Mrs. Lawton as if she were her mother, and with tearful eyes they separated.

"Soon Seraine was on her way to report to Mr. Davis, President of the C. S. A., as she had promised to do, and also to effect an early exchange of prisoners if possible. Her trip was a dreary one. She remained as quiet as possible, having no one to cheer her on her way. On arriving at Richmond she again stopped at the Virginia Hotel, and there again met Capt. Redingson. He expressed pleasure at seeing her, and tendered his services as escort and protector while in the city. After detailing some of her experiences on her journey, and thanking him for his former politeness, and also for his present proffered services, she requested him to bear her compliments to President Davis and ask for an early interview, as she had promised to return and report to him. The Captain readily assented, and on returning that evening informed her that he would be pleased to accompany her to the Executive Office the next day at eleven A.M., at which hour President Davis would see her. She was very anxious and quite nervous until the time arrived. Exactly at eleven o'clock the next day the Captain came for her with a carriage, and very kindly attended her to the presence of the President.

"Mr. Davis met her with cordiality. He spoke to her about her perilous undertaking, and hoped she had been treated kindly by his people. He also inquired as to her success in finding her friend, to all of which she responded that her treatment was kind, and her efforts were so far crowned with success. She gave him an account of her journey and visits to the prisons; her examination of them, and finally her success in finding Henry at Pine Forest. She told him the truth about the prisons, the food, raiment, and treatment of the prisoners. He answered in a manner rather tender, and feelingly expressed his desire

to have matters in this direction improved, but regretted
the impossibility of doing all things as we might desire to
have them done.   He spoke of the barbarism of war and its
attendant cruelties.   But he soon changed the subject,
after thanking her for her honesty and for having the
nerve to tell him the truth.

"He then inquired what she desired in reference to her
friend.   She asked for his release as the only means of saving his life.   He responded that he would order his exchange at once, and promised her that he should be on the
first boat or train sent North with prisoners.   He also gave
her permission to write to Mrs. Lawton on this subject,
provided she did not use his name in connection with this
promise.   He then gave her a letter of safe conduct through
his lines and detailed Capt. Redingson to go with her to our
lines.   Having accomplished the object for which she had
gone South, and reported fully and truthfully to Mr. Davis
as she had promised to do, she took leave of him with her
best wishes for his personal welfare.   He bade her farewell
and God-speed in a very kind and tender manner, so much
so that Seraine has ever spoken kindly of him as a man.

"She repaired to the hotel and told Capt. Redingson that
she desired to leave early the next morning for the Headquarters of the Union army.   He said he would call for her
as requested, and they separated.   Seraine, after going
to her room, wrote to Mrs. Lawton and inclosed a note to
Henry, merely telling him that she was well and on her way
home, encouraging him to bear up under his sufferings, etc.

"The next morning Capt. Redingson called according to
his promise, and they were off at once for the lines of the
armies.   On arriving at the Headquarters of the Confederate army, they were nicely entertained by the commanding
General.   They partook of a good meal and then rested
for the night, Seraine being cared for at a farm house near
by.   The next morning, on being provided with a pass
through the lines, they were conducted under a flag of truce
to the Headquarters of the Union army, some twenty miles
away.

"Seraine was received by the commanding General and

taken care of. Capt. Redingson, after having delivered his
charge, returned with Seraine's blessing for his kindness to
her. After she had taken a rest she conversed with Gen.
Meador, who was then in command, and related to him her
experiences, at the same time keeping her promise to speak
of nothing pertaining to the Confederate army or any
movements of the same. After a night's rest she was sent
under charge of an escort to Washington city, where she
stopped for several days, until she could see the President
and Secretary of War. She finally managed to have an interview with the Secretary, and, after explaining who she
was and her mission South, he replied with some nervousness:

"'Henry Lyon! Is he a son of Daniel Lyon, of Allentown, Ind.?'

"On being answered in the affirmative, he exclaimed:

"'My God? what affliction that family has had! His oldest son died recently, being the third son he has lost since
this war began.'

"This was the first knowledge that Seraine had of the
sad distress in the family. She sighed and dropped a tear.
The Secretary at once understood the situation, and told
her Henry Lyon should be looked after and properly cared
for. She asked if, when he was exchanged, he could not
be discharged from the service. She said that Mr. Lyon's
seven sons were all in the army, and three having lost their
lives, she thought one ought to remain at home to comfort
the parents during their terrible trials. She struck a tender
chord in the Secretary's heart, and he replied: 'Yes; when
he returns, you write me and it shall be done, if he con-
sents.'

"This brought joy to her very soul. She bade the Secretary good-by, saying as she left that he would hear from
her in due time.

"She then called at the President's and sent in his own letter which he had given her when she started South, that
she might thereby be recalled to his memory. He sent for
her at once. As she entered his office he arose and greeted
her most affectionately, calling her 'my child,' and bidding

her be seated. He commenced plying her with questions, and she told him the whole story. When she related what she had seen in the rebel prisons, his countenance saddened and tears fell from his eyes. He said:

"'This must be remedied somehow. Humanity revolts at retaliation in kind, but in an instance like this it might be justified.'

"She told him what she desired, and what the Secretary had promised. He replied:

"'My dear child, it shall be done. My old friend Lyon is making more sacrifices than should be demanded of any one. I hope you will see him soon, and when you do, tell him that I often think of him and his family, as well as what they are doing for their country.'

"The President was a man of generous impulses. He had a very kind heart, full of sympathy for humanity.

"She left the President with feelings of the deepest affection and gratitude, having every assurance that her wishes would be complied with. As she left, he bade her good-by, calling her his 'little heroine.' From Washington she went to Baltimore, learning that some prisoners who had been exchanged were to be landed there. She remained at the Burnett House, most of the time in her room, not wishing to make any acquaintances, but watching the papers closely to ascertain the time for the arrival of the prisoners. One evening she learned that a vessel had come into port with 200 prisoners. She hastened to the dock; arriving all out of breath, and seeing the large crowd that was waiting she became very much excited, and observing an officer in uniform she ventured to speak to him. It was Gen. Shunk, of Ohio. She told him who she was, and also for whom she was looking. He answered her very cordially, and said he knew Mr. Daniel Lyon, formerly of Ohio, and inquired if the person in question was one of his sons. She said he was, and he told her to wait and he would see, as he was then in command at Baltimore. In a few moments he came back with the glad tidings that Henry Lyon was among the prisoners. She was going to rush on board the vessel, but the General detained her, informing her that it was not allowa-

ble under the orders, but he would bring Henry to her as
soon as possible. Soon she saw Henry coming from the vessel, leaning upon the arm of a comrade. He seemed to be
very weak, and still looked like a mere shadow. He was
brought where she stood, trembling and almost fearing
to meet him lest his mind might have given way somewhat
under the trying ordeal through which he had just passed.
She threw her arms around his neck and wept aloud. A
carriage was procured, and she accompanied him, by permission, to the hospital where he was ordered to go. Reaching there, he was placed in a nice clean ward. There they
talked matters over, and Henry agreed to the discharge
from the service. Seraine left him with the nurses, saying
that she would return as soon as possible; at the same time
he was not to let his people know anything of his whereabouts. She left that night for Washington.

"The next morning at the earliest hour that she could see
the Secretary of War, she made her appearance. On meeting the Secretary he recognized her, and asked if she was
after the discharge about which she agreed to write to him.
She replied that Henry was now at Baltimore, having been
exchanged. Then she told him of his condition. The Secretary at once ordered the discharge made out, and as soon
as it had passed through the proper officers' hands and was
returned to him he handed it to her, saying:

"'You deserve this yourself, without any other consideration.'

"She again thanked the Secretary, and at once repaired
to the President's Mansion. When she was admitted, on
seeing her the President guessed from her bright countenance the whole story, and congratulated her most heartily.
She told him all, and showed him Henry's discharge and
thanked him for his kindness. He said:

"'May God bless you, my child, and give you both a safe
journey home!'

"Returning to Baltimore, she made arrangements to
have Henry placed in a clean car and taken to Allentown.
After they were under way she told him about the discharge, and he was delighted. She telegraphed me to meet

her at the depot, but did not say one word about Henry. I
read the dispatch to the family, and many were the conjec-
tures. Peter said she had not found Henry, and a great
variety of opinions were expressed. My wife burst into
tears, fell down on the sofa, and cried, saying she felt that
Henry was dead. Ham, hearing what was being said, concluded it was his turn to guess; so he began:

"'You's all off de track. Ham sees it all frough de glass
in he head, he do.'

"'Go 'long wid you, you ole fool: since you's free you
'spec' you is big and knows a heap. You doesn't know
nuffin, you don't,' said Aunt Martha.

"'Well, alright, Marfa; 'spec' me not know bery much;
but, sho's you is born, dat boy all right; you see, you jes'
wait. I say no mo', but I see what is de matter. You jes'
wait, dat's all you got to do.'

"The next morning I went down to the depot with a
carriage, and there found Seraine and Henry waiting for
me. I embraced my poor boy, overcome with grateful
emotion. My joy was complete in finding him alive. He
was a living skeleton. We were not long in driving to the
house. All were out on the portico to see Seraine, no one
but Ham expecting Henry with her. As they all saw
Henry the family leaped with joy, and rushing out to meet
us, but seeing Henry's ghastly appearance a sudden sadness came over all. We helped him out of the carriage.
He was completely overcome when he saw his mother. She
clasped him in her arms and cried piteously. He was assisted into the house and laid upon the sofa. All seemed
to have overlooked Seraine in their great joy over Henry's
return. I introduced her to each one of the family including old Ham and Aunt Martha.

"'Didn't I see dem in my glass, Marfa; didn't I? What
you got to say now?'

"'I 'spects you did, Ham; dey is heah, sho.' Bress de
Laud; he bring dis boy home. I not see him afore dem
pizen Sesh fix him dat way! Dey starve him. What did
dey do to him to make him look like dat?'

"Soon we all got settled, and after breakfast we heard

Seraine's story. She was our heroine, and no mistake. No one of us could do too much for her. My good wife wanted to have her for a daughter at once. She could not let her go out of her sight for a moment. She hugged her, kissed her, seemed almost to want to take her in her lap as a child; in fact, we all loved her. She had gone through great perils to save our dear boy, and why not love her! For some days we did nothing but talk over her journeyings and what she saw and did. She was the idol of our household. When Henry had gained strength enough to bear up under the double shock, we told him of the death of David and James, which painful news he had not heard before. It took him many days to rally after this melancholy intelligence of the fate of his dear brothers. After Henry was strong enough to walk about without help Seraine thought she must leave us for a time and return home. This saddened our hearts, as we had grown much attached to her. But she and Henry talked the matter over, making their own arrangements, and the next day Jackson escorted her to her home in Michigan. When she left, no family ever wept more in sorrow at the departure of any one than did ours.

"There was a mystery connected with her periling her life in the way she did that I could not then solve, but I made no inquiry into her secret.

"Of the few left to us they were now once more nearly all together, and further plans were in order."

At this point Dr. Adams said: "The horrors of those rebel prisons have ever been like a specter before me whenever I hear them mentioned."

Judge Reed here interrupted, saying: "I indorse every word of Miss Whitcomb's description of these prisons. I endured their horrors and inhumanity for nine months, and she does not tell the half that might be told. To show that Seraine's statement is not in the least exaggerated, I have saved an article from the Sumter (S. C.) *Watchman*, published in reference to the Florence Prison at that time, which seems to have equaled the Pine Forest.".

Being asked to do so, Dr. Adams read as follows:

"The Camp we found full of what were once human beings, but who would scarcely now be recognized as such. In an old field, with no inclosures but the living wall of sentinels who guard them night and day, are several thousand filthy, diseased, famished men, with no hope of relief, except by death. A few dirty rags stretched on poles give some of them a poor protection from the hot sun and heavy dews. All were in rags and barefoot, and crawling with vermin. As we passed around the line of guards I saw one of them brought out of his miserable booth by two of his companions and laid upon the ground to die. He was nearly naked. His companions pulled his cap over his face and straightened out his limbs. Before they turned to leave him he was dead. A slight movement of the limbs and all was over—the captive was free! The Commissary's tent was close by one side of the square, and near it the beef was laid upon boards preparatory to its distribution. This sight seemed to excite the prisoners as the smell of blood does the beasts of the menagerie. They surged up as near the lines as they were allowed, and seemed, in their eagerness, about to break over. While we were on the ground a heavy rain came up, and they seemed to greatly enjoy it, coming out *a puris naturalibus*, opening their mouths to catch the drops, while one would wash off another with his hands, and then receive from him the like kind of office. Numbers get out at night and wander to the neighboring houses in quest of food.

"From the camp of the living we passed to the camp of the dead—the hospital—a transition which reminded me of Satan's soliloquy—

> "Which way I fly is hell; myself am hell,
> And in the lowest deeps, a lower deep,
> Still threatening to devour me, opens wide."

"A few tents, covered with pine-tops, were crowded with the dying and the dead in every stage of corruption. Some lay in prostrate helplessness; some had crowded under the shelter of the bushes; some were rubbing their skeleton limbs. Twenty or thirty of them die daily; most of these, as I was informed, of the scurvy. The corpses laid by the roadside waiting for the dead-cart, their glaring eyes turned to heaven, the flies swarming in their mouths, their big-toes tied together with a cotton string, and their skeleton arms folded on their breasts. You would hardly know them to be men, so sadly do hunger, disease, and wretchedness change 'the human face divine.' Presently came the carts; they were carried a little distance to trenches dug for the purpose and tumbled in like so many dogs. A few pine-tops were thrown upon the bodies, a few shovelfuls of dirt, and then haste was made to open a new ditch for other victims. The burying party were Yankees detailed for the work, an appointment which, as the Sergeant told me, they consider a favor, for they get a little more to eat and enjoy fresh air.

"Thus we see at one glance the three great scourges of mankind—war, famine, and pestilence, and we turn from the spectacle sick at heart, as we remember that some of our loved ones may be undergoing a similar misery."

"This publication," said Col. Bush, "made in one of their own papers at the time, proves that all that has ever been said of their treatment of our prisoners is true."

"Yes," said Uncle Daniel, "and much more."

"Uncle Daniel," said Dr. Adams, "this Miss Seraine Whitcomb was, indeed, a true woman, and, as the President well said, a 'little heroine.' I take it she was rather small, from this expression of his."

"Yes, she was rather small, but a pure jewel."

"She was a woman of great determination, and loved purely and strongly. There are but few instances of such pure devotion and rare patriotism to be found in the annals of history. What feelings she must have had while traveling through the Confederacy in such anguish and suspense. She was a jewel, sure enough."

Col. Bush here interrupted, saying : "The condition of our poor soldiers in the prisons she visited must have driven her almost insane. It certainly drove many of the poor sufferers into a state or condition of insanity, in which numbers died in their ravings and delirium."

9

"Is it not wonderful," said Dr. Adams, "how soon these barbarities and inhumanities are forgotten by our people?"

"Yes," said Col. Bush; "but you must remember that our people are moving too rapidly to look back upon scenes of distress. Money and power are now the watchwords—throw patriotism to the dogs. It is not needed now to save their property and their rights. You must remember that a man like Hibbard, the deputy at Pine Forest Prison, who allowed men to be shot down like dogs and starved like wild beasts, is now looked upon with more consideration and favor than Uncle Daniel, who gave his whole family as a sacrifice for his country. Did not this same Hibbard travel all through our country last Fall making speeches? Was he not received with shouts by our very neighbors, within a stone's throw of this dear old man, whose son was starved near unto death in Pine Forest Prison by this man? Has he not held high positions in his State since? And I would not be surprised to hear that he had been appointed to some Foreign Mission, in order that he may represent our country abroad in the true Christian spirit of our advanced civilization!"

"Yes," said Uncle Daniel; "when he was North on his stumping tour I mentioned the fact of his inhumanity, and only received jeers from those who heard me—some young students who were not old enough to be in the war, and now feel that it must never be mentioned except in a whisper. It seems that all the treason, infamy, and the barbarities and cruelties practiced during that bloody period are now condoned, and the persons who practiced the greater wrongs are made thereby the more respectable. Oh, that I had not lived to see these things! It makes me almost doubt my own existence. Sometimes I feel that it is all a dream."

Maj. Clymer, in order to draw the aged man's mind away from this unpleasant theme, inquired if he knew what became of Mrs. Lawton.

"I cannot tell," said Uncle Daniel; "she and Seraine corresponded for a number of years after the termination the war. The last we ever heard of her she had marri

with an Englishman and located in Canada. God knows, I
hope she may yet be living and happy. She was a noble
woman. I fear, however, that she, too, has passed away,
as we have had no tidings of her for many years."

Uncle Daniel at this time becoming weary and very melancholy, we excused him for the present, and asked permission to return again, when he promised that he would continue his narrative, and, bidding him good-night, we left,
with an increased desire to hear more from his honest and
truthful lips.

CHAPTER XV.

" The earth had not
A hole to hide this deed.— SHAKESPEARE.

SOME weeks having elapsed since Uncle Daniel was excused, we were anxious to hear him further, and assembled again at Mr. Wilson's house. Uncle Daniel
was feeling quite well, greeted us pleasantly, and
asked that we be seated. After the compliments of the
season, we inquired if he was ready to continue his story.
He replied that he was, and began by saying:

"After Jackson had returned from escorting Seraine to
her home in Detroit, we discussed the question as to what
steps should now be taken. Gen. Anderson was still quite
feeble, his wound being very painful. It was thought that
it would require considerable time for him to recover sufficiently to again be able to take the field. He thought it
would, perhaps, be several months. Jackson, after reflection, thought he would continue his investigation of the
Golden Circle conspiracy, and to do so satisfactorily deemed
it best for him to go to England and get on the track of
their allies in that country, and see what preparations were
being made abroad in connection with the leaders in this
country. Gen. Anderson thought this a good plan.
Henry, who had been growing stronger, said to Jackson,
that while he (Jackson) was making his voyage of discovery through parts of Europe, he would go to Canada as
soon as he was able to do so, and carry out the plans left
unexecuted by Jackson at the time he returned from New

York. This arrangement being understood by all, we sent Ham out to the farm, in order that Dent might be summoned to Allentown to give us what information he had gathered, if any, during our afflictions and consequent suspension of our operations in that direction,

"We directed Ham to bring Mr. Dent back with him the next morning. At ten o'clock Joseph Dent and Ham arrived from the farm. As soon as we could conveniently do so, we had an interview with Dent as to what was transpiring in his immediate neighborhood among his friends, the Knights of the Golden Circle. He related to us the facts in reference to a meeting held two nights before, about which he had intended to come in that day and tell us, if Ham had not come after him. The facts, as he stated them to us, were these:

"A person by the name of Harris stated to his confederates that he was just from Richmond, Va., at the same time claiming to be a member of the Confederate Congress from Missouri. (A part of Missouri believed that it had seceded, as you may remember, just as a few Counties in Kentucky thought they had.) Harris had passed through the lines, coming through West Virginia and Kentucky, as any one could have done at any time, and as many doubtlesss did. His statement, as Dent told it to us, was this: That he was sent by the President of the Confederate States (so-called), and was on his way to Indianapolis to lay a plan before the leaders in this and other States; thence he was to pass into Canada and meet the leaders there, and in that way have prompt action and co-operation assured. His greatest desire seemed to be to meet Mr. Thos. A. Strider, who, he said, was one of their best and shrewdest advisers. His headquarters were to be at Windsor, Canada. He directed the Lodge to which Dent belonged to be ready at a moment's notice to do whatever might be directed from the Supreme Council. He told his hearers to spread the alarm wherever they could without being suspected, that there was to be a great destruction of property in the North; that, he said, would terrify leading men and property holders; and, in order to satisfy his confederates that there was a basis for this statement, he disclosed a part of a plot that had been proposed to Jefferson Davis and was soon to be carried out. It was that a discovery had been recently made by a professor of chemistry, one McCullough, by which towns and cities, and vessels coming in and going out of our ports, could be easily burned without danger of discovery. With this newly-discovered combustible material a general and wholesale destruction of all kinds of destructible property was to be inaugurated. Harris said that agents were to be employed all over the country, who were to be selected from the members of the Knights and to be made up of the most reliable and tried men; that this matter had been duly considered and determined upon by the authorities at Richmond; that Jacob Thomlinson, C. C. Carey and others were now on their way to England to meet Mr. McCullough, who was already there, and where the destructive material was to be manufactured and brought in an English vessel to Canada, as there was no way of getting from the Confederate States to the place from which they wished to operate without running the gauntlet, and perhaps meeting with dangers not desirable to be encountered. This man Harris also instructed all who heard him that the penalty now fixed by the authorities in the Councils of the Knights for disclosing any of their secrets was death, which might be inflicted by any of the Order ascertaining the fact so that no doubt could exist as to the guilt of the person who had played traitor to them.

"This, I could see, alarmed Dent and made him cautious and hesitating at times when we would give expression to our utter abhorrence of the use of such villainous means as seemed to be in contemplation by our enemies. We constantly assured the old man, however, that he need have no fears of any of us, which, of course, he had not; yet he was somewhat timid. He could not tell which way Harris started from their meeting, nor how he was traveling. This ended his recollection of Harris's statement. We then got Dent again to repeat the signs, grips, passwords and instructions to Gen. Anderson and Capt. Jackson, as well as to Henry, and so they found themselves well posted. Then, thanking Dent and encouraging him to persevere in his discoveries, we allowed him to go and make his arrangements with David's widow about matters at the farm and then return home.

"The next day I wrote to the President, giving him the history of matters as detailed to us by Joseph Dent; also, the plan we had laid out for the future. In a few days I received a note from Washington, unsigned, merely saying, 'the plan is approved.' I knew from whom the note came, and was well satisfied to have the plans carried out.

"The next day we received a letter from Peter, informing us that he was well, and that the Army of the Center was in camp and were expecting a long rest after the two great battles. This delighted my wife, as she felt that while they were not moving, her boys were safe. By this time all necessary arrangements had been made for Jackson's departure, and after bidding his mother and the rest of us good-by he left for New York; from there he expected to sail for Europe. On arriving at New York he called upon Mc-Masterson and B. Wudd, and made satisfactory statements to them as to the reasons for not going to Canada. After obtaining letters of introduction to Jacob Thomlinson they proceeded to discuss the situation, and from them he learned that preparations, such as had been detailed to us by Dent, were evidently being made for great damage to towns, cities, and property generally. He also obtained letters from McMasterson to some important persons in London, where he professed to be going on some mission for the rebels. The letters, as before, introduced Mr. Jackson, of Memphis, Tenn.

"He sailed the following day and had a pleasant voyage. While on board the vessel crossing the Atlantic he made the acquaintance of one Capt. Redingson, a jolly, gentlemanly companion. They were very suspicious of each other for some time, but finally Capt. Redingson gave him the sign of the Golden Circle, to which Jackson responded. The friendship was then at once established. Jackson carefully felt his way,—as you have seen, he was a cautious man,—and finally discovered that Capt. Redingson was

well acquainted in Memphis. This rather placed Jackson
in a dilemma, as his letters located him at Memphis. Finally
he turned the conversation in the direction of building
railroads, and finding that Capt. Redingson knew nothing
about railroads, he mentioned that he had been employed
in engineering work on the Memphis & Chattanooga Railroad. He said he lived in Ohio, but claimed Memphis,
Tenn., as his residence, inasmuch as he was a rebel and

JACKSON STARTS FOR EUROPE.

would have nothing whatever to do with the North while
they were making war against his friends, as his people
were all natives of Virginia, he himself having been born
there. This statement made all things right, and the two
had a jolly good time together the remainder of the voyage.

"During one of their conversations Capt. Redingson, in
relating some of his war experiences, made mention of the
fact that at one time, not long past, he had met a young
lady from Michigan in search of her sweetheart, and that

he had been her escort while she was at Richmond, and
through their lines to ours. At this moment Jackson told
me that he came very near spoiling everything by his agitation, but by rising and taking a glass of water had time
to recover, and then listened to the story with great interest, asking a question occasionally. Capt. Redingson finally
took a small book from his pocket and read her name, 'Seraine Whitcomb,' and that of her lover, 'Henry Lyon,' and
remarked, that he intended, if ever he should have an opportunity, to find out the history of the two, as she had
impressed him very favorably, and, in fact, had excited his
admiration,—she was so gentle and frank, and withal so
brave. Jackson said at this point he again became very
thirsty.

"Very soon the conversation took a turn in another direction, and Jackson inquired if the Captain thought there
were any persons in London looking after the interests of
the Confederacy, to which the Captain replied that Jacob
Thomlinson, C. C. Carey, and one or two others that he did
not know, were there on a secret mission, the nature of
which was not fully known to him, as he had only returned
to Richmond from Mexico on one day and left under orders
the next, and had to run the blockade in order to get
away. His description of the passing of our vessels in the
night out from Wilmington in a vessel laden with cotton ;
the darkness, the stillness of the night, the lights on our
vessels, the fear of being discovered and overtaken, the joy
he experienced when they had passed our line and were
covered by one of their fast-running cruisers (the Susque-
hanna) was indeed quite graphic. Jackson said that although the Captain was a rebel, and perhaps engaged in
running the blockade frequently, yet he was cheerful, and
took everything that seemed to be working against their
success so philosophically that he enjoyed his company,
and rather liked him. During the trip Capt. Redingson
learned to like Jackson also, and made him a confidant,
promising to introduce him to many friends after they
should arrive, among whom he included Jacob Thomlinson,
Carey, and many others. He finally disclosed to Jackson

the fact that he was sent by the authorities at Richmond to London and Paris with a large amount of Confederate bonds for sale, and that he would take Jackson with him to visit the bankers, and also get him introduced, so that he might be admitted to some of the Gentlemen's clubs, where he could hear much discussion pro and con about the war. It seemed that Capt. Redingson had been across several times on business for the Confederacy.

"When the vessel reached port, and all was ready, the two went out together, and from Liverpool to London were engaged in conversation as to how they could best manage to enjoy themselves while in London, and at the same time attend to the business for which they were abroad. Jackson had satisfied the Captain that he was going more to find out how the people there felt, and the probabilities of the English Government rendering aid to the Southern Confederacy, for the purpose of his speculating in bonds and stocks, than for anything else, and at the same time to aid if he could the friends of the Confederacy everywhere; and to use all means, no matter what, for their success. They had not noticed any of the important points until they came within some ten or twelve miles of London, when their attention was attracted by the church and school buildings of Harrow, beautifully situated on a hill rising from a plain. This celebrated institution is one of the first in the Kingdom. It was founded in the reign of Queen Elizabeth. Many distinguished men have been educated there, among whom were Lord Byron, Sir Robert Peel, and Lord Palmerston. After this the Captain and Jackson took much interest in the historic objects presenting themselves till they reached London.

"On arriving they engaged rooms at the Charing Cross Hotel. During the next day Capt. Redingson found his friend Jacob Thomlinson and brought him to his room. Very soon after this he invited Jackson in and introduced him as Mr. Wm. Jackson, of Memphis, Tenn., a good and true friend of the Confederacy, who was willing to do anything to aid in making the rebellion a success. Mr. Thomlinson received him with much cordiality, and conversed very

freely, but cautiously.   He was not quite as free and easy
as Capt. Redingson.   Finally Mr. Thomlinson invited them
to visit him at his hotel, 'The Palace,' near Buckingham
Palace, on the following evening, stating he would have
some friends who would be pleased to meet them.   Jackson
was very desirous to accept this invitation, as perhaps the
opportunity would be afforded to get some information of
value, and was consequently delighted that Capt. Redingson promptly indicated their acceptance.

"In good season they made their toilets as if they were
to meet the Queen of England or the Prince of Wales, and
set out for the Palace Hotel.   On arriving at the hotel and
notifying Mr. Thomlinson of their presence, they were
ushered into his apartments, which they found were most
elaborate and elegant.

"On entering they were presented to Mr. C. C. Carey,
Prof. McCullough, and Dr. Blackman, of Kentucky.   These
men had the appearance of the Southern aristocrats, except Prof. McCullough, whose manner and speech denoted
Northern antecedents.   Jackson noted this particularly,
and in the subsequent conversation he learned that the
Professor was of Northern birth and education, having
been, prior to 1860, professor of chemistry at Princeton
College, N. J.   For a time the conversation ran on the
voyage and the many interesting places that should be
visited by all travelers.   Before the evening was over, however, the topic was changed, and the success of the Confederacy (as they were pleased to call it) became the en-
grossing subject of discussion.

"Jackson was here tested and found not only sound in
this, the most interesting of all questions to them, but it
was thought he might be made very useful in assisting
them in perfecting and executing their plans.

"Mr. Thomlinson and Captain Redingson discussed the
selling of bonds, etc.; Thomlinson stating that the intention of the authorities at Richmond was to have given
him the bonds, but that they were not prepared in time, as
he had to leave at a certain date to escape the blockade, on
account of his previous relations with the United States

Government. Captain Redingson replied that he knew
nothing about the business except from his instructions,
and he could not do otherwise than to obey them.

"After many suggestions it was finally understood that a
meeting of the gentlemen then present should be held every
evening at the same rooms, except when engagements otherwise should interfere. Capt. Redingson and Jackson then
took leave of the other parties and returned to their hotel.

"After going to their rooms Captain Redingson remarked
that he wished Jackson to stay with him and be his guest,
as he feared he might need a friend in future in reference
to his business; that he desired him to witness his trans-
actions in reference to the sale of the bonds in his custody.
At the same time he asked Jackson if he had heard what
Thomlinson stated in reference to his (Thomlinson) being
the one who was to have placed the bonds. Jackson responded that he had. Redingson said :

"'Mr. Jackson, I intend to deal honestly with my Government (meaning the Confederacy) in this whole matter,
and I do not intend that these bonds in my possession shall
be a missing 'Indian Trust Fund?'

"Jackson remarked, 'Why, Captain, what do you mean
by Indian Trust Fund?'

"'Oh! nothing,' said the Captain; 'it was a mere idle
remark.'

"This, however, opened a flood of light in upon Jackson's
mind in reference to matters of the past, in connection with
certain frauds upon the United States Government. He
pretended not to understand the Captain, however, and
there the conversation on this subject dropped. Jackson
thanked the Captain for his generosity, but declined to accept his offer,—that of being his guest while in London,—
but said he would remain with him as long as he could do
so. They agreed that the next day they would visit some
few points of interest while resting and before starting into
business matters, and separated for the night. After Jackson had retired to his room he jotted down what he had
seen and heard, the names of those whom he had met, etc.,
and at the same time he concluded there was a chance for a

fair-sized row between Jacob Thomlinson and Capt. Redingson. Evidently, the latter had but little confidence in
the former, and was determined to look well to his own
matters of business.

"The next morning, after they had breakfasted, a programme was arranged and they started out in a cab sight-
seeing. The first place of interest visited was the monument at Fish-street Hill, near London Bridge, which stands
as the enduring monument to London's great fire in 1666.
The next place, which is usually the first one visited by
travelers, was Westminster Abbey—the shrine of the ashes
of some of the most illustrious and greatest of England's
dead. They then visited the Temple, being next in anti-
quarian interest; then St. Paul's Church, the Middle and
Inner Temple Hall, Middle Temple Library, Temple Gar-
dens, and one or two of the principal parks. By this time
they had whiled away the most of the day, and therefore
returned to Charing Cross Hotel.

"After dinner that evening they again visited the rooms
of Jacob Thomlinson and found the same friends of the
evening before. After salutations, and the ordinary chat
about London and the points visited by each, the conversation again turned on the war at home. On this occasion
ways and means were discussed very freely. The Professor
and Dr. Blackman seemed to be really fiendish in their feelings and suggestions. The Professor was very anxious that
money should be obtained at once, in order that the plan
agreed to at Richmond should be entered upon without
delay, which was, as heretofore stated, that the material
was to be made in large quantities wherewith towns, cities
and other property could be easily burned without detec-
tion. Jackson inquired of the Professor what his combustible was, to which he replied:

"'There are but two men who have the secret; it cannot
be given without the consent of both and in the presence
of both. I can,' he continued, ' burn the city of New York
in one day or night by throwing this preparation in eight
or ten places at the same point of time, and no power can
prevent its success in making destruction certain. The

person throwing it can, by a certain gauge, give himself plenty of time to be entirely out of the sight of any one who might chance to be near. In that way he would not even be suspected. When the explosion takes place the flames will instantly cover an entire block of buildings. It has been so thoroughly tested that there is now no longer any doubt of the destructive power of the material.'

"Capt. Redingson here interposed a question, desiring to know if this would come within the range of civilized warfare ?

"'Civilized warfare!' said Dr. Blackman; 'what do I care for the rules of civilized warfare? Have not these Yankees destroyed our property ? Are they not setting our slaves free? Is not that destruction of our property rights ?'

"'Yes,' said Capt. Redingson ; 'but this is retaliation on property and persons that are not doing any injury. You must remember that we have many good friends North, and this mode of warfare would be the destruction of women and children.'

"'Very well,' said Dr. Blackman; 'let that be so. If those people are, as you say, our friends, let them join in and help us. They can stop this war if they want to do so. No, sir! they are only pretended friends. They are after the dollar, and play between the lines !'

"Jacob Thomlinson here spoke up, saying: 'You are quite right, Doctor; we cannot look for help from any of those people, and the sooner we light up their cities with a grand and bright light the better !'

"'Very well, gentlemen ; I was merely wishing to understand the matter,' said Capt. Redingson.

"Dr. Blackman by this time was walking to and fro across the room somewhat excitedly. Halting in front of Capt. Redingson, he said : 'I presume that your Christian sentiments would revolt at my proposition, and to which the authorities have already assented.'

"'What is that ?' quickly inquired Capt. Redingson.

"'It is to spread disease in the Northern cities and through the Northern army.'

"The Captain promptly replied : 'Well, sir, this would

be a novel way of fighting battles. I had supposed that physicians were educated in the line of preventing and curing diseases, and not in the practice of how to spread them.'

" ' Yes, sir ! as a principle, that is so ; but in a case like this, where is the difference between shooting a man to death and poisoning him to death ?' said the Doctor.

"'Doctor, I can see a very great difference. In the one case you fight him, giving him an equal chance with yourself ; in the other, you murder him in the most dastardly and cowardly manner.'

" ' I am greatly surprised at you, sir,' said the Doctor. ' I thought you were one of our truest men ?'

"'So I am,' responded the Captain. 'But, Doctor, we had better not discuss this matter further. I shall obey my orders ; but please excuse me from anything more than to do so in the direction of which you were speaking.'

"During this discussion Jackson had remained silent. The Doctor, turning to him, said :

"'Mr. Jackson, what are your views on the subjects under discussion ?'

"To this Jackson replied that, being unacquainted with the usages of war, he was not competent to decide, but he thought while all parties implicitly obey orders, he did not see that individual opinions cut very much of a figure in the operations of a great war.

"Thomlinson said that was the most sensible solution of the question ; that he presumed there were a great many questions upon which we might all have very different shades of opinion.

"'But, Doctor,' said Jackson, 'there is a difficulty in my mind as to how you are to carry out your proposed plan.'

"'Not the slightest difficulty, sir. I have already made arrangements with all the smallpox hospitals of England, so that instead of destroying or burying in the ground the towels, sheets, covers, blankets, and under-clothing, they are all to be boxed up tightly and covered with clean blankets and sent to an out-of-the-way place which I have prepared. I am to pay for them on delivery. I have persons employed, all of whom have passed through the most malignant forms of the disease. They are collecting and having brought to this out-house those infected goods. When I have a sufficient quantity of them I shall purchase a large amount of material used by soldiers, such as handkerchiefs, stockings, underwear, sheets for hospitals, etc., mix them with the infected goods, box them up and ship them to the Sanitary Commission in New York by way of Canada for distribution to the Union Soldiers, post hospitals, and sanitariums. I shall go to the Charity Hospital Association here and get permission to send them in their name; in fact, I have the permission now. They, of course, do not know they are infected goods, but I have given them the list of goods I intend to purchase, and they will give me the letter I wish, turning the goods over to me as their agent to take them to New York and present them to the Sanitary Commission for the Union armies. I have given to them the name of James Churchill, of London.'

"'But, Doctor, how will you take them on board ship without danger to the people on the vessel?'

"'Very easily, sir. There is not the slightest danger in doing so. I will pack them inside fresh linens and blankets, with cotton and paper outside of them, making the boxes of good material and very close in the joints. I shall leave for New York in about one month, and I have no fears that I will not succeed in doing great damage to the army, and also to the members of the Sanitary Commission who handle the goods. I regard the Commission as a set of scamps and hypocrites.'

"Jackson here interrupted, saying: 'Doctor, you seem to have your scheme pretty well planned, and it looks as though it might be a success.'

"This Dr. Blackman seems to have been a communicative individual, and Jackson having sounded him all that he wished at that time, the Captain and Jackson took their leave and repaired to their hotel. When there the Captain walked into Jackson's room and stood for a moment looking straight into Jackson's face. Finally, he spoke in about these words:

" 'Mr. Jackson, I am a rebel ! I am what is called a traitor
to the United States Government. I am in favor of the
whole country becoming one universal wreck before I would
submit to go back into the Union. But, sir, I want you to
remember, if you should ever think of Capt. Redingson in
the future, that his mother was a Christian woman, and
taught her son to have some of the instincts of humanity.
No, sir; I am no murderer; no city burner; no poisoner !
I have listened to all these things and remained partially

BURNING OF THE WILL-O'-THE-WISP.

silent. But, as God is my judge, I will not be a party to
any of these schemes. I will obey all legitimate orders, so far
as money is concerned, and as a soldier will do my duty;
but no man has a right to order me to commit murder or
to perform inhuman acts, and I will not do it !'

"Jackson listened to him, and then gave him his hand,
saying:

" 'Captain, you are a man, and a gentleman, with true
appreciation of what may be justified in war, and that
which cannot be.'

"The Captain said he would go the next day to see the syndicate that was to take the bonds, and as soon as he could arrange his matters he would leave London.

"Jackson told him he would go with him, and they parted for the night with that understanding.

"The next day the Captain made a visit to the office of the syndicate, where all the preliminaries were arranged. Jackson, at the Captain's request, and in pursuance of their former understanding, accompanied him. An arrangement was made for the Captain to meet these gentlemen the next day at the Bank of England, where the bonds were to be verified with papers sent by the Secretary of the Treasury of the Confederacy. Being quite weary they did not that evening visit the rooms of Jacob Thomlinson. After the Captain retired Jackson wrote to me a detailed statement of all that had transpired, and directed his letter to his mother, so that no suspicion could attach, not knowing what might happen.

"I will digress here a moment to say that the letter was received in the due course of the mail. The statements it contained as to the proposed schemes were so revolting that they struck terror to my very soul. I left for Washington the next morning. On arriving there I laid the letter before the President. He read it and seemed to be dumfounded. He finally said :

"'Is it possible that such men live in this day and age ?'

"He sent for the Secretary of War. The letter contained a minute description of Dr. Blackman and Professor Mc-Cullough. Certain reliable officers were at once detailed and dispatched to New York, with proper authority to arrest either or both of these men, if they or either of them should chance to enter that city. The President talked freely with me after this was done, asking me many questions about the feelings of the people. As soon as I could leave Washington I did so. Having performed my errand I returned home and found Henry sufficiently recovered to undertake his promised trip to Canada, and the day following my arrival he started. I have wandered from the subject, however, and must get back to London."

"It is all interesting, Uncle Daniel," said Dr. Adams.

"Yes, yes! but I must get back to London. The day agreed upon the Captain (Jackson accompanying him), met the gentlemen of the syndicate of the Bank of England, and then and there the bonds in the possession of Capt. Redingson were verified and found correct according to the Secretary's letters. The bonds taken by the syndicate amounted to several millions of dollars, and, much to the surprise of the Captain, the syndicate had instructions also from the authorities at Richmond to place two millions in the Bank of England to the credit of the Treasury of the Confederate Government, one million in the Bank of France to the same credit, and one million in the Bank of England to the credit of Jacob Thomlinson, and the remainder ($50,000) to be paid to Capt. T. P. Redingson. This he placed to his own credit. He then took a statement of the whole transaction from the bank. After giving his signature, so that he might draw for his money, he was then ready to leave. When asked if he knew Mr. Jacob Thomlinson, he replied that he did, and then in turn asked the bank officer the same question. He answered that Mr. Thomlinson was well known to the bank, and, in fact, was then in the back room in consultation with some other gentlemen. This seemed to nettle the Captain, as he felt that he was watched by Thomlinson. Jackson asked the Captain if he was ready to return. He signified that he was. They took leave of all the gentlemen, and left for their hotel.

"That evening they visited the rooms of Jacob Thomlinson. Before starting the Captain spoke rather angrily about Mr. Thomlinson's conduct and about the amount of money placed to Thomlinson's credit. Jackson, being a very deliberate man, advised the Captain not to have any discussion with Thomlinson, but to take everything for granted and to agree to whatever plans the gentlemen at the rooms might suggest ; that he could leave the country whenever he wished, and not meet them at any point in the United States or Canada. The Captain, with some warmth, said :

"'Mr. Jackson, I will not meet them anywhere away from here to assist in carrying out their murderous plots and schemes! Thomlinson has the money to his credit, and can buy and pay for what he pleases. I will no longer be responsible; and the fact that so much money is placed to his credit causes me to have suspicion that these schemes, as they say, have been indorsed by the authorities at Richmond. Now, my dear sir, if I knew that to be true, so help me Heaven, I would renounce the whole concern, as much of a rebel as I am. I would go to Mexico or some other country and live. What! I, Thomas P. Redingson, a man of reputation, born of Christian parents, assisting in spreading disease amongst poor soldiers, who are merely obeying the orders of their Government? No, sir! no sir! never! I do not believe that the All-seeing God will allow this infamy to prosper.'

"Jackson then said: 'Captain, let us go; they may be waiting for us.'

"They proceeded to the meeting place. Upon entering they found all present, and apparently feeling very much gratified at something. The champagne was flowing freely and the conversation became quite loud. A new face appeared in their midst. They were introduced to him. His name was given as Dr. Mears, formerly of Washington City. In the course of the evening it was disclosed that he was the man referred to by Prof. McCullough as the only man other than himself possessing the secret of the discovery of the great combustible that was to burn up the world. Jackson excused himself from taking any wine on account of his head not being in good condition. After many bumpers they all sat down to review the situation.

"C. C. Carey said that the first thing now, since the necessary money had been provided, was to ascertain what length of time would be necessary to perfect the arrangements, as well as for Dr. Blackman to complete his collection.

"Dr. Blackman, always loquacious, spoke up instantly, 'I will be ready in two weeks.'

"Prof. McCullough thought it would require a greater length of time for him and Dr. Mears to make proper preparations. He thought that four weeks would be sufficient time.

"So it was finally decided that the three should make their arrangements to be ready to sail within four weeks, and that they would sail on the same vessel for Montreal, Canada. Jacob Thomlinson and C. C. Carey were to precede them and have matters all prepared for taking care of and storing their materials. The time was not then fixed for these gentlemen to sail, but it was understood they should go in advance and make all the necessary arrangements for quick and effective work as soon as the Professor and the two Doctors should arrive in Montreal. The plan was that agents were to be selected from their sworn friends of the Golden Circle, who were known to be tried and true men of great daring and courage. These men were to be placed at different points, where they were to be furnished with the material and instructed by Prof. McCullough and Dr. Mears on their arrival. Their operations were to be from Canada. The agents were to operate against New York and New England towns and cities from Montreal; also, against Buffalo and interior cities in the State of New York from Toronto, and against Cleveland, Cincinnati and Chicago from Windsor.

"These preliminaries having been settled, the next inquiry was as to how the money was to be placed to defray all the expenses. Mr. Thomlinson made inquiry as to the amount that would be required. The estimates were made at once by Dr. Blackman for his part, and by Prof. McCullough for the 'fireworks,' as Redingson now called them. The two estimates footed up $109,000. Thomlinson thought that would be very extravagant. The Professor inquired if he knew the material to be used. Thomlinson admitted that he did not.

"Jackson saw that Redingson was regarding Prof. McCullough, with a look of intense curiosity. Nothing was said for some moments. The silence was finally broken by Mr. Carey saying that he thought it might be a good plan to have one of the party who was to remain in London to have the amount placed to his credit somewhere, so that he could act as Treasurer for the two divisions of labor, and draw all the checks or drafts necessary. Dr. Blackman spoke to Thomlinson, saying that he thought well of that plan.

"'Well, gentlemen,' Mr. Thomlinson said, 'whom will you select?'

"Prof. McCullough said: 'I do not care; I am willing that Dr. Blackman shall act if he will do so. What say you, Dr. Mears?' The Doctor assented, and it was so arranged.

"Jacob Thomlinson said: 'All right, gentlemen; on to-morrow I will make the deposit, and then Mr. Carey and myself will take the first chance for getting to Canada, in in order to make the arrangements as now understood.' At the same time he asked Capt. Redingson when and where would his orders take him.

"The Captain replied that he should return to Richmond as soon as he could get through the lines. Speaking to Jackson, he said: 'I suppose you will remain in London for the present.'

"'Yes,' replied Jackson; 'I shall look around the country some little before returning.'

"They all agreed to have one final meeting the next evening, prior to separating for their various destinations. Bidding each other good-night they left.

"Capt. Redingson and Jackson wended their way to their hotel. After arriving at their rooms Capt. Redingson commenced the conversation. You will notice that these two men never talked on the street, or elsewhere than in their room. Redingson said to Jackson:

"'Did you see how loath Thomlinson was to put money in any other hands than his own?'

"'I saw some hesitancy,' said Jackson.

"'Well, sir, he proposes to spend only what is absolutely necessary. None of it will ever find its way into the Confederate Treasury. He loves money equal to any Yankee. But now, Mr. Jackson, what do you propose? Will you return to New York, or will you remain here for a time?

"Said Jackson, 'I ought to return very soon, but I have learned but little as yet in reference to the sentiments of the people in England, and am thinking of remaining for a short time longer.'

"'Well, sir, if you have no objections, I will remain for a time with you. I would like to see and learn more than I have about several matters. Let us go to-morrow and take a look around. What do you say?'

"'Very well,' replied Jackson.

"'Good night,' said the Captain.

"When Jackson was alone, he wrote again under cover of his mother's name, without signing his own, giving full details of the plan of attack on the cities named, agents to be employed, etc. He gave the names of places in Canada from which the attacks with fire were to be made. Thomlinson and Carey's headquarters were to be at Montreal; therefore Jackson suggested that I send for Henry and put him on the track, and for him to discover the agents so they could be arrested, etc. This, he thought, could not be risked in a letter to Canada. Hence, I wrote to Henry to come home. He came at once. I gave him Jackson's letter and he studied it, making diagrams, etc., and then returned to Canada, determined to get in with these men and learn who their agents were, etc. I could not visit Washington at that time, so I took the chances of a letter to the President. He received my letter and took the proper precaution to have careful watch for the developments of the dreadful wickedness.

"Now, let me return to the Captain and Jackson. According to their agreement when we left them, the following morning they started out and spent a day of great interest to them. While riding in a cab the Captain said : 'I have a proposition to make to you, Mr. Jackson, which I will do to-night. The more I reflect upon what certain men are going to attempt, the more atrocious it appears to me.'

"Jackson looked at him, but with his usual caution made no response, except that he would be glad to hear what he had to say. That night when all the parties met at Jacob Thomlinson's rooms, as per engagement, all were good natured and full of hope and belief as to their success and the future triumph of the Confederate cause. In the conversation it seemed that the Professor and Dr. Blackman had come to the conclusion that they could be ready perhaps a week sooner than they had at first thought. Jacob Thomlinson said: 'All right, gentlemen, the sooner the better.'

"He then revealed to them that he had that day chartered for safety a fast-running steamer called the Will-o'-the-Wisp, to transport them and their supplies of material from Liverpool to Montreal. The Captain and officers were, he said, their friends, and ready to aid them in anything. To Dr. Blackman he said: 'Take this letter; in it you will find full instructions and memoranda, so that you can at any time communicate with the Captain of the vessel. You had better send your material along with some discreet person as rapidly as possible, and leave for Montreal the first moment you can do so.'

"He also stated that he and Mr. Carey would leave London in the morning to take passage from Liverpool to Montreal. The Messenger being the first steamer to leave, they were going over in her. After some further talk of no great importance, the Captain and Jackson bade good-by to all and withdrew.

"After entering Jackson's room the Captain said: 'Mr. Jackson, I told you last night that I could not see how the Living God could allow such inhuman plans to succeed. Now, what I propose is this: for you and me to remain and find if any vessel will leave for Montreal near the time, but later than the Will-o'-the-Wisp, and that we take passage on her and follow them. I am resolved that I will prevent this inhuman scheme from being carried out. I do not believe that you will betray me, therefore I tell you this. I do not now know how I am to do it, *but I will do it!* What say you, sir? Are you a Christian man?'

"Jackson responded, saying, 'I am a man of but few words, and therefore only say, give me your hand.'

"They clasped hands and pledged fidelity to each other.

"'Now,' said the Captain, 'let us off for Paris to-morrow. We will not see these men any more while here. We can watch the papers and learn about the vessels, when they leave, etc.'

"This being agreed upon, the next day they were off.

They visited Paris and quite a number of points of interest during the delay of their friends in London. Finally, the Captain came to Jackson with the Liverpool *Gazette* and showed him the advertisements. The Will-o'-the-Wisp leaves Liverpool for Montreal, Canada, on Thursday, —— day of ——.

"'We must leave for Liverpool at once,' said the Captain, and in an hour they were en route to London.

"Here they took the cars for Liverpool, and arrived the morning of the departure of the parties with their fireworks, poisoned clothing, etc., on the Will-o'-the-Wisp. She was a beauty—very long, with a sharp prow. She sat in the water like a seafowl, and sped away out of port as if she expected to attract the admiration of the immense throng on the wharf. They soon ascertained that the Fairy Queen, a very fast-going steamer, would leave the same evening for the same place,—Montreal, Canada,—and at once engaged passage and went on board of her.

"During the day the Captain said : 'Mr. Jackson, you are not as much of a talker as our friend Blackman. I do not believe there is one of the friends whom we have met in London who could tell your full name, where you were born, what your business is or has been, or where you intend going.'

"'No, sir,' replied Jackson; 'I never intrude myself upon any one. These gentlemen all seemed unreserved in their conversation, did they not? How did they know that I could be trusted with their secrets?'

"'Oh! they knew that I would not have introduced you unless I knew you were all right. And they do not seem to appreciate the enormity of what they are doing. Oh! I did not tell you the curious dream that haunted me in my sleep last night?'

"'No,' replied Jackson; 'will you tell me what it was?'

"'Yes, sir. It was this: I dreamed that Dr. Mears and the Professor had committed a murder in London, and were tried, convicted and hanged; they were both cremated, and that you and I were invited to see it; that their bodies were in a blaze like tinder, and soon became nothing but a small quantity of ashes.'

"Jackson said that was a very singular dream.

"'But that was not all. I thought that Dr. Blackman was a perfect sight to behold with smallpox, and that he was delirious, and jumped into the Thames, and that you and I rescued him, took him to the hospital, and had him attended to. I then awoke. The whole thing was so vivid to my mind that I believed it to be true for a moment. What say you to this? I believe somewhat in dreams, and fear that these reckless men will get into trouble with their infernal machines, or fireworks, and poisons. They must not be permitted to carry out their hellish purposes, as I told you, and you agreed that they shall not do it. I will suffer death before I will see these plots succeed and carry the guilty knowledge on my conscience through life. I swear, if President Davis has sanctioned this, I hope the Confederacy may sink into utter nothingness. What say you?'

"Said Jackson: 'I agree to all, except I do not believe in dreams.'

"'Well, well, we shall see,' said the Captain. 'It is a warning of some kind.'

"That afternoon the vessel moved out of port in majestic style. The steamer Fairy Queen was stylish and noted for speed. Nothing transpired to cause any excitement until the sixth day out. They had spoken several vessels on the voyage and found them moving on all right. On this day they discovered a vessel far in advance of them. The Captain and Jackson were on the deck, and concluded that it must be the Will-o'-the-Wisp. That night they were coming close to her, when the Captain of the Fairy Queen told them that the vessel in sight was the Will-o'-the-Wisp, and that she was moving slower than usual.

"During the night, perhaps about two o'clock, they were aroused by fog-horns and various noises. They arose and went out. It was dark and the fog so dense that nothing could be seen. The fog-horns indicated that the vessels were coming dangerously near to each other. The running to and fro and the language of the Captain of the ship all betokened danger.

"By this time the passengers were all up and out in so many different garbs that it was laughable, though the danger was imminent. The two vessels were nearing each other in spite of all that could be done by officers or crews. Finally the Fairy Queen was turned and run in the contrary direction from her course, and by that movement we got out of the swing of the Will-o'-the-Wisp. All remained up, filled with alarm.

"In the morning the fog lifted, and again they could see their way. The Will-o'-the Wisp was still in view, but seemed to be struggling. Nearing her again they found she was crippled in some way. The Captain of the Fairy Queen spoke her and inquired her trouble, when he found one of her shafts was broken. The arrangement was being made to get her tow-line and aid her on her way. Just as they were fastening it they saw a stream of fire pour from her that looked as if the whole ocean was in a blaze. Their vessel had to cut loose and move rapidly to save herself. The fire seemed to leap into and out of the water, like great burning shafts, seemingly reaching the very heavens. It would then play on the surface of the water and reach apparently miles away.

"There was no possible means by which any assistance could be rendered. No one could live near her, nor could a vessel of any kind approach. They could hear such frightful shrieks as would have made a demon shudder. Finally nothing could be seen save sheets of sulphurous flame jumping and skipping over the water as if playing with the waves. Then all became dark, and a streak of suffocating smoke hung over the water, as if a lake of burning brimstone was belching forth over the sea.

"All on the Fairy Queen stood aghast and looked as though stricken with paralysis. When the dark cloud of smoke had passed away there was nothing in sight save one small boat, perhaps a mile away. The Will-o'-the-Wisp was gone forever, and it looked as though all on board had gone with her. The Fairy Queen steamed up and steered in the direction of the small boat, and found that it contained but two persons. It was found that one sailor and

Dr. Blackman had escaped by cutting loose with the little boat when the first signs of trouble were discovered. The doctor knew what was coming, and made away for dear life.

"When Jackson and Capt. Redingson made themselves known to him he was greatly surprised. They then talked the matter over, and all agreed that all the schemes of the Professor and Dr. Blackman were at an end.

"Capt. Redingson turned to Jackson, saying, 'There is my dream.'

"Blackman said Dr. Mears and the Professor were lost, and their great secret with them.

"Capt. Redingson asked how this fire could have occurred.

"'The Doctor thought some of the Professor's material must have ignited in some way. 'The truth is,' he said, 'the ship was wrapt in flames in an instant. I saw this sailor jump into the life-boat, and I followed him. We are the only ones of all on board that are saved. The rest were all burned to death before they could possibly get from the vessel into the sea. There has never been any such combustible made before, and perhaps never will be again. But it is lost."

"He seemed very despondent all the rest of the voyage. When they arrived in Montreal and conveyed the sad intelligence to Jacob Thomlinson and Mr. Carey, they were overwhelmed with disappointment. Their schemes were all blasted and they were bewildered.

"Finally, after some days of talking and consulting, they concluded to send Dr. Blackman to Richmond for instructions as to further operations. The first news that reached Richmond of the burning of the Will-o'-the-Wisp created great consternation. The loss of Prof. McCullough and Dr. Mears was thought to be the severest blow they had received.

"Dr. Blackman left Jackson and Capt. Redingson to go to Richmond, but which way he went they never knew. Capt. Redingson took passage for Nassau, there to run the blockade, and was never heard of again by Jackson. I hope he is alive, as I think he was at heart a good man, full of noble impulses. Jackson was very fond of him, rebel as he was."

Col. Bush said : "Well, Prof. McCullough and Dr. Mears got their just deserts ; their own fireworks did the business."

"Yes, yes ! but the innocent officers and crew suffered with them."

"Yes," said Col. Bush, "but this had to be ; the Lord did not intend that such infamy should be permitted to succeed."

"But," said Maj. Clymer, "there was Dr. Blackman, just as bad as either of the others ; he escaped most miraculously."

"Yes," said Col. Bush ; "his material, however, was all lost, and he had a warning against trying the same thing again. There was no great secret in his material to be lost; but there was in the others', and the gain to mankind was in the loss of their diabolical secret."

" Uncle Daniel, what became of this vile conspirator, Dr. Blackman ?" asked Dr. Adams.

" Well, Doctor, I am sorry to be compelled, with shame, to state the fact, but nevertheless it is a fact, that this same man, Dr. Blackman, has been made Governor of one of the States since the war, and at the same time his record was known by his constituents. But it did not seem to lose him any friends with his party, but, on the contrary, seemed to help him. Yes, yes, my friends, this is the sad phase of the whole matter. It matters not what a man did if he was a rebel; but if a Union man, and he did the slightest wrong, he was disgraced forever. None of the great and inhuman wrongs are remembered against the individual rebels who violated every instinct of humanity."

Here the old gentleman became silent, and placing his hands over his face, wept like a child. At length he continued :

" I, with all my sacrifices, even here at home would be thrust aside in order that the citizens might pay homage to the men who would have afflicted their own household with loathsome disease, and at the same time mocked at their calamity. If God wills, let it be so. I do not believe, however, that He is doing more than trying the Nation, to see if our people are worthy of such a Government as ours."

CHAPTER XVI.

A HAPPY WEDDING.—MARRIAGE OF SERAINE WHITCOMB
AND HENRY LYON.—FIRE AND PLAGUE.—THE PLOT-
TING IN CANADA TO BURN CITIES AND SPREAD DIS-
EASE.

*"I did not FALL in love—
I ROSE in love."*—BULWER.

"AFTER Jacob Thomlinson and C. C. Carey had recovered somewhat from their alarm and demoralization, they spoke freely to their friends in Montreal (and they had many there) about the burn-
ing of the Will-o'-the-Wisp, saying it was a great loss to their
interests, without specifying in what way. In a few days
Jackson, (after finding that they had invited Valamburg,
of Ohio, Strider, Bowen, and Bryan, of Indiana, for consultation,) could remain no longer, as he would be known by
Valamburg at once. He bade his friends good-by, saying
he would travel through the West and would return if it
became important to do so. He left for Toronto, remained
there a day or so, and then came to Windsor, where he remained for several days. Finally he met Henry, who had
just returned from Montreal to Windsor, where he was
known as Henry Davis. He was introduced by Henry to
one Samuel Wintergreen, who was in the employ of the
Confederacy, or, in other words, of the rebels, getting
everything ready for raids on the cities and villages in Ohio
and Illinois. This man was very shy of Jackson, but spoke
freely on all subjects save what he was himself doing.
Henry and he were chums and seemed to understand each
other perfectly.

" Wintergreen was from Thomlinson's town in the South,
and was fully trusted and posted by him with all their

plans and schemes. The only remark he made to Jackson
was that he knew, from Mr. Thomlinson, who Jackson was,
and merely asked if he saw the burning of the Will-o'-the-
Wisp ; to which Jackson replied in the affirmative. Jackson and Henry had arranged so that they should leave for
Detroit the next day. Henry informed Wintergreen that
he must visit Detroit on matters of importance, and that
he might, perhaps, be detained for some considerable time,

THOMLINSON AND HIS FRIENDS IN CONSULTATION.

but that he would keep his eyes and ears open at all times
during his absence. The next morning Jackson and Henry
met in accordance with their agreement and immediately
left for Detroit. Upon arriving they drove directly to the
house of Mr. Whitcomb, where they found the old gentleman, his wife, and Seraine ; James, her brother, now a
Lieutenant and Aide-de-Camp to Gen. Anderson, having
some time prior left for Allentown, in order to be with the
General, where he had since remained, giving to him every
attention. While spending a pleasant evening at the home

of Mr. and Mrs. Whitcomb, in conversation, in reference to the army, Henry remarked that he longed to be in the cavalry service once more, so that he might get even for the suffering he had experienced at the hands of our enemies while nearly starving to death in Pine Forest Prison.

"Miss Seraine here spoke with much feeling, her eyes filling with tears as she said : 'I think there are quite a sufficient number of your family already in their graves by the hands of the rebels without any more of you taking the chances of death that must be taken in the army.'

"'Yes,' said Jackson ; 'and there seems to be one less at almost every turn. I feel that my time will surely come sooner or later, before this war closes.'

"This was uttered in such a sad and melancholy tone that Henry could not for a moment control his feelings. Recovering, he said :

"'It does seem that our family are struggling against fate ; just think of the barbarous manner in which Harvey was killed, and see how, recently, the fiendish bushwhackers murdered poor brother Stephen. Would you not desire to be avenged on such wretches as these ? Ever since I heard this, which was but a short while ago, (first told me by Seraine,) I have felt almost desperate, and certainly very revengeful.'

"'Yes,' said Jackson, 'revenge is said to be sweet ; but suppose you cannot get it, and instead of being revenged, you lose your own life ?'

"'That is not all, Capt. Lyon,' as Seraine called him by his title; 'Mr. Henry Lyon promised me that he would not enter the service again, but that he would stay at home and take care of his father and mother, and I hope he will do so, and not break his promise to me. I have periled my life for him, and would do the same again.'

"Henry clasped her in his arms and said : 'Seraine, I will do anything for you, and now I want to say right here, in the presence of my brother, that I am now and ever have been, ready to fulfill all of my promises to you.'

"Seraine looked him in the face and said : 'I have never doubted you, Henry, nor do I now.'

10

'Jackson here interrupted, and turning to Henry, said :
'What are your promises to Seraine ?'

" 'That she and I would become man and wife whenever
she should say that the time had arrived to have the marriage take place. Is it not so, Seraine ?'

" 'Yes, Henry, that is true ; but I have never thought
that the proper time had arrived.'

" ' Well,' said Jackson, ' if you will allow me to suggest, I
think the time has now arrived. Seraine, your father and
mother are growing old; your only brother is in the army and
may never return.' And to Henry he said: 'Our mother and
father are also growing feeble from so much grief. Mother,
I think, cannot survive very much longer, and all of us
who are now left, save yourself, are in the army. From our
experience thus far the future is not full of hope. You and
Seraine may soon be all that are left of both families, except,
perhaps, some one or more of our parents. Now, Seraine,
let us get your father and mother to go with us to Allentown, and there, in the presence of both families who yet
remain above the sod, (save brother Peter, who cannot be
with us,) have this marriage solemnized. Henry, our
mother and Jennie would be very happy over this, and so
would Mary Anderson and the children, all of whom love
Seraine very much.'

" By this time the tears were rolling down Seraine's
cheeks. Henry stood looking at her, and grasping her by
the hand, when Jackson had finished, he led her into the
presence of her father and mother and told them the proposition, and asked them to consent. They gave Seraine to
Henry, and blessed them both as their children. Seraine,
in answer to Henry, thought, in consideration of the whole
situation, that the time had come, and that she would
acquiesce in the arrangements as proposed by Jackson, who
was happier now than he had been since the beginning of
the war, and so expressed himself to Seraine and Henry.
The next day being agreed upon for their departure for
Allentown, Jackson repaired to his room, leaving Henry
and Seraine together to talk over the details of their pro-
spective marriage.

Leaving Detroit the following morning they arrived at my house in the afternoon and found a warm welcome awaiting them, my wife and the two other ladies of my household doing everything to make Seraine's father and mother feel that they were more than merely welcome. When we were all together Jackson became spokesman, and waxed quite eloquent over the whole affair. When he had finished Gen. Anderson cried out:

"'Bravo! Bravo! Henry and Seraine!'

"My wife drew Seraine to her bosom as she would have taken a child, and embraced her and wept, until, from sympathy, we all were overcome with emotion. The family congratulated Henry. The two little girls did not quite understand it all, and began plying us with questions until we had to explain all about it, and tell them Seraine was going to be their 'aunty.' This delighted them, and they commenced climbing upon Henry's lap, and questioning him about their 'Aunty Seraine,' until finally he made his escape from the house.

"The preliminaries were soon arranged, and Mr. Whitcomb and I procured the necessary license. I then called in our minister, the Rev. Mr. Lowe, who performed the marriage ceremony in the parlor of our home. We were very happy that evening in celebrating Henry's and Seraine's wedding, and seemed to have forgotten for the time being all our misfortunes and griefs. In speaking of Seraine's success in visiting the Southern prison-pens and rescuing Henry, I came very near letting out the secret kept from her father and mother about the visit of Mary Anderson to the President in order to rescue her brother, but caught myself in time and changed the conversation. Our minister, a truly loyal man, was most enthusiastic over the marriage, insisting that this was just as it should be, and at the same time expressing some surprise that it had not taken place before. I said to him that I felt so, but had not interfered. I had allowed the two young people to arrange the matter to suit themselves. I must confess, however, that I was well pleased, and certainly should never have been satisfied if Henry had not married Seraine. No more devoted woman ever lived.

"Just at this moment Aunt Martha announced tea. We all entered the dining-room and sat down to tea, as she called it, but found, instead, a right royal wedding feast, which all enjoyed exceedingly. Young James Whitcomb, who had been very quiet during the evening, though very attentive to his mother and father, now asked the minister if he thought it right for him to keep from his parents anything pertaining to himself which might distress them in his absence.

MARRIAGE OF HENRY LYON AND SERAINE WHITCOMB.

"Mr. Lowe replied that he thought they should know all. All turned and looked at each other with surprise. The young man was silent for a moment, and his great blue eyes filled with tears. He said:

"'I have never heretofore kept anything from my mother, father or sister, and I am now fully determined to tell them all about myself.'

"We enjoyed our dinner, however, and joked Henry by telling him that Seraine would have to look after him, as she had been doing all through the war up to this time.

"Here Aunt Martha had to come in; we could not stop her. She said:

"'Yes, sah; dat gal takes kear of Marsa Henry. If it not done been for her he done starved to deff, he would. Dem Sesh, dey be affer dis fambly. Dey done kill mos' all, and am still affer you. I tells you, dey am; I knows dem, I do. Marsa Henry, you mus' stay home wid de folks, you mus'.'

"At this my wife became much distressed. I told Aunt Martha to stop, which she did. Aunt Sarah then referred to Peter, saying that her dreams were now entirely about him, and that she was sorely troubled on his account. Ham stood near by, listening, and said:

"'No mistake, Marsa Peter all right. I see him las' night in my head glass when I's sleep. He all right, sho'.'

"By this time we had finished dinner, or tea, and were returning to the sitting room, when James Whitcomb took his parents out on the veranda and told them all about his trouble, the kindness of our family, Mary Anderson's trip to see the President, his clemency, etc.; his present situation, and how he obtained his position. We thought that this was a mistake, but he felt relieved, and his parents and sister, after they were satisfied of his having done no wrong intentionally, felt that it was the best for them to know it. We had intended it should be kept from them, but it was now no longer a secret in my family, and it was perhaps best that his father and mother should know all.

"The next day Mr. and Mrs. Whitcomb thought that they must return home. Mr. Whitcomb said to Henry and Seraine that they must come as soon as they could do so to their house and make it their home, as he and his wife being alone at such a time it was very hard, and made them discontented. They thanked all of us for our watchfulness over their only son, and it seemed that they could not thank the General and his wife sufficiently for what they had done for him. They bade us all good-by and separated from Henry and Seraine with many regrets.

"After they had gone Jackson entertained us by a recital of his visit to Europe, and, in addition to what he had written me, he gave us all he had seen and heard. His recital of the burning of the Will-o'-the Wisp was quite graphic, and excited Henry and the General very much. No one except those who were in the secret knew what she had on board, nor the importance to the Confederacy of the men that were lost with her. The language used by Gen. Anderson against such fiendishness as Jackson's statement disclosed I will not attempt to repeat. It was strong and denunciatory, such only as men like himself, versed in letters, could employ.

" I requested Jackson to make me a detailed report from the day·he left my house up to the date of his return, which he did. I retained a copy of his report, and still have it. We did not call on Henry for his report that day, but on the next told Henry that if he could leave Seraine long enough (you know how young people are), we would like him to tell us what he learned in Canada. I really did not suppose that he could tell us a very great deal of interest, as I presumed he had spent much of his time in Detroit, as there was an attraction for him in that place which would naturally draw him thither. He said, however, that he was ready to tell us all that he had discovered in reference to the conspiracy; that when he went to Canada he formed the acquaintance of a Mr. Samuel Wintergreen, and soon they became great friends, as he satisfied Wintergreen that he was ready to carry out any plan to aid the Confederacy. The passwords, signs and grips of the Golden Circle seemed to be all that any one needed in order to be at once recognized as a friend to those people. In Canada the people, almost without exception, were in sympathy with the rebellion. After traveling for quite a while he came back to Windsor, and there again met his friend Wintergreen. Remaining there for some time and talking with many persons without any material results, Wintergreen invited Henry to accompany him to Toronto, and finding nothing of importance there, they left for Montreal. On arriving at Montreal they found Jacob Thomlinson, C. C. Carey, and many other distinguished men. Wintergreen met Jacob Thomlinson. and reported to him that his friend of whom he had written was with him. Thomlinson asked

him to come to his rooms, and to bring his friend Davis.
That evening they visited Mr. Thomlinson, and found
Mr. Carey and two other gentlemen—a Mr. Landers and
Ben Wudd. Henry was presented as Henry Davis, one
of the agents under Mr. Wintergreen who was to assist (as
it was then understood) in carrying out such plans as might
be agreed upon in the interest of the rebel or Confederate
Government.

"They remained together till a late hour discussing various points. One of the topics was the great loss the Confederacy had sustained in the burning of the Will-o'-the-
Wisp, in the material, and by the death of Prof. McCullough and Dr. Mears, as they alone held the secret of manufacturing the wonderful explosive. Thomlinson and
Carey insisted that there should be no let-up, and that they
must now resort to other means, in which the other gentlemen agreed. It was thought best to try releasing prisoners
and arming them and such others as would join them, and
make portions of the North a desolate waste, as they said
was now being done in the South by the Union army.
Thomlinson said in reference to releasing prisoners that he
intended in a very short time to make preparations in Illinois for an attack on Camp Douglas, near Chicago.

"'I think,' said he, 'that will result in the burning of the
city. It is one of the worst places in the North. The influence of Lincoln over the people there is very great, and extremely bad for us, and that city must be destroyed by some
means. If the Will-o'-the Wisp had not been lost, Chicago
would now be in ashes.'

"After some further discussion on this subject, all went
their way for the night, with an understanding that there
would be a meeting of delegates from the Northern States,
called by Jacob Thomlinson, to assemble at St. Catharines
in one month from that time, where many matters of interest
would be discussed and considered. Henry and Wintergreen then returned to Windsor with the understanding
that they would attend the meeting at St. Catharines. At
Windsor, Henry and Jackson met, and that which followed
their meeting I have already stated. What Henry ascer-

tained in Canada was only important in this, that it had opened the way for discovering that which was important to know, which probably would occur afterwards. I requested Henry to do as Jackson was doing,—to write out his statement in full. After both were prepared, I sent Henry with them to the President. He thought it a little hard to be sent so summarily away from his bride. The President received Henry with great kindness, and told him to inform me that the whole matter had been more skillfully and successfully managed than anything in this line since the war began. He also said, that he and the Secretary of War could breathe freer since they had learned the fate of the cargo of the Will-o'-the-Wisp, and that McCullough and Mears had their deserts.

"The President requested Henry to continue his investigations, and especially to attend the meeting of the leading Knights of the Golden Circle, who were soon to meet at St. Catharines, in Canada, and send through me, without delay, his report. The President inquired very particularly about all our family, including Gen. Anderson and Jackson. He also desired to know what had become of James Whitcomb and his sister. Henry explained fully about them all, and when he mentioned that Seraine was his wife, the President shook his hand most heartily, and told him that he was a very fortunate man.

"When Henry returned home and had sufficient time for rest we held a consultation, and agreed to the following plan : Henry was to start at once with his wife for Detroit, leave her with her parents, and pass over to Windsor, and there, in company with Wintergreen, visit all places that Wintergreen might suggest, and then go to St. Catharines to the meeting arranged for the delegates from the Golden Circle of the Northern States ; that when he had obtained information of any value, he was to return to Detroit, write his report in full, give it to his wife Seraine, and she was to come in person with it to me."

"She was a jewel," said Dr. Adams.

"Yes," said Col. Bush ; "there were but few like her."

Uncle Daniel continued : "Our lines of communication

now being safely established, we were all anxious for Henry's departure; therefore, Henry and Seraine left for Detroit, leaving all of us almost heartbroken to be forced to give them up. But the hope of seeing them very soon again reconciled us to some extent. The two children said they loved their Aunty Seraine so much that they did not wish her to go away any more. After they were gone, it now being far into the Winter—in fact, Spring was approaching—Gen. Anderson said he felt that he could again take the field and perform his duty without endangering his health, and therefore must make preparations for returning to his command. We tried to dissuade him from it, but it was of no avail, so the next day he told the family that he should leave very soon. In the conversation he said that he had felt all the time that there was a void in his military family that could not easily be filled. He felt the loss of Capt. Day very much, but said he would try James Whitcomb thoroughly and had great hopes of him. Aunt Martha was near by and heard what was said. She immediately hunted up Ham and said : ' Marsa Gen'l is gwine off to fight dem Sesh agin, and I 'spect he want Ham to go, too.'

" Ham said: ' Well, Marfa, maybe he not want me any more. I's not well; I's got dem pains in de knees and de breas' and de shouldars and de stomach. What is it dey calls dem pains?'

" ' Rumatiks, you ole fool; doesn't you know nuffin'?'

" ' No, Marfa, I not know nuffin'; you know I doesn't. I 'spect you better told de Gen'l, Marfa, I's sick. I go off and die wid dem pains, den what you do, Marfa? You be all by yerself, and don't you see dat won't do, Marfa. No, indeed, dat won't do.'

" ' Well, now, Ham, I's not goin' to tell Marsa Gen'l no such way as dat. No, sir. Ham, you jes' got to go wid de Gen'l; dat's what you do, so you needn't be tucken sick jes' for to skeer me, kase I know you, Ham. You no get kill. No, sah, no danger; so you jes' go, dats what you do.'

" ' Well, Marfa, jes' as you say. If you say Ham go, he goes, dats all; but de good Laud love you, Marfa, I's powerful sick, sho'.'

" 'No you isn't; you play dat afore. I knows you, Ham; you knows I do. You jes' stop dis rumatiks and go wid de Gen'l, dat's what you do. When did you get sick? I not hear it afore. You not sick. Let me see you walk.'

" Old Ham hobbled off and Martha laughed at him. This nettled the old man and he straightened up and said: 'Well, I guess I's not bery bad, but I's not well, all de same.'

" I came up to them, and nothing more was said.

" I told Ham to go out to the farm and ask Joseph Dent to come into my house in the morning. His sickness all left him and he did the errand. The next morning Dent came in with Ham and we interrogated him on the question of his friends and what they were doing. He said that two days prior to this they had a meeting and were notified that they must change their name to the 'Sons of Liberty'; that the object of their organization was becoming too well known, and that they could not operate any longer under their old name. This was being done all over the country and in Canada. He also stated that Thos. A. Strider had ordered them to send delegates to Indianapolis secretly, in order to assist in appointing delegates to go to St. Catharines, in Canada, in a few days, to consult as to the best means to be adopted to aid their friends, as they had met with a great loss. They had lost a ship and a valuable cargo, as well as their most important men who were to operate in burning cities. This was so true of what had occurred that we no longer had any doubt as to their certain communication one with another, as well as their perfect organization. This was all they did at that time. We excused Dent, and he returned home.

" That evening at tea my wife (Aunt Sarah) said to Jackson and the General that she wished Peter to come home.

" 'But,' said Jackson, 'mother, you must remember he has been promoted, and is now a Brigadier-General commanding a brigade, and he cannot very well get away. He might lose his command by leaving.'

" 'Well,' said his mother, 'I want to see him. I am dreaming about him whenever asleep, and I feel there is

something sure to happen to him. I have seen all the rest
of you who are alive, and I want to see him.'

"Here Jennie broke down and cried, remembering the
death of her poor husband when mention was made of all
being present who were then alive. Jackson spoke to Jennie and his mother and quieted them. We all repaired to
the sitting-room and talked over Gen. Anderson's returning
to his command. This was Saturday evening. So he instructed Capt. Jackson and Lieut. Whitcomb to be ready
on Monday morning, as they would then leave for Chatteraugus. They were well pleased with the General's determination. His poor wife was depressed, and said she
felt as though he had made so many narrow escapes that
perhaps he might not escape again. But grief and sorrow
had been such constant visitors at our house that we were
all prepared for almost anything, and always looking for
the worst. We enjoyed ourselves, however, as best we
could until Monday. Jackson took in the situation, and
kept us interested by giving accounts of many things seen
and heard by him in England. This was very interesting
to us, but more especially to the ladies and little girls.

"On Monday they left for their command. The parting
with the family was one of those affecting scenes natural
under the circumstances. When poor old Ham bade good-
by to all, after kissing Aunt Martha, his wife, he turned to
my wife and Mary Anderson, and said: 'You need not to cry
no mo.' I be 'sponsible for de General and Capt. Jackson.'

"This was too much for Mary Anderson. Although
weeping, she could not restrain a smile, nor could the others;
but Ham was in good faith, poor old man.

"After they had gone I felt keenly, and drove out to the
farm, and there spent the rest of the day with Joseph Dent.
He, however, knew nothing more than he had disclosed to
us, about which I have already spoken. On returning in
the evening I found all the family very lonely and solemn.
They felt the loss of that portion of our family who were
compelled to leave. Our little children climbed upon my
knees and talked and chattered about their Uncle Henry
and Aunty Seraine, as well as the General and Jackson,

but 'Aunty Seraine' seemed to be the favorite. I did the
best I could to gratify them by trying to answer their questions. Some two weeks had passed in this way when one
morning I was notified to meet Seraine at the depot. I did
so and brought her to the house. When the very hearty
and affectionate greetings were over, and the two poor little girls had gotten through climbing on Seraine and asking her questions, which she did the best she could to answer, she gave me a paper which was Henry's report, accompanied by a good letter from him, stating that he
would come soon himself. This was not signed.

"I carefully examined his report, and was almost dumfounded at some of his statements; but he had gone into
such minute details and given such indubitable proofs that
no one could for a moment doubt. Henry said that on his
arrival again at Windsor he met Wintergreen, and after
preliminaries were arranged they traveled about the country from one town to another, until the time had arrived
for the assembling of the prominent friends of the rebellion
at St. Catharines in accordance with Jacob Thomlinson's
request. They started for that place, and on arriving
stopped at the Victoria Hotel, where they met a great
number of persons, strangers to both, but well known in
the Circle. Henry, on recovering from his prison starving
and sickness, had grown quite stout, and was so different
in his appearance from what he had ever been prior to his
recovery that his own acquaintances would not have recognized him, therefore he did not feel that he was in any
danger of being detected. He had heretofore claimed to
Wintergreen that he was from Parkersburg, W. Va., and
having been raised near there in Ohio could speak quite
understandingly of the country thereabouts, as well as
about a number of people.

"On Wednesday, being the day fixed, quite a number of
men from different parts of the country assembled. Quite
a large room in the rear of the Victoria Hotel had been procured, in which the gentlemen were to meet, and Wintergreen, having been designated by Jacob Thomlinson for
that purpose, notified the various delegates of the time and

place of meeting. When all were assembled each one was required to give the signs, grips and passwords of the Golden Circle, or the 'Sons of Liberty,' as the name had been changed within a few days from the Knights of the Golden Circle to the Sons of Liberty. Henry did not find the slightest difficulty in being recognized, as he had perfected himself in all the signs, grips and passwords of the order in his travels with Wintergreen.

"After Jacob Thomlinson, Mr. Carey and their committee were satisfied as to those present, they were called to order and seated in as regular a manner as would have been done in any deliberative body, by Mr. Valamburg, of Ohio, who, in taking the chair, said that as Grand Commander of all the Sons of Liberty in the United States, Canada and the Southern Confederacy he desired to occupy the time of the delegates for a few moments, in order that he might explain the object for which they had met. The assembling at that place, he said, was in order to be without the jurisdiction of the United States; that while together and out of the way of danger they were to deliberate in reference to matters that were best calculated to effectively aid the Southern people, who were struggling for an independent constitutional government; that the Government of the United States had become intolerable in its oppressions and tyranny. He made a long speech, presenting a list of abuses by our Government against the Southern people, and urged the necessity for aid to the South at once, in some way that would be most potent. When he took his seat he was loudly applauded by all his hearers. In this meeting were B. Wudd and McMasterson from New York, Mr. Woodsen and Mr. Moore from Pennsylvania, Valamburg and Massey from Ohio, Dan Bowen and Dorsey (who was a substitute for Thos. A. Strider) from Indiana, N. Judy Cornington and a Mr. Eagle from Illinois (both from Chicago). Other States were represented—Missouri, Kentucky, Iowa, Wisconsin, Maine and Massachusetts; but Henry did not give the names of the delegates from those States.

"Many propositions were discussed. Jacob Thomlinson

gave the full details of what Prof. McCullough and Dr.
Mears were preparing to do; their loss by the burning of
the Will-o'-the Wisp; also, Dr. Blackman's proposition and
the loss of his goods, and he now wanted to see what could
be devised as substitutes. All of the representatives present seemed to deeply deplore the loss to the Confederacy of
the secret only known to the men who went down with the
Will-o'-the Wisp.

"Jacob Thomlinson explained that he had been instructed by the authorities at Richmond to lay several
matters before this or any meeting they might have of
representative men from the North. It was desirable to
have these matters fully understood, so that the friends of
the South in their meetings could commit all who were
willing to aid the South in carrying out the various
propositions. First, he would lay the message of President
Davis on only one important subject before this meeting.
It was dated January 13, 1863, and was in reference to the
Proclamation of Emancipation by Mr. Lincoln.   Thomlinson said:

"'Mr. Davis claims that "by it the negroes are encouraged to general assassination of their masters by the insid-
ious recommendation to abstain from violence unless in
necessary self-defense. Although our own detestation of
those who have attempted the most execrable measures
recorded in the history of guilty man is tempered by profound contempt for the impotent rage which it discloses so
far as regards the action of this Government on such criminals as may attempt its execution, I confine myself to
informing you that I shall, unless in your wisdom you
deem some other course more expedient, deliver to the
several States' authorities all commissioned officers of the
United States who may hereafter be captured by our
forces in any of the States embraced in the proclamation,
that they may deal with them in accordance with the laws
of those States providing for the punishment of those
criminals engaged in inciting servile insurrection."'

"At the conclusion of the reading of this extract loud
cheers went up for Jeff Davis. Jacob Thomlinson continued reading:

" 'On the first day of May last the Confederate Congress passed a series of resolutions. The fourth resolution declares that every white person, being a commissioned officer, or acting as such, who during the present war shall command negroes or mulattoes in arms against the Confederate States, shall be deemed as inciting servile insurrection, and shall, if captured, be put to death. The seventh resolution declares that all negroes and mulattoes who shall engage in war, or shall be taken in arms against the Confederate States, or shall give aid or comfort to the United States, shall, when captured in the Confederate States, be delivered to the authorities of the State or States in which they shall be captured, to be dealt with according to the present or future laws of such States.'

" After reading the message and resolutions, he said that in order to understand the full scope of both, it would be proper for him to state that the laws of all the Southern States for the crime of inciting servile insurrection fixed the penalty of death, so that the meaning of the whole proposition is, that any white man commanding negroes or mulattoes, who shall be captured, shall suffer death, and it will be the same when negroes or mulattoes are captured in arms against the Confederacy. With this explanation he submitted these documents, which were all printed and distributed in confidence, and in this way Henry was enabled to give the whole proceedings. Mr. Valamburg decided that the proposition might be debated, and on this being so determined, Dan Bowen, of Indiana, arose and made a most inflammatory speech. He said he was born in Virginia, and would stand by her in her trials. He was in favor of Jeff Davis's message, and not only so, but would favor the hanging of any white man who would lead negroes against his Southern friends, and would sustain them in any measure of punishment that they might adopt in such cases.

" Mr. Eagle, of Illinois, made quite a speech on the same line. He was from Kentucky originally, and was for the South getting their rights at any cost. He said: ' Let blood flow like rivers, sir. Yes, sir; let fire rain upon Northern cities, and let the destruction of property become general, if necessary to produce the desired result. You must make the Northern people feel poverty, sir, if you wish to succeed. They care more for their property than for their lives. You must touch their pockets and then you touch their hearts. They are a fast-going people. I would just as lief as not they would know after the war is over, if it ever is, that I was in this meeting. No matter how the war may terminate, they will forget it all in a month, especially if times are good and money shall be plenty.'

"This caused a great laugh, and the speaking ended. The question was taken and decided unanimously in favor of the proposition. None but delegates were allowed to vote.

"Mr. Carey then presented his views, which were that their Northern friends must encourage raids and guerrilla warfare in their own States, and that they must commence it themselves. Burning must be resorted to when it could be done. He said that it had been so managed at Camp Chase in Ohio, by their friend, the Grand Commander of the Sons of Liberty, that a great many very excellent Confederate officers had made their escape, and were ready at any time to take command of men whenever their friends were ready, and that those officers were brave and fearless men ready to undertake any kind of enterprise or daring exploit. He did not look for any more foolish expeditions like the one made by Gen. Morganson. That it was not successful is easily understood. The Southern people were in too great haste in trying raids by large bodies of men where there were no lines of escape or retreat."

"Yes," said Col. Bush; "they counted their chickens before they were hatched."

"I think they were stale eggs," said Capt. Inglesby.

"Mr. Carey said," continued Uncle Daniel, "'We have now entered upon a system of small raids and destruction of property, so as to be very effective. And although we fear that we cannot repair our loss in the kind of material we had secured and had on board of the Will-o'-the-Wisp, yet we may, by good management, in some degree compensate for it, and, in order that you may understand how we propose to operate, I will read to you the order of the Secretary of War of the Confederate States to one J. C. S. Blackman, the brother of Dr. Blackman, whose poisoned goods were lost on the Will-o'-the-Wisp. The order is dated Richmond, 1863, and signed J. A. Seddon, Secretary of War, C. S. A., authorizing Blackman to enlist a company of men, not to exceed fifty in number, for special service on the Mississippi River. In lieu of pay or other compensation they are to receive such percentage of the value of all property of the United States or loyal people destroyed by them as may be awarded by an officer selected by the Department in charge of such duty, but in no case to exceed fifty per centum of the value.'

"Carey said that under this order it was understood as soon as Blackman should enlist twenty-five men for this purpose he was to receive a commission in the provisional army without pay. This commission was for his protection in case he should be captured. Said he:

"'We are now issuing quite a number of these commissions, and much good has already resulted. Blackman has destroyed a great quantity of property on the Mississippi and Ohio Rivers. A man by the name of J. G. Beall, who holds a like commission, has destroyed a great amount of supplies and other property on the Chesapeake. He is near here now, has a vessel, and is recruiting men for the Sons of Liberty in New York city, with a view of running over to St. Albans, in Vermont, and is not only to destroy property, but is to terrify those rich old Vermont Yanks out of their wits. It is by such means that we must alarm the Northern property-holders into peace measures and into voting the anti-war ticket. This is the only sure way to success, in my opinion.'

"They all laughed and agreed that a St. Alban's raid would be a splendid thing, as the old Yankees would do anything to save their money and property. Mr. Carey continued:

"'I think Mr. Beall is known to Mr. Wudd and Mr. Mc Masterson.'

"They both replied that they knew him well, and he could be relied upon to do whatever he should undertake.

"'Now,' said Mr. Carey, 'the prisoners at Camp Douglas, near Chicago, Ill., and at Camp Chase, in Ohio, must be released. Mr. Thomlinson has the money to pay all expenses. Cannot you men in the Northern States assist in this? Can you not get up organizations such as Blackman and Beall have done? The Richmond authorities will pay the same percentage for the destruction of all property necessary for the use of the army, as they do Blackman and Beall. Why, gentlemen, crops enough might be destroyed in one night by a simultaneous move to very badly embarrass the prosecution of the war.'

"A man by the name of Burnett H. Yonkers, who was present, said he would undertake to release the Camp Douglas prisoners if the gentlemen here from Chicago would render their assistance, to which the gentlemen replied that they would give any aid in their power; that already there had been arms sufficient for this purpose secured by Thomlinson and placed in the hands of a friend in Chicago by the name of Wall; that if Mr. Yonkers should go to Chicago on that business he should stop at the Richmond House and inquire for Mr. John Wall, Mr. Morris Buckner, or either of the gentlemen present; that any of the clerks of the Richmond House would know where to send for either of the persons mentioned.

"Mr. Walters, of Arkansas, being present, (the same that Gen. Anderson met in Colestown, Ill.,) and being one of the chief Organizers, was asked in reference to the condition of the Sons of Liberty. He said he had been traveling for more than a year in the Northern States. He had never been molested, nor had he been questioned as to his business. He had organized thousands of Lodges and found the friends—that is to say, the common people, who connected themselves with the order—ready and willing to act at any time, and willing to do anything that was required. The only trouble he found was in the cowardice of the leaders. To illustrate what he meant, he said: 'I came from Indianapolis here. Thos. A. Strider promised me faithfully that he would be here, but you do not see him. He is the one man of all others in the West who is expected to advise and suggest.'

" Dan Bowen here interrupted, saying: 'Strider has been at work. He has been in Washington, and has sown seeds of dissension in the army; has created jealousies between the Eastern and Western commanders, and produced much trouble on account of the Emancipation Proclamation.'

" ' Yes,' said Col. Walters, 'that I believe to be true; but why is he not here? I see he sends a substitute; is he afraid? Mr. Eagle was correct when he said the people of the North will forget all about the war in a month, if you will only give them a chance to make money. I can go into any city and proclaim myself in sympathy with the rebellion, and no one will molest me. If we should fail, and our cause go down, it would not be one year before Jeff Davis would be invited to attend agricultural shows North, so as to draw a crowd and increase the gate money.' This caused great laughter. ' I want now to ask my friend Bowen why his friend Thos. A. Strider is not here.'

" ' Well,' said Bowen, 'I cannot say. I had hoped that he would be here, but I find he is not.'

" Mr. Eagle, who seemed to be rather sarcastic, said he understood Strider was compelled to stay at home on account of a cow case in which he was employed. They laughed at this, and then proceeded to business. The propositions and suggestions were all indorsed, and many promises made on the part of each one present as to the part he would take in the matter when he returned home.

" Jacob Thomlinson said to Mr. Yonkers that he wished him to remain a day or so longer, as he desired to confer with him about the prisoners at Chicago. He then made quite an address to those present, saying the success of the Confederacy depended largely upon their friends in the North ; that if the war continued two or three years longer the supply of men and money would fail. All their available men were in the army, and there was now nowhere whence they could draw recruits. Their friends in the North must wake up and help. They had friends enough in the North to make the Confederacy a success in six months, if they would only come up to the work manfully.

"'Let our friends do as our friend Carey suggests, get up raids, organize companies for spoils; this is seductive and calculated to gather in young men. We will release our men who are now prisoners and turn them loose full of fiendish revenge, and alarm our enemies into peace measures. You who are our friends in the North must go home determined to carry the next election. This is important. If we can defeat Lincoln at the next Presidential election we are safe. The watchword must be that the war has been a failure; that the North cannot subdue the South; that foreign countries are ready to recognize the Confederacy, which will involve the United States in other wars; that the people are being taxed unmercifully; that the war should stop and the unbearable taxation cease. Your next Democratic platform should start out with the proposition that the war has been prosecuted only for the freedom of the negroes, and not for the Union, and that their freedom can only be maintained by the Union armies being entirely successful, and that during years of horrible, bloody war the Government has failed to conquer the rebellion and must continue to fail. Do this, and stand by it with a good candidate, and you must succeed. I would suggest that you take your "Little Napoleon," General Mac, for your candidate. He is exceedingly popular with the soldiers of the East, and with the people also, as I am told. The sympathy will be with him, having been relieved from the command of the Eastern armies because he could not whip us, which was no fault of his, as none of their commanders will succeed in doing that on our own ground. We were foolish to undertake an invasion of the North. But no matter, we will soon make up for this. If you will take up Little Mac there will be no trouble in your giving him the nomination, and then one united effort on the part of our party will send him into the White House. If he can be elected that will end the war, as he is a peace man and a Democrat. We would then have another advantage. Many of the officers of the Union army of the East do not

believe in our subjugation, and are bitterly opposed to the
Emancipation Proclamation. Some of them have large
commands. For instance, there is Gen. Farlan, who is a
friend of mine of long standing ; he is violently opposed to
the Lincoln administration, and would at once favor a
cessation of hostilities. So also is Gen. Smite and General
Cross, both leading Generals. I may also mention Gen.
Fitzgibbon. He has been ready for some time to stop the
war, because he is thoroughly satisfied that we have been
wronged and oppressed. He is in favor of putting Little
Mac in as President. He would be ready for peace on our
terms, which would be to withdraw the Union forces and
let us alone. We have been robbed of our property, but
should we gain our independence we care nothing for this,
as we would reclaim our slaves, such as have not been
stolen by the Abolition army. This, gentlemen, is what we
desire and expect you to aid us in securing. If these things
all fail us we will, in our desperation, make the homes of
many of your Northern men miserable and desolate.'

"When he was through with his suggestions they all
cheered him, and each one, by short speeches, pledged a
faithful adherence to the Confederacy. When they adjourned it was to meet again at some place in Canada to be
named by Jacob Thomlinson, and the representatives to be
notified by Mr. Valamburg. They separated with three
cheers for the Confederacy."

Dr. Adams said: "I am desirous of knowing if Jacob
Thomlinson and Mr. Carey are the same persons whom
your son Jackson met in London?"

"Yes; they are the same men who were engaged in procuring explosives and poisoned clothes, of which I have
heretofore given you a full account."

Col. Bush asked if this man Blackman, who took out a
commission in order to depredate and plunder, is still
living?

"Yes, he is not only living, but is now holding one of the
highest positions in the United States, as a Reformer."

"What?" said Dr. Adams.

"Yes, sir, as I once before have stated, his brother, who

was to distribute poisoned clothing to our soldiers and in our
hospitals, was made Governor of one of the adjacent States,
and this marauder has been given one of the highest and
most honorable positions. But why? You look surprised,
Doctor. Has this not been so ever since the war ? The
most desperate and reckless men have been given the highest
places by the opponents of the war, while our people, many
of them, are only too glad to find something against one of
our good soldiers as an excuse for laying him aside as use-
less furniture."

Said Maj. Clymer: "Valamburg is dead, I believe."

"Yes; he shot himself accidentally soon after the war,
and died of his wound."

Uncle Daniel proceeded by saying: "I made my arrangements to leave for Washington at once, in order to have
this information in the hands of the President as soon as
possible. I requested Seraine to remain with the rest of
the family until I should return, as I might wish to send
some word to Henry. When I arrived at Washington and
called upon the President I told him the reason I had not
visited him recently, and why I had sent my son with the
last report. Our afflictions had been severe and my wife
was in such a condition, both in mind and body, that I
really feared to leave her, except under very extraordinary
circumstances. The President was very glad to see me and
very grateful for what my sons were trying to do for our
country He asked after the health of my family, Gen. Anderson, and all of whom he knew as in any way a part of us,
and the poor man seemed almost as much grieved over our
misfortunes as myself. He seemed to be full of hope, however, and spoke to me very freely about the war and our
chances of final success.

" He strode across the room and, turning to me, said: 'We
are now on the right road, I think. I have rid myself of
some of those Generals that we spoke about when we last
met, and I intend to be rid of them for the remainder of
the war. If they want dictators, and will not obey the
President, they will have to organize outside of the army.
I have now a new commander for the Army of the East

who seems to be doing well. I hope he may continue as he began. He won the battle of Gotlenburg and broke the rebel army to pieces. 'I think,' said he, 'that Gen. Meador should have followed up his victory; but perhaps not. If he should not exactly fill the bill my eye is on a Western man who seems to know what he is about, and I think of bringing him East and giving him control of all the armies; but I will determine this later.'

"I then gave him the statement made to me by Henry. He read it over carefully, and in an excited manner ordered a messenger to go for the Secretary of War. He soon arrived, and after greetings the President handed the statement to the Secretary. He also read it carefully. They then discussed the matter, and concluded to order an additional force to Camp Chase, relieve the commandant, and place a more careful and efficient officer in his place. This was done by telegraph, with a warning to the new commander to look out for an attempt to release the prisoners.

"The Secretary said to the President: 'The rebels are desperate, and since they lost their shipload of explosives and poisoned clothes, with their two friends who were to carry out their plans, they are determined to attempt something else equally desperate, and we must look for raids, fire and plunder. By the way,' said the Secretary to me, 'that was rather a nice thing your son Jackson did in finding out all their schemes in London. Had it not been for his discovery we never would have known the desperation and infamy to which those men were driven.'

"'Yes,' said the President. 'Mr. Lyon, is he your eldest son now in the army?'

"'I have but two left in the army—Jackson and Peter. The latter you promoted for gallantry at Middleton Ridge. Jackson is now my oldest son in the service.'

"'Mr. Secretary,' said the President, 'you will make out a commission for him as Brigadier-General, and give it to Mr. Lyon to take home with him as an evidence that we appreciate the services of his family, and especially Jackson's great service in this most important matter.'

"I was visibly affected. The President saw it as he stood by a window for a moment. I arose and thanked him. He said:

"'No, the obligation is the other way.'

"Just then a dispatch was handed the President, stating that quite a number of prisoners had escaped from Camp Chase. He gave it to the Secretary, saying:

"'I guess we were a little late in removing the commander of Camp Chase; it ought to have been done sooner. Mr. Lyon,' said the President to me, 'we will have to watch those fellows. They are doubtless up to some game.'

"He asked me to keep Henry in Canada if I thought he could do good by staying there. I promised him to do so, and after getting Jackson's commission and bidding the President good-by I left for home, feeling gratified at the recognition given me. Arriving at home, I found my wife better, and when she found that Jackson had a commission as Brigadier-General she seemed so happy that we felt that she would entirely recover.

"I placed Jackson's commission in an envelope with a letter explaining how the President came to promote him. When the boy returned from the post-office he brought me a morning paper containing an account of Beall's raid on St. Albans, Vt.; how he had sacked the town, robbed the banks and alarmed the people. I said to Seraine, 'There it is! They have carried out the first part of their program, and we will soon hear of trouble in all the prison camps. I regard this as the beginning of desperate work.'

"'Yes,' said Seraine; 'Henry was very sure that they were desperately in earnest; but I thought, perhaps, the warning we had given to the President might save any further disaster in that direction.'

"Seraine remained about a week longer, and then left for Detroit. I sent a letter to Henry, directing him to remain in Canada as long as necessary to find out when, where and how they were to move and operate. My poor wife was soon taken ill again, and was quite feeble and almost helpless for some weeks. Aunt Martha was constantly by her bedside, waiting on her, as well as trying to entertain her with her curious interpretations of dreams and her experience while in slavery. My friends, this did not last a great while. More sorrows soon came to us."

CHAPTER XVII.

> *" One day thou wilt be blest,*
> *So still obey the guiding hand that feuds*
> *Thee safely through these wonders for sweet ends."*—KEATS.

"AFTER the battle of Middleton's Ridge some rest for Papson's troops was indispensable. As soon, however, as it could be done consistently with the condition of things, Gen. Silent issued orders from his headquarters, then at Nashua, to Papson and Sherwood for a disposition of the troops to be made so as to protect the lines of communication between Louis City, Nashua and Chatteraugus north, and from Chatteraugus to Bridgeton, Huntersville and De Kalb west. This distribution was speedily made. The enemy was in no condition for serious offensive movements, and contented himself during the Winter with a continuous harassing of our troops whenever found in squads or small commands not sufficiently strong to make effective resistance.

"Near Huntersville a man by the name of John Cotton, with somewhere between fifty and one hundred men, was constantly raiding small corrals where only a few guards were left to watch them. His business seemed to be to steal mules and wagons, being one of the parties operating under a contract to plunder for fifty per cent. of the property so taken. He had the same authority and character of commission from the authorities at Richmond as Blackman and Beall, of whom I have heretofore spoken. During the Winter this man crossed the Little Combination River near

Painter's Rock, and made a raid on Gen. Chas. Ward's corrals. Ward had been notified of the intention of John Cotton by a Union man named Harris, who resided near Huntersville. Gen. Ward had a company of infantry under cover near the corral, and about midnight Cotton made his appearance. The men who were watching for him remained quiet until he was near the corral, and then fired a volley into his raiders, killing three and wounding ten. They then rushed at Cotton, and he, with nine of his men, were taken prisoners. The wounded were cared for and the dead buried. The next day Gen. Ward organized a drumhead court-martial and tried those captured who were not wounded. The nine men claimed to have been forced into the service by Cotton, and were sent to Nashua and put to work, under sentence. John Cotton was treated differently. He was not troublesome again during the time that our troops remained at Painter's Rock. The understanding South and North among the friends of the rebellion was that raids were again to commence whenever they could be made at all advantageous to our enemies.

"The Knights of the Golden Circle, or 'Sons of Liberty,' began to be open and bold in their utterances and their villainous work. In New York they aroused their friends and got up mobs of such magnitude that they could only be suppressed by withdrawing troops from the field to operate against them. The recruiting offices were mobbed, offices and papers burned, and the officers brutally beaten; houses were set on fire in great numbers and destroyed. Many large stores were broken open and plundered by the mob. All helped themselves to dry goods, clothing, jewelry, watches, and whatever they discovered. Innocent men were brutally murdered in the streets. Women were driven from their houses and insulted in every possible way. Hospitals and asylums for orphans were plundered and burned, and the poor, helpless inmates driven into the streets. Children were clubbed and brained by brutes for no other reason than that they were colored. Wounded and sick soldiers were thrown on the sidewalks and left without aid or assistance of any kind. Poor negro men were taken from hacks and wagons and hanged to lamp-posts. In one instance a poor man was cut into halves as if he were a slaughtered beast. Men were sent from Canada, employed by Thomlinson and his co-conspirators, to come to New York and aid in this inhuman butchery."

"My God! What brutality and inhuman cruelty! It does seem impossible that such things could have trans-pired in a civilized community!" said Dr. Adams.

"Yes," continued Uncle Daniel, "it would really seem so. Yet these things did not only take place, but were carried on here in the North by the anti-war party, and were well known by all who were old enough at the time to understand matters; but they are now forgotten. Why, sir, mob violence was resorted to in many places. Inflammatory speeches were made in every community where they would be tolerated. Our people were alarmed everywhere in the North, and were preparing for great trouble at home in the absence of the army. Indiana was stirred up to white heat. Many outrages were perpetrated on the State soldiers who returned home on a furlough, and in many instances they were murdered. One old man by the name of Banty, who had two sons in an Illinois regiment—they being residents of that State at the outbreak of the rebellion—was tied to a tree in the woods some distance from home, and remained in this condition till rescued by his wife. It became so intolerable that troops were held at Indianapolis for protection to the city and country. The Governor, as well as other citizens, were threatened.

"In Ohio the same condition of things existed. Camp Chase was about to be attacked. Troops had, of necessity, to be sent for the safe keeping of the prisoners.

"At Coleston, Ill., the Knights of the Golden Circle attacked a squad of Union soldiers, who had just returned home from the army on furlough, and killed seven of them. In one county further south in Illinois, the name of which I have forgotten, there were quite a number of soldiers killed in secret. A man by the name of Geo. Akers, who had once been Sheriff of the County, but at the time of which I am speaking was the Head Center of the

Golden Circle in that part of the country, was so strongly suspected of having soldiers quietly 'put out of the way,' that a search of his premises was made by a Provost Marshal, and in his mill, which was on his place, were found many suits of Union soldiers' uniforms, evidently taken from dead bodies. He was put in prison, but was aided to escape by his brother conspirators. In the same County a soldier by the name of Stacks, while home on a furlough, was called to his own door in the night and shot by one Honeycliff. I give these instances merely to have you understand the feeling and determination of the men in the North who sympathized with the rebellion, to aid it in all ways and by any means, no matter how foul or vile."

"Uncle Daniel," said Col. Bush, "I know about Akers and the cases you mention in Illinois, as I was sent there at that time with a battalion to look after those fellows, and you do not tell one-half the trouble there was in that part of the country."

"No, I presume not; I only remember these facts in regard to matters in that State that fastened themselves irrevocably upon my mind."

Said Dr. Adams: "It seems incredible that such things could have happened in the North, where the same men now claim to have been loyal then."

"But, Doctor," said Col. Bush, "all these things did occur, though they are now forgotten by many, and our young people, who know very little about the war, except such things as they may gather from imperfect and distorted histories, doubt the truthfulness of these facts, being unable to understand why traitors should go unpunished. Why, Doctor, many of the men who were harassing and alarming the people then as Knights of the Golden Circle, are now the leading men in the communities where they were then the most offensive to Union people and disloyal to their Government. They have so managed as to be at the front politically, and if affairs continue as they are now, and seem tending, very soon the same men will claim that they put down the rebellion. They have already deceived many by their self-assertion. You see, Doctor, the

policy of not allowing ourselves to speak of the war nor any
of its concomitants, leaves the young people in ignorance
of what we suffered during its existence."

"That is true, I am sorry to say," replied Dr. Adams;
"but we who do know all about it should teach the present
and coming generations these very important facts.   The
difficulty is, however, that when you undertake it many
people insist that they wish to forget all about it, and that
they do not want their children to know anything of its
horrors.   But, Uncle Daniel, please continue what you
were telling us."

"The Richmond authorities," said Uncle Daniel, "had
detached a portion of Biggs's command under Gen. Brice,
some 20,000 strong, and sent them into Missouri, where they
had made the homes of many Union people desolate, and
spread terror throughout that State and a portion of
Kansas.   Brice had organized bands of marauders and
bushwhackers, as they were termed, in the same way and
under the same character of agreements as made with
Blackman and others.   Quartell's and Stringfinder's bands
were the most destructive to life and property, murdering
Union men as they moved, and making the country a desolate waste through which they passed.   The smoke rising
from houses, barns, etc., could be seen in every direction.
It could well have been termed 'a pillar of cloud by day
and a pillar of fire by night.'

"At the same time the rebel cruisers were a terror on
the high seas.   The Alabama, the Florida, and the Shenan-
doah were a dreaded scourge among our merchantmen.
Our commerce was being driven from the seas and passing
under the flags of other countries.

"All these things were very discouraging to the loyal
people of our country, and at the same time greatly encouraged the rebels and their allies and friends in the
North.   The demagogues of the anti-war party traversed
the whole country, haranguing the people, preaching peace
and crying high taxes, and insisting that the war had so
far been a total failure, and that it would not be any better
in the future.   In fact, they were carrying out to the letter

that which had been suggested by Valamburg and his friends at St. Catharines, in Canada, at the meeting about which I have heretofore spoken. Many of our best men had to return home from the army for a brief period and canvass as stump orators before the people, in order to quiet their apprehensions and fears as to the chances of our ultimate success."

"Yes," said Capt. Inglesby, "I well remember the very great anxiety then amongst our people. I returned home about the time mentioned, and the question was constantly asked me if I thought we could ever suppress the rebellion. All our successes during the Summer and Fall before seemed to have had only a temporary effect upon our people. In fact, they were easily discouraged during the whole period through which the war was continued."

"Yes, Col. Bush, that is easily accounted for. We left behind us an element nearly or quite a majority; certainly so in many parts of our country North, which was constantly decrying the war and the means which were being used against the rebellion. Their constant talk in the same direction could not help having a great influence, especially on the minds of weak men, and in many instances on those whose nearest and dearest relatives were in the army taking the chances of their lives; and, as you all well know, these pretended friends to our faces were in their hearts wishing and praying for the success of our enemies."

"Yes, that is true; and it was strange and hard to understand at the time, as these same people could have gained nothing by the success of the rebellion. They lived North, and would have been equally despised by the rebels (if they had succeeded) as a part of the Yankee Nation."

"Doubtless that would have been so, but it was not particularly the love that they had for the rebels or their cause, but their hatred for the party in power. They had been in power so long, that being ousted by the voice of the people made a number of the leaders who had lost in the political contest feel a desire to see the people who had beaten them lose in the contest against the rebellion. They had said so many bitter things against Mr. Lincoln

and prophesied war and final separation between the slave
and free States, that they were willing to see the country
destroyed in order to be considered among the people as
wise oracles and political prophets; so that they made it
their interest politically that the rebellion should succeed.
Many people were followers of these men in all the States
North. Out of this feeling grew and prospered the Knights
of the Golden Circle, or Sons of Liberty."

"Well, gentlemen," said Dr. Adams, "I agree with all you
have said; but I am growing somewhat impatient to again
hear Uncle Daniel."

All were again listeners, and Uncle Daniel proceeded:

"I was speaking of the alarming condition of the country and the dangers that were menacing peaceful citizens,
as well as their property. I became very much alarmed for
the safety of the two families left in my charge. I sent a
letter to Henry to come with his wife and make my house
his home for the present. He and Seraine came at once,
and were willing as well as happy in remaining with us for
a while, Seraine feeling satisfied that, as her parents were
two such quiet people, no harm could come to them. After
the excitement and confusion created by the delight in the
household over their arrival subsided, Henry took me aside
and related his experience since leaving home.

"He said that he remained quietly in Detroit for some
time at his wife's home. Then he went to Windsor, and
there learned that the people of the Confederacy were very
much disheartened, but were making a desperate effort to
harass the armies of the Union, without fighting great battles, until their armies were recuperated and filled up with
new recruits; that the plan was for their friends to confuse
and excite the Northern people, just as they were doing. He stated Jacob Thomlinson's plans just as they
were being literally carried out. After these plans were
well on the way in the direction of being fully executed, C.
C. Carey left for Richmond, and Jacob Thomlinson for
London, accompanied by Mr. Wintergreen, who was to act
as his private secretary. On separating from Carey the
understanding was that they would remain away from

Canada until the political canvass for President had well advanced and until after the nominations by both parties had been made. During their absence they were to ascertain what new plans were being executed and what new schemes could be put into operation during the Fall and Winter following. Henry said the one mentioned was the only one matured, and that was being carried out.

"Gen. Silent had now been promoted and ordered East, and Gen. Sherwood put in command of the Center, with orders to make a campaign South, pushing and pressing the enemy at every point possible. This movement was to and did commence at the earliest possible moment in the Spring following. Simultaneously with this a movement was made in the East against the capital of the Confederacy.

"One evening, a few days prior to Gen. Silent's departure for the East in pursuance of his orders, while walking out on the bank of the Combination River a short distance from Nashua, as the shadows of night were quietly gathering about him, a form seemed to stand before him, which, from its appearance and the flowing white robes in which it was arrayed, he at once recognized as the strange specter that had appeared to him while sitting on a stone beneath a tree at Chatteraugus. Gen. Silent was startled for a moment, but stood still with eyes fixed upon the apparition. Finally a light, beautiful and dazzling, shone around the figure. He did not move. It approached him, saying in a subdued, soft and melodious voice:

"'Gen. Silent, you have been selected to forever wipe out the crime of slavery. This can only be done by suppressing the rebellion now in progress against your Government, which must be completed within fourteen months from this day or all will be lost. Start East at once; take no rest with either of your great armies until this is accomplished. All is with you. The matter is exclusively in your hands.'

"After speaking thus, the specter disappeared and all was still. He stood for a moment, bewildered. When he had collected his thoughts he turned and walked rapidly

11

to his quarters, which were at the Nashua House. He entered his room and sat for some time in deep meditation. While at Victor's Hill he had thought of moving his army across to Mobile, and thence to Savannah and North to the rear of Richmond. He was not a superstitious man, but at the same time was forced by what he had seen and heard that night to consider well that which seemed to be before him. The condition of the armies of the Union, and also that of the rebels, was taken in at one grasp of the mind. The East and West were carefully considered, and a plan seemed to be placed before him that would certainly be successful. The whole question of the suppression of the rebellion seemed to be disclosed to his mind, and indelibly photographed thereon, as if in a vision from on high. He could see his Army of the West and Center combined under one commander, making their way against obstinate resistance to the sea; and then coming north to the rear of Richmond, breaking the shell of the Confederacy as it marched. At the same time he saw the great rebel army of the East, under Laws, in Virginia, melt away before him, driven, demoralized, and finally captured. This all seemed to be a dream, and yet it was the true method to pursue in order to put down the rebellion. These things were at once firmly fixed in his mind, and thus he would undertake to bring success, should he be selected as the commander of all the armies of the Union, as had just been indicated to him.

"Just then a rap was head at his door. 'Come in,' was the response, and Gen. Anderson entered. Gen. Silent met him with great cordiality and asked him to be seated. They conversed for some time on the subject of the war and the probabilities of success.

"Finally Gen. Anderson said : 'General, this war can be concluded in but one way, and that is by desperate fighting. The armies on both sides are made up of Americans, each believing they are right, and numbers and endurance will finally determine the contest, provided our people do not become alarmed at the constant cry for peace by the Northern Golden Circles and other sympathizers with the South.'

"'That is true,' said Gen. Silent; 'I feel more bitterness towards those Northern croakers and sympathizers than I do toward the rebels in the South, who take their lives and put them in chance for what they believe to be right. Wrong as they are, they are better men than those who are behind us trying to discourage us, and to encourage the rebels, without the nerve to fight on either side.'

"'Yes,' said Anderson; 'I fully agree with you. Allow me to ask at about what time will our Spring campaign begin?'

"'At the very first moment that we can move on the roads in safety. I am now sending Sherwood with what troops are within his call from Victor's Hill east to Meredith, breaking railroads, destroying bridges, etc., so that when we commence our movements in the Spring, Biggs will have no line save the one due south or east. We will then force him into the extreme South or cause him to make a junction with the army in the East, under Laws, where our Army of the West and Center must pursue him. The destruction of the two great rebel armies must be our task. This done, the rebellion will be at an end. This must be accomplished within the next fourteen months; sooner if we can, but within that time we must succeed, if at all, and I have no doubt whatever of a final triumph. The Almighty is only permitting the continuation of this struggle in order that the people shall become thoroughly satisfied with the destruction of slavery. Whenever that time comes He will give our enemies over into our hands.'

"'Gen. Silent, your faith is certainly very strong.'

"'Yes; I am now thoroughly convinced in my own mind that within the time mentioned our enemies will be at our feet. I am going East, where I am ordered by the President for some purpose. I intend to lay my whole plan before him and urge its adoption, believing that if followed the rebellion will end as I have stated. Would you like to go East, Gen. Anderson, if I should wish you to do so?'

"'I would certainly not disobey your orders, Gen. Silent, but I have a good command, and one with which I am well acquainted, and perhaps I would be of more service by remaining with it than by taking a new one. I did have a great desire to be ordered East when I was sent here, but the reasons for that desire do not now exist.'

"Gen. Anderson then, in confidence, related to Gen. Silent what had transpired at McGregor's headquarters the evening after the battle at Antler's Run, which astonished Gen. Silent. He sat for some time without making any remark. Finally he asked if the President and the Secretary of War had this information.

"Gen. Anderson replied that they had.

"Gen. Silent smiled, but said not a word. The conversation on this subject then dropped. Gen. Silent inquired if he believed in dreams.

"Gen. Anderson answered in the negative; at the same time he said he had heard on one or two occasions of very strange dreams, and one especially that he was watching closely to see if it would turn out in accordance with an interpretation given to it by a person whom he well knew.

"Gen. Silent then asked him if he had ever seen anything that he could not understand or account for.

"'No, sir,' replied Gen. Anderson.

"Gen. Silent said no more, and it then being quite late they separated. Gen. Silent left early next morning for the East. As soon as he could reach Washington he appeared at the Executive Mansion and had an interview with the President, when he was informed that he had been ordered East with a view of putting him in command of all the armies of the United States. He did not exhibit the least surprise at this, but at once proceeded to lay his plans before the President and Secretary of War. The plans were the same as suggested by him to Gen. Anderson. After careful consideration they were approved.

"The President told Gen. Silent he now should have the full support of the Government, with supreme command, and that the President would hold him responsible for the suppression of the rebellion, and expect that the enemy would be dispersed at an early day.

"Gen. Silent replied that the rebellion would end within fourteen months.

" ' Why fourteen months ? Could you not say twelve? '

" ' No, sir,' replied Silent; ' I put it fourteen. I hope to see it accomplished at an earlier date, but within this time it will be done.'

" ' Gen. Silent, I have a strange reason for saying twelve months,' and the President laughed at the idea of having a superstition about dreams, ' but, General last night I had such a curious dream that I must tell it to you. I thought a strange man appeared in the presence of the Armies of the West, riding upon a large brown horse, and that where-ever and whenever he appeared the armies were successful; that this strange man would disappear without uttering a word. This same strange man had appeared at the East, and at his appearance the rebel armies laid down their arms and sued for peace. In my dream peace was restored, but it lasted for only a short time; the citizens of Maryland and Virginia conspired together and swept down upon Washington, cap-tured the city, burned the Government records, and mur-dered many of our leading men, amongst whom was your-self. What do you say to this, General ? Can you inter-pret it ?'

" ' No, Mr. President, I cannot. I do not allow myself to think but very little about dreams. They certainly can be nothing more than the wanderings of the mind during sleep. But, Mr. President, since you have taken me into your confidence I must confess that I am sometimes startled by what seems to be an unfolding of events in the future.'

" Saying this much he relapsed into his wonted silence. After some further conversation they separated. The next morning Gen. Silent left for the Army of the East. He was received on his arrival in a manner that showed their confi-dence in him as a great commander. He established his head-quarters in the field near Meador, and at once commenced giving directions in his quiet way for reorganizing the troops and preparing in every way for an early advance. His army was soon organized into three corps,—Second, Fifth and Sixth,—commanded respectively by Gen. Hanscom, Gen. Sedgewear and Gen. Warner; the Ninth (Independent) Corps, under Broomfield, with the cavalry under Sherlin, who had been ordered to the East from the Army of the Center.

"My son Jackson, having been spoken of very highly to Gen. Silent by Gen. Anderson, had also been ordered to the East and placed in command of a brigade under Gen. Hanscom.

"The armies both in the East and the West being reorganized and in good condition, Gen. Silent began his arrange-

GENS. SILENT AND MEADOR IN CONVERSATION.

ments for an immediate movement. The Armies of the West and Center now being combined under the command of Sherwood were to move from Chatteraugus directly down the railroad against Biggs,—or rather Jones, the new commander of the rebel forces. The movement of the combined armies, East and West, against the enemy, was to take place on the same day. The rebel army East was admirably posted for defensive operations, provided they were to be attacked in their position. Laws had his army divided into three corps, commanded respectively by Ewelling on the right, A. P. Hiller on the left, and Longpath (who had come from Biggs) as reserve in the rear; his cavalry by J. E. Seward. His army was on the south bank of the Rapidan, and in rear of Mine Run, and extending east to the spurs of the Blue Ridge, on the west and left flank, protected by heavy earthworks. His forces and his movements were covered by streams, forests, hills, and by a very heavy chaparral or copse for miles in extent.

"Silent would not attack in his front, as Laws expected, but concluded to plunge immediately into the chaparral and threaten Laws's right. This would compel the enemy to give battle at once or retreat. So orders were issued for the Army of the East to move at midnight, cross the Rapidan, and march into the dense woods by the roads nearest the rebel lines. The troops moved, and by dawn the next morning had possession of the crossings and were passing over the river. By night of that day the army had crossed with most of their trains. The cavalry had pushed forward and camped near Sedgewear, who had gone into bivouac on the hill after crossing the Rapidan. During the day our signal corps had read the signals of the enemy, which were that Laws had discovered Silent's movements and was making preparations to meet them.

"Silent had ordered Broomfield to move at once and make night marches so as to be up in time. Sherlin was to move forward and attack the rebel cavalry at Chancellor's City. Three times this army had crossed the Rapidan before and as many times had been driven back. The question in the minds of all was, 'Will Silent go on, or will he be forced to recross the stream?' Laws was very confident that he would force him back.

"That night Silent received a telegram from Sherwood at Chatteraugus, saying that his army had moved out that day and was near the enemy; also, from Crooker and Boutler; all had moved. Thus Silent had all the armies of the Republic, wherever they might be, at the same hour moving against the enemy aggressively. No such movements had a parallel in history. The enemy were menaced

in every front, so that no portion could give aid or re-enforcements to the other.

"Laws, when he saw the situation, determined to attack,
believing that he could assault Warner and drive him back
before Hanscom (who had crossed some miles from Warner)
could come up to join on Warner's right. That night
Warner and Ewelling lay facing each other, nearly together.
They might easily have divided rations, though hidden
from each other by the dense forest. Yet, like the knowledge we all have by instinct of our near approach to
danger, they were each aware of the other's presence.

"Gen. Silent ordered a change, so as to move his head of
column direct for the right flank of Laws's new position.
Warner moved, with cavalry in advance, to Craig's Meeting House, his left resting at Chaparral Tavern. Sedgewear was to join on his right, Hanscom to move from
Chancellor City to his support, and Sherlin on the left and
in rear of Hanscom.

"Early in the morning the enemy appeared in Warner's
front. One regiment of cavalry had already been hurled
back. Meador had made his disposition in accordance with
Silent's instructions. Broomfield was now crossing the
river, and Silent waiting at the ford to see him; but learning of Laws's movement, he went forward at once to Chaparral Tavern. This tavern was in a low place, densely
surrounded with trees and underbrush. Here Silent
placed his headquarters in the rear of Warner's Corps.
The woods and chaparral were so dense in all directions
that neither army could distinguish the line of the
other.

"By 9 o'clock an occasional shot could be heard, and
then the rattle of musketry, as though a company or so
had discharged their pieces. Presently a few skirmishers
would come back to the main line, asserting that the enemy
were in force in our front. Then orders would be given
to advance the skirmish-line and feel for the enemy.

"About 10 o'clock a shot from the artillery of the enemy
announced the fact that he was posting for resistance. Our
line at once advanced as best it could in the direction of

the enemy. The musketry opened and continued to increase until one whole division of our troops were engaged. The artillery opened on both sides and roared as the mighty thunders. Musketry rattled like hail on the housetops. The enemy in our front, Ewelling commanding, was driven in great disorder for some distance by Griffith's division, but the underbrush was so dense that no alignment could be made with the troops. Regiments and brigades could not find each other. It became impossible to have any unity of action. This same cause prevented Sedgewear from joining on Warner's right or connecting with Griffith. This left Griffith's flank exposed, and the rebels at once taking advantage of this, forced him back again with the loss of some of his guns and quite a number of prisoners. The rebels made no attempt to follow up their advantage, but began at once erecting earthworks.

"Laws was attacked before he anticipated, although making a show of readiness; but he was resting on ground familiar to him and wholly unknown to our troops. Silent was notified of our repulse. It was apparent that Laws's whole army was on the field, and meditated an attack before our army could be brought into action. Sedgewear's troops were not all up ; Broomfield had not arrived, and Hanscom was not yet on the ground. This was not quite what Gen. Silent had been accustomed to. His commands heretofore were always at the spot on time when ordered, and generally before the time appointed.

"He at once mounted his horse and rode in person to the front, in order to get a view of the situation. He followed Warner on a narrow road, which was thronged with troops in great disorder. Slight works thrown up by both sides, in intervals of the fight, were very close together. He at once saw from the nature of the surrounding country the importance of maintaining Warner's position. On his return to his headquarters he dispatched officers to hasten Sedgewear's and Broomfield's troops with all possible speed. His wish now was to bring to bear as large a force as possible against Laws's left, in order to prevent the discovery of the great space between Warner and

Hanscom. Laws, however, had detected this gap, and was forming Hiller's Corps to move through it.

"Geddis was now ordered to move at once and hold this part of the line with his division of Warner's Corps against all force that might come against him. This was the breathless time during the day. Geddis took the position. Hiller moved against him, but Geddis held the point. Hanscom came up, but his corps was far away to his rear. It was nearly two o'clock before his troops came in sight, certainly none too soon. He at once formed on Geddis's left. There was but one spot, on account of the density of the forest, where artillery could be put in battery or used to any advantage. Here Hanscom put all his artillery. At 2:30 he received orders to attack Hiller at once in conjunction with Geddis, which he did. This compelled Hanscom to move two of his divisions in support of Geddis, Burns and Motley. The two lines had both approached until they were exceedingly close together.

"The battle now commenced in great earnest on both sides, and was of a most destructive and deadly character. The musketry firing was continuous along the whole line. The remainder of Hanscom's Corps was ordered up and went into action, having no time for protecting themselves. Several desperate assaults were made by Hanscom and Geddis, but the enemy, having the cover of the chaparral, were able to inflict great damage on our forces.

"Silent, learning that our forces could not dislodge the enemy, sent a force from Warner's left to relieve the troops who were so hotly engaged. Accordingly one division under Gen. Walworth and one brigade under Roberts were sent through the woods to the sound of battle. But they could not see fifty yards before them on account of the underbrush. The roar of the battle was like a continuous peal of thunder. Gen. Walworth tried to penetrate the thick woods to relieve his comrades, but did not arrive until nightfall.

"Sedgewear had now taken position on the right of Warner, and both of their corps had been engaged during the afternoon. Sherlin had struck the rebel cavalry near

Ford's House and driven them back. He now held the
country to the left of Hanscom on the road to Spottsylvania. The night had closed in and the two armies rested
facing each other. The killed, wounded and dying were
strewn between the lines like leaves.

" Gen. Meador and others came to Silent's Headquarters
that night. One corps in each army had not been engaged
during the day, and so the battle had but fairly commenced. Silent gave orders to assault the enemy the next
morning at five o'clock. Longpath on the side of the enemy, who had not been engaged during the day, was moving
that night to the support of Hiller, evidently intending to
crush our left. Geddis was ordered to remain with Hanscom ; Walworth was to assault Hiller's left, while Hanscom
made a front attack. Broomfield was to move to the gap
between Walworth and Warner's left. But Laws was
preparing also for an attack, and made his assault on
our right a little before Hanscom made the attack contemplated by Silent.

"The battle commenced by Ewelling assailing Wight.
The fighting became furious along Sedgewear's entire front
and over and along Warner's line. Burns and Motley, of
Hanscom's Corps, advanced upon the enemy and assaulted
him with very great energy. Walworth now assaulted
where he was directed. The contest was a desperate one.
The smoke rose through the woods like a dense cloud. The
artillery was brought to where it could be used, and from
both sides it belched forth its iron hail and sounded as if
the earth was breaking into a thousand fragments. The
musketry rattled and showered the leaden missiles of death
in every direction. The yells and shrieks of the wounded
were enough to strike terror to the souls of the strongest,
during the whole time of this great battle of blood and
death.

" The enemy were driven at every point, and retreated in
great confusion. Our troops undertook to pursue them
through the thick woods and became broken up and confused. Sherlin was now engaged with Seward's cavalry,
near the Todd House, in a terrible contest. The firing and

shouting could be heard by Hanscom's troops. Sherlin was victorious and Seward retreated.

"Up to this time Longpath had not taken the position assigned him, but now moved rapidly against Hanscom's left. The contest was renewed. Silent and Meador rode out to the front and looked over the ground. Silent never lost confidence in the result for a moment.

"Longpath now assaulted with great vehemence; our advance brigade was swept like chaff before the wind. The density of the brush was such that Hanscom could not make his proper formation, and therefore had to fall back to his position held early in the day. Walworth was driven back, and in trying to rally his men was shot through the head and instantly killed. Sedgewear's right was assailed and turned, losing many prisoners. He rallied, however, and drove the enemy back again. Longpath being now severely wounded, Laws led his corps in person.

"A simultaneous attack was now made by our forces. Broomfield assaulted for the first time during the day, and the enemy were forced back. In this assault my son Jackson, leading his brigade, was wounded and taken to the rear. This was late in the afternoon. The woods had been on fire several times during the day, but at this time the breastworks of some of our men having been constructed of wood were fired by the musketry and blazed up, catching the timber and leaves with which the ground was covered. The fire became general and drove men in every direction, both Union and rebel. The shrieks and screams of the poor wounded men who could not escape the flames were heartrending.

"Darkness came on and the contest ceased. During the night Laws withdrew the rebel army to his old line of works and gave up the idea of driving Silent back across the Rapidan. Gen. Silent repaired to his headquarters, where he received the reports of the commanding officers. Some were sure that Laws would attack again the next morning. Some thought that we had better retire across the Rapidan. At this Silent said not a word, but smiled. He finally gave orders to be ready to meet the enemy the next morning, and to attack him if he had not withdrawn. When he spoke of the enemy withdrawing a look of surprise was on the faces of many.

" After they had all repaired to their respective quarters he went out to look around, and while listening under a tree in order to hear any movements that might be making in the enemy's lines, he was again startled by the same spectral form that had appeared to him twice before. It pointed in the direction of Richmond and spoke these

A SCENE IN THE TRENCHES.

words, 'Move on to-morrow,' and disappeared. He was strangely affected by this, and became quite nervous for a man of his stoicism.

" He returned to his tent and inquired for his Adjutant-General. When he reported, he asked if any further reports had come in, and was told that a messenger had just arrived with dispatches announcing that Boutler had moved on City Point, capturing it; that Sherwood expected to attack Jones at Rocky Head on that day. Silent then went to bed and slept soundly.

"The next morning there was no enemy in sight. Gen. Silent advanced his troops well to the front until satisfied that Laws had withdrawn. He gave orders for taking care of the wounded and burying the dead. The wounded of both armies were thickly strewn all over the battlefield. Many had perished from the smoke and fire in the woods. It was a sight I do not wish to describe if I could.

"That day Silent issued his orders for the army to make a night march by the left flank in the direction of Spottsylvania. He and Meador started, with the cavalry in advance, late in the afternoon, and as they passed along the line going in that direction the boys understood it and cried out, 'Good! good! No going back this time; we are going to Richmond,' and they made the woods resound with shouts of joy.

"The next day about noon Sherlin was directed to move with his cavalry to the rear of the enemy, cut the railroads, and destroy all the enemy's supplies he could find. He moved at once. Silent notified Broomfield of the resistance being made to our further advance, and ordered him to move up as rapidly as possible. Skirmishing and sharp fighting between isolated divisions and brigades occurred. Many officers and men were killed. Gen. Sedgewear was among the killed on this morning, and Gen. H. G. Wight was assigned to the command of his corps. This was the 9th day of the month, and the armies had been marching and fighting five days.

"Silent's lines were now formed and ready to attack or resist. Thus they lay during the fifth night. On the next morning orders were issued to assault the enemy's center at 10 o'clock. Some movement of the enemy delayed the assault, and about 1 o'clock the enemy pressed forward to attack, which they did with great vigor. They were repulsed with great loss and fell back in confusion. They reformed and came forward again. The contest now became fierce and even terrific. They made their way close up to Hanscom's front and delivered their fire in the very faces of our men. Our line did not waver, but now opened such a terrible fire of musketry on them that they broke in great disorder.

"In the very heat of the contest the woods had taken fire again, and the flames were leaping along with frightful rapidity, destroying nearly everything in their pathway. Our troops on this part of the line were compelled to fall back, leaving many poor fellows of both sides to perish. Soon, however, the skirmishers were re-enforced and drove the enemy for a mile into their entrenchments.

"It was now determined to make the assault contemplated in the morning. So about 4 P.M. Silent ordered the assault. Warner and Wight were to move simultaneously with Warner's and Gibbs's divisions, Motley to advance on the left of Wight's Corps. Our troops had to advance up a densely-wooded hill. Silent and Meador took position on an elevated point, but could see little of the field, it was so overgrown with bushes.

"The battle had again commenced, our troops assaulting. A cloud of smoke hung heavily over the field, lighted up occasionally by flashes from artillery. The shouts of the commanders giving their orders, the yells of the soldiers on both sides, as well as the groans of the wounded and dying, could be distinctly heard in every direction. Across an open field, then through heavy woods, across a soft morass in front of one division of the enemy near the stream, went our lines, struggling forward under a most galling fire until lost to view in a copse of wood and the smoke of battle. Only our wounded now came staggering and crawling out from under the cloud of smoke to the rear. These few moments of suspense were terrible. Looking, listening and waiting, our troops at this moment ascended the hill and stormed the enemy's works, but could not hold them against the destructive fire. They fell back to their original line.

"On our left, at that moment, a great victory was being accomplished. Col. Upson and Gen. Motley formed a storming party of some twelve regiments, and drove right against the flank of the enemy. They rushed with such impetuosity against the rebels that they could not withstand the assault. Our forces captured an entire brigade and one battery of the enemy. Hanscom now assaulted and broke the enemy's line, capturing many prisoners. At six P.M. Broomfield attacked. Night closed with our columns within one mile of Spottsylvania Court-house. The fighting of this day was desperate, and the loss on both sides terrible. The suffering was great; many were burned who had fallen wounded on the field.

"This was the sixth day of blood and death. Our forces held some 4,000 prisoners, while the enemy had taken none from us save a few stragglers. That night Boutler reported great success. Sherlin had got in the rear of the enemy, destroyed ten miles of his railroad and nearly all of his supplies of food and medical stores. Silent now ordered rest and reconnoitering for the next day.

So, on the following day, our lines were adjusted and reconnoissances made, with full preparations for the ending of the great contest. Hanscom was to move in the night so as to join Broomfield, and they were to attack at 4 A. M. of the 12th. They moved into line not more than two-thirds of a mile from the enemy. The ground was heavily wooded and ascended sharply towards the enemy. In the morning a heavy fog lay close to the ground, but at 4:35 the order to move forward was given. Burns and Barrow moved in advance. The soldiers seemed to be urged forward by some kind of inspiration, and finally broke into a double-quick, and with irresistible force over the earthworks of the enemy they went. Both divisions entered about the same time, and a most desperate battle here ensued. Muskets were clubbed and bayonets and swords pierced many bodies on both sides. The struggle was short, however, and resulted in our forces capturing some 5,000 prisoners, twenty pieces of artillery, and thirty colors, with two General officers. The rebels broke to the rear in great disorder, our men pursuing them through the woods. Shouts of victory rent the air.

"Silent was now by a small fire, which was sputtering and spitting, the rain coming down in uncomfortable quantities. Hanscom had taken and was now holding the center of their line. He reported: 'Have just finished up Jones and am going into Ewelling; many prisoners and guns.'

The enemy made six assaults on Hanscom, which were repulsed. Broomfield now reported that he had lost connection with Hanscom. Silent wrote him: 'Push the enemy; that is the best way to make connection.'

"Desultory fighting continued until midnight, when the enemy gave up the task of re-taking their lost line and retreated. Thus ended the eighth day of marching and most desperate fighting ever known.

"The next morning an assault was made in order to take possession of high ground near the court-house, which was a success, without any considerable resistance. The rain was now falling in torrents. The roads became so muddy that they were impassable, which prevented any further movement for the present. The collecting of the wounded and burying the dead was a sight to behold. The whole country back for miles was one continuous hospital. Our losses were over 20,000, and no one could ever ascertain the loss of the enemy; but it could not have been less than 30,000—including prisoners.

"The howl that was set up by the Sons of Liberty and Copperheads excelled anything that had ever been heard. Silent was a 'murderer,' a 'butcher,' a 'brute,' an 'inhuman monster.' The enemy, however, were all right. They were 'humane friends,' 'good Christians,' etc. The hypocrisy of this world is perfectly amazing.

"At this time take a glance at the rebel capital. Boutler was within ten miles; Sherlin's troopers were, many of them, inside the works on the north side of Richmond. Sherwood was forcing the rebel Army of the Center. Gen. Crooker had cut all railroads between Tennessee and Richmond. All lines of communication with Richmond were severed, and confusion and terror reigned in the rebel capital. Jeff Davis contemplated flight, but was prevented by those surrounding him. With all these evidences of our final success and failure on their part, the anti-war party in the North could find no words of contumely too severe for our successful commanders.

"Henry and I left for Washington, and in the confusion of everything I finally found a surgeon by the name of

Bliss, who informed me where I could find my son Jackson. He had been brought to Washington and placed in the Stone Mansion Hospital, on Meridian Hill. We lost no time in visiting that place, and by permission of the surgeon in charge visited Jackson. We found him with a high fever and some evidence of erysipelas. His wound was in the right groin—a very dangerous wound. He talked quite freely, and gave all kinds of messages for his mother, the family, and Gen. Anderson, but said to us that he could live but a few days.

"'The fates are against our family,' said he. 'We will all go down sooner or later. Mother is right.'

"We remained in Washington and gave Jackson all the attention we could. We merely paid our respects to the President. He was so busy we could not interrupt him. Joy was in the hearts of all loyal people, while curses were upon the lips of every disloyal and anti-war Democrat in the whole country.

"Jackson died from erysipelas on the sixth day after our arrival. This shock almost broke me down. Henry was nearly frantic. Jackson was his favorite brother. They had both been wanderers alike from home. We took his remains to our home, had his funeral services in the church to which his mother and I belonged, and buried him by the side of my son David, in the Allentown Cemetery.

"You must imagine this blow to our family; I will not undertake to describe our distress. His mother almost lost her mind, and for several days she talked incessantly about Peter. She seemed to lose sight of all else. Scraine was deeply affected. She thought very much of Jackson, he being the one who brought about her union with Henry much sooner than, perhaps, it would have occurred."

Just then Mrs. Wilson came in. We could see that she kept a close watch over Uncle Daniel. He took her in his arms and said :

"My darling, I was just speaking of the death of your Uncle Jackson."

"Yes, Grandpa; I well remember when you and Uncle Henry came home from Washington with his remains; how we were all distressed ; how Grandma's mind was affected ; and how poor old Aunt Martha cried and spoke of him. I remember also that he was buried by the side of my poor father."

She ceased speaking and wept and sobbed, and finally she took her grandpa by the hand and led him to his room.

CHAPTER XVIII.

" We die that our country may survive."—LYON.

"GEN. SILENT was now in command of all the armies
of the United States, having his Headquarters
with the Army of the East, so that he might
have the immediate supervision of it. Sherwood,
having been placed in command of the Armies of the West,
commenced organizing and concentrating his forces for the
Spring campaign, under the general plan suggested by
Silent and approved by the President and Secretary of
War. The condition of things in the North was as heretofore described. Sherwood was kept continually on the
alert, in order to meet the many raids that were being
made in his Department.

"About the 1st of April, Gen. Forrester, with a large
cavalry force, again moved north, marched between Big
and Little Combination Rivers, and made his way unmolested to Paduah, and there assaulted the Union garrison
held by Col. Heck, by whom he was badly beaten. He
made his retreat, swinging around to Conception River, and
following that down to Fort Pillston, which was held by a
very small garrison of colored troops. After capturing the
post the unfortunate troops were most barbarously and in-
humanly butchered, no quarter being given. The poor
colored soldiers and citizens were shot down like so many
wild beasts. Some were killed while imploring their cap-
tors for mercy; others were tied to trees, fires built around
them made of fagots, and in that way burned to death.

The sick and wounded fared no better. Such brutality is seldom resorted to by the most barbarous of the savage Indian tribes. What do you suppose would have been the fate of any Union officer who would have permitted such conduct on the part of his command?"

"Why," said Col. Bush, "the officer would have been dismissed the service in utter disgrace, and would not afterwards have been recognized as a gentleman anywhere in the Northern States."

"No, sir," said Dr. Adams; "such officers would have been compelled to change their names and to find homes in the mountains, where they would have been unobserved."

"Yes," said Uncle Daniel, "that would have been so with any of our troops; yet you never hear this fact alluded to. It is lost sight of, and if you should mention it publicly, you would only be criticised for so doing. Our tradesmen and merchants want their Southern customers, and therefore, no matter what their crimes may have been, they are hushed up and condoned. But to return to my story.

"Sherwood had made his disposition for an advance, and on the same day that the Army of the East commenced its movement to cross the Rapidan, his army moved out against Gen. Jones, who had displaced Biggs and was in command of the rebel Army of the Center. Sherwood's army moved in three columns from and about Chatteraugus—Scovens on the left, Papson in the center, and McFadden on the right. Papson moved directly against Turner's Hill, and McFadden, by way of Gadden's Mill, to and through Snake Gap, against Sarco. Papson had encountered the enemy at Rocky Head, and failing to dislodge him, was ordered to the right in support of McFadden. Jones fell back to Sarco and made a stand. Hord's Corps assaulted him in front, Scovens on his right, Papson and McFadden on his left, McFadden gaining the high ridges overlooking the fort and opened a destructive artillery fire against it.

"Late in the evening, as night was closing in, Gen. Anderson ordered a part of his command to assault and charge their works near the river, south of the town. This was executed in gallant style, Gen. Ward leading the charge. The firing all along both lines was picturesque. As volley after volley was discharged, it reminded one of a line of Roman candles shooting forth. Soon our troops succeeded in dislodging the enemy and capturing his works, with many prisoners. This closed the contest; and that night Jones, with his army, retreated, destroying bridges and all else behind him.

"He was vigorously pushed by our army. Two days later Papson's head of column struck the rear of the enemy between Caseyville and King's City. Skirmishing commenced, and was kept up during the night. At this point Jones had collected his whole army—three large corps, commanded by Harding, Polkhorn and Head, numbering nearly as many men as Sherwood's forces. During the night, however, the enemy retreated, and did it so handsomely that the next morning there was nothing to be seen as evidence of an enemy, save fresh earthworks.

"After remaining there several days waiting for supplies, etc., our forces resumed their advance and moved rapidly in the direction of a town on the Powder Springs road called Dalls; McFadden on the extreme right, Papson in the center, and Scovens on the left. Hord, of Papson's army, in moving to the crossing of Pumpkin Run, met the enemy, and was soon engaged in what turned out to be a severe battle, lasting until quite in the night. This checked the movement of the army under Papson, and changed the point to be gained to Hopeful Church. There was continuous skirmishing and fighting at this point at close range behind works for about five days. The losses, however, were not very considerable on either side, both being under cover of earthworks. The troops here were so situated in their lines and works that both sides kept well down behind their cover. Finally our boys gave it the name of 'Hell Hole.'

"McFadden having moved to Dalls, as ordered, was some miles away to the right of the remainder of the forces. The enemy seeing this, concentrated two whole corps and hurled them against the Fifteenth Corps, and one small division on its left. The assault was made by Harding and Polkhorn on the morning of the 28th of May, and lasted until late in the afternoon. This was a fierce and very bloody battle, with quite a loss on both sides. The enemy broke the line of our forces on the right and poured through the gap like bees swarming, but the commander of the corps of 'Forty Rounds' was equal to the occasion, charging them with reserve troops and driving them back with great slaughter. From that time on, the day was in our favor. The General who commanded the corps came down the line where bullets were thickest, with hat in hand, cheering his men on to action and to victory; with a shout that could only be given by that old, well-drilled corps, which had never known defeat, they rushed forward against the enemy and routed twice their number. Men who were in this battle say that the soldiers and officers were more like enraged tigers than men. No power could stay them when it came to their turn during the day to make an assault, the enemy having made the first one.

"Two days after this brilliant victory they were ordered by Sherwood to their left to join the right of Hord's command. The army now being in compact form confronting the enemy, he withdrew to Bush and Kensington Mountains, in front of Henrietta, covering the railroad to Gate City. Gen. Sherwood moved his army on a parallel line to Shantee, covering the railroad to the rear, being our line of communication, directly confronting the enemy on the Mountain ridge. The position of the enemy was a good one; much better than our troops occupied. Thus, our forces were 100 miles south of Chatteraugus. During the whole march it had been one succession of skirmishes and battles, from Rocky Head to Kensington Mountain. The skirmishes and battles were generally fought in dense woods, and doubtless, in the rapid movements, many of our poor men, and also of the enemy, were wounded and left to die in the forest. The enemy's lines were several miles in length, covering those spurs—Kensington, Bush and Pine Mountains. Our troops were pushing up as close as possible under a continuous and heavy fire. While advancing our lines our forces could see the signals of the enemy on the mountains, and very soon learned to read them.

"In one of the forward movements on our extreme right a very sharp artillery duel took place between Davies' artillery and Polkhorn's, who formed the enemy's left. During this engagement Polkhorn was killed by one of our round shots. Our signal officers interpreted the enemy's signals stating his death. Our boys sent up a great shout.

The enemy thereby discovered that our men could read their signals and at once changed them, much to the chagrin of our Signal Corps.

"The railroad bridges that had been destroyed in our rear by the enemy on their retreat having been repaired, the trains began running and bringing up supplies. One day a train came in drawn by a very powerful engine. The engineer concluded that he would tempt or alarm the enemy, so he put on a full head of steam and started down the track as though he was going directly into their lines. As soon as he came in sight—which was unavoidable, as the road ran through an open field directly in front of Kensington Mountain, and then curved to the left through a gap— they opened a battery directed at the engine. Peal after peal was heard from their guns, but the engineer ran the engine down to our skirmish line and there held it for some moments, keeping up meanwhile the most hideous whistling and bell ringing. The number of guns that opened fire and their rapidity in firing was such that all along both lines they believed a battle was raging. The engineer returned his engine to the train amid the shouts of thousands of our troops.

"Our skirmishers were now close, approaching nearer and nearer every day and night, the advance being made by regular stages. Several attempts were made to double the skirmish-lines and move up the slope of the ridge, but this could not be accomplished. Finally Gen. Anderson asked permission to make a reconnoissance to our left and to the right and rear of the enemy, or at least to find where his right rested. This was permitted, and Gen. Anderson struck the enemy's cavalry some five miles to our extreme left, driving them around the point of the mountain and capturing very nearly two regiments. This at once disclosed the fact as to the exposed flank of the enemy. He then moved back to his position in line and waited further orders.

"Just about this date Gen. Sherwood received information that the expedition up Blood River had failed, and that Forrester had defeated Sturgeon and was now preparing to raid the railroads in our rear. This was not very encouraging to our forces, but caused great joy in the rebel camp in our front, as our forces learned. The next day the enemy made a feeble attack on our right, but was handsomely repulsed by Gen. Hord's Corps. Sherwood seemed determined to try to dislodge the enemy,—a flank movement seemed to others to be the way to force the enemy from his lines of works on the crest of the mountain.

"On the 27th of June, he ordered an assault on Little Kensington Mountain. Our troops at the same time were to make demonstrations on all parts of the line. McFadden assaulted, by order of the commander, the face of the mountain, where there was no possibility of success. He was hurled back, losing many officers and men. Papson assaulted on his right, where the mountain sloped down to a low foothill with no rugged heights. Here the enemy had strong earthworks, with an almost impenetrable abatis. One division after another and one corps after another were hurled against this breastwork, where fell many brave and gallant men and officers on that fatal day. Papson did not believe our troops could take those strong works, posted as the rebels were, but obeyed orders from his superior officer.

" Towards noon our losses were heavy, and it seemed like leading men into the very jaws of death to attempt another assault. Some of the officers, as well as men, openly said it was most cruel and cold-blooded murder to force men up against works where one man behind them would equal at least four of the assaulting party. Yet another attack was ordered, and about the middle of the afternoon all were ready. Sherwood was on a high hill a good distance in the rear, where he could see all that was going on.

"The order was given to move forward. Gen. Anderson was put to the front, my son Peter in command of his advance brigade. On, on they went, well knowing that many a brave boy would fall to rise no more. Not a word was spoken save the one of command. The line moved right on, the enemy pouring shot and shell into our ranks. Our brave boys fell like grass before the scythe. As our ranks thinned and gaps were made by shot and shell the solemn command could be heard, 'Close up, my brave boys!'

"Gen. Anderson rode in full dress, with a long black plume in his hat. On and on, to the very jaws of hell they went. When close up to the enemy General Anderson raised his sword, the gleam of which could be seen afar in the sunlight. He ordered a charge, and well was it made. Up, up, and into the jaws of death they moved. But to take the works was impossible. The whole line was now engaged. Finally our forces fell back. Gen. Anderson held his men in their line. They were not dismayed. He was finally ordered to fall back, and did so. Peter, my son, was shot through the lungs. Sullenly and coolly did our men fall back, with curses many and loud against the blunder.

"This was the first repulse to our army, and forced the commander a few days later to do what should have been done without the loss of so many men. He moved around against Jones's flank, which caused him to abandon his line and fall back to Chatham River, into his heavy intrenchments prepared some time before.

"My son Peter, during the evening after the battle, had been conveyed to the hospital. As soon as Gen. Anderson could do so, he started to find him. He found young Whitcomb with my son, whom the General had sent earlier to look after him; also, old Ham, who was in the rear during the engagement, not far from the hospital. When the General entered, Peter recognized and greeted him, but added:

"'General, my time has come. When I go, that will be the last finger but one. My mother's dream; O! how true! how true! This is not unexpected to me, my dear General.

I have been waiting for it. This morning, when I found what our orders were, I committed my soul to God, and felt this to be my time.'

"The General said to him that he thought there was a chance for him to get well.

"'No, no,' replied Peter; 'I may linger some time. The doctor thinks there is a chance for me; but, no; I am sure this is only the fulfilling of my mother's dream.'"

At this recital the old man wept and walked out of the room. Very soon, however, he returned, and continued:

"Why should I grieve? I will soon see them all. I am very sure that I will meet my good and brave family again in a better world."

"Amen!" said Dr. Adams.

Uncle Daniel said: "Peter always believed there was something in his mother's dream; and while Gen. Anderson was trying to encourage him, old Ham spoke up:

"'Marsa Gen'l, dey's no use. I tell you dat dream am a fac'. It is, sho', an' Marsa Peter he know it. I 'terpret dat for him; 'deed I did. I not fool on dat. But, den, we mus' take keer ob him. I 'spec' he go home an' see he mudder and fader. I 'spec' me better go wid him and tend to him. Don't you t'ought so too, Marsa Gen'l?'

"The General told Ham he would see about it. Peter began to improve, and it really seemed as if he would recover. I was informed by Gen. Anderson of Peter's misfortune, but kept it from my family, except Henry, who was at home, as I before stated, in order to aid me in protecting the family, the country being in such an alarming condition. The growing belief in the final success of Silent against Laws was quieting the people somewhat.

"I made an excuse to the family, so that Henry was sent South to see Peter and bring him home if he should be able to stand the journey. I obtained a pass for Henry from the President by letter, and he started to find his brother. He told Seraine, however, before he started, what his mission was. She was discreet, and did not speak of it to any one.

"During this time Sherwood moved out, McFadden on

the extreme right, Scovens in the center, and Papson on the left. About six miles on the road leading to the crossing of the Chatham River Papson encountered the enemy and passed the compliments of the Fourth of July with them, firing his artillery loaded with shell into their lines. The celebration was kept up in this way by both sides during the day, but the loss was not great on either side.

"Just at this time Gen. Russell, under orders, left De Kalb, Ala., with 2,000 cavalry, passing through the country and meeting but little obstruction on his way. He finally struck the railroad west of Opelima and destroyed it for many miles, making a successful raid. He reported to Sherwood at Henrietta, with hundreds of horses and mules, supposed to have followed him, on his return.

"Stoner was also to the west of our forces hunting for railroads, bridges, etc., which might be useful to the enemy. McCabe was with his cavalry on Soap Run, and one other division under Garner at Ross Mills, to the left of our main army.

"McFadden with his army now moved to the left, by Ross Mills, across Chatham River and down to De Kalb by way of Stonington's Mountain. Scovens crossed the Chatham River near the mouth of Soap Run, and thereby occupied the center. Papson crossed at or above the railroad bridge. The whole army was now safely across the river and moving in the direction of Gate City. McFadden had reached De Kalb and there connected with Scovens, who had extended near to the Howland House. Papson was not so far advanced, leaving quite a distance between him and Scovens.

"As Papson lay at Crab Apple Run, the men carelessly taking their rest in fancied security, they were furiously attacked by Head's Corps. At first our men were scattered in confusion, but were soon in line again, and the battle raged with great fury. After some two hours' hard fighting the enemy fell back and again occupied their breast-works. The losses on both sides were heavy for the length of time they were engaged.

"On the same afternoon Gen. Legg's division had a very

sharp contest for a high hill in an open field to the left and
south of the railroad from the east to Gate City. Legg secured this hill, which overlooked the city and was the key
to the situation on the east side.

"On the 22d a great battle was fought over this ground
by McFadden's army, which was severe and bloody, lasting
well into the night. Thousands were slain on both sides.
The field almost ran with blood. Gen. McFadden fell early
in the day, and the command then devolved upon another.
The battle was a success to the Union troops. It was a
great victory. Many prisoners and a great quantity of
munitions of war fell into the hands of our troops. Gen.
Sherwood for some reason remained at the Howland House
during this battle, with Scovens, whose forces were not engaged. This battle cannot be properly described in this
narrative, nor will I attempt it.

"On the 28th another great battle was fought by the
same gallant army as on the 22d, without assistance, at a
place called Ezra's House, on the extreme right of our
lines. Having been ordered to move round to the rear of
Scovens and Papson, after the 22d, they struck the enemy.
During this engagement the enemy made as many as seven
different assaults upon our line, but were repulsed with
great loss each time. Night closed in and ended the contest. The next morning the dead of the enemy lay in front
of our lines in rows and in piles. The enemy having retreated during the night, our troops buried their dead,
which numbered hundreds. One of their Color-Sergeants,
of a Louisiana regiment, was killed, and his flag taken by
a boy of an Ohio regiment within twenty feet of our lines.

"Skirmishing and fighting continued around and about
Gate City for nearly a month, during which time the losses
on both sides were very serious. The latter part of August
a general movement to the flank and rear of the enemy was
made by the whole of the united forces. McFadden's army,
now commanded by Hord, moved on the right in the direction of Jonesville, and a terrific battle ensued, lasting for
some four hours. They fought against two corps of rebels,
which were driven back and through Jonesville to the
southward.

" Late in the night a great noise of bursting shell was heard to the north and east of Jonesville. The heavens seemed to be in a blaze. The red glare, as it reflected in beauty against the sky, was beyond brush or word paint-ing. The noise was so terrific that all the troops on the right felt sure that a night attack had been made on Pap-son and that a terrible battle was being fought. Couriers were sent hurriedly to the left to ascertain the cause, and about daylight information was received that Head—who was in command of the rebel forces, having succeeded Jones—had blown up all his magazines, burned his store-houses of supplies, evacuated Gate City, and was march-ing with his army rapidly in the direction of Loveland Station.

" Thus the great rebel stronghold, Gate City, had fallen and was ours. The joy in our army was indescribable. Sherwood moved on Loveland Station and skirmished with the enemy during one afternoon, but no battle ensued ; why, has often been asked by our best-informed men. Our troops moved back on the same road by which they had advanced to and around Gate City, and then went into camp, remaining during the month of September with but little activity.

" One day, at Gen. Sherwood's headquarters, Gen. Ander-son was asked by Sherwood if he was ever in the Regular Army. Gen. Anderson replied in the negative.

" Sherwood said : ' I am sorry for that, as I would like to give you a larger command. You are certainly a good soldier.'

" ' Well,' said Gen. Anderson, ' is it not good soldiers that you want?'

" ' That is true,' said Sherwood; ' but we are compelled to make this distinction, where we have those who are or have been in the old army, or have been educated at the Military Academy.'

" ' But, General, suppose a man is or has been in the Regular Army or educated at the Military Academy, and is not a successful General, how will you then decide?'

" ' Well, Gen. Anderson, we have studied war and know

all about it; you have not. We must rely upon those who make it a profession. Papson, Scovens and myself have considered the matter, and we cannot trust volunteers to command large forces. We are responsible, you know.'

" 'But, General, you seem to trust volunteers where there is hard fighting to do, or where there is any desperate assault to be made.'

" 'Yes, that is true; but we cannot afford to allow volunteers to be put over Regular officers; Regulars do not like it, and we cannot do it.'

" 'I have seen some of your volunteer officers and soldiers succeed where your Regulars have failed. Should not such men be as much entitled to the credit as if they were professional or Regular Army soldiers ?'

" 'There may be cases of that kind; but we will not discuss this further. I can only say that while we have Regulars to command our armies, we will see to it that they are given the places.'

" Gen. Anderson was very angry, but said no more except ' good-by.'

" By this time Peter had so far recovered that the Surgeon felt it to be safe to remove him. Henry, who had remained with him all this time, now brought him home, with old Ham's assistance. Henry had kept me posted by letter, and it was very hard at times to explain his absence. But when he reached home, and the truth was revealed to my good wife, she was almost frantic, and was unable to sit up. She talked continually of her dear son, and was haunted day and night by her dream. Peter gained strength very rapidly. The members of the household were at his service at all times. The children could not understand so many coming home shot as they termed it, and little Mary Anderson was continually inquiring of her mamma about her dear papa, and if he was shot again ! Our family had all become so nervous that I was continually on the alert for fear of sickness being produced by the constant strain.

" Old Ham and Aunt Martha had many things to say to each other. Ham's experiences in battle very greatly amused Aunt Martha. They were both very kind to Peter, but wore very serious countenances in our presence. Ham would only talk to me about Peter, and would always say : ' I hopes dat Marsa Peter git well, but I fears. Marsa Lyon, I tell's you dat dream of de Madam, dat am bery bad. I fears de time am mighty nigh come.'

"Aunt Martha did not express any opinion, but would shake her head. Peter kept the two little girls by him nearly all the time, petting them, but conversed very seldom. He would talk to his mother occasionally, to keep her mind away from her horrible dream.

"About the 1st of October we learned of the movements of large bodies of the enemy's cavalry in Tennessee, raiding the railroads to the rear of Sherwood's army. Head had thrown his army across Chatham River, below Gate City, to the north, and moved parallel to the railroad, so that he could strike and destroy our lines of communication at various points. Sherwood was compelled to follow him. Our forces were stationed on the railroad at many places. Gen. G. B. Ream, with one division, held Carter Station, Etwan Bridge, Alletooning, Ainsworth, King's City, Adamsville, Sarco, and north to Dallytown. Chatteraugus was held by Gen. Sleman with his division, and Romulus by Cortez. All had orders to support any point that should be attacked. Gen. Ream was of the opinion that Head would strike the railroad at Alletooning, where a great quantity of supplies were stored.

"Sherwood left Somers with his corps at Gate City and started north. He arrived at Henrietta just as Gen. Ream had got Cortez with his command at Alletooning. Head was advancing on Alletooning by rapid marches. He assaulted the garrison at once on his command's arrival. The assault was made with great determination, but it was not successful. His loss was very great. He drew off and at once moved in the direction of Romulus.

"Gen. Sherwood reached Carter Station, and was directing his movement in order to protect the railroad and no more. Gen. Ream insisted to Gen. Sherwood that Head's next move would be against Sarco. Sherwood did not think Head would cross the Cussac River, and so commenced his march on Romulus by way of King's City, and left the matter of protecting Sarco to Gen. Ream, who procured trains and started all the troops he could get together for that place. That night on the way they found the track torn up. This was soon repaired, and the troops proceeded. At five o'clock Gen. Head arrived in front of Sarco and demanded its surrender. Gen. Ream, learning this, took the troops from the cars and marched from Cahoon, sending the trains back for more re-enforcements. By daylight our troops were in the fort and on the skirmish-line at Sarco.

"Ream at once sent word to Gen. Sherwood that Head was present with his army in front of Sarco, and would like to pay his respects. About daylight Head opened his artillery upon the forts, and sent forward his skirmish-line. In the garrison every effort was made to impress Head with the idea that Sherwood's main force was present. Every flag was displayed on the forts and along the skirmish-line. Head kept up a continuous fire on the forts during the day. Late in the afternoon re-enforcements arrived. There were but 500 ; this was enough, however, to show that re-enforcements were coming. The firing was kept up the most of the night; the next morning the enemy was gone.

"He passed around Sarco and struck the railroad north of this place and dismantled it for many miles, capturing every garrison north from Sarco to Turner's Hill. Turning west from there he passed through Snake Gap, moving in the direction of Alabama. Gen. Sherwood arrived at Sarco very soon and was gratified that the place, with its great quantity of supplies, was safe. He at once pushed out through Snake Gap in pursuit of Head.

"The next place that Head presented himself with his army was in front of our garrison at De Kalb, Ala. He withdrew, however, and crossed into Tennessee, where he rested for near a month, collecting supplies and recruiting his army.

"Sherwood halted his army, and while resting made
12

such dispositions as were in accordance with the plan to be followed out in the near future.

"In the meantime the excitement in the North was very great. Jacob Thomlinson had returned from Europe and was again in Canada with a large sum of money, which was freely used in all the States North in attempting to elect the Democratic candidate, 'Little Mack,' for President—the man that Thomlinson had suggested in the meeting of the leaders of the 'Sons of Liberty' at St. Catharines, Canada, of which I have heretofore spoken. Mobs were now frequent, and bad blood was stirred up all over the country.

"Finding the condition of things very unsatisfactory, I suggested to Henry that he make a short visit to Canada. He did so, and returned to Allentown four days before the Presidential election. He had met Wintergreen, who had returned from England with Thomlinson. He disclosed to Henry the fact that the rebels were greatly depressed, and were using all the money they could to defeat the war candidate, Mr. Lincoln; and that the night before the election a raid would be made on all the Northern prisons, so that released prisoners might burn and destroy, and thereby cause such alarm on the day of the election as to prevent as many as possible from going to the polls. At the same time their friends were to be in possession of the polls wherever they could. In this way they had hopes of carrying the election.

"I sent this report to the President by letter, which he received in time to have all the prison guards re-enforced. The attempt was made, however, but defeated in every instance. In Chicago they were very near accomplishing their designs. They had cut the water pipes and were making preparations for the burning of the city. But the attack on the camp was thwarted, and the leaders arrested and put in prison. John Wall, of whom I have heretofore spoken, was one of the leaders, and was captured and imprisoned.

"Mr. Lincoln was triumphantly elected. Mr. Jacob Thomlinson's friend, 'Little Mack,' as he called him, was ingloriously defeated. This indorsement by the people of the war measures and the manner of their execution was cheering to our loyal people, as well as to the armies and their commanders.

"Soon after the election Sherwood abandoned pursuing Head, leaving the States of Tennessee and Kentucky, with Head's army scattered along the main thoroughfares, to be looked after by Papson, with his forces, preferring himself to take the Armies of the Tennessee and Georgia and cut loose and march unobstructed to the Sea. On the march, food for the troops and animals was found in abundance, making this march really a picnic the most of the way.

"While Sherwood was making this march, matters of great interest were going on in Tennessee. On the last day of November the enemy, maddened by disappointment in their failure in the North to carry the election and have their Confederacy recognized, concluded to risk their all in a great battle for the recapture of the State of Tennessee. Head, then in command of an army increased to nearly 50,- 000, moved across Goose Run and against our forces at Franktown, where he at once assaulted Scovens, who had been sent to oppose his advance. Our troops were behind intrenchments. He attacked with fearful desperation. At no time during the war did any commander on either side make a more furious and desperate assault than was made by Head. After forming his lines in double column, he moved right up to our works, where his men were mowed down by the hundreds. Gen. Pat Cleber charged time and again with his division, and hurled them against our works only to be as often driven back with great slaughter. At last, in a fit of desperation, he led his men up to the very mouths of our cannon and the muzzles of our muskets. He drove his spurs into his horse until his forefeet rested on our parapet. In this position he and his horse were riddled with bullets and fell into the trench, which was literally running with blood. The desperation of the enemy was such that they continued their murderous but ineffectual assaults until their men were exhausted as well as dismayed at their great loss. Thirteen of his commanding officers fell killed and wounded. Night forced him to desist.

"The next morning his men could not be brought to the slaughter again. The bloody battle ended and Scoven's men withdrew to Nashua, three miles to the South of which place Papson's army was intrenched. Wellston, in command of about 8,000 cavalry, covered both flanks of our forces. It was now getting along in December. The enemy moved forward and intrenched in the front and within two miles of Papson. The weather became very bad for any kind of movement. It rained, hailed, and sleeted until the country around and about them became very muddy and swampy, and at times covered with a sheet of sleet and ice. Papson hesitated to attack and Head could not retreat; so there the two armies lay shivering in the cold, suffering very greatly, both fearing to take any decisive steps.

"Gen. Silent became quite impatient, believing it to be the time to strike, as the enemy could not get away. Finally he concluded to relieve Papson, but notified him of his order. Papson now made ready for an assault. His command was posted as follows: Gen. A. J. Smithers on the right, who was to assault the enemy's left, supported by Wellston's cavalry; Ward was to support Smithers on his left, acting against Monterey Hill, on the Hillston road; Scovens was to hold the interior line, being the defense of Nashua. When the time arrived, all being in readiness, the order was given. The enemy seemed to be totally unaware of the movement. Smithers and Wellston moved out along the pike. Wheeling to the left they at once advanced against the enemy. The cavalry first struck the enemy at the Harden House, near Rich Earth Creek, and drove him back, capturing many prisoners. One of Smithers's divisions moving with the cavalry, captured two of the enemy's strong advance positions, with about 400 prisoners.

"At this time Scovens's Corps was put in on Smithers's right, and the advance was then made by the whole line. Ward's Corps now found the enemy to Smithers's left, and Gen. Anderson led his command against Monterey Hill and

carried it, capturing a number of prisoners. Ward's Corps
at once advanced against the main line of the enemy, and
after a bloody contest carried it, capturing a great many
prisoners, a number of pieces of artillery, and many stands
of colors. The enemy was now driven out of his entire line
of works and fell back to a second line at the base of Har-
pan Hills, holding his line of retreat by way of Franktown.
Night closed in and stopped again the play of death. Our
forces were now in possession of sixteen pieces of artillery,
with many officers and 1,200 prisoners, not including
wounded. Our troops bivouacked on their line of battle in
order to be ready for any movement in the morning.

"Ward's Corps at six in the morning moved south from
Nashua, striking the enemy and driving him some five
miles, to Overton's Hill, where he had thrown up works
and was making a stand. Gen. Sleman now moved rapidly
to Gen. Ward's left. Scovens remained in his position of
the last night. Wellston moved to the enemy's rear and
drew up his line across one of the Franktown roads.

"About two o'clock one brigade of Ward's Corps, supported by Sleman's division, assaulted Overton's Hill,
which was the enemy's center. One of Sleman's brigades
was composed of colored troops. The ground over which
they had to assault was open. The enemy re-enforced his
center. The assault was made, but received by the enemy
with a terrible shower of grape, canister and musketry.
Our forces moved steadily on, not wavering in the least,
until they had nearly reached the crest of the hill, when
the reserves of the enemy arose from behind their works
and opened one of the most destructive fires ever witnessed,
causing our troops to first halt and then fall back, leaving
many dead and wounded, both black and white indiscriminately, in the abatis and on the field.

"Gen. Ward immediately re-formed his command, and
all the forces of the army moved simultaneously against
the enemy's works, carrying every position, breaking the
lines in many places, and driving him in utter rout from
his position, capturing all his artillery and thousands of
prisoners, among whom were many officers, including four

Generals. Ward and Wellston pursued the fleeing enemy until by capture and other means Head's army was entirely destroyed and wiped out of existence as an organization. It appeared no more in the history of the great rebellion. Thus were destroyed all the formidable forces of the enemy in the West. The army of Papson now went into Winter quarters at different points which were thought necessary to be garrisoned.

"Peter, by this time, was growing very weak, having had a relapse, resulting in a very serious hemorrhage. At his request I had telegraphed Gen. Papson, stating his great desire to see Gen. Anderson. Upon the receipt of which, leave was immediately granted the General and he came home, bringing Lieut. Whitcomb with him. On the way home people greeted him everywhere with shouts of joy. They could now see that the end was near, and they were overflowing with gratitude and good feeling.

"On their arrival you can imagine the joy of our household. The meeting between him and Peter was most touching. Both wept like children. All were much affected; even the two little children wept and sobbed aloud at the bedside of their Uncle Peter. My wife was quite feeble. She greeted the General as one of her own sons, and said:

"'Our dear Peter is not going to live. I see it all, and I pray God that he may take me also.'

"The General encouraged Peter all he could. Ham and Aunt Martha were as delighted to see the General as were any of his family. We all tried to be cheerful and in good spirits, but it was very hard to do this under the circumstances.

"The next day after the General reached home he inquired of Ham why he did not return to the army. Ham said:

"'I fuss done thought I would, and den I knowed I be no use, kase you so far off, and I feared I not jes' safe gwine frough dem Sesh lines down dar; and den I knowed, too, dat you kin git as many niggers as you wants dat am jes' as good as Ham is, 'ceptin when you done wants good tings to eat, sech like as chickens. Ham can allers get dem when dey is 'round and skeered of the Sesh. I all de time noticed dey is powerful feared ob de Sesh, Marsa Lyon. De General know dat am so.'

"'Well, Ham, you must be ready to go back with me when I return.'

"'Oh, yes, Marsa; oh, yes! I go all right; I will, sho' as you is bawn. But I tells you dat Marsa Peter am powerful bad, he am, sho'. I dream it all out las' night. Missus, she be right in dat. He be agoin' dis time, and no mistake. Dat dream ob de Missus be all come 'round.'

"'That will do, Ham; you go and talk to Aunt Martha about your dreams.'

"''All right, Marsa, all right, sah; but you mine what I tole you.'

"The next day Joseph Dent came in, and we had a long conversation on the subject of the war, the Golden Circle and the Sons of Liberty. He said that they were alarmed, and quite a number had refused to meet recently, but that the Grand Commander had issued a call for a meeting to be held in Canada some time soon, where many of the leading men were again to assemble and take into consideration some new plan for aiding the rebellion. After he left for home the General, Henry and I consulted as to the best plan to get at what those men in Canada were working up. They had tried mobs and riots in New York and other places, had tried releasing prisoners, burning and destroying cities, scattering disease in our hospitals, and army raids, guerrilla warfare, etc., and had failed in all. Now what next? We thought that it would be best for Henry and Seraine to return to Detroit; that Henry again should visit Canada, and, by him the information could be communicated to me. This being understood, they left the next day. James Whitcomb, having gone immediately home on his arrival at Allentown, would be with his parents and Seraine, while Henry should visit in Canada.

"Peter was now apparently improving and we felt he might possibly recover. The news of Sherwood's safe arrival at the Sea having been received, the people were

greatly rejoiced.   They felt that the Spring campaign
would probably end the rebellion.   The country was full
of hope and the drooping spirits of anxious people were
much revived.   Things went on in this way and our family
enjoyed themselves as best they could.   Mary Anderson
and Jennie Lyon, David's widow, and the two little girls,
made our home as pleasant as possible   But my poor wife
grew weaker all the time. which gave us much concern.

"Henry had arrived in Canada, and again found his
friend Wintergreen.   They were now visiting different
places.   Henry had written Seraine and she came down to
Allentown, spending two days with us, and at the same
time posting the General and myself as to the movements
of the conspirators.   Thomlinson had called the leaders of
the Northern Sons of Liberty to again assemble at St.
Catharines the last Thursday in January.   Henry had
concluded to remain and learn fully their intentions and
schemes.   I told Seraine to say to him that his proposition
to remain was approved.   I sent to the President the information and Henry's intention, in answer to which I received a very kind and touching letter from one of his
Secretaries, exhibiting great sympathy for my family and
deploring our misfortunes.

"Time moved on, and the General was preparing to
leave for his command, when Peter became very much
worse; and, also, my wife was growing weaker and losing
her mind.   Peter was coughing very often and having
slight hemorrhages.   The physician pronounced him to be
in a very critical condition.   One morning Aunt Martha
came running into the parlor where the family were sitting,
and with much anxiety cried out:

"'Marsa Lyon and Marsa Gen'l, come to Marsa Peter,
quick; 'cause he bleed to deff if you not hurry.'

"We ran to him quickly.   He was bleeding profusely,
holding his head over the edge of the bed.   He could only
speak in a gurgling whisper.   He took me by the hand and
said:

"'Father, it is all over with me; soon there will be but
one finger left.'

" We laid him back on the pillow, and without another word or struggle he passed away. Good bless my poor son ! "

"Amen ! " said Dr. Adams.

Uncle Daniel soon proceeded, saying : "But, my good friends, this was not my only grief. We tried to keep his death from his mother. She, in her delirium, was constantly speaking of her dear son Peter, and crying. She seemed to

MRS. LYON DIES AT PETER'S COFFIN.

have no thought except of Peter and the constant shadow of her dream. The day of Peter's funeral her reason seemed to return and her strength revived. She asked for all of us to come into her room, and we did so. When she saw that Peter was not with us, she inquired why. I answered that he could not come. I then broke down and left her room weeping. She saw it, and, with strength that she had not shown for many weeks, arose, and leaping to the floor rushed past all into the parlor, and there saw Peter lying a corpse. She shrieked and fell on his remains. We lifted her and carried her back to her bed. She was dead!"

Uncle Daniel sank back into his chair overcome with his sorrows. The severe trials through which he had passed, re-called again, opened the flood of sorrow, which well nigh swept him away. We withdrew for the present, with intense sympathy for the old hero and a feeling that the Government had sadly neglected him.

CHAPTER XIX.

" I could a tale unfold, whose lightest word
Would harrow up thy soul, freeze up thy young blood."
—SHAKESPEARE.

"THE death of my son Peter and my beloved wife
cast such a deep gloom over our household that
it seemed we never could rally again to do anything for ourselves or our country. Gen. Anderson returned to his command a sad and despondent man.
He had left Ham to look after things for us at home, our
family now being reduced to Jennie Lyon, Mary Anderson,
the two children, Ham, Martha and myself. We were
lonely in the extreme, and seemed, for some cause undis-
coverable to us, to be drinking the bitter dregs from the
poisoned chalice. Ham and Aunt Martha saw my distress
and tried in their honest and simple way to pour consola-
tion into my soul. The little children, in their childish
simplicity, seemed to be the only fountain whence I could
drink draughts of comfort in my lonely hours of distress.
Seraine came to our house to attend the funeral, as Henry
could not reach home in time to be with us and see the
last of his mother and brother. I wrote him by his wife
and directed him to remain. He came to Detroit terribly broken down with grief, and returned, sad and de-
jected, to Canada. He was frequently interrogated as to
the cause of his melancholy, but parried it as best he
could.

"About the 12th of February he returned to Detroit, and, bringing Seraine with him, came to my house. Our meeting was mixed with joy and sadness. The ladies, as well as my myself, were very much gratified at having dear Seraine (as we all called her) with us again. She conversed so sensibly on the subject of our misfortunes that she made us almost feel that they must be for our good.

"As soon as we could do so, Henry and I sat down to talk over the situation in Canada and the schemes of the conspirators. He reported to me all he had seen or heard on the question of the war, stating in the beginning that there was no time to lose. When he found Wintergreen they set out for a trip through Canada. After visiting many places and meeting various persons from the South who had been in Canada for the purpose of aiding in carrying the Presidential election in favor of the anti-war or Democratic party, but who had not been able to return since the election, and were waiting, Micawber-like, for something to turn up, they had finally arrived at Montreal, where they again met Joseph Thomlinson and quite a number of faces to them unfamiliar. These persons were evidently there for some purpose looking to the success of the rebellion. Thomlinson received them kindly, inquired of Wintergreen how he felt since his return from London, and asked many questions about certain people at Windsor. Henry was also interrogated as to how matters looked to him, to which he answered that the signs were not so favorable as heretofore.

"Thomlinson went into a long disquisition on the recent campaigns. He denounced Gen. Head, who had been so utterly destroyed by Papson, as a 'brainless ass,' and spoke of Gen. Laws as having lost much of his vigor and daring. He said that if Gen. Wall, their greatest General, was alive, he would drive Silent out of Virginia in one month. He said that the re-election of Lincoln was a severe blow to them; that they had been deceived by their Northern friends. They had been led to believe that there was no doubt of Little Mac's election, with a liberal expenditure of money; that he had drawn checks and paid out for that purpose on behalf of the Confederacy $1,100,000, and seemed to think that unless measures were taken at once to strike consternation into the hearts of the Northern people all would be lost; that the President of the Confederacy and his Cabinet had been all along expecting some great result from the efforts of their Northern allies, and especially from the efforts of Valamburg and Thomas A. Strider.

"'True,' he said, 'Valamburg had been very much hampered by the suspicions resting upon him in the minds of the people, but it was not so with Strider. He could have done a great deal more if he had not been so timid. He (Strider) seemed to think that he could secure the success of the Confederacy by crippling the U. S. Government in opposing legislation and breeding strife and jealousies in the Union armies. 'But,' he continued, 'Lincoln is an old fox, and soon smelled out those little devices of Strider. He has completely checkmated him and his friends who were acting on his line, by relieving from command all those who were playing into Strider's hands, and has put in their places a set of fanatics, who are fighting on moral grounds alone.'

"He spoke of Silent as a man who did not value life or anything else, saying that he was a superstitious man, who believed that he was merely an instrument in the hands of the Almighty to wipe out slavery. Not only so, but believed that he was guided and directed in all his movements by the mysterious hand of Providence. So he (Thomlinson) could not see the use of relying longer on any satisfactory result to come from the course being pursued by their Northern friends. He said they must act more openly, energetically and promptly, if they were to help the Confederacy.

"There were two men present that Henry thought he had seen somewhere before, but could not place them. One was a medium-sized man, with rather dark complexion, dark hair, eyes and mustache. He was introduced as a Mr. Wilkes. The other was a young man, perhaps thirty years of age, slight, with brown hair, blue eyes and no

beard, named John Page. These two men seemed nervous
and uneasy; they conversed but little. The man Wilkes
remarked that there was but one way, which was a part
of every insurrection, and he was in favor of that way.
Page agreed with him, both seeming to understand the
proposition; yet it was not stated in the conversation at
that time what Wilkes meant by 'but one way.'

"Thomlinson made no answer to Wilkes or Page, but
continued by saying:

"'I have called the leading men of our organization to
meet again at St. Catharines, on the first Tuesday in February, and at that time there must be some scheme devised
and agreed upon that will turn the scale, or all will be lost,
and we will all be wandering vagabonds over the face of the
earth.'

"Henry inquired if Mr. Carey was in the city. Thomlinson said no; that he was in Richmond, but would be at
their meeting if he could get through the lines, in doing
which they had met with no trouble heretofore. Wintergreen said that the people where he had been, who were
friendly, were now very despondent and greatly alarmed
for the safety of Richmond, as well as the Confederacy;
that everything seemed to be against them of late.

"'Yes,' replied Thomlinson, 'we have much to discourage
us, and at the same time all can be regained that we have
lost if our friends will settle upon some good plan and
carry it out. But it does seem that all our plans and
schemes so far have been abortive. Our first great scheme
of burning the Northern cities failed by the burning of the
Will-o'-the-Wisp and the loss of Dr. Mears and Prof. McCullough; and also of the material accumulated by Dr. Blackman. We stirred up riots in New York city and elsewhere
in opposition to the draft, with a promise from Valamburg,
Strider, McMasterson, and B. Wudd that our friends would
come to the rescue and make resistance everywhere. But
these men failed to stand by their promises. The inaugu-
rating of riots and the employment of men to engage in
them cost the Confederacy $500,000. We undertook to re-
lease prisoners from all the Northern prisons. We pur-

chased arms and smuggled them to our friends sufficient to
have armed all the prisoners. This was all that was wanting, our friends North stated to me; but when the time
came, which was the last night before the Presidential
election, at Camp Chase the effort was too feeble to be
recognized, and at Chicago, where we were assured that
the prisoners would be released and the city burned and
destroyed, what was the result? They cut one or two
water-pipes, and Wall, Greenfel and Buckner were arrested.
All our arms were found in Wall's cellar, and taken possession of by our enemies. Mr. Eagle and Mr. N. Judy Cornington were not on hand, neither as actors nor advisers;
and so it is. The arms, ammunition and hire for smuggling
them through cost a half million dollars. This kind of
work will not do. It is not only expensive, but fruit-
less.'

" He then stated to those present that he wished them
all to attend the next meeting, as mentioned, and to study
up in the meantime, some well-defined plan for successful
operations. Henry and Wintergreen left for other points,
and returned to St. Catharines on the day appointed for
the meeting, where they met with many additional persons,
strangers to both of them. The delegates assembled in the
same hall, in the rear of the Victoria Hotel, as before.
They were called to order by the Grand Commander of the
Sons of Liberty, Mr. Valamburg, of Dayburg, O. All were
seated and the roll was then called by Wintergreen, who
was the Secretary.

"Illinois was first called. Wm. Spangler and John Rich-
ardson answered; from Indiana, Messrs. Dorsing and Bow-
lin; Ohio, Valamburg and Massey; Pennsylvania, Wovel-
son and Moore; New York, McMasterson and B. Wudd;
Missouri, Col. Burnett and Marmalade; Kansas, String-
felter; Iowa, Neal Downing; Wisconsin, Domblazer; Ne-
braska, Martin; Arkansas, Walters; Connecticut, Eastman;
Vermont, Phillips; Massachusetts, Perry; Maine, Pillbox;
Rhode Island, no answer; New Jersey, Rogers. From
Richmond, for the South, there were Thomlinson and C.
C. Carey, the latter having just arrived. Other names, not

remembered, save those of Messrs. Wilkes and Page, who were admitted as representing the District of Columbia.

"After the necessary examinations were made by a committee, the persons mentioned, with several others, were admitted to seats in the assembly. Henry was selected by Wintergreen to assist him in his duties as Secretary. The preliminaries being settled, the Chairman (Valamburg) was quite severe in his strictures against Dan Bowen, Thos. A. Strider, C. H. Eagle and N. Judy Cornington for not attending, saying he had letters from each of those gentlemen promising to be present. He characterized their conduct as cowardly and they as sunshine friends, which was loudly applauded by all.

"After remarks by quite a number of delegates on the situation and probabilities of the success of the Confederacy, which were generally tinged with ill-forebodings, a committee of five was appointed to take into consideration and report to the assembly ways and means by which the rebellion could be materially assisted. This report was to be submitted the next day at 12 o'clock. The meeting then adjourned until that time.

"During the evening a variety of discussions were indulged in by various delegates in favor of different schemes. Some went so far as to favor the assassination of many of our leading men. Wilkes, Page, and quite a number of persons from the South were in favor of assassinating the President and Gen. Silent, with such others as the necessity of the case demanded. And so the conversation and discussions ran until the meeting of delegates the next day.

"At 12 o'clock the assembly was called to order by Valamburg. When the roll had been called and all were quiet, the Chairman inquired of the committee if they were ready to report. The Chairman, Mr. Carey, arose with great dignity and responded that the committee, after due consideration of the many suggestions submitted to them, were now ready to report. He was invited to take the stand, which he did.

"He said that, preliminary to reporting, he desired to make an explanation, which was as follows: That on his return from Montreal to Richmond, since the Presidential election, in viewing the many disasters that had recently befallen the Confederacy, the authorities at Richmond suggested to him to ascertain if he could communicate in some way with the newly elected Vice-President, and discover his attitude towards the people of the South. This was accomplished by sending one of the Vice-President's old friends from North Carolina to Nashua, who being a citizen, and not in any way connected with the Confederate army, easily passed through the Union lines to Nashua, where the Vice-President-elect was residing at the time. There was no difficulty in agreeing to an interview between himself and Carey, it being understood that Carey was to pass into Nashua in disguise and let the Vice-President know in some way where he was stopping, and the interview was then to be arranged. In pursuance of this agreement, Carey made the trip to Nashua disguised as a Louis City merchant, and passing by the name of Thos. E. Hope. He had no difficulty in getting into Nashua, but for fear of recognition, went directly to the house of a rebel friend by the name of Hanson, and remained in a room in the rear of the second story of the house. Through the lady of the house the Vice-President-elect was informed of the presence of Mr. Carey.

"The next morning the Vice-President visited the house of Mr. Hanson, and he and Carey had the contemplated interview. Carey said that in the interview the Vice-President contended for peace on the terms of a restored Union, but agreed with the Democrats of the North that the restoration should be on the basis of the old Constitution. Carey said that in answer to the question as to what he would do if he were President, the Vice-President said that he would restore the Union if he could on the old basis, but that the people were tired of war and taxes, and that unless Silent could drive Laws out of Richmond, capture it, and destroy the Confederate army during the next Spring campaign, the Confederacy must be recognized and the war ended.

"At this the assembly heartily cheered. Carey also said that in answer to the question as to the powers of the Vice-

President, in case of the absence of the President, if he should be so situated that he could not return to perform the duties of the office, the Vice-President replied that such a case as stated would certainly come under the provision of the Constitution, wherein it is recited that in case of the death, resignation, or inability of the President to discharge the powers and duties of the said office, the same shall devolve on the Vice-President ; that under such circumstances he should at once assume the duties of the office, but hoped that such a case would not arise while he was Vice-President.

"Carey stated that the Vice-President said that he had always been a Union man, but that he was a Democrat, and had never been anything else, and did not propose to be; that he was placed on the Republican ticket without being consulted. Therefore he did not feel under any obligations to that party. He also stated that he recognized the fact that when it was evident that the Union could be held together only by subjugating the people of the South, it was statesmanship to let them go, and stop further bloodshed. This also brought applause.

"Carey further stated that the Vice-President expressed a willingness to meet privately with any of our leading men of the South at any time when and where it could be done without danger to either party. With this the interview ended. When the parties separated the Vice-President bade him good-by and grasped his hand in the most friendly and cordial manner. He said if Carey should experience any trouble in getting back to Richmond to let him know.

"Carey left the next morning, and returning to Richmond reported the interview precisely as it occurred, at which the authorities were greatly pleased, and thought it opened a way for success, knowing the character of the man, his stubbornness, his egotism, and that he possessed a belief that he was destined to be President of the United States at some time. It was not intended to say any more to him than to ascertain his views on a given state of facts, and having accomplished this much, the authorities at

Richmond felt sure that if the President of the United States could by some means be captured and spirited away, and Silent also, or either of them, the success of the Confederacy would be assured beyond question. In the event of the capture and hiding away of the President, the Vice-President would surely assume the powers and duties of President. The friends of the Confederacy in Congress could then so cripple the Government that no doubt could longer exist of success. He said it was thought that in the event the President could not be captured, a party could be organized who could, without much risk, surprise and capture Gen. Silent. This done, Laws would at once assume the aggressive, drive Meador and his army back on Washington, and continue the war beyond the next Spring, so that the friends of the Confederacy could regain strength, and, with the Vice-President in favor of the recognition of the Confederate Government, it could not be longer postponed. But the great thing to be accomplished, he said, was the capture of Mr. Lincoln; that would end all controversy.

"This seemed to strike the audience, and they cheered the proposition. Carey then stated that this was the first proposition the committee desired to present. He had other important ones, however, that must be considered by the assembly. While in Richmond he found many men of great courage and daring who were ready to do anything to bring success if they could be sustained and protected. The authorities gave him the proposals and directed him to lay them before this assembly.

"The second was made by a foreigner—a man of good family in Europe, and a most daring and courageous man, an educated soldier, who had been successful in very many daring enterprises heretofore. His proposition was read to the assembly, being a verbatim copy of the one this party had made to the President of the Confederacy through the Confederate Secretary of War, which was as follows:

"'SECRETARY OF WAR OF THE SOUTHERN CONFEDERACY.

"'SIR: In reference to the subject upon which I had the honor to converse with you yesterday, and on account of which you bade me call to-day, I take herewith the freedom to address this most respectful writing to you. Your Honor seemed to hesitate in giving me an affirmative answer to my statement because I was unknown to you. Permit me to remark that, notwithstanding I can give you no references in this country, I am, nevertheless, worthy of your high confidence. My grandfather, Maj. Baron De Kalb, fell in the Revolutionary War of this country. * * * I received an education proportionate to the means of my parents, and served in the Crimean war as Second Lieutenant of Engineers. * * * I landed in Quebec, Canada, in November last, and arrived in Washington, D. C., about three weeks ago. I cannot perceive why you should require any references or confidence, for I do not expect personally to reap any benefit before the strict performance of what I undertake. The task I know is connected with some danger, but never will it, in any event, become known in the North that the Southern Confederacy had anything whatever to do with it.

"'The whole matter resolves itself, therefore, into this one question: Does the Southern Confederacy consider the explosion of the Federal Capitol at a time when Abe, his myrmidons, and the Northern Congress are all assembled together, of sufficient importance to grant me, in case of success, a commission as Colonel of Topographical Engineers, and the sum of $1,000,000? If so, your Honor may most explicitly expect the transaction to be carried into execution between the 4th and 6th of the month. * * * I trust you will not press in regard to the manner in which I intend to perform it, or anything connected with the execution.

"'In case of an affirmative answer there is no time to spare; and to show you still further my sincerity, I will even refrain from asking for any pecuniary assistance in carrying the project through, notwithstanding my means are, for such an undertaking, very limited, and that some funds would materially lighten my task, diminish the danger, and doubly insure success. * * * I intend to throw myself at a convenient place into Maryland and to enter Washington by way of Baltimore.

"'Very respectfully, your obedient servant,

"'(Signed) C. L. V. DeKalb.'

"Carey said that this man was in the employ of the Confederacy, but that the authorities would not adopt his scheme without the indorsement of their Northern friends, so that those friends could have warning and not be endangered at the time. This man being a foreigner, and not understanding the situation, regarded all Northern men alike and would destroy one as soon as another. Therefore, those having the authority to do so, would not accept the proposition unless due notice could be secretly given, under the obligations of the Sons of Liberty, to their friends in Congress. Carey said he thought this a very dangerous undertaking on account of the friends who might be imperiled, but felt that there was no doubt but it could be accomplished.

"Walters spoke up at this point, saying this proposition was not feasible at all, and a number assented to his remark.

"Mr. Carey said the third proposition was also in the form of a communication, and was placed in his hands by the authorities in Richmond for consideration by the Northern friends, and was in the following language, which he proceeded to read:

"'BOSTON P. O., GA.
"'JEFFERSON DAVIS.

"'SIR: Having a desire to be of benefit to the Southern States is the only excuse I can offer for addressing you this letter; and believing the best plan would be to dispose of the leading characters of the North, for that reason I have experimented in certain particulars that will do this without difficulty; although it is quite an underhanded manner of warfare, and not knowing whether it would meet with your approbation or not, prevents me from giving you a full account of the material used, although I believe any one of them would take the life of a Southern man in any way they could. If you wish, write to me and get the whole process.
"'Hoping for your good health and future victory.
"'(Signed) J. S. PARAMORE.'

"Said Carey: 'This man was sent for and closely examined as to what he proposed, and by the experiments made by our best scientists they were of opinion that his plan could be made a success, as the process was without doubt effective. The question, however, was not as to the process by which this could be done, but must we resort to it? Had all other means failed?'

"The other proposition was on the same line, but proposing a different mode of execution, which Carey also read:

"'HEADQUARTERS 63D GA. REG'T.,
"'NEAR SAVANNAH.

"'TO PRESIDENT DAVIS.

"'MR. PRESIDENT: After long meditation and much reflection on the subject of this communication, I have determined to intrude it upon you, earnestly hoping my motives will constitute a full vindication for such presumption on the part of one so humble and obscure as myself, though I must say that the evidences of your Christian humility almost assure me. I propose, with your permission, to assist in organizing a number of select men, say not less than 300 to 500, to go into the United States and assassinate, for instance, Seward, Lincoln, Greeley, Prentice, and others, considering it necessary to the chances of success at this time. I will only say a few words as to the opinion of its effects. I have made it a point to elicit the opinion of many men upon this subject, in whose good sense I have great confidence, and while a difference of opinion to some extent is almost inevitable, most have confidence in its benefit to us. The most plausible argument seems to be that to impress upon the Northern mind that for men in high places there to wield their influence in favor of the barbarisms they have been so cruelly practicing upon us is to jeopardize their lives; for distinguished leaders there to feel that the moment they array hordes for our desolation, at that moment their existence is in the utmost peril—this would produce hesitation and confusion that would hasten peace and our independence. With these meager suggestions upon the subject I will leave it for this time. If you deem the matter worthy of any encouragement, and will so apprize me, I believe I can give you such evidences of loyalty and integrity of character as will entitle it to your consideration. So far as I am concerned, I will say, however, that I was born and raised in Middle Georgia. All my relationships and affections are purely Southern. I was opposed to secession, but am now committed to the death against subjugation or reunion with men of whose instincts and moral character, till this war, I was totally ignorant. If I have insulted any scruple or religious principle of yours I beg to be pardoned. I neglected to state in the proper place that I am an officer in the volunteer service.

" 'Begging your respectful attention to this communication,

" 'I am, your Excellency's most obedient servant,
" 'H. C. DURHAM, 63d Ga.'

"The reading of this communication was received with cheers from quite a number of those present, principally Southern men. Carey said that the Secretary of War had sent for Durham, and that he was then at Richmond. He was a fine looking, intelligent man, terribly in earnest. This was thought, although there was hesitancy about it in the Cabinet, to be a much more feasible undertaking than the attempt to explode the Capitol at Washington. The necessity for some radical measure to be adopted and put into execution at once was the reason for these documents having been taken from the archives and placed in the present hands in their original form.

"Lieut. W. Alston, of Sulphur Springs, Va., who was present, as stated by Carey, also proposed to the authorities at Richmond to undertake to rid the country of the Confederacy's most deadly enemies, and authorized the committee to say that he, here and now, renewed his proposition; all of which Carey submitted to the assembly for their consideration.

"The propositions having been submitted in due form, the Chairman stated that they were before the assembly and open for consideration. Jacob Thomlinson opened the discussion, and said that these propositions were of the most vital importance; that the success of the Confederacy hung upon the action of this assembly. The authorities were waiting with bated breath until they could hear what their Northern friends would consider proper and feasible to be at once entered upon. He wanted no more promises without performance. He would save the Confederacy by any means if he could, and would consider himself justified. If some of these measures had been resorted to much earlier it would have been better. He said that war was mere barbarism and cruelty; that plunder, burning, pillage and

assassination were merely the concomitants, and a part of
the system, of all wars; that when men make war it means
crime, rapine and murder, and those engaging in it should
so understand. Each party is expected to capture all of the
enemy that can be so taken, and to kill all that resist. It was
proper to pick out and deliberately shoot down the Generals.
He asked if it would be any worse to secretly capture Lincoln and Silent, the two leaders and commanders of all the
United States forces, or to assassinate either or both of
them, than to shoot them near our lines. He contended
that if either or both of them should be seen near the Confederate lines they would be shot down, and the persons
doing it would be rewarded with medals of honor, and
would go down into history as great patriots for performing the act. If this were true, as all must concede, why
should it be considered a dark and damnable deed in time
of war, when a great and dire necessity required, for two
such tyrants to be put out of the way in the cause of
liberty? He insisted that no difference could exist, save in
the minds of individuals morbid on the subject of human
life. He said that he had witnessed enough shamming,
and heard enough shallow professions, and wanted no
more of either; that the promises of some of their Northern friends, already broken, had cost the Confederacy millions of dollars in coin, and had left him individually bank-
rupt and impoverished. There had been nothing but a
series of failures growing out of the pretenses of some of
their Northern allies. He was very severe on many of
them, especially on Cornington and Eagle, of Chicago, and
Strider and Bowen, of Indiana, all of whom he charged
with getting large sums of money for use in the late election and for other purposes. He said they neither
accounted for its disposition, nor had they entered an appearance, after promising on their obligation to do so.
This he considered the most unwarranted course of conduct
of which any one could have been guilty—no less than the
deepest-dyed perfidy. When he closed his speech he was
cheered to the echo."

Dr. Adams said: "This man Thomlinson was a very

brutal man in his instincts. He seemed also to have been out of humor with his co-conspirators. He was certainly very angry and much disappointed that his schemes had all failed. But how an intelligent man could argue and justify assassination, as he seemed to do, I cannot understand."

Col. Bush replied : "Doctor, you must see that this man, no matter what he may have been in former years, had become a hardened, inhuman wretch. Do you not remember that he was the same person who employed men to gather poisoned clothes for the distribution of disease, as well as his attempt to have our cities burned, but was thwarted by Divine Providence, in my judgment?"

"Yes, I remember all this, and God knows that seemed the extreme of barbarism and inhumanity ; but his last proposition in his argument was deliberate, cold-blooded murder in order to gain a political end ; and to think of Northern men listening at any time to such propositions without remonstrance or disapproval in any way makes me shudder."

"They seemed to indorse it instead of manifesting disapproval," said Ingelsby, "and I have no doubt they favored it, and in some way assisted in trying to have it carried out."

"Yes, yes," said Uncle Daniel ; "the half of the treachery and diabolical deeds of many of our Northern men, now leaders, is not known or understood ; but, my dear friends, I will continue my story :

"When Thomlinson had concluded his remarks, Valamburg followed in a like strain, and concluded with a 'so help him God' that he was ready for any enterprise to serve the Confederacy, no matter how dark nor how desperate and bloody. This was received with a wild shout, as though some rebel victory had been announced.

"Walters, of Arkansas, then addressed the assembly. He said he was in favor of the first proposition ; that there seemed to be something practical in it. Since their last meeting he had been all over the North, even in Washington city, and there was not the slightest difficulty in passing to and fro without any questions being asked. He said he saw the President riding out beyond Georgetown with only one person accompanying him ; that there would not have been the slightest trouble in five men capturing him and crossing the river into Virginia, or retreating into Maryland and passing along on byways with him to where he could have been securely kept until a chance was afforded for conveying him to some more secure place. So far as putting him out of the way was concerned, there would not be the slightest difficulty in doing that, but he thought the other the best, taking all things into consideration. The one would be considered a clean trick, and perfectly legitimate warfare, while the other would not, and would arouse the Northern people to more energetic measures. He said that he did not think there would be very great difficulty in capturing Silent ; that he had made inquiry about him, and found that he seldom had anything more than a few men as escort, and kept but a small company as his head-quarters guard ; that 100 good, picked men could capture him almost any night. If they even failed, it would only make those who attempted it prisoners of war, so that they would be exchanged. This, if accomplished, in case of either Lincoln or Silent, would secure the Confederacy. With Lincoln captured, the Vice-President would only be too glad to have an excuse for the recognition of the Confederacy. With Silent captured, Gen. Laws would again be master of the situation. Silent was the only match for him in the United States. So far as the Vice-President was concerned, he was in a bad humor with the whole administration. He (Walters) had seen him and conversed with him since the time mentioned at which Mr. Carey had his interview. Walters had been at Nashua, and remained for several days unmolested, and had talked freely with quite a number of persons who were intimate with the Vice-President, and who were conversant with his views and knew his feelings. He said that the Vice-President suggested to him to get through the lines and go to Richmond, and say to the authorities there that if he were President he would recognize the Southern Confederacy ; but he (Walters) did not then have full confidence in what he was saying, as he was rather in his cups at the time. But since he had heard what Mr. Carey had learned in his interview with him he had no further reason to doubt his sincerity.

"Mr. Wilkes here interposed and asked whether the whole question of recognition by the Vice-President did not entirely depend upon the capture and successful spiriting away of Lincoln.

"Mr. Walters answered in the affirmative.

"Wilkes then said: 'Suppose this scheme should fail, what then?'

"Walters remarked that that was a question to be determined by this meeting, and that he did not wish to decide it in advance.

"Mr. Spangler, from Illinois, said that he did not desire to detain the assembly with a long speech, but he wished to impress upon the minds of the delegates present that in the State from which he came, he did not think the assassination of Lincoln and Silent would be indorsed, as it would raise such a storm there that all their friends would be driven from the State. He was in favor of their capture and, in fact, anything that was thought necessary; but as he lived in the same town with Mr. Lincoln, he would not like to be forced to stem the torrent if he, Lincoln, should be assassinated. He would cheerfully vote for the first proposition, and at the same time pay $100 into the general pool for that purpose. This brought down the house—money seemed to be the one thing they greatly desired. He said: 'Now, Mr. Chairman, who is the Treasurer?'

"The Chairman answered that Mr. Thomlinson had the disbursing as well as the authority to receive all funds for the carrying out of the objects of the meeting.

"'Then,' said Spangler, 'here is my $100,' handing it to Thomlinson. This started the ball, and in a few minutes $5,000 were raised and handed over to Thomlinson, who thanked the friends for their liberality.

"The debate here closed and the vote was taken on the propositions. The Chairman said he would put the third, or last, proposition first, which was, whether the assembly would indorse the proposition of Capt. Alston and Mr.

Durham, who proposed to organize a force and assassinate the leading men of the North who are prominent in the war against the South, and recommend the authorities of the Southern Confederacy to carry out the proposed project. The question being stated, the vote was taken. Being very close, the roll had to be called, and the proposition was lost by three votes.

"The next proposition was the one submitted by De Kalb to the Confederacy, to blow up the Capitol at Washington when Congress should be in session. The vote being taken, this proposition was lost; it being deemed inexpedient on account of the danger of destroying so many of their own friends.

"The last proposition to be voted on was whether the assembly would recommend to the authorities at Richmond to organize a force and capture Lincoln and Silent, or either of them, and hold the captive or captives until the Confederacy should be recognized. This question was taken and carried unanimously with a great hurrah and three cheers for the man or men who should accomplish this most desirable object.

"After the proposition had been agreed to, Mr. Page and Capt. Alston both desired to know what was to be done, if anything, should this attempt to capture those men fail. Quite a discussion here arose, during which considerable feeling was shown on the part of some of the Southern men. Finally they determined to recommend that Wilkes, Page, Alston and Durham be put in charge and organize for the purpose mentioned, and that they receive their instructions directly from Jacob Thomlinson. One of these men should go to Richmond with C. C. Carey, and there meet Durham and consult with the authorities as to the route to be adopted in getting into and out of Washington, and the means to be resorted to for their assistance and protection; also that, in the event of failure in capturing either of those men, then in that case they, or some of them, were to return to Canada and confer further with Thomlinson; and whatever measures he and they should adopt that looked like bringing success were to be carried out, with the understanding that the assembly here and now assented to it; which it did, and appointed Mr. Thomlinson with power to act as fully as if the matter had been laid before it and agreed to by a vote.

"This concluded the business of the delegates, and they adjourned to meet on the call of the Grand Commander at any future time when necessary for the benefit of the cause of the Confederacy. Henry remained a day or so in order to note any further developments. Carey and Page left at once for Richmond, intending to make their way in disguise by rail into West Virginia, and from there to Richmond. Wilkes started for New York and Alston for Buffalo. They were to make their way to Baltimore, and meet there on a certain day and remain until Page should return from Richmond with Durham. They were then to have an understanding as to how they should operate. Before leaving they all had a secret meeting with Thomlinson, but what instructions they received of a private nature Henry did not know, except that he learned if their scheme should fail, one or more of them were to return at once to Canada and consult further with Thomlinson as to their future operations.

"I required this to be written in full by Henry, and leaving him and his wife, Seraine, with what of our family was now left, I telegraphed to the President:

"'Stay indoors; important; am coming!
                    (Signed,)   DANIEL.'

"I at once left for Washington, feeling that time was important. The desperation of these men was such that they would undertake an enterprise of any kind, and the condition of the Confederacy such that nothing less than some heroic remedy would avail anything.

"When I arrived at Washington it was early in the morning. I directed my steps toward the Executive Mansion. On arriving at the door the usher recognized me, but said that the President had not been to breakfast.

"I said: 'I do not wish to disturb him, but it is very important that I see him before a crowd comes in. I will remain here.'

" He stepped in and very soon returned, and at once showed me to the President's office up-stairs. He was waiting for me, and as I entered he came forward with both hands extended, and said, 'My dear friend Lyon, how are you?'

" I answered him as to my health in a sad tone. He spoke of my great afflictions in the most tender manner, and inquired as to the telegram.

" I said : 'Mr. President, this paper,' handing him Henry's report, 'will explain it.'

" He said : ' This is a long paper—as long as a President's message,' and laughed, saying, 'I expect you have been writing one for me?'

" I replied that it was an important message for a President. At this he laughed, and said :

" ' That is quite good, and is a very wise distinction; but,' said he, 'we will not read it now. When we get our breakfast, that will do, will it not?'

" I replied : ' Yes, perhaps it will.'

" He would have me take breakfast with him. His family only were present, and we all conversed freely, but principally about the late election and our success in the West against Head, and the prospects of Silent against Laws. He was feeling very happy and confident of final victory. He told me about having just returned with the Secretary of State from Hampton Roads, where they had met the Vice-President of the Southern Confederacy and others on a peace mission; 'but,' said he, 'it was the same kind of peace that the Copperheads have been preaching, under instructions from Richmond and the rebel agents in Canada, for three years.'

" After breakfast we returned to his office. He instructed his usher that he could see no one for the present. Being seated, he drew the paper that I had given him from his side pocket and commenced reading. Very soon he exhibited some little excitement, rang his bell and sent for the Secretary of War, who soon came in. After the Secretary had exchanged compliments with me, the President continued reading. When he had finished he turned to me and said :

"'This is the most extraordinary thing that I have ever read or heard of, in or out of history. Mr. Secretary, please read this.'

"The Secretary read it very carefully and remarked : 'This is what they are coming to; they will stop at nothing. But the most surprising part of all is the attitude of your

UNCLE DANIEL CONFERRING WITH LINCOLN AND STANTON.

Vice-President. What can he mean by hob-nobbing with those traitors and having interviews with one of their principal leaders inside of our lines?'

"'Yes,' said the President; 'this is strange, indeed.'

"After further conversation it was determined to have the Cabinet officers meet that day. The President also directed the Secretary of War to ask Gen. Silent to be at the Executive Mansion the next morning. He asked me to remain in Washington and come to see him the next day at 10 o'clock, and not to fail. I left, went to the Owen House and took a room.

"While there I met a man in rather delicate health, who said his name was Alston, that he was a Canadian, and had come to Washington on account of the mildness of the climate. He was about five feet ten inches in height, hazel eyes, light hair, with small goatee; was quite a nervous man, moving his hands, or sitting down and immediately rising again, picking his teeth, or pulling his goatee. I remembered the man's name as that of one of the conspirators, and marked him well. On inquiry I found he had arrived the day before and was intending, as he said, to remain for some time in order to test the climate in his case. I stepped up to the War Department, and finding my friend, the Secretary, in, I asked him to send a detective with me, and he did so. I put him on the man and said no more to any one until I met the President and others the next day.

"At 10 o'clock the following morning I appeared at the Mansion and was admitted at once. On entering the President's office I met Gen. Silent. Having previously met him at Chatteraugus and elsewhere, he recognized me, and after the usual compliments asked about Gen. Anderson. I told him about my misfortunes, the last of which he was not aware of. He said no more for a short time; he then asked me if Gen. Anderson would not like to come East and have a better command. He said he did not think he had been given a command equal to his ability; that he would order him East if agreeable. I wrote the General as soon as I returned to my hotel.

"The conversation was then turned to the report of Henry. The President seemed serious, and said the astounding statement about the Vice-President worried him, and yet, he said, it was almost incredible.

"Gen. Silent said he could believe it, but was very much surprised at his having the interview and disclosing his opinions to our enemies. Silent said he made some curious statements to him while he was making his headquarters at Nashua, but he attributed it to Tennessee whisky more than to any wrong motive in his mind, until he repeated the same things over more than once. He thought strange of it, but did not mention the conversation.

" 'But,' said the Secretary, 'what do you say to the attempt they are to make to capture you two gentlemen?'

"Silent said: 'That scheme has already failed. Our knowledge of the fact defeats it. You must have a guard of at least one company of infantry at or near the White House, and the officers must be notified, in confidence, why they are placed here. There must be a company of cavalry ordered here for escort to the President, and he must not go out of call of the guards without an escort.'

"The President said: 'This will not look well, but I suppose I must do it for safety. I do not like this Vice-President's talk; it worries me. But how about yourself, Gen. Silent; they seem to be after you as well.'

" 'Yes,' said the General; ' but you must remember that I am surrounded by an army, and this notice protects me. I will look after that hereafter. The truth is, they might have caught me napping, as I have heretofore had but a small guard. I will make it large enough when I return. My fears, however, are very much increased, as I see that there were many of those conspirators in favor of taking the proposition to assassinate instead of capture. That can be done in spite of guards, by reckless men who will take desperate chances. This is what we must look out for. I see that they are to take orders from Jacob Thomlinson, who is a most reckless man, without any of the instincts of humanity, and utterly without any regard for the rules of civilized warfare. He is a very dangerous man if he has about him those who will do his bidding. So look out, Mr. President; my judgment is that you will be in imminent peril.'

" 'Yes,' said the President. 'Gen. Silent do you remember the dream I repeated to you when you came to Washington?'

" 'Oh, yes,' said Gen. Silent, 'perfectly; and in that dream I was to be murdered as soon as the rebellion should be ended. But I do not feel alarmed about myself; dreams, you know, Mr. President, go by contraries.'

" 'Yes,' said the President, 'I will not say that I believe in dreams, neither do I; yet they make an impression on my mind.'

13

"Gen. Silent said no more on the subject, and the conversation on that topic was dropped.

"I was asked if I would send Henry back to Canada to watch further developments. I assented. They all thought that perhaps in this way we would be able to head off any further scheme as the one reported had been.

"I then related what I had discovered at the Owen House, and suggested a close watch on this man Alston. The President took up the report, and finding the name, thought there might be something in my suggestion. They sent for the detective that I had placed to watch him, and he informed us that this man drank pretty freely, and had disclosed to him while in his cups the night before that he was from St. Catharine's, Canada; that he had plenty of money in gold, and was desirous of finding some five or six good, active, bold and daring young men, who would be likely to be fond of an adventure. The detective was sent back at once with instructions to arrest him and have him taken to Old Capitol Prison. If any questions should be asked, he was to answer that the Secretary of War had directed it. The next morning it was telegraphed all over the country that a Mr. Alston was arrested in Washington for attempting to hire men to kidnap the President; and so the scheme was exploded.

"The next day I bade the President and the Secretary good-by, at the same time warning the President of his great danger. He could not thank me enough, he said, for my interest. Silent had left for the army. Just as I was leaving, the President said to me in a whisper:

"'Look out for a great battle soon, and with it you will hear of the fall of Richmond.'

"I thanked him for his confidence in me and left. On arriving at home I found all well and very anxious to see me, as this had been my first absence since the death of my wife and Peter. Henry had seen the notice of Alston's arrest, and when I described him he said he was the right man. I wrote to the President what Henry said, and Alston remained in prison.

"In a short time I heard from Gen. Anderson. He was

willing to go East. I telegraphed Gen. Silent and he ordered him to report at once. He came by home on his way and remained over several days. Lieut. Whitcomb was with him. While there I related all that had taken place. He thought Henry should return at once to Canada, leaving Seraine with us. He said it would be dangerous since Alston's arrest to risk writing, so Henry would have to come to my house with any information that he might have. Henry left at once and the General the next day.

"We were alone again. The women and children were weeping over the departure of Henry and the General. Aunt Martha came in and said:

"'Bress de good Laud, chil'n, what is you cryin' 'bout. De Gen'l all right ; dars no danger 'bout him ; he am safe. De Laud protect him. He dun sabe him all dis time for good. Don't you see de Sesh git whip whareber he goes? Dey all done killed down whar he bin, and now dey jest' take him ober by whar Marsa Linkum am, and de Sesh all git smash up ober dar de same way as what dey is down whar he bin afore.'

"Old Ham chimed in : 'Yas, Marfa, dat am de fac'. You see, when I goes wid Marsa Gen'l, he gets shotted nearly ebery time. I not understand dis, but he not git any time hurt when I's away. How is dat, Marfa? Guess it best for me not be wid him. I tell you I guess I see it all now ; de Laud want me to stay here wid dese womens and dese chil'ns, and Marsa Gen'l he not t'ink ob dat, so de Laud jes' let him git hurted, so he hab to come and stay wid de folks and hab me heah? Is dat it, Marfa?'

"'Yes, dat am de case ; and I 'spec you is glad, kase you is a powerful coward, Ham ; you knows you is.'

"'Marfa, you neber see me fightin' dem Sesh. Else you not say dem hard words 'bout Ham. No, indeed, you not know 'bout me.'

"'I 'specs dat's so, Ham. How many of de Sesh does you 'specs you is killed ?'

"'Don' know, don' know. I neber counted em ; war too busy, Marfa.'

"This was getting Ham into a close place, and he retired.

"In a few days Henry returned and reported that the arrest of Alston had alarmed the conspirators in Canada very greatly. Carey and Page were still in Richmond. Wilkes had returned to Canada and had been at Montreal with Thomlinson, but Henry could get nothing out of him, as Thomlinson thought it best not to have any one know what was to be attempted unless they could aid in carrying it out; but he said the country would be startled very soon. Henry surmised what he meant, and as soon as he could get away from Wintergreen he left for home.

"I sent him to the President with this information, also a letter calling the President's attention to his great danger, and the danger in which the country would be in the event that anything should occur that would put the Vice-President in power. This was the last communication I ever had with the best of all Presidents."

CHAPTER XX.

COLLAPSE OF THE GREAT REBELLION.—LAWS' ARMY SUR-
RENDERS.—THE ASSASSINATION OF PRESIDENT LINCOLN.

> *" After life's fitful fever, he sleeps well;*
> *Treason has done his worst; nor steel nor poison,*
> *Malice domestic, foreign envy, nothing*
> *Can touch him farther."*—SHAKESPEARE.

"WHEN I left off speaking of Gen. Silent and his command in the East, and continued my story about the West and Center, you will remember that he had passed through eight days of bloody contest with Laws. We must now return to him and understand the condition of things on his line while these events were transpiring in the North, in Canada, and in Sherwood's department, of which I have given you a history.

"Silent moved out in the night time the last of May, and on June the first found a heavy force in his front. Fighting at once began again. Sherlin was in the advance, and by direction held his ground through that night. By daylight support reached him and his position was secure. Silent now established his headquarters at an old tavern, under wide-spreading trees, at Cool Haven, some ten or twelve miles from the rebel Capital, and at once assaulted Laws in his works. The Union troops charged with great dash and heroism, taking the enemy's first line of rifle-pits; but the enemy, falling back to his shorter and stronger line, was enabled to hold his position and force our troops to abandon the assault. The contest continued during the afternoon and evening. Our losses were quite heavy.

"On the next day a general assault was made, which resulted in our repulse. The enemy being behind heavy earthworks, it proved too great a task to dislodge him. Our army was now intrenched, and heavy skirmishing continued for several days. Laws made two assaults on our lines, but was repulsed with severe loss on both occasions.

"A few more days of skirmishing and desultory fighting, and the campaign closed for the season. During the Summer, Silent had succeeded in holding Laws close to Richmond. The Copperhead press and orators of the North made him the especial target for their calumny during the Presidential campaign. This course was evidently directed from Richmond and Canada.

"The following September, Silent, with his usual vigor, began active operations against the enemy. Sherlin was now in the valley of the Shannon, operating against the rebel Gen. Dawn, and Silent was holding Sentinel Point as his headquarters, and directing operations from there. On the morning of the last day of September Boutler moved from Deep Valley. Orden's Corps moved by the Veranda road close to the river, Burns by the new Sales road, and the cavalry by the Derby road to our right. All our forces were now moving in the direction of the rebel Capital.

"Our troops struck the rebel works and attacked them at five o'clock P. M., and after desperate fighting for hours Fort Harris was taken, with its fifteen guns and all its garrison; also, the line of works running down to Champ's farm, with several hundred prisoners. Thus again the work of war had begun in earnest. Silent stood on the side of the fort, and could with his field-glass view the whole line of rebel works now held by them, as well as see the church spires in Richmond. Our cavalry had advanced on our right to within six miles of the Capital. This was very encouraging. Yet many a bloody battle must be fought before the prize could be ours.

"Burns now made a gallant assault against the enemy's works in front of his advance, but, unfortunately, was repulsed. This checked the advance of our troops on this part of the line. Boutler's position now extended from the river (James) to the Derby road, fronting Richmond.

Meador's command was in front of Petersville. In the afternoon of the next day Parker's Division of Warner's Corps was attacked near Boyd's road. He was promptly re-enforced, and the rebels were repulsed with great loss. Fort Harris was also assaulted with a view of recapture, as it was a very important position. The attempt failed, and we still held the fort.

"Our right and left wings were now being slowly advanced in the direction of the Capital, under the very eye of Laws, the rebel commander. He had the advantage in this, that it would require a day for Silent to move from one flank to the other, while Laws, holding the chord of the circle, could re-enforce any part of his line in a few hours. Laws could not by any possibility stretch his line much farther, while Silent was steadily acquiring more ground.

"The greatest consternation now prevailed in the city of Richmond. Its evacuation was seriously contemplated. The publication of the newspapers was suspended, and the printers were called out to defend the city. Some of the city police fell into our hands.   Offices and shops were closed. The church bells sounded the alarm. Guards were sent into the streets to impress every able-bodied man. Members of the Government were sent into the trenches, and all between the ages of fifteen and fifty-five were ordered under arms. Laws stubbornly held his position. He could plainly see that Silent was determined to fight it out and settle the contest in and about Richmond, without being driven or drawn away, unless some alarm at Washington should cause a change of his campaign.

"After many movements, counter-movements, and much fighting, of all which I cannot speak in this narrative, Laws concluded to set Ewelling at the work of threatening our Capital. He crossed the Potomac and turned and threatened Washington, expecting Silent's army to be at once ordered to its defense; but this made no impression on Silent. He sent Wight's Corps to meet Ewelling and to follow him, which was done, and the danger to our Capital passed. Ewelling struck for the Valley of the Shannon, passed into Maryland and the border of Pennsylvania, levying contributions as he marched through towns and country, returning with much booty to the valley mentioned, joining Dawn. In the meantime Wight was following him. Sherlin was sent to take command of these forces. He fell upon Ewelling and Dawn, and almost annihilated their commands, driving what was left of them entirely out of that part of the country, and making such a desolation that another movement in that direction by the rebels would be wholly impracticable. Leaving a sufficient force to prevent any further movement, he returned to the army near Richmond, destroying railroads, canals, and in fact nearly all the enemy's lines of communication of any advantage to him.

"In the meantime an attempt was made by our forces in front of Petersville to mine and blow up some of the enemy's main forts. The main sap was run some 500 feet, until it was under a fort on Cemetery Hill. Wings were constructed to the right and left of the sap or tunnel, so that about four tons of powder were placed under the fort, tamped with sand bags and wood. The intention was to explode the mine, and at the moment of the explosion to open with all the artillery in this front on the enemy's lines, and to rapidly move a storming column through the crater and carry the high ground in rear, which, if in our possession, would command the city and the enemy's works. At about 3:30 on the morning of the 30th of July the fuse was lighted, but no explosion followed. Many attempts were made before the powder ignited. The suspense was great. Silent was quietly waiting to see the result.

"Finally the smoke was seen and the dead, heavy sound was heard, like unto the mutterings of distant thunder or the rumblings of an earthquake. Following this the whole surroundings were darkened, and up far in the air were sent guns, gun-carriages, caissons, picks, shovels, timbers and human beings. They went up in a confused mass and came down as though falling from the clouds in fragments. Many poor fellows were blown to atoms. Our artillery opened, and the cannonading that followed perhaps was never equaled during the war. A column of infantry

charged into the crater and there hesitated and halted
after capturing those who were left alive. This hesitation
gave the enemy time to recover from their astonishment
and alarm. They rallied and opened a terribly galling fire
into the crater. Support was sent in, which only made the
confusion among our men the greater. A cross-fire was
now poured into them in the breach, and it was turned
into a great slaughter-pen. Both sides were slaughtered in
great numbers. Rebel and Union troops, white and colored
men, were mixed together, crying to one another for help.
The scene, as described by those who witnessed it, was one
upon which no one could wish to dwell. Our people felt
this disaster as much as any during the war. It was used
by our enemies everywhere to prove our commander to
be a heartless butcher.

" About this time an ordnance boat loaded with supplies
of ammunition was exploded at or near Silent's headquarters at Sentinel Point. The report alarmed every one
for miles around. The earth shook and trembled as if this
globe was dissolving. Fragments of shell, wood and human
beings fell about the locality like hail coming down. Men
shrieked and ran wildly about, thinking that the final end
of all things was at hand. Silent was near by, but uttered
not a word. He entered his tent, quietly sat down, and
wrote a dispatch describing the disaster.

" Time wore on without any very great results either
way, until the armies were all ready for the final movement
in the Spring following. Silent was still steadily gaining
ground to his left, and holding Laws close to his lines, at
the same time keeping his cavalry in motion, to the great
annoyance of the enemy. In February, 1865, when I was
at the Capital, where I met the President, Secretary of
War and Gen. Silent, the campaign of Sherwood north to
the rear of Richmond was about commencing; but I was not
then aware of it. Gen. Silent was also getting ready for
his final move against Laws, though he was waiting for
Sherwood and Scoven to make a junction at or near Goldsburg, in North Carolina.

" In the meantime Charleston had been evacuated;

Columbia, S. C., surrendered, and many of our starving prisoners were there released from their deadly and poisonous prison-pens, not fit for pigs, even, to live in. Cotton had been piled in the streets of Columbia by the retreating rebels and set on fire. When our troops entered the city they put the fire out, as they thought. In the evening, however, the smoldering fire was fanned into flames by a strong wind, and the burning flakes of cotton lighting on and against houses, set them on fire. One division of our forces worked hard to subdue the conflagration, but in vain. The flames leaped from housetop to housetop, as if some unseen hand was aiding in the terrible work of devastation. Men, women and children left their houses in their night-dresses, screaming and crying for help. Nothing could be done to allay the destruction. A great portion of the city was laid in ashes, and many people were in the streets houseless and homeless. The troops of Sherwood did all in their power to alleviate the suffering, by dividing blankets and food, and also by taking as many families as could be placed in the wagons to a point from whence they could take shipping North, where, on their arrival, they were amply provided for.

"Again moving forward rapidly, Sherwood's left wing struck Harding's rebel corps at Averyville, and drove it in rout from its position. Our left wing then moved by rapid marches on the Burton and Goldsburg road, the right wing moving on a shorter and more direct route in the same direction, many miles to the south. At Burton's Cross-roads the head of column of the left wing struck the rebel army under command of Gen. Jones, who had again been placed at the head of the forces collected together since Head's defeat at Nashua. His forces were now commanded by Harding, Biggs, Chatham and Hamden, the latter commanding his cavalry. The Union forces, under Gen. Somers, discovering that a large force was in their front, deployed two divisions and attacked, but could not drive the enemy from his position. Somers hastily constructed earthworks and held the enemy in his position until the right wing, or a portion of it, could come to his

relief. The word was soon sent to the General commanding the right wing, and the Fifteenth and Seventeenth
Corps were dispatched at once to Burton's Cross-roads.

"They arrived early on the next morning, having received the order late at night. The General commanding
the Fifteenth Corps, which was in the advance, at once
formed his leading division (Gen. Charles Ward's) and
charged the enemy's works. His men went on the run
over the works and right into his trenches, the General
commanding the corps leading and leaping his horse over
the parapet in the midst of a shower of deadly missiles.
Our men captured the rebels who were in their front, and a
general stampede of the enemy followed, and in a short
time Jones and his whole command were hastily making
their escape across Mill Run. The march was not any farther impeded, and Sherwood's army marched to Goldsburg,
where, as before stated, they joined Scoven, and thus
ended the hard fighting of Sherwood's army.

"The President and Vice-President had been inaugurated, and the message of the President was so mild and
conciliatory, breathing forgiveness and charity in such an
honest and earnest spirit, that many thought it might have
some influence on the feelings of the enemy in respect to
the Union in which they had lived and controlled so long
to their own advantage. But no; the more he expressed
sentiments of respect for their opinions the more bitter
they became, denouncing every expression of kindness as
an insult to their people; so that it was determined there
should be no let-up in any way whatever—no armistice nor
rest, but when the movement commenced, to let that end
the rebellion before ceasing. The country was now up to
this point, and all were ready and fully prepared for the
result.

"Gen. Silent had now directed Papson, as well as Sherwood, to keep their cavalry at work in destroying lines of
communication, bridges, and supplies of the enemy. Will-
ston in the West was operating south of Tennessee, cutting
off all chance of re-enforcements from that direction, and
Sherwood's cavalry in the direction of Augusta and north-

ward, performing the same character of service, while
Sherlin was again marching with 10,000 cavalry around
Laws, making the whole country untenable for want of
facilities in gathering supplies, of which at this time the
enemy was in great need.   The whole coast from Savannah
to Newbern, with forts, gunboats and munitions of war,
was now in our hands, with 100,000 as good soldiers as ever
marched or fought a battle almost entirely untrammeled,
well supplied, and ready to drive Jones or any opposing
force north back to Laws, where the whole could be
crushed at one blow. Sherwood was to so conduct his movements as to detain Jones in his front until the 10th of
April, and then he was to move directly against him and
drive and follow him; but if possible, to get to the Roanoke
River, so as to hold Laws in his position.

"While Silent was preparing for his final movement
against the enemy, which was to commence on the 29th of
March, Laws, suspecting the movement, on the morning of
the 25th, selecting the weakest point in our lines, as he
thought, assaulted the right of Meador's position in front
of the Ninth Corps. The point assaulted was a small fort
known as Fort Sleman, where the two opposing forces
were not more than 200 yards separated from each other.
At dawn of day the rebels moved against this point with
Gadden's Corps, re-enforced by Bush Jones's division.
Parker's pickets were overwhelmed and the trenches taken
by the enemy, so that the main line of the Union forces
was broken. The rebels now seeing their advantage
wheeled to the right and left, sweeping our lines before
them, and capturing our batteries, which they at once
turned upon Fort Sleman. The fort made all resistance
possible, but, being assaulted in front, flank and rear, was
compelled to surrender. The guns of the fort were now
turned upon our own lines on either side with great effect,
driving our men and taking complete possession of this
part of our intrenchments.

" General Parker at this juncture came upon the scene,
brought up artillery on the hills commanding the point attacked, and ordered his forces to occupy the fort. General

Hartley also moved up and massed his division and assaulted the enemy as they were moving along our line. He checked their advance, and, being re-enforced, drove Gadden's Corps back, recaptured the fort and all our abandoned lines, with 2,000 prisoners. Meador arrived on the field and at once ordered Wight and Hume to advance on Parker's left, which was promptly done, and that part of the enemy's picket-line was taken, with many prisoners; so that the temporary success of the enemy proved very expensive to him in the end. This was the only unprovoked assault that Laws had made since the campaign of the Summer before.

"On the night after this assault Gen. Meador, General Orden and several other Generals were at Gen. Silent's headquarters, discussing the contemplated movement to be commenced on the 29th. The President had also been down to see Silent, and agreed in every particular to his programme. Gen. Tom Anderson was also present, having been ordered to Sentinel Point for assignment to duty. He was introduced by Gen. Silent as an able and brave officer. Gen. Orden said to Gen. Silent that he would be pleased to have him assigned to his command; to which Silent answered that he would speak to Anderson.

" When the movement was understood, preliminary thereto Gen. Orden was directed to move the next day to the extreme left, in connection with and in support of the cavalry under Sherlin, designed to prevent Laws from finally retreating in that direction, as was thought he might attempt, in order to make a junction with Jones and fight Sherwood's forces instead of Silent. This was not desired, as the General commanding wished the army that had always confronted Laws to have the honor of the capture of him and his army.

" When all had left for their respective headquarters, Gen. Silent spoke to Gen. Anderson of Gen. Orden's request.

" Anderson replied : ' General, assign me anywhere ; I will try to do my duty wherever I may be placed.'

" Gen. Silent then wrote the order and handed it to him,

saying : ' You will proceed to join Gen. Orden in the morning; he will move to the left during the day.' Silent said
that he would give him a larger command in a few days,
but could not do so then, as they were on the eve of the
movement in contemplation.

"Gen. Anderson expressed entire satisfaction, and directed
Lieut. Whitcomb, who was with him, to have preparations
made for starting at daylight the next morning.

"During the evening, they being entirely alone, General
Silent said : 'Gen. Anderson, do you remember a conversation we had at my rooms the night before I left Nashua for
the East ?'

" 'Very distinctly, General; I was much impressed by
what you then said as to your views in reference to crushing this rebellion within a certain time, and the mode to be
adopted for the accomplishment of this end.'

" 'Well, we will do it within the time mentioned. But
do you remember my asking you if you believed in dreams,
and if you had ever seen anything that you could not explain or understand ?'

" 'Yes, General, I well remember that also.'

" 'Well, sir, I desire to make a confidant of you in this
particular. I do not wish what I say known at this time.'

" 'You can do so; I will not betray your confidence.'

" 'I intended telling the President to-day,' continued
Gen. Silent, 'but was so taken up with other matters that
I forgot it; and I feel a strange kind of superstition that I
may not see him again. He and I are both in great
danger, but I feel that I can protect myself better than he
can himself. I do not desire to tell this story to any of
my family, as I do not want them, or either of them, to become superstitious. It is so easy for any of us to become
so. I find even the President, as strong a man as he is,
somewhat so inclined.'

" Gen. Anderson said: 'I am surprised at this. I did not
suppose he was so; but many strong people are, and many
claim to have cause for being so.'

" Gen. Anderson then related my wife's dream to Gen.
Silent, and told him Peter's interpretation of it, and said

six of her sons were now dead—one only (Henry) remaining alive.

"At this Gen. Silent became melancholy, and quietly responded, ' 'Tis strange, indeed!' He then related to Gen. Anderson the fact of his having seen a strange form in the night-time while under a tree at Chatteraugus; also, the night that he met him at Nashua, as well as in the night near his quarters while fighting the battle of the Chaparral, its indications at Chatteraugus, and its indications to him at Nashua and in the Chaparral. He said:

" 'I have also seen the same spectral form to-night, saying to me: " Move to the left rapidly; the enemy are all in your hands, and in half a moon all will be prisoners." Gen. Anderson, what is this ? Am I dreaming, or am I laboring under some disease of the mind ? I hope you will speak freely to me as to what you think. I could not keep it longer. I must tell some one. I feared I was becoming broken down in my brain power,—I have studied over the military situation so much.'

" 'No, General, you need not have any fears of that. You are as vigorous in that respect as any man living. I cannot, however, explain this ; nor can I understand it. I will ask you, however, if you had this character of campaign in your mind before you saw this strange apparition? '

" 'Yes, I had a thought of it; but somehow this seemed to influence me not to deviate in the least, and to give me faith and confidence in our final success ; and yet I cannot but believe this to be only an optical illusion. It must be ; it cannot, it seems to me, be otherwise.'

" 'There is one thing, General : it appears to be leading you, or, at least, helping your faith, in the right direction.'

" 'Yes ; but, Gen. Anderson, it harasses me by day and by night. I cannot keep it from my mind. I try to throw it off, but cannot. But we will speak of this no more at present. I feel that my mind is greatly relieved since I have given you my secret. What a strange feeling this is; but I believe it is so with every person.'

" 'Yes, General, that is true. Things pent up in the mind

and heart become oppressive, and wear the mind until relieved. This seems to be our safety-valve.'

"The conversation here ceased on this subject, and both retired to rest. The next morning Gen. Anderson and his companion, Lieut. Whitcomb, left very early for Gen. Orden's headquarters. As they were leaving Gen. Silent came out and spoke many kind words to Gen. Anderson. He said:

"'I feel much better this morning. I will be at the front to-day, and will see you, perhaps.'

"With a good-by they separated. When Gen. Anderson arrived at Gen. Orden's headquarters he was ready to move his command to the left. He had been telegraphed by Silent of Anderson's assignment, so the orders were ready, and Gen. Anderson at once took command of a splendid division, getting acquainted as best he could on the march that day. His command was in the lead. Late in the afternoon he met Gen. Sherlin, who was overjoyed to see him, saying:

"'Anderson, you have no time to learn the situation, but I want you to be close to me. I will speak to Orden.'

"Their lines were formed that evening and all was in readiness for action. On the afternoon of the 29th the Union line was continuous from Appomattox, and still moving to the left. Silent said:

"'I feel now like ending the matter, if it is possible, before going back.'

"The army of Silent was located about as hereinafter stated. Parker and Wight held our line in front of Petersville, and Orden's line reached to the crossing of Hatcher's Run. Hume had moved to the left of Orden, by change of orders, and Warner was on the left of the moving column. Sherlin was now at Dinwiddie, on our left flank, some five miles separated from the left of our infantry. This movement was made late in the afternoon. Our lines now covered the ground from Appomattox to Dinwiddie Courthouse. Silent said:

"'Now, let us see what we can do with the enemy.'

"This portion of the country was covered with forests and swampy streams. During the night the rain fell in torrents, and by the next morning it seemed impossible for man or beast to move without sticking in the quicksands. The rain continued, and a deep gloom seemed to settle over our army. Some who were in Silent's confidence suggested a return to our former lines, but Silent could not see how we could go back if not forward.

"Just at this moment Sherlin came riding up, through rain and mud, and suggested that an advance was sure of success. Silent at once gave him orders to return and take possession of Five Forks. The enemy was now confronted by our army at every point.

"Sherlin, on his return, at once sent one of his divisions forward. The conditions of the roads prevented any serious assault with cavalry. Warner was now advanced, extending his left across the Boydton road, He fortified his position, but did not attack ; the enemy were too strong in his front. Hume, meanwhile, attacked the enemy and drove him from his advanced position. On account of mud and bad roads no further movement was made during that day.

"On the next day, however, as Silent had suggested to Meador, the enemy made a heavy assault on Warner's left, and pressed his whole corps back some distance. Hume sent Milo with his division to Warner's support. The rebels were now checked. The Second Corps was sent to Milo and the enemy were attacked in flank in front of Warner, and were driven back to their original line. Warner now moved up, supported by Milo, and gained a lodgment on the White Oak road. Sherlin was attacked near Dinwiddie and a severe battle ensued, which continued until dark, Sherlin holding his ground.

"Both parties lay upon their arms that night within a stone's throw of each other. During the night the Fifth Corps was ordered to the support of Sherlin. The enemy, discovering this movement, retreated early in the morning, Sherlin following and assaulting them at every opportunity. Laws had instructed his infantry and cavalry that Five Forks must be held. Sherlin well knew the importance of this position; Petersville must fall with this in our possession. He ordered Mullet to assault in front with his cavalry, while the Fifth Corps, and McKenon, with his cavalry, were to hold the White Oak road and to drive the enemy back toward Petersville. At five o'clock the assault was made. The cavalry dismounted and fought on foot. The division of the Fifth Corps under Griffith and one brigade under Ames charged the rebel ranks, and under the inspiration of the bands playing and the lead of the intrepid Sherlin, the works were stormed by our men and the rebels routed, leaving 6,000 prisoners in our hands. Five Forks was ours, and a noble day's work had been accomplished. This was the first great battle fought in the last campaign against the rebel Capital.

"Gen. Silent now ordered the enemy's works assaulted at three points at four o'clock the next morning, April 2. Promptly on time Wight and Parker moved against the strong works of the enemy in their front. They broke over the enemy's picket-line with ease; but now in their front frowned heavy earthworks and forts. They moved under a galling and deadly fire, tearing away abatis and all kinds of obstructions until they came to the main works. Here the contest was severe and bloody. Bayonets clashed and musketry rattled; but our troops seemed to know that the end was near, and nothing could stay or resist them. They climbed and leaped over parapet and wall and into the enemy's trenches, capturing men and guns. The advance of our men could not be stopped. They pressed forward to the railroad, tore up the track, and turned and swept right and left down the enemies' lines. Soon the whole line, from the point of attack to Hatcher's Run, and all the artillery and forts were in our possession.

"Parker made his assault near the Jerusalem road. His column stormed and carried the works in his front, capturing twelve pieces of artillery and about 1,000 prisoners.

"Orden now assaulted, Gen. Anderson's division leading. The fighting was severe, the rebels saw that this kind of fighting meant the capture of Richmond. Anderson led his men in person, and was one of the first to scale the enemy's works. The enemy retreated in great haste. Anderson again recognized Joseph Whithorne leading one of the brigades in retreat.

"'My God?' he exclaimed, 'am I always to meet this man in battle!'

"Orden turned his command to the right and joined on with Wight, and they now made their lines strong in order to resist the enemy, as they expected him to attempt a recapture. It had now become one continuous battlefield, from Petersville to and beyond Five Forks. Silent now determined to face Meador's entire command, as well as Orden's, in toward Petersville, and take it if possible. The entire rebel army was rushing to the defense of Petersville. Sherlin was moving on the White Oak road toward the city. Laws was exerting himself to stay the tide. Gadden was ordered to drive Parker back from his line. Hiller and Mahoney were gathering all the fragments of commands that they could find and reorganizing them. Longpath, who had not been engaged, was ordered to cross the James River to the south side, for the defense of this portion of the line. Laws telegraphed his chief, the President of the Confederacy, of the imminent danger to his army.

"The enemy now assailed Parker's line, which was on both sides of the Jerusalem road, and several desperate efforts were made to dislodge him, but being re-enforced he held his position. His line included several forts, and also commanded the main bridge across the Appomattox, almost the only exit then left to the enemy. The rebels were now concentrating their forces within an interior line of very heavy works immediately surrounding the city. There were, however, two strong forts outside of this line not yet captured by our forces—Forts Gregg and Baldwin. Orden was directed to take Fort Gregg, and two of his brigades, commanded by Turnlee and Forest, made the assault. After one or two repulses they succeeded in storming and capturing the entire garrison. Both sides fought gallantly. It was finally taken at the point of the bayonet.

"Milo was now attacking the enemy near the intersection of the White Oak and Claiborne roads, but finding him too well intrenched, had to fall back some distance.

Late in the afternoon Sherlin, with the Fifth Corps and a portion of his cavalry, struck the enemy who had repulsed Milo in their works that day, taking them in flank. He routed them, capturing nearly 1,000 prisoners. He pursued, and struck them every opportunity, until finally they threw away their arms and took shelter in the woods. Night covering their retreat the darkness saved them. The day's work left about fifty pieces of artillery and 12,000 prisoners in our hands.

"All west of the center of Laws's army had been driven by Sherlin across the Appomattox, and the rest had been forced inside the interior lines around Petersville, from which there was no escape save by bad roads—country highways. Laws was now struggling to get his army out and escape, so as to join Jones, and get the best terms he could after one more short campaign.

"Gen. Hiller, of the rebel army, fell that day. Laws had him buried that night, and after the last rites were paid, he rode with his staff out of the city, and in accordance with orders previously given, the whole rebel army, save a small picket-line, filed out and moved in the direction of Amelia Court-house. Parker, under his orders to feel the enemy during the night, discovered the movement, captured the rebel pickets, and the city was surrendered at four o'clock the next morning. Laws burned behind him the small bridges on the Appomattox and blew up his forts on the James River.

"The next morning Silent ordered Meador immediately up the Appomatox River. Sherlin was ordered to push for the Danville Railroad with Hume and Griffith and all the cavalry. Orden was directed to push south-west, on the Cox road. Silent waited until he got news of the surrender of the rebel Capital and the flight of Davis and his Cabinet; then he pushed out on the road to his army marching to intercept Laws. Mullett, being in the advance, came upon the enemy at Deep Run, on the 3d of April, and then a battle ensued, in which the rebels were defeated and put to flight. The road was strewn with caissons, ammunition, clothing, and all kinds of material used by an army.

This was evidence of the great demoralization of the enemy.

"At 5 P.M. on the 4th, Sherlin, with the head of the column of the Fifth Corps, arrived at Geterville, capturing Law's dispatch to Danville for rations, his army being entirely destitute of food. He was at Amelia, but our forces were in his front and in possession of the Danville road.

"On the 5th, Silent received information from Sherlin, that Laws and his whole army were at Amelia, and that he (Sherlin) had possession of the road to Burkesville. He sent Davies' division on a reconnaissance in the direction of Painstown to see if any movement was being made by the enemy. This command struck a train of wagons, burned them, and captured five pieces of artillery and several hundred prisoners. The enemy moved out a stronger force and renewed the contest, but were driven back.

Meador had now arrived with his force and joined Sherlin, but failed to attack, he being the senior and then in command. Silent rode late in the night to Sherlin's headquarters, and at once ordered an attack at four in the morning, but said that Laws would steal away that night. The next morning he was gone, and changing his course, was now heading for Lynchburg. Pursuit was immediately made. Hume struck the rear of the enemy at Deatonville, and at once attacked him. Crooker and Mullett attacked the enemy's wagon train in flank. Orden had arrived at Rice Station, and was intrenched, so as to prevent any further movement of the enemy south. At four o'clock Wight's Corps came up and at once went into action and carried the road two miles south of Deatonville, breaking the enemy in twain. Hume was on his rear and Sherlin on his flank. Hume here moved to the right after one of the fragments, in the direction of the Appomattox,

"Wight now drove the enemy in his front two miles into a swampy, marshy bottom of Sailor's Run. The cavalry were now to the left, where they were burning and destroying the wagon trains of the enemy. The rebels in front of Wight's Sixth Corps had crossed the run, and were throwing up breastworks. Sherlin ordered the stream crossed

and their works assaulted. This was done by two divisions.
The fight was a desperate one. The works were carried on
the enemy's left, but a division of the enemy came sweeping down on our flank and drove the troops of the Sixth
Corps back across the stream.

"Just at this moment Mullett's division of cavalry came
charging down on the enemy's rear. The Sixth Corps
again advanced, and a most desperate and bloody hand-to-
hand bayonet and saber contest now took place. Our artillerymen opened on the lines of the enemy some twenty
guns. Our lines were now closing around them. Crooker
had come up with his command and closed the gap. The
enemy threw down their arms and surrendered—7,000 men
and fourteen pieces of artillery, with Gen. Ewelling and
his seven subordinate Generals. This utterly destroyed the
entire command that was covering Laws's retreat.

"Hume had pursued the fragment of the enemy which
he had opposed in the morning to the mouth of the run,
some fifteen miles, attacking and fighting—a running battle all the day—as well as fording streams, building
bridges, etc. The last stand of the enemy was stubborn.
Hume's command was victorious. His captures during the
day were four pieces of artillery, thirteen stands of colors
and about 2,000 prisoners. Night now drew her curtain
over the scene, and our troops lay down to rest.

"The next day was used almost entirely in winding the
coil more closely around Laws's army. Hume and Crooker
were on the north side of the river confronting Laws;
McKenon was at Prince Edwards; the cavalry column was
moving in the direction of Appomattox Station; the second and Sixth Corps were moving to the north side of the
river to attack the next day; Mullett was pushed to the
south side to Buffalo Station; the Fifth and Twenty-fourth
Corps were moving on Prospect Station, south of the river,
to prevent Laws from escaping in that direction; Orden
was following Sherlin, having taken with him Griffith, with
instructions to attack the head of Laws's column. The
next morning news was received that Stoner had entered
Lynchburg and was holding it. During the greater part

of the night the armies of the Union were moving in the direction assigned them. Gen. Silent occupied the old tavern at Farmville, where Laws had slept the night before.

"After the last of his forces on this line had passed, Silent was sitting quietly on the porch, thinking Laws must surrender the next morning. He concluded to send him a note suggesting his surrender, to stop the further effusion of blood, stating that the last few days must convince him of the hopelessness of his cause. He sent the note. Soon after this he was about to retire, when he heard his name pronounced. He looked and saw the same form as heretofore mentioned, which spoke in these words:

"'Laws will not surrender if possible to escape with any portion of his force. Do not let your army rest until he is surrounded completely.'

"Silent returned to the porch, and did not retire that night. About midnight he received Laws's reply, saying he did not feel as Gen. Silent thought on the subject of surrender, and during the night again moved out in order to escape.

"On the morning of the 8th our forces moved at once. Slight contests only occurred during the day. At night the head of our cavalry column reached Appomattox Station. The enemy were coming in quite a force for supplies, there being at the station four heavily-loaded trains, which had just arrived, for Laws's army. One train was burned, and the others were sent to Farmville. The enemy made an assault on our forces, but were repulsed, 25 pieces of artillery and many prisoners falling into our hands.

"Sherlin was here, with no force as yet save two divisions of his cavalry. He moved a force on the road in the direction of Farmville and found Laws's whole army moving to Appomattox. Orden and Griffith were marching rapidly to join Sherlin, and by marching all night reached Appomattox at 6 A.M. on the morning of the 9th, just as Laws was moving his head of column with the intention of brushing away Sherlin's cavalry and securing the supplies. Laws had no suspicion of infantry having joined our cavalry at

Appomattox. Orden was the senior and commanded the two corps of infantry—his own and Griffith's, formerly Warner's. These troops were deployed in line of battle across the road where Laws must pass, the cavalry in front covering the infantry. Crooker moved out and was soon hotly engaged with the enemy. He fell back slowly, and finally our cavalry moved off to the right, leaving the road apparently open to the rebels. They, seeing this, sent up a shout and started as if to pursue the cavalry, when, to their utter amazement, Gen. Tom Anderson came charging down at the head of his division upon the head of Laws's column, and at the same time our battle line advanced. The enemy were rolled back in great demoralization, our lines pressing them on every side.

"Anderson was assaulting them in front. Griffith was on one flank, and Sherlin, moving around quickly on the enemy's left, was just ordering a charge, when Laws sent a flag of truce and asked for a cessation of hostilities. The cordon was now complete. Laws and his army were at our mercy. Laws surrendered his army that day, and thus the rebellion virtually ended.

"The news sped on the wings of lightning, and the joy that found vent throughout the North no pen could do justice to by way of description. Old and young wept, embraced and shouted aloud, with their hearts full of the glad tidings. None but the class of rebel sympathizers before mentioned mourned at the sad fate of the enemy.

"The next day after the surrender of Laws, Gen. Anderson and his staff were riding around the field taking observations. While passing down near Longpath's Corps, suddenly a man in a rebel General's uniform, with two other officers, came dashing up to the General and halted. It was Joseph Whitthorne. He cried out:

"'Tom Anderson, is that you?'

"Gen. Anderson responded affirmatively, at the same time saluting him in proper military style. At this Whitthorne drew his pistol and was just in the act of firing at the General, when Lieut. Whitcomb rushed at him and ran him through with his sword. He fell from his horse and expired. Gen. Anderson shed tears, but did not disclose to anyone present the close relationship existing between them. This occurrence was of such a character as might have caused trouble with the troops, so it was kept quiet. The officers present on both sides deemed this course the best under the circumstances. Lieut. Whitcomb never knew of the relationship, Gen. Anderson's wife, Whitthorne's sister, always thought her brother was killed in one of the last battles. The General revealed the facts only to myself.

"The joy that now pervaded the North lasted for but a brief space of time before sorrow and deep mourning took its place.

"You remember that Alston, one of the Canadian conspirators, had been arrested and placed in prison at Washington on the charge that, he, with others, were intending to attempt the capture of the President. This having failed, doubtless the last resort had been agreed upon by Thomlinson, Carey and their allies. Page had returned from Richmond with Durham and met Wilkes at Baltimore, where this diabolical scheme was agreed upon. The President, the Secretary of State, the Secretary of War, and Gen. Silent were all to share the same fate. Wilkes, doubtless, with his picked few, were to dog the President, Page the Secretary of State, and Durham the Secretary of War, and others to in some way destroy Silent. My son Henry returned from Canada on the 14th of April, and stated to me that Wintergreen said the three above named were near Washington and would do their work well, each selecting his man; that Thomlinson and Carey had left for Europe on the 6th of April.

"Henry left that night for Washington with this information for the President and his Secretaries. His trip, however, was for naught, as on that night the assassins did their work in part. Wilkes did his, and Mr. Lincoln, the noblest of all men, fell by the bullet of his murderer. Page tried his hand, but failed to complete his task. Durham failed entirely from some cause.

"Henry arrived in Washington the next evening, when

he saw the Secretary of War. He told him to say nothing, as they would all be put on their guard by these facts being made public. Gen. Silent only escaped, as it seemed, by a miracle, as he had agreed to accompany the President that night and was only prevented by his wife's trunks with her wardrobe being carried by Washington to Baltimore that afternoon.

" The intelligence of Mr. Lincoln's death, as it trembled along the wires on the morning of the 15th to every portion

THE SHOOTING OF PRESIDENT LINCOLN BY WILKES.

of this Republic, coming as it did in the midst of universal rejoicing, firing of cannon and unfurling of banners, struck dumb those who a moment before were shouting with joy. Language nor pen can adequately express the horror and grief with which the people were stricken. A Nation's shouts of joy and triumph at one moment, were the next turned into grief and sorrow. The people were bowed down and bathed in tears. The shadows of gloom were on every countenance. The flags that were floating in triumph one moment were the next at half-mast. Almost

Instantaneously all houses were draped in mourning. Women ran into the streets wringing their hands and weeping aloud. Children ran to and fro to learn the cause of the great change from joy to overwhelming grief. Each family wept as though for the loss of their first-born. The soldiers in the field had lost their idol; the colored people had lost their deliverer from the wilderness of slavery.

"The people gathered in their places of worship and mingled their tears with their prayers. A dark pall hung over the whole land. The people seemed to lose heart. The very earth seemed to groan and cry out against the horrible deed. The enemies of the Government were alarmed and shocked at this terrible crime, growing out of their own course of conduct. Foreign Governments were horrified at the atrocity of the fiendish resentment shown. Many men became alarmed and hastened to leave the country. Some left for Mexico, some for South America, and some for Europe.

"The Vice-President had now taken the oath of office and had entered upon the duties of President. Lincoln was dead ; the last act in the bloody drama on the program of the conspirators had been played."

CHAPTER XXI.

" Forgiveness to the injured does belong,
But they never pardon who have done the wrong."—DRYDEN.

"JONES surrendered to Sherwood. Mobile had fallen
and all the minor commands in rebellion were trying to see which could get in first. The President of
the Confederacy had been captured by Wellston.
Our great armies were mustered out of the service, and
peace once more reigned throughout the land. The then
President had by his declarations shown such bitter hos-
tility toward the leading rebels that they were greatly
alarmed, and many were leaving the country. The General
of our armies had established his headquarters at Washington, and all matters pertaining to the future were now
in the hands of the civil authorities.

"Gen. Anderson had returned to my house, where he
found joy and happiness in our little family at his safety
after passing through the storm of this great struggle. His
wife and little Mary, as well as little Jennie, seemed as
though they would never get through kissing him. Henry
and his wife (Seraine) were now with us. Lieut. Whitcomb
returned to Detroit to his parents. Gen. Anderson and
Henry were all who were left of the eight of my household
who had entered the service. You can imagine the sadness
this brought back to me.

"David's wife (Jennie) became melancholy and more depressed than usual. She was stricken with fever and died in about three weeks after the General's return. This left this dear child "—pointing to Jennie Wilson—"alone in the world, without a protector, save her poor old grandfather. Mary Anderson, the General, Henry and Seraine were all kind and willing to do anything for her that they could. She was sole heir to her father's farm, which had been left in my hands, and naturally looked to me, and so we have ever since lived together.

"Henry, Seraine, Gen. Anderson and his family stayed with me until the General could determine whether he would remain North or venture to return to his old home in Mississippi. Old Ham and Aunt Martha, after the murder of Mr. Lincoln, seemed to have lost all energy, and were unusually silent and melancholy, seldom speaking to any one, save in the expression of their great joy at the safe return of their 'Marsa Gen'l.' One day, while we were sitting on the porch, the General said to Ham, who had come to the front of the house:

"'Ham, what is the matter with you and Aunt Martha? You seem to be in a serious mood all the time, since my return?'

"'Yes, Marsa Gen'l, we is monstrous serious, sah. We feels bad 'bout Marsa Lincum, what dem 'Sesh kill. He war our bes' frien', He make us free, and we feel dat dar am some wrong somewhar, dat dem 'Sesh starve de Union sogers; dey shoots dem when dey wants to, and dey kills our President, and none of dem get hunged for dis. If dis is de way dat matters is a-gwine, what am goin' to 'come of de darkies? Whar am dey gwine? What am gwine to 'come ob Marfa and Ham? Dat's what am worryin' us.'

"'Well, Ham, you need not worry about that. You will be taken care of. I will see to that.'

"Just then Aunt Martha came into the house, and hearing the conversation, the good old woman became greatly excited. When she heard what the General said to Ham she caught hold of the former, and in her way gave expression to her feelings. She said:

"'Marsa Gen'l, I's mighty feered somethin' bad gwine

to happen to us poor colored folks. Dar frien's seem de only ones what get kill, and when dey do de folks do nuffin wid de 'Sesh. Dey send dem home agin, so dat dey do jes' what dey please. You mind what Aunt Marfa say, dem 'Sesh do wid de darkies what dey wan' to in less den no time. Dey is free; I know dat; but who dey work for? Mus' dey be under de same ones what sell dem before de 'bellion? If dey is, den de 'Sesh make dem young darkies what's comin' on b'lieve anything dey wants to; and afore dey is growd up dey be helpin' de 'Sesh, and den what we do? I tells you dis bin on my min', and in Ham's head, too. We trus' in de good Laud; and you, Marsa Gen'l, you kin fix dis. I's sure you kin. De good Laud spare you for dis; I know he do. I's sure dar was six mans in dis family, all kill, my good old missus die, den my good young missus, she die; dey was all kill and die 'ceptin' you, and I knows dat you are save to take keer of us darkies, or you bin kill long afore dis!'

"'Well, aunty, I will do all I can for everybody. You and Ham shall be cared for; have no fears about that.'

"'Dat be good. I always know you look after us, Marsa Gen'l, case we sabe you life; but, den, my chillens, Laud knows whar dey is. Ham and me bin talkin' 'bout dat. We wants dem to get 'long, but we not know dem, nor whar dey am. Maybe we see dem some day.'

"'All right, aunty, we will talk about this hereafter.'

"Poor old darkies! They both went back to the kitchen better satisfied and much happier."

Dr. Adams said: "Uncle Daniel, Aunt Martha did not miss it very far, did she?"

"No; the poor old woman had a presentiment that matters would not be as peaceful and well for the colored people as was anticipated.

"Just at this time old man Joseph Dent rode up to the gate. He was as glad to see the General as if he had been one of his own family. We talked over the war, and praised the old man for the part he had played in assisting us in discovering the plots of the conspirators. He returned to the farm greatly delighted that his work was appreciated.

" We all remained at home for some time trying to shake off our many sorrows. Mary Anderson and Seraine tried to make it pleasant for all. The General interested us in giving his experiences, and Henry in turn his with the conspirators. Time wore on, and finally Gen. Anderson concluded to go to Colorado for the purpose of seeing what he could do in the mines, leaving his wife and daughter still with me. Henry remained with us ; he and Seraine visiting occasionally with his friends at Detroit.

" Congress was engaged in trying to agree upon a plan for the reconstruction of the South, as well as to reorganize the army. When the law was passed for the latter purpose I was written to by the Secretary of War in order to ascertain Gen. Anderson's whereabouts. I wrote him, giving his address. The General was tendered a position in the army. He came home and consulted his wife, but finally declined it. He recommended Lieut. James Whitcomb, his Aid-de-Camp, Seraine's brother, for a position, and he was appointed a Lieutenant in the cavalry arm of the service. He is still alive and in the army, but transferred, as I understand, to a different branch of the service.

" The General concluded to go to Washington city, where he remained some weeks. On returning he thought he would settle there in the practice of the law. His wife did not wish to go until he had tried the chances of success. So it was arranged that his family should remain with me, his wife wishing to return to her old home when she felt that it was safe for the General. He returned to Washington, and did very well.

" By this time there seemed to be some friction between the President and Congress. This condition of things continued, with ill-feeling, and the breach still widening. The President differed widely with the Republican majority, as well as the Secretary of War and the General of the Army, as to the reconstruction of the States recently in rebellion. Every measure that Congress would pass with a view of taking charge of the colored people or aiding them in their perilous condition, was rejected by the President, and had to be passed over his veto. It was the same with matters in reference to reconstruction. He began haranguing the populace from the balcony of the Executive Mansion, in order to create an ill-feeling and prejudice in the minds of the people against their representatives.

" He, however, very suddenly changed his views as to the proper treatment for the leaders of the rebellion. Instead of wishing them tried and punished, as formerly, he thought a portion of Congress should be tried and punished. He turned his back on his Union friends and made the leading rebels and their sympathizers of the North his confidants. Jefferson Davis and all those under arrest for treason were, under his new programme, released. He denounced leading Republicans as conspirators and traitors. He was cajoled by every conspirator of the late rebellion. Finally the visits of certain men from Maryland and Virginia became so frequent that it aroused a suspicion in the minds of the Secretary of War and the Chief of Staff to the General of the Army, and very soon this suspicion extended to the General himself that a new conspiracy was being organized. The General was led to believe this, first, on the ground that the President at one time wanted all the leading men who had been paroled by the General arrested and tried by the U. S. Court in Virginia. This the General of the Army had resisted in such a manner as to cause quite a coolness between the two. The same men that he at one time desired to see hanged had now become his companions, confidential friends and advisers.

" Information was received about this time, through a source that could not be doubted by the Secretary of War nor by the General of the Army, of a programme which had been agreed upon by the President and certain rebels claiming that their States were sovereign, were States now as ever, with all their rights—that of representation included. The President determined to issue his proclamation for an election of Senators and Members of the House of Representatives from all the States lately in rebellion, and if they came to Washington claiming their seats, and should not be admitted by the Republican majority, he would organize a Congress with the Southern members and the Northern Democrats, and as President would recognize them as the Congress of the United States and send his messages and communications accordingly.   If the Republicans resisted he would disperse them by force, and thereby make them the rebels against the lawful Government, as he claimed, and in that way turn it over to its enemies and their sympathizers, with himself as their chief instead of Mr. Davis, holding the Capital and all the Government archives.   If he could induce the General of the Army to obey his orders he could carry out this scheme; if not, he would get rid of the General and try and find some other officer upon whom he could rely.   To be prepared in case he could not use the Commander of the Army, a force was to be organized in Maryland and Virginia, which was to sweep down upon Washington and take possession before outside forces could be organized against the President's authority, using in connection with this force such of the army as would obey him.   He tested the General of the Army and found he could not use him to aid in starting a new rebellion.   He then concluded that he would send him away to Mexico, and put in some pliant tool as Secretary of War, and then put this scheme in operation.

"Just about this time an application was made to the General of the Army, without coming through the Secretary of War, by the State of Maryland, for its quota of arms.   This at once struck the General as strange.   He went to the Secretary of War, and upon consultation the application was placed among the relics of the past.   In a day or so the President inquired of the General if he had received such an application.   The General said he had, and was asked what he was going to do.   He answered that it would be looked into.   This seemed to the General very unusual, for a President to be looking after such things.

"I had gone to Washington to look after pay that was due three of my sons when killed.   While sitting with Gen. Anderson in his room, soon after my arrival, a knock was heard at the door.   A boy entered with a note from the Secretary of War, saying he had just heard of my arrival and desired to see me.

14

"The next morning as soon as I could I went to his office.
When I met him he was very cordial with me; conversed
about the murder of Mr. Lincoln and the utter collapse of
the rebellion, as well as the great loss in my family. I spoke
to him about my business, and he at once directed matters
so that it would be attended to without delay. The Secretary then said to me that it was through my direction that
Mr. Lincoln and himself had been able to thwart the late
conspirators in many of their diabolical schemes during the
war, and that they failed only in one—that of preventing
the murder of the President.

"In speaking of this sad calamity the great tears stood
in his eyes. 'But,' said he, 'my dear friend Lyon, we are
now standing upon the verge of a volcano, and this time,
if the schemes of the conspirators can be carried out, we
will be in more danger than ever; and we who have just
put this great rebellion down will be compelled to play
the part of rebels ourselves in the next great drama.'

"I was almost struck dumb by this announcement, and
thought the Secretary was perhaps unnecessarily alarmed
at some minor matter. He rang his bell for a messenger,
and sent him across the street for the General of the Army.
He soon came in, and after pleasant greetings we all retired to the Secretary's private room. There he was about
to make me acquainted with this whole matter, when the
General said to the Secretary that he desired his Chief of
Staff to be present. He was sent for, and soon entered.
I was put under a pledge of secrecy, and then the whole
scheme was revealed to me as I have told it to you, except
that it was given to me more in detail. The name of their
secret informant was given. and I was then truly surprised
and could no longer doubt the facts as to the conspiracy
for the second rebellion. The man who had unfolded the
scheme to the Secretary of War and to the General of the
Army was a man of reputation in a marked degree; had
held a high position in the Confederate service, but had
seen enough of war, and also respected his parole to the
General of our Army.

'The General did not know at what moment he might

be relieved from the command of the Army, and was therefore anxious that the Secretary of War might in some way
be prepared for the emergency, should it arise ; but said
that he could not personally be a party to any preparations
for such an event while he was subject to the orders of the
President. So he said that he would retire, but would
leave his Chief of Staff, who, he said, seemed to be bel-
ligerent enough for any purpose. When the General withdrew the Secretary said :

" ' Now, Mr. Lyon, what can you do to aid us, or what
do you suggest ? '

" I said : ' Give me until this evening to reflect upon the
matter and I will meet you gentlemen here at any hour
that may be agreed upon.' So eight o'clock was designated,
and we separated.

" During the day I made inquiry of Gen. Anderson about
the disbanded soldiers ; how they, or some of them, could
be organized in an emergency, and supposed the case of
the rebels trying their rebellion over again. He laughed
at the idea, but said there was but one condition of things
that could possibly bring about such a result, and that was
if the President should undertake the restoration of all the
rebel States without the action of Congress, as he had
heard hinted by some leading rebels who had recently
been in Washington.

" I asked him if it would not be well for some men of influence to be on the alert.

" ' Yes,' he replied ; ' there ought to be a secret force in
Washington and elsewhere, until the reconstruction of the
rebel States is complete.'

" I said no more to him at this time on the subject. Gen.
Anderson said he would call and see the General of the
Army in a day or so, as he had only visited him occasionally since in Washington, but that his calls were always
made very pleasant.

" At eight o'clock sharp I went to the War Office and
found the Secretary and the Chief of Staff to the General
waiting for me. We at once entered into conversation on
the subject of the conspiracy. I made the same suggestion

that Gen. Anderson had intimated to me, which was at
once discussed and thought to be a good proposition. But
how could it be done without the whole matter being made
public in some way? The Secretary thought this was a
matter that should be kept within the knowledge of a very
few discreet men.

" 'True,' said I; 'but you must have a nucleus here in
Washington if you can find the man to organize it. I know
a man who would be perfectly safe, but I have a suggestion
in connection with him that I think better. It is this:
My son Henry is very anxious to go to the Black Hills, but
that country being unsafe, on account of the Indians, I
have been thinking that a large number of discharged
soldiers would jump at an enterprise of this kind. They
could be organized and have it so arranged that they could
be got together quickly for any emergency; and if the emergency should not arise, when the danger should be passed
the General of the Army could properly issue an order preventing any organization or combination of men from
entering the Black Hills country, and instruct the army in
that part of the West to carry out the order. This would
let the men at the head of the organization out of the scrape,
and would afford them an ample excuse for abandoning the
enterprise.'

"The Secretary said: ' This seems feasible; who could
you trust with this management ?'

" I replied: ' Gen. Tom Anderson.'

" 'Just the man,' replied both gentlemen.

" The Secretary said : ' This part is in your hands. We
do not wish to see anyone but you on this part of the plan.
We will give our confidence to no one else. We hope you
will not delay. We will look out for Washington. You
need not hesitate ; these two men, Gen. Anderson and your
son, will be amply compensated.'

"The Chief of Staff to the General then remarked: ' I
think I know the man to take hold of matters in Washington.' He then named a man who had been a Union officer,
and who was then in the city. He was sent for and had an
interview the following afternoon with the two gentlemen

mentioned. I immediately returned, met Gen. Anderson, and asked him to go with me to my room. When there I laid the case before him fully, imposing entire secrecy, should the terrible threatened disaster be averted, saying to him that Henry, my son, being young and thoughtless, must not know the inside, but must look upon it merely as a matter of precaution, and with the intention of carrying out the Black Hills scheme in order to get into that rich mineral country.

"The General readily assented to all, and at once prepared to return home with me. He visited the General of the Army the following day.

"The next morning I again visited the Secretary of War, and explained to him the General's readiness to act. He was delighted with the arrangement, and said to me that I must return in two weeks and let him know how matters were progressing; that it would not do to communicate in writing. I bade him good-by, and the General and I left for home.

"On our arrival his wife and the two children were greatly delighted, as well as the rest of the family, including Ham and Aunt Martha. His wife, finding that he was to remain at home for some time, was extremely happy. Henry was now called into council and put in possession of a part of our plan. They at once went to work diligently, and in a very short time had made up a secret organization with a view, as understood, of going to the Black Hills, and by moving about in the country found that any number of good soldiers could be rendezvoused at Indianapolis ready to move by rail in any direction required. the Black Hills being the objective.

"Gov. Morton was sent for and had an interview with the Secretary of War. What arrangement or understanding was had between them I did not know, nor did I ever learn. The only thing he ever said to any of us was to Gen. Anderson, that there were plenty of arms, etc., in Indianapolis, and if he should ever have to start for the Black Hills to let him know at once. I suspected that he was fully posted.

"I returned in about two weeks to Washington. In the meantime the President had attempted to send the General of the Army out of the country into Mexico, on some civil mission. The General had positively refused to go. By this time there was quite a bitter feeling. The President expressed himself freely. The General was silent.

"The Secretary of War had been requested to resign, which he had refused to do, and the excitement was warming up considerably. Many telegrams were coming to the General of the Army from his old soldiers, saying they were ready to come to Washington in case of trouble with the President on the question of the enforcement of his views against the action of Congress. The General would destroy these telegrams as fast as they came. I told the Secretary of the progress of Gen. Anderson and Henry in reference to the Black Hills. He was very much gratified at the result.

"I was invited to come to the War Office at about 8:30 o'clock that evening. On arriving I was admitted by the Secretary himself. Inside the door I found a sentinel with musket in hand, regularly on duty.

"I said to the Secretary, 'How is this?'

"His only reply was: 'It looks warlike, does it not?'

"On entering his private room I found the Chief of Staff to the General of the Army and two other gentlemen. One was a man whom I knew well, the same mentioned by the parties as being the one to take care of Washington city. The other gentleman I had never seen. He was a resident of Washington city, had been a Colonel in the Union army, and was now acting as Adjutant-General and organizer under the former. These men remained during every night in the War Department with the Secretary of War, having spies out in Baltimore and Richmond, as well as in Washington, and knew of every movement that was going on. They also knew of every meeting of leading rebels with the President. I learned that their organization, secretly armed and equipped in Washington, amounted to over 2,000 men, the object of which was not disclosed to the men more than that it was a military organization in favor of the Union, and to be ready on call for any emergency.

" If the President had attempted to carry out his scheme, and any movement had been made from either Baltimore or Richmond, or from any part of any State, the first prisoner would have been the President. The Secretary of War determined that his Department should not go into the hands of any one who would be subservient to any set of conspirators, or the President, who was to be at the head of them.

" I returned home the next day full of alarm for our country. I greatly feared another scene of blood and desolation. I was so worried over the situation that my family thought me ill.

" Gen. Anderson returned that night from Indianapolis, and Henry from near Fayette. I told the General what I had seen and learned. When I told him how the gentleman in charge of the secret forces in Washington seemed to feel, and that he would make the President a prisoner the first thing if any move was made, he remarked :

" ' That is the way to do it ! Cut off the head the first blow, and the body will soon die.'

" Things went on in this way for a time. The President had copies of telegrams given him from the telegraph office, which were sent from different parts of the country, tendering the services of different organizations of soldiers to the General of the Army. He also discovered in some way that he would be in danger should he attempt the use of force.

" The House of Representatives now presented articles of impeachment against him. This alarmed his co-conspirators, and the embryo rebellion collapsed.

" I have no doubt that if the President at that time had had a General of the Army and a Secretary of War who could have been used by him to further his and his co-conspirators' schemes, within ninety days from the time when I first went to Washington, as stated, this country would have been plunged into another bloody rebellion with an unscrupulous, courageous and desperate man at the head of it, and at the same time in possession of the Capital of the Nation. The country has never known what it escaped

and what it owes to those men—the Secretary of War and
the General of the Army and his Chief of Staff—for standing as they did against these machinations."

"Uncle Daniel," said Dr. Adams, "why was this matter
kept so profoundly secret?"

"There were two reasons: First, the country was easily
excited at the time, and on that account, when the danger
was passed, it was thought best to say nothing, and all who
knew of it had been put upon their honor not to disclose it.
Second, it could not be verified as to the co-conspirators in
Maryland and Virginia, and the plan agreed upon by them,
without involving a man heretofore mentioned, in high position among the very persons who were conspiring to do the
deed. His exposure would doubtless have cost him his life;
and I hope you will not now ask me to say whether he is
living or dead."

"I will inquire no further on this subject," said Dr.
Adams, "but would like to know what became of the Black
Hills scheme?"

"That scheme failed at or about the same time of the
collapse of the new rebellion.

"Time passed, and finally the country got rid of this President by electing the General of the Army. We all, or
many of us at least, breathed more freely. The reorganization of the South became a fixed fact, and the machinery
moved smoothly for awhile. My son Henry was still anxious to go to work and try his fortune in the Black Hills
country. About this time his wife bore him a fine son. He
therefore left her with me and started fortune hunting.

"Gen. Anderson made a visit to his old home in Mississippi and was, to all outward appearance, well received.
He returned home, and, after talking the matter over with
his wife, they thought it would be safe to return. The
Union men were at that time in power in Mississippi, and
many Northern people were flocking there and purchasing
property. Very soon the General and his family got ready
to leave Allentown for Jackson, Miss. When the time came
for them to leave, the sorrow with us all was very great.
Mary Anderson and Seraine wept, and held to one another,

instinctively fearing that this separation was forever. The two children, little Mary and Jennie, shrieked and screamed, and begged not to be separated. The scene was heartrending. I felt as though my last friend was leaving me. The General and I acted like children. We both wept and embraced each other—neither could speak. I held poor little Mary in my arms and bathed her blessed cheeks with my tears. Old Ham and Aunt Martha would go with 'Marsa Gen'l.' They both wept and heaped blessings upon us all. As far off as we could see the poor old people, they were bowing and bidding us good-by. God bless their poor souls; they were as good and as kind a couple as ever lived!

"Seraine and I had procured good help before they left, and were, in that particular, in excellent shape; but when the General, his wife, little Mary and the old couple left, it was desolate, sure enough. We were lonely in the extreme. We had been so long together, and had passed through so many trials, had grieved, and had experienced so many sorrows together, that no one could describe our feelings. The General, however, felt that he could do well again at his old home, and he thought the people down there were reconstructed and satisfied with their wrong course.

"I spent most of my time out at the farm. I would take my Jennie, as I called my granddaughter, with me and explain everything to her, as much to employ my own mind as hers. Henry wrote us very often. He was delighted with the country and was doing quite well; had made money, and was investing it in property in Yankton. Seraine's father and mother visited us frequently, and we were living as happily as we could under all the circumstances.

"In a few months Gen. Anderson visited us. He was feeling satisfied with his home and was doing well. He gave a glowing description of old Ham and Aunt Martha's happiness now that they could see other colored people. The President had offered him (Anderson) a foreign mission, which he had declined on account of his fine prospects in his profession in Mississippi.

"The next year after Henry left us he returned, but was determined to make his new home his permanent one, and insisted on Jennie and I going with him. He said he would not leave us alone, and would stay in Indiana if we could not go with him and Seraine. He could not think of leaving Seraine and his fine baby boy any more. I thought I ought not to interfere with the boy's prospects, so I agreed to go with them. I rented my house, made arrangements about the farm, and we all left for Yankton. Henry had purchased a nice place, and we lived there very happily together. We kept up our correspondence with Gen. Anderson and his family.

"One day Henry came into the house very much excited, saying that he had just seen Wintergreen on the street, who pretended not to recognize him. The town was settling up and growing very fast. Many people from the South were coming into the Territory as well as the town. I told Henry to beware of this man ; that he, knowing that Henry had his secrets, might, through fear, if nothing else, do him some harm. One day there were quite a number of persons near a billiard hall, in a dispute about some matter. Wintergreen was in the midst of the crowd. Henry stepped up out of curiosity to ascertain the cause of the trouble. Wintergreen spied him, drew his revolver, and shot him dead.'

Dr. Adams exclaimed, "My God! Your last son!"

"Yes," said Uncle Daniel with a tremulous voice, "this was the last of my dear family. So you see, gentlemen, as I first stated, my home is desolate. Why should I wish to buffet the world longer? This was the fulfillment of my good wife's dream—the seven fingers were now gone.

"Wintergreen escaped. The distress of Henry's wife, as well as my own grief, I will not undertake to describe. We conveyed his body to Allentown and there laid him to rest with his mother and brothers. Gen. Anderson, learning of our affliction, met us at our old home. Seraine and I remained with our little family at Allentown, I getting back my house. I broke down under this last sorrow, and was confined to the house for more than a year. Seraine cared for me as she would for her own father, and this child here, my dear Jennie, was with me and by my bedside nearly the whole time of my sickness. God bless her!"

"So say we all!" was the response from those present.

"Gen. Anderson visited me several times during my illness. His wife and little daughter came and spent a month with us, which added greatly to what happiness we could then enjoy.

"The men who had been in rebellion now began to show their feeling and take hold of the politics of the South. Gen. Anderson was very prominent as a lawyer and a leader in political affairs in Mississippi. The rebels now commenced to organize secret societies similar to those that were in the North during the war. Another Presidential canvass came on, and the then President was re-elected. Very soon political matters in that part of the country, in State affairs, became very exciting. Prominent men were threatened; colored men were whipped and driven away from meetings; raids were made upon their houses in the night-time and many were murdered—some white men sharing the same fate.

"Gen. Anderson used all of his influence to stay this tide of oppression and wrong. He was threatened with violence, but did not believe they would assault him. He was a brave man, and could not think of leaving his friends, but determined to stand by them. Quite a number of Northern men were driven from that part of the country, and their property destroyed. A perfect reign of terror prevailed.

"The General moved into another county, so as to be out of the excitement as much as possible. At a political meeting near the capital of the State, Gen. McKee, a Northern man, without any provocation whatever, was brutally assaulted and almost murdered for making a Republican speech. This character of conduct continued until one day in court, where some of these men were being tried for their outrages, the General denounced this course as brutal, and such as ought to make barbarians blush. A mob collected around the court-house and made threats of violence against him, denouncing him as a —— Yank and not fit to live. They then and there notified him to leave the State within five days, and that if found there longer than this his life should pay the forfeit.

" He had determined not to leave, so he prepared himself
and remained at home.   At the end of the five days a mob
collected about his house and demanded that he leave at
once.   They were boisterous and threatening.   One of his
neighbors was at his house and prepared to assist the
General in defense of his home and family.   His wife and
little girl were so much alarmed that they screamed and
cried for help.   Finally the General, standing in his door,
flatly refused to leave.   A volley was fired at him, one shot

MURDEROUS ASSAULT UPON GEN. ANDERSON AND FAMILY.

taking effect in his right thigh.   His little daughter ran to
him and threw her arms about his neck, shrieking and
begging for her papa.   His neighbor fired from a window,
wounding one of the mob.

" This was like fanning the flame.   They rushed upon
the house, firing indiscriminately.   The General was shot
three times and fell dead.   His little daughter, with her
arms about his neck, received a shot in her left breast, from
which she died in a few minutes.   His neighbor, Gibson,
was as brutally murdered in the house, being riddled with

bullets. Old Ham ran out of the kitchen to make his escape and was shot dead in the yard. Mary Anderson fell senseless to the floor. Old Aunt Martha was the only soul left to do anything. She was on her knees praying while the mob was doing their desperate and bloody work. They retired yelling like Indians after taking scalps. Poor old Martha ran to one of the neighbors for help, but could get none from white people. A few old colored people gathered at the house and cared as best they could for the dead.

"For two days this family of dead and stricken lay without a white person coming to the house to aid or assist. The enemies would not, and the few friends were afraid to do so. The General, little Mary, and Mr. Gibson were buried by the colored people in the best manner they could. Mary Anderson became a raving maniac and died in about one week after, and was buried by the side of her husband and daughter, a minister and a few women having come to look after her since the interment of the other dead. Old Ham was laid away by the colored people. Aunt Martha was grieved beyond expression, and alarmed for fear she also would be murdered. She prayed night and day to be brought back to her 'Marsa Lyon.'

"The colored people, having great respect for the General and his family, made up money enough to send Aunt Martha back to my house. A young colored man ventured to come with her, for which I remunerated him. This poor old woman's story was enough to melt the most obdurate heart. She talked constantly of the General, his wife, little Mary, and poor old Ham, and felt that the 'good Laud' had deserted them for some reason."

We were all dumfounded at the recital of these barbarous murders.

"My God!" exclaimed Dr. Adams, " what is this people coming to?"

Col. Bush shed tears, but could not speak. All were silent. Uncle Daniel left the room, but returned in a few moments and said:

"My friends, you can now see why I so often have said, 'What have I to live for?' Why should I desire to remain here and brood over my great misfortunes and sorrows longer ? "

Finally Col. Bush walked the floor, and in a most subdued tone, said : " For such a man and so noble a family to die in such a villainous manner ! Did no one suffer punishment for this diabolical crime ? "

" No, not one was punished. The matter was investigated, but that was all."

" Well, I have asked myself heretofore the question, why did I give my right arm for such a Government ? That such a man, who had served his country as faithfully as he, could be thus brutally murdered, with his family, and no one punished for it, is a marvel to me ; and no doubt some of his murderers are now holding high official position ! "

" Yes," said Uncle Daniel, " one of the instigators of this crime has held office ever since, as a Southern patriot who nobly assisted in ridding the South of one of those Northern Yankees."

" Uncle Daniel, what became of Aunt Martha ? " inquired Maj. Clymer.

" Poor old woman, she lived with Seraine and me for about three years after her return, when she sickened and died. When she spoke on any subject she would finally get to these murders. They preyed upon her mind constantly, and I think hastened her death."

" How strange that all who were connected with your household during the war should have had such a fate ! "

" Yes, my friends, it has been the one unaccountable mystery in my life. Poor old Joseph Dent died in the same year, and I was left almost alone. My dear Jennie, a few years ago, married Mr. Wilson, and I came to live with them in Oakland. Seraine went to her father and mother in Michigan. They are both alive and she remains with them. Her son Harvey—named for his uncle, my youngest son, who was murdered at the battle of the Gaps, if you remember—is now in Chicago working as one of the cashboys in a dry-goods store. I thought, as he was the last link in our family, that the Government owed it to us to send him to the West Point Military Academy, but I could not get him into the school. The member from here was not favorable, inasmuch as he was an anti-war Democrat during the rebellion. Harvey is making his own living now and I hope he may have a bright future. He often comes to see us. Poor Seraine; when the boy could not get into West Point, it almost broke her heart. She said to me :

"'Father, how shallow is this world. You, his grand-father, lost seven sons, six in the army. This boy's father was starved near unto death in Pine Forest Prison. I, his mother, risked my life in going through the rebel lines to obtain his release. He was murdered by one of the conspirators; and now we are forgotten. No one cares what we suffered during and since the war. My son cannot even have the poor privilege of being educated by the Government, when the sons of nearly every rebel General who tried to destroy the Union are now under the guardianship of the Government, being educated either at West Point for the army, or at Annapolis for the navy.'"

Dr. Adams said: "This is hard; it is uncharitable, and shows a great want of the proper gratitude that should be due under the circumstances."

Col. Bush said : "What does the Government or people care for those who made the sacrifices ? We are so far away from the war now in space of time, that we are not only forgotten, but regarded as pests in society. Are the people not grumbling about what has been done for the soldiers ? Do they not complain about our pensions ? A few years more, however, and all of us cripples, one-armed and one-legged and those who are wholly armless and legless, will have passed away out of sight. The recognition now is not to the victors, but to the vanquished. If you wish to be respected by a certain class, North or South, only make it appear that you headed a band of marauders during the war, dealing death to Union men and destroying their property, and you will be invited to agricultural shows, to the lecture halls, and upon the stump; and if still living in the South, you will either be sent to the United States Senate, made Governor, or sent on some foreign mission."

"Uncle Daniel, what became of Thomlinson and Carey, the Canadian conspirators," inquired Inglesby.

"They are both dead, and many of their co-workers also. There has been a very great mortality among the leaders of the rebellion. That is to say, the older men—those who were somewhat advanced in years when it began."

"Are many of the Northern men of whom you have spoken in your narratives as rebel sympathizers, Knights of the Golden Circle, or Sons of Liberty, still living?"

"Yes, they were generally young or middle-aged men, and with few exceptions are still living, and are, almost without an exception, in some official position—some of them in the highest and most honorable in our Nation.'

"This could not have occurred in any other Government than ours, and is passing strange," said Dr. Adams.

"Yes, that is true; but do you not remember my mentioning the fact that Hibbard, who was connected with one of the rebel prisons during the war, came North last Fall to teach us our duty? I also said that probably he would be sent abroad to impress some foreign country with our Christian civilization."

"Yes, I well remember what you said."

"Well, I see by the papers that he has been appointed to a Foreign Mission. I also see that a man of great brutality, who is said to have been connected with one of the prisons in Richmond, has been put in charge of all appointments in the greatest Department of the Government—the Treasury."

"Are these things so? Can it be possible?"

"Yes, these are truths. This is merely testing us in order to see how much the people will bear; and they seem to bear these things without a murmur. The next will be stronger. If the people of the South see that they are sustained in this by the people of the large cities North, on account of a fear that they may lose Southern trade, what may they not demand? Certainly, very soon nothing less than Vice-President will be accepted, and the same people who sustain these things now will cry out that this is right!"

"It does look so. I have been studying this question since you have been reciting your experiences and giving the views of yourself and others, and am now prepared to agree that greed is at the bottom of all this. This same greed is one of the several dangers that threaten our country's institutions to-day. It causes crimes and wrongs to be overlooked, and in many cases defended, in order to gain influence with the people who are determined by any means in their power to control the Government."

"Yes; and see the progress they are making in this direction. As I have said, there is not a man, with but very few exceptions, North, who denounced the war and those who were engaged in prosecuting it, who is not in some official position. Turn to the South. So far as they are. concerned it may seem natural for them to select from their own class; but why should the North fall in with them? You have given, in your answer to me, the only reasonable answer—that of greed and gain; but to see this great change in the minds of the people in so short a time is strange indeed. Twenty years ago they were thundering at the very gates of our Capital. To-day they control the country. There is not a man, save the President of the Southern Confederacy and a very few of the leaders in the war made to destroy our Government, who is not now in some honorable position if he wishes to be. We find them representing us in the first-class missions abroad, in the second-class and in the third-class; and there not being high places enough of this kind, that the world may know the Confederacy has been recognized fully by our people since its downfall, those who were in high positions under it now take to the Consulships and are accepting them as rapidly as can well be done.

"You find your Cabinet largely represented by their leading men, and many of your Auditors, your Assistant Secretaries, Bureau officers, etc., are of them. This not being satisfactory, all the other appointments South are made up of those men to the exclusion of every one who was a Union man before, during, or since the war. The Government not furnishing places enough, all the State, county, and city offices South are filled in the same manner by this same class. This still does not satisfy, and all men sent to the United States Senate or to the House of Representatives from the South, with only one or two exceptions, are of the same class. In fact all of Jeff. Davis's Cabinet, his Senate and House of Representatives, and his Generals that are living, and who desire, are holding official positions of some kind. What does this argue? Does it not notify us who have made sacrifices for this Union that our services are no longer desired, and that we are waste material, of no further use for any purpose?

"Who could have believed, while the war was going on, that this state of things could ever have existed? Suppose this picture had been held up before my seven dead sons when they entered the service. Suppose they could have seen their mother's dream realized—all in their graves beside their mother, and their father living on the charities of a grandchild, laughed at in the streets by young men when speaking of the wrongs inflicted by the rebellion, and told that this is of the past—how many of them do you suppose would have gone right up to the enemy's guns and been shot down in their young manhood?

"Suppose Gen. Tom Anderson could have seen a howling mob murdering his family and no punishment for the murderers; would he have risked his life hunting up the Knights of the Golden Circle and chancing it in battle, as he did, for his country, that the rebels might control it, and that, too, through the influence of the North, whose all was at stake, and whose fortunes were saved and protected by such men as he? I doubt if patriotism would have gone so far. Can you find me the patriot to-day that, deep down in his heart, likes this condition of things?"

"Yes; but Uncle Daniel, these men are not rebels now. They are Democrats," said Maj. Clymer.

"Yes, true; but they are no more Democrats now than they were then, and they were no less Democrats then than they are now. But I should not say more; I have had trouble enough. Why should I grieve for the condition of things which were not expected? I and mine have

paid dearly for this lesson. I hope it may never fall to the
lot of any one else to pass through such an experience. I
shall see but little more trouble. May God forgive all and
protect the right."

DEATH OF UNCLE DANIEL.

Uncle Daniel here ceased speaking and sank back in his
chair. His granddaughter came into the room. Seeing
him, she screamed and fell upon his neck. We moved
quickly to him. He was dead.

THE END.